Tonight,
Somewhere in
New York

ALSO BY CORNELL WOOLRICH
AND EDITED BY FRANCIS M. NEVINS

Night and Fear

Tonight, Somewhere in New York

The Last Stories and an Unfinished Novel by

CORNELL WOOLRICH

Edited with an Introduction by
FRANCIS M. NEVINS

CARROLL & GRAF PUBLISHERS

NEW YORK

For Carlos Burlingham (1925–2004)
muchas gracias, mi amigo, y buena jornada

Tonight, Somewhere in New York
The Last Stories and an Unfinished Novel by Cornell Woolrich

Carroll & Graf Publishers
An Imprint of Avalon Publishing Group Inc.
245 West 17th Street
11th Floor
New York, NY 10011

AVALON
publishing group incorporated

Selection, Arrangement, General Introduction and Introductions to individual selections copyright © 2005 by Francis M. Nevins

Individual Cornell Woolrich selections copyright © 1958-2005 J. P. Morgan Chase Bank, Trustee, the Claire Woolrich Memorial Scholarship Fund

First Carroll & Graf edition 2005

Library of Congress Cataloging-in-Publication Data is available.

ISBN-13: 978-0-78671-530-5
ISBN-10: 0-7867-1530-8

10 9 8 7 6 5 4 3 2 1

Printed in the United States of America

Interior design by Jamie McNeely

Distributed by Publishers Group West

CONTENTS

INTRODUCTION

He was the Poe of the 20th century and the poet of its shadows, the Hitchcock of the written word. What he originally set out to be was the second F. Scott Fitzgerald. In 1934, when he abandoned all hope of mainstream prestige and began writing crime-suspense tales for magazines like *Dime Detective*, he was consumed by a frenzy of white-hot creative energy that sustained him in his empty life and gave birth to much of the literature that we now know as *noir*. Then, sometime during 1948, it died away. He didn't stop writing but slowed down radically and, although he didn't know it at the time, entered his final period. His twilight.

What brought an end to that burst of creativity we can never know for sure, but if we know enough about Cornell Woolrich, and about his parents, an educated guess is possible.

• • •

Many of the mysteries about his ancestry on his father's side have been cleared up thanks to Peter Woolrich, a Canadian who is related to the master of suspense through common great-great-grandparents and has exhaustively researched his family's roots. Briefly, James Woolrich (1761–1823), an Englishman born in Yorkshire, emigrated to Montreal, in the Canadian province of Quebec, and became a prosperous dry goods merchant as well as a shipowner, banker, and land speculator. In 1791 he married Magdeleine Gamelin, a union that produced nine children. One of their sons was Thomas Hall Woolrich (1802–1842), whose marriage to Mehitable Shaw of Nova Scotia produced Thomas Hopley-(or Hopply-) Woolrich. This man, who was born in Quebec in 1829 or 1830 and lived until at least 1916, migrated from Canada to the Mexican state of Oaxaca, where he had eleven children by at least five women. His first wife, Aurora Sandoval, was the mother of his son Genaro, who was born some time in the early or middle 1870s.

This man, who was Cornell Woolrich's father, was a complete enigma until, late in the 1990s, chance put me in touch with his half-nephew Carlos Burlingham (1925–2004), a psychiatrist whose mother was a daughter of Thomas Hopley-Woolrich by his fifth marriage. To put it another way, Thomas, whom Carlos described to me as "a man who hung around many women," was both Carlos's maternal grandfather and the paternal grandfather of Cornell Woolrich. In the early 1940s, when Carlos was in his teens, he lived with his Tío Genaro for more than a year. The memories he shared with me before his recent death provide the only solid information we have about the man whose only son became the greatest writer of pure suspense fiction that ever lived.

Thomas, or Tomás, Hopley-Woolrich was prosperous enough not only to support children by five marriages but to subsidize

North American educations for them. "My grandfather sent all his children to different schools in the United States," Carlos told me. After completing his education Genaro "went to work building the subway system in New York City." It was probably in 1901 or 1902 that he met Claire Attalie Tarler. Claire's father, George Abelle Tarler (1849–1925), was a prematurely white-haired Russian, the son of a rabbi. After emigrating from his native Odessa to Panama and then Mexico, he settled in the United States and became a pioneer in the import trade with Central America, dealing in real estate as a sideline. He married Sarah Cornell (1855–189?) early in 1874 and Claire was born on November 29 of the same year. She married Genaro a few years after her mother's death, and their first and only child, Cornell George Hopley-Woolrich, was born in New York on December 4, 1903.

Genaro, so Carlos told me, was not happy living away from his homeland. "Every child that my grandfather had, they always could not stand the environment. They always wanted to come back to Mexico. Genaro was exactly that way. . . . He said to Claire: 'I have to go. I don't like this place. Your role is to follow me.' " They left New York in 1907, taking three-year-old Cornell to Mexico with them. The marriage did not long survive the move. When the couple separated it was decided that the boy would stay with his father at least until adolescence. Claire Attalie Woolrich (as she continued to call herself for the rest of her life) returned to New York and the Tarler household.

Woolrich and his father must have had a very rocky relationship. According to author Lou Ellen Davis (1937–   ), who knew Woolrich in the 1960s, "he told me that near where they lived . . . there was a bigger kid, and that he paid this bigger kid to let Cornell beat him up where Cornell's father could see it. . . . Here was this skinny, frail, very gifted, very artistic kid, and here was this macho guy, and the kid so wanted macho approval." Carlos Burlingham gave me another anecdote about the young Woolrich that one of his many uncles told him generations ago. "There was a situation that happened in the city of

Oaxaca. I don't know how old Cornell was, but he was probably walking around in the park or something like that, came back to the hotel where he and Genaro were staying, and found his father with a woman in his bed. He created a mess and became quite upset and angry, because his idea was that his father was very loyal to his mother even though they were separated. Perhaps Uncle Genaro never spoke with him regarding the trauma of the separation and the finality of the separation. He probably had this idea that sooner or later they were going to get back together."

From his perspective as a psychiatrist Carlos looked back on Genaro as "somewhat schizoid, extremely withdrawn, extremely silent . . . He had a custom of getting up late in the morning. Before dinner he would have two or three shots of rum, and then some more after dinner and some more before supper." One can't help wondering if Woolrich's own withdrawn personality and problems with alcohol were the dark side of his inheritance from his father.

In early adolescence Woolrich underwent the experience that was to mark him forever. It happened, he says in his autobiographical manuscript *Blues of a Lifetime*, "one night when I was eleven and, huddling over my own knees, looked up at the low-hanging stars of the Valley of Anahuac, and knew I would surely die finally, or something worse." This, he tells us, was the beginning of "the sense of personal, private doom" that has been with him ever since. "I had that trapped feeling, like some sort of a poor insect that you've put inside a downturned glass, and it tries to climb up the sides, and it can't, and it can't, and it can't." There is no more perfect description of our situation in the world as Woolrich sees it. From that feeling springs almost everything in his fiction that is most distinctive and intense and chilling.

A few years later his painful life below the border with Genaro came to an end and his life as a New Yorker with his mother and the Tarlers began. For the first ten years or so after his return to the States, Woolrich's home address was 239 West 113th Street, an imposing house near Morningside Park, completed at the turn of the century and occupied ever since by Grandfather Tarler and other members of his family. George Tarler was the only man other than Genaro who played a major role in shaping Woolrich's life and world. Even in his own last years he recalled countless details about his grandfather: that he spoke "four of the main European languages" and loved opera and kept several glass cases in the house crammed with curios from his travels in Mexico and Asia. It was Tarler who, on a visit to Mexico City, had taken the eight-year-old Woolrich to see a performance of the then-new opera *Madama Butterfly*, introducing the boy to color and drama and the world of tragic love and unhappy endings in an intensely visual ambience—elements which were to become building blocks in his own fictional world—and it was Tarler who, after the adolescent Woolrich had come up to New York, took him to the movies once a week, introducing the teenager to the medium which over the years was to teach him how to write visually.

Woolrich was still living with his mother and maternal grandfather in 1921 when he enrolled as a freshman at Columbia University, just a short walk from 239 West 113th Street. He was alone in the house one day a few years later when the doorbell rang, and he went downstairs and found in the vestibule a uniformed policeman who announced bluntly that Grandfather Tarler was dead. We know from the *New York Times* obituary that the date was April 25, 1925, and that George had died of a heart attack as he entered his lawyer's office downtown, at 41 Park Row. "It was the first time I'd ever come up against death," Woolrich wrote decades later in *Blues of a Lifetime.* When his first novel sold to a major publisher, he left Columbia and spent the next several years writing the mainstream novels and short stories with which he hoped to establish himself as the next Fitzgerald.

In the early 1930s George Tarler's children sold the house on West 113th Street and Woolrich and Claire took an apartment together in the Hotel Marseilles, a comfortable Victorian pile at Broadway and 113th Street: the prison cell where he was to serve a twenty-five-year sentence. During the first fifteen years of that sentence he wrote the eleven novels and the 200-odd stories of pure suspense that earned him his reputation as the Hitchcock of the written word: "Johnny on the Spot" (1936), "Dusk to Dawn" (1937), "Three O'Clock" (1938), "Guillotine" (1939), *The Bride Wore Black* (1940), *The Black Curtain* (1941), *Phantom Lady* (1942), *The Black Angel* (1943), *Deadline at Dawn* (1944), *Night Has a Thousand Eyes* (1945), *Rendezvous in Black* (1948), and countless others.

On January 12, 1948, Genaro died. When Woolrich in New York heard the news, no doubt from some relative in Mexico, he reverently set down in the 1937 desk diary he used as a sort of portable file cabinet, "my father's resting place—Panteón Español, Cuartito IV (Spanish Cemetery, Section IV), Mexico City, Mexico," and noted that the grave was "marked with a tile plaque, on which his name is written." To whatever extent his son's career was a plea for Genaro's attention and respect and love, and an attempt to build a bridge on which his long-parted parents might reunite, its *raison d'etre* was gone now. The fire of creative passion which had sustained Woolrich for almost fifteen years was stamped out. With his mother almost seventy-five and in worsening health, and with the virtual guarantee of steady money from paperback reprints and movies and radio and soon television, why should he keep writing novels and stories which deep in his mind and heart he considered garbage?

Still, he continued to write. He couldn't not write. Much of the best work of his last twenty years is collected here.

• • •

If one judged only by the number of times his name appeared in print and media credits, he seemed to be prolific as ever. But he had nothing to do with the movies and radio and television dramas based on the novels and stories of his prime, and the collections of his short fiction that continued to be published on a regular basis were overwhelmingly of older material. *Six Nights of Mystery* (as by William Irish, 1950) claimed to collect five of Woolrich's classic pulp tales and one story that had never been published before. In fact, "One Night in Zacamoras" was simply his 1940 pulper "Señor Flatfoot" under a new name. This was the first instance of a practice Woolrich was to indulge in throughout the 1950s, passing off revisions and expansions and sometimes verbatim reprints of old work as brand new. The three new Woolrich novels published during this period—*Fright* (as by George Hopley, 1950), *Savage Bride* (as by Cornell Woolrich, 1950) and *Strangler's Serenade* (as by William Irish, 1951, but expanded from the 1945 novella "Four Bars of Yankee Doodle")—were universally panned as well below his standard and haven't been reprinted in generations.

From early 1953 until mid-1958, Woolrich's total output of new published work added up to exactly one short story, which is included here. Yet thanks to his continuing popularity in the reprint markets and the visual media (principally television), his annual income kept on a respectable level: just over $8,000 in 1953, just under $10,000 in 1954, about $20,000 in each of the next two years, around $13,500 in 1957, and a bit more than $18,000 in 1958 when some fresh Woolrich material finally got into print. Some of that money he really didn't earn. When Flying Eagle Publications launched the new and well-funded mystery magazine *Manhunt*, Woolrich promptly sold its editors "The Hunted," a tale set in Japan and supposedly fresh from his typewriter. On its appearance in the magazine's premiere issue (January 1953), a long-memoried reader wrote in to point out that Woolrich's contribution had appeared fifteen years before as "Death in the Yoshiwara" (*Argosy*, January 29, 1938; collected in *Night and Fear*, 2004). The editors were not amused.

In December 1953 Woolrich turned fifty. From then on he left the Hotel Marseilles almost never, just to get a haircut or a few drinks, or perhaps to see a movie. Occasionally he would run into Lee Wright, the editor who had bought his first suspense novels for Simon & Schuster. "Every time I saw him," Wright told me in

1979, "he would tell me how lonely he was, that nobody loved him. And I would say to Cornell: 'Well, it's probably your own fault. I mean, you sort of put people off. You're too shy. Why can't you be more outgoing? You'll find that people will like you very much. You're very likable.' And he would say: 'You're so wonderful.' Not me! You know, you could never believe a word he said, really, although *he* believed it at the time."

Alfred Hitchcock's *Rear Window*, the best-known and most successful of the dozens of movies based on Woolrich material, was released in 1954. Woolrich made very little money from the film, and there is no reason to believe that he and the great director whose background and unique talents and tormented soul were so much like his own ever discussed the film while it was in production or even met each other. "Hitchcock wouldn't even send me a ticket to the premiere in New York," Woolrich complained near the end of his life. "He knew where I lived. He wouldn't even send me a ticket." Since Woolrich is unlikely to have paid for a ticket with his own money and since he died before its first showing on network TV, it's quite possible that he never saw the movie at all.

His one serious writing project of the 1950s was his most ambitious attempt at mainstream fiction since the books he had written in the Jazz Age. He wanted to do an episodic novel about the birth, youth, prime, middle age, decline, and death of a New York hotel much like the Marseilles, with each chapter taking place in the same room at different moments in the building's life span. Except for one segment, published as "The Black Bargain" (*Justice*, January 1956) and included in this book, its chapters had nothing to do with crime or suspense and therefore were unmarketable to genre magazines, but they failed to interest the editors of mainstream periodicals either. Woolrich kept plugging away at the project as and when he could.

His creative life had gone stale and his physical environment had become appalling. The Marseilles was turning into an urban dunghill as successive managements kept finding new corners to cut. According to *Blues of a Lifetime*, the building's floors were coated with "ingrained and ineradicable grime," the airshaft was filled with combustible debris, and the tenants were plagued with everything from blown fuses and crawling elevators to mice in the walls and frequent burglaries. The fire stairs were littered with fruit peels, beer cans and pages from old newspapers, and since every bulb had been stolen from the walls, going down those steps was like "running in a box in the dark." Near the end of his long tenancy, he says, there wasn't even a phone connection between his apartment and the lobby because in the latest economy move the downstairs switchboard had been taken out. By 1957, "as the concentration camp of Harlem burst apart its barbed-wire boundaries," the hotel's population was almost completely black and Woolrich and his mother were the only whites on their floor. Their neighbors included a prostitute, an alcoholic welfare mother, and some of the poorest of the working poor. "We were all just people together. Some poor, some better off than that; some young, some older than that; some healthy, some (like my mother) sick almost unto death." Surely the Woolriches could have afforded to leave this dismal and dangerous cage, but, if for no better reason than inertia, they stayed.

Claire had suffered a massive heart attack in the spring of 1956. Afterward, although she could still move around freely within the apartment, she was unable to go outdoors. From then on her son was as surely a prisoner of the Marseilles as if a turnkey had locked him in each night. Eventually she had to be hospitalized, and Woolrich began haunting her bedside. She died on October 6, 1957, at the age of eighty-three. A service was held at the Walter B. Cooke Funeral Home on West 72nd Street, and her body was interred in the family crypt at the Ferncliff Mausoleum in Hartsdale, near White Plains. Her death brought Woolrich that much closer to his own.

He wrote nothing for publication about his reaction to the loss, and even in *Blues of a Lifetime* he dismissed the subject in four words: "She is gone now. . . ." Elsewhere in the manuscript he says:

"I didn't cry when my mother died, though my arm shook and my whole body too, as I stood up with a brandy and toasted her, somewhere sight unseen. But you don't have to cry to love someone, to miss them." A year or two later he told an editor that every night he "set out a bottle of champagne and two glasses, one for him and one for his mother, and drank a toast to her."

Her death devastated him but liberated him at the same time. Either while she was dying in the hospital or shortly afterward, Woolrich moved out of the Marseilles to an apartment in the Hotel Franconia, at 20 West 72nd Street, just off Central Park, a huge leap forward in terms of physical environment. A widowed sister of his mother's moved in with him and tried to take Claire's place but didn't last long. One night while his aunt was still living with him, Woolrich went out drinking with fellow crime novelist Dan J. Marlowe (1914–1986). "He didn't drink much," Marlowe told me, "but I learned quickly that any amount was too much for Woolrich. He simply went to pieces, and I learned later that this was his pattern. . . . [A]t this time he weighed perhaps 120 pounds and every drink probably hit him three times as hard as it did a larger man. . . . I never saw him again, although we did exchange a few notes from time to time. There was a wit in his notes sadly lacking in his person. . . ."

In the wake of *Rear Window,* Woolrich had contracted with the Dodd Mead publishing house to assemble two new collections of short stories, each volume to include tales from previous collections, old magazine stories not previously collected, and new thrillers never before published anywhere. Whether Woolrich ever intended to write new material for the books or was deceiving Dodd Mead all along is unclear. Both *Nightmare* (1956) and *Violence* (1958) were advertised as including two new stories apiece. All four in fact were revised versions of old pulpers, one of them included here.

The episodic novel on which Woolrich had worked in fits and starts while his mother was dying was published by Random House in July 1958 as *Hotel Room.* It was dedicated:

To
Claire Attalie Woolrich
1874–1957
In Memoriam
This Book: Our Book

The story of the Hotel St. Anselm's birth, adolescence, maturity, old age, and death, as told through the stories of the people who checked into Room 923 at various points in time between 1896 and sixty years later, represents Woolrich's last sustained attempt to break into the mainstream and win again the acceptance he had enjoyed in his early twenties. It failed. The book wasn't even reviewed in the *New York Times* as almost all his suspense novels and collections had been, it wasn't picked up by a book club or paperback house, it earned pitiful royalties for a few months, and then the novel died like the hotel it described. No one has seen fit to resurrect it since. But in *Hotel Room* more than in any other late work except perhaps the 1950 novel *Fright*, Woolrich created a form in perfect harmony with the vision of a man who had confined himself in an urban box for most of his adult life.

In December 1958 he turned fifty-five. He was unable to write any more of the suspense classics that had made his reputation and equally unable to produce the sort of mainstream fiction that literary critics would accept as serious, but if he completely stopped writing he would die, and even though he had lost his mother and was utterly alone, he wasn't ready for death. He went back to dabbling in the genres of exotic adventure and horror and the occult that he had explored sporadically since his first sales to the pulps. The result was a trio of paperback originals that are full of his distinctive motifs and stylistic quirks but sadly deficient in his legendary word power. *Death Is My Dancing Partner* (1959) shows the unmistakable Woolrich hallmarks of episodic structure, feverish romantic dialogue, tinny insult humor, south-of-the-border settings, and popular song lyrics to evoke mood, but it's by all odds the worst novel he ever wrote, with characters beyond laughability, dialogue

11

beyond goopiness, and a nonexistent plot. *Beyond the Night* (1959) is a collection of six occult horror tales, three of them advertised as never having been published before although in fact two were resurrected pulpers from the 1930s. The only genuine new tale in the book was "The Number's Up," a gem of *noir* set in 1929 in a New York hotel room (suggesting that this tale too might originally have been intended as a chapter of the 1958 episodic novel) and included here. *The Doom Stone* (1960) was also advertised as brand new, but in fact three of the four installments of this episodic novel had first come out in *Argosy* back in 1939 as the four-part serial "The Eye of Doom." Anthony Boucher in the *New York Times* described the plot with perfect succinctness as "heaven help us, about the diamond stolen from the eye of a Hindu idol in 1757 and the curse it brings on successive owners in Paris during the Terror, in New Orleans under the carpetbag regime and in Tokyo just before Pearl Harbor." Only the Tokyo episode was new. Copies of all three of these disasters are worth a mint today.

Woolrich hadn't left New York City in decades, but during 1960–61 he spent seven months in Canada: Whether in search of his father's roots or for some other reason remains unknown. On a visit back to the city he had his attorney prepare a new will for him. The document, dated March 6, 1961, left his entire estate in trust to establish a Claire Woolrich Memorial Scholarship Fund at Columbia University. The Chase Manhattan Bank was named executor and trustee.

Late in April 1961 Woolrich went to the Astor Hotel for the Mystery Writers of America annual dinner, the first he'd attended in years. After the banquet he went drinking with Donald A. Yates (1930–   ), a young professor of Latin American literature at Michigan State University and a fan and scholar of mystery fiction. That was the start of one of the closest approximations to a friendship Woolrich ever experienced. He loved talking with Yates about Hemingway and Faulkner and (of course) F. Scott Fitzgerald but refused as if on principle to talk about himself. "He was made uncomfortable by references to his own work," Yates told me in

1987. "I honestly think that he thought it was so much garbage." When Yates tried to explain how much he admired the other's work, Woolrich said: "Well, that's your mistake. There's nothing I can do about that."

After the breakup with Claire, Genaro Hopley-Woolrich had had liaisons with many other women. The last and longest was with Esperanza Piñon Brangas. Their daughter Alma was born in Nogales, Sonora on June 17, 1938. "I learned I had a brother who was a writer when I was fourteen," Alma said in an interview conducted with her on my behalf by the Argentine author Juan Jose Delaney. "My aunt used to tell me about him, saying that my father had made a silver cup for him and that someday we would meet." In 1961 Alma came up from Oaxaca to New Jersey to visit her uncle Carlos and his family, staying with the Burlinghams more than a year. Carlos wrote to Woolrich, expecting that he'd want to meet the half-sister he'd never seen. "When I wrote to him that Alma was with me," Carlos said, "he wrote me from New York, or probably an attorney wrote for him. He mentioned in this letter that he knew his father had never married again and never had any daughters. . . . He flatly refused to accept the fact." One day Alma went to New York in an attempt to meet her famous half-brother. "But he wouldn't receive me. . . . I remember that he sent out his secretary saying that he didn't want to see me." Woolrich never had a secretary. Juan Jose Delaney told me that the word Alma had used in their interview was *secretario*. It was a man who turned her away from Woolrich's door. Almost certainly that man was Woolrich himself. How could he or anyone else have resisted the temptation to sneak a peek at his only close relative without revealing himself? If he had died without a will, his half-sister who speaks no English would have inherited the copyrights in all his work by intestate succession.

Woolrich was dying by inches, but two editors did everything in their power to draw him out of his shell and get him functioning as a writer again. One was Frederic Dannay (1905–1982), co-author of the Ellery Queen novels and founding editor of *Ellery Queen's*

Mystery Magazine (*EQMM*), in which he had reprinted Woolrich stories regularly since Volume I, Number 1. The other was Hans Stefan Santesson (1914–1975), editor of *The Saint Mystery Magazine*. Most of the few new tales Woolrich managed to complete during the 1960s were published in one periodical or the other.

In 1964 the sight in his right eye began to fail and he underwent cataract surgery. Lou Ellen Davis visited him in the hospital and brought him a stuffed mouse with polka-dot ears to cheer him up, but it wasn't quite the gift he was looking for. "I remember he was trying to get the people who came to see him in the hospital to bring him alcohol," she told me.

At the end of April 1965 he felt spry enough to attend the Mystery Writers of America annual dinner at the Biltmore Hotel. Being Woolrich, he didn't bother to purchase a ticket in advance or to dress or even shave for the banquet. Being the living legend that he was, he got the best seat available. That same week he had his first and only meeting with Anthony Boucher (1911–1968), the critic who, earlier and with more enthusiasm than anyone else, had recognized Woolrich's unique gifts and praised them again and again, first in the *San Francisco Chronicle* and later in the *New York Times*. It was a strange evening to say the least. "Tony was delighted that he had finally met Woolrich," his widow told me, "and at the same time thought that it wouldn't do his nerves any good to see too much of him. . . ."

After recovering from his eye surgery Woolrich moved into the last hotel room of his life, a comfortable if spartan suite on the second floor of the Sheraton-Russell at 45 Park Avenue, on the corner of 37th Street. Don Yates, who continued to visit whenever he was in town, described the suite for me.

As you face the hotel from across the street . . . it would be on the extreme left corner. It consisted of a large sitting room in which there was a screen that he'd drawn across. A very small kind of a kitchen which was adjacent to the corridor outside. On the wall facing 37th Street was a sofa and a coffee table in front of it. . . . Looking out over south Park Avenue was a writing table and a lamp. There was a TV in the corner to the right of the writing table, and a few occasional chairs, [and] a closet which he seemed always to keep locked, next to the kitchenette. And then, occupying the space between the sitting room and the 37th Street end of his apartment were, on the right, a small bathroom, and on the left, at the very corner, his bedroom. I never saw a book in his apartment. Never saw any kind of reading material, not a magazine, not a newspaper.

He did still write now and then but left unfinished a great deal more than he completed. When the darkness fell he would come down from the second floor and, in the words of the Sheraton-Russell's rooms manager, become "part of the lobby." Sitting in the same chair every evening, looking out at the street lights, saying nothing. A few of the older waiters in the hotel dining room remembered how he would come in and sit at a table in an alcove where almost no one could see him and quietly eat his dinner.

The last collection of his short fiction published in his lifetime was *The Dark Side of Love* (1965), which consists mainly of mediocre stories he couldn't place with magazines but does offer a concentrated dose of how the world looked to him as he approached death. The collection closes with "Too Nice a Day to Die": a faultless gem of *noir*, its facets perfectly reflecting a world in which chance is god and beams fall, which is included here too.

Thanks to reprint sales and continuing media interest in his decades-old classics, he never had to worry about where the next drink was coming from. His total income for 1965 topped the $18,000 mark despite the fact that he was publishing next to nothing new. The briefest excursion out of New York seemed to terrify him. Over and over again Fred Dannay and his wife would invite Woolrich to spend a Sunday afternoon with them in Larchmont, which is forty minutes by train from Grand Central Station.

Woolrich might answer with a yes or a no or a maybe, but he never came.

In June 1967 the Scott Meredith agency, which represented him at the time, assigned his account to a young man named Barry N. Malzberg (1939–   ), who went on to write countless novels and stories of *noir* fantasy and science fiction. What he feared even more than death, Woolrich told Malzberg, was "the endless obliteration, the knowledge that there will never be anything else. That's what I can't stand, to try so hard and to end in nothing." In a powerful chapter in his book *The Engines of the Night* (1982) Malzberg gives us vivid glimpses of Woolrich's last years, of how he "lived alone . . . on the second floor of the Sheraton-Russell Hotel . . . surrounded by cases and cases of beer cans and bottles of whiskey and invited the staff to come up and drink beer with him and watch television."

Now his slow march to the grave quickened into a trot. An ill-fitting shoe led to a bad case of gangrene which, "untreated," as Malzberg put it, "turned his leg to charcoal." His life became even more zombielike than before. He "would stay in his room and drink almost all the time and stare at the television looking for a film from one of his novels or short stories which came on often enough and usually after 2 A.M.; between the movies and the alcohol he was finally able to find sleep. For a few hours. Until ten or eleven in the morning. When it would all start again."

This was his life, if you want to call it living, until the first week of 1968. "At the end," Malzberg writes, "amidst the cases and the bottles and the empty glasses as the great black leg became turgid and began to stink there was nothing at all." Someone finally called a doctor but too late. On or around January 10 Woolrich was carried out of the Sheraton-Russell and taken to Wickersham Hospital, where his leg was cut off above the knee. He was released until the stump had healed and then readmitted in April for the fitting of a prosthesis. In June he left the hospital with an artificial leg on which he could never learn to walk. His last few months were spent at the Sheraton-Russell in a wheelchair. But at least he had the help of a magnificent hotel staff. "They came to his door with trays, snacks, food, messages, advice," Malzberg writes. "They took good care of him. They helped him down on crutches to the lobby and put him in the plush chair at the near door so that he could see the traffic from the street. . . . They brought him to the dining room and they brought him out. They took him upstairs, they took him downstairs, they stayed with him. They created a subterranean network of concern. . . ."

Thanks to their concern, Woolrich was still alive late in June when the first major theatrical film based on his work since *Rear Window* had its New York premiere. *La Mariée Etait En Noir*, directed by the world-famous François Truffaut and based on Woolrich's 1940 breakthrough novel *The Bride Wore Black*, opened on June 25 at the Festival Theatre, on 57th Street and Fifth Avenue, about a mile from the Sheraton-Russell. Truffaut had made the trip from Paris in hopes of meeting him, but Woolrich refused to see either the director or the film.

In the summer of 1968 he looked decades older than his sixty-four years. He had, says Malzberg, "the stunned aspect of the very old. Where there had been edges there was now only the gelatinous material that when probed would not rebound." But his eyes were still "open and moist, curiously childlike and vulnerable." On the evening of September 19 he suffered a stroke and was found unconscious in the hallway of the Sheraton-Russell. He remained in a coma until, six days later, two and a half months short of his sixty-fifth birthday, the specter of Anahuac came for him, the glass was lifted and the fly released from life.

The last new story Fred Dannay bought from Woolrich and probably the last he completed was "New York Blues" (*Ellery Queen's Mystery Magazine*, December 1970; collected in *Night and Fear*, 2004). Its storyline is all but invisible and at the same time pure *noir*. A nameless man who has killed the woman he loves, or perhaps another woman, or perhaps no one at all, sits in the dark of a room on the second floor of a New York hotel and looks out at the night and waits in terror for the Them, who

are death personified, to take him. Within this minimalist frame-
work Woolrich reprises virtually every motif, belief, and device
that had pervaded his fiction for generations: flashes of word
magic, love and loneliness, madness and death, paranoia and total
despair. "Each man dies as he was meant to die, and as he was
born, and as he lived: alone, all alone. Without any God, without
any hope, without any record to show for his life." If this was the
last story Woolrich completed, he couldn't have ended his career
more fittingly.

The handful of tales he finished in his last years was only a frac-
tion of his twilight work. Among his papers were found a "collection of personal memoirs" he called *Blues of a Lifetime* and
incomplete typescripts of two novels. One of these, with a beginning and ending contributed by crime novelist Lawrence Block
and an afterword by me, was published as *Into the Night* (1987).
The completed chapters of the other, with running commentary
by me, are included here, along with two chapters from *Blues of a
Lifetime.*

"I was only trying to cheat death," he wrote in a handwritten fragment found among his papers. "I was only trying to surmount for a
little while the darkness that all my life I surely knew was going to
come rolling in on me some day and obliterate me. I was only trying
to stay alive a little brief while longer, after I was already gone." This
collection shows that, almost forty years after his death, he succeeded. He is still with us. Haunting us.

TONIGHT, SOMEWHERE IN NEW YORK

In the last years of his wretched life Woolrich worked intermittently on two novels, neither of which he lived to finish. The one closer to completion at his death was published almost twenty years later as *Into the Night* (Mysterious Press, 1987), with beginning and ending provided by Lawrence Block and an afterword by me. The other novel-in-progress was still a long way from completion when Woolrich died, but given enough time and care it too might have developed into a first-rate *roman noir* that only he could have written. His original title for it was *Tonight, Somewhere in New York,* which he eventually X'ed out and replaced with a perfect Woolrich self-description: *The Loser.* The publisher and I agree that the earlier title is more evocative and should be used here. A casual reference to the year 1966 in one of the completed chapters suggests that that was when he began work on the book. Clearly he didn't get very far with the project: Several sequences exist in more than one draft, and a number of characters and situations overlap with people and events from *Into the Night,* as if he couldn't make up his mind what belonged in the one book and what should go into the other. The surviving chapters, however, show us the direction in which he was headed and hint that it might have grown into a fascinating novel.

The first chapter exists in two versions: a finished draft of seventeen typed pages—which was included in *Nightwebs* (Harper & Row, 1971), the first posthumous Woolrich collection, as "Life Is Weird Sometimes"—and a variant version, only nine pages long and nowhere near as well developed and dramatic. We pick up the nameless protagonist-narrator just after he's killed the woman he once loved.

CHAPTER 1

Have you ever seen a woman die? I hope you never have to, never do. I mean in violence, at your own hands. It isn't a good thing to see. When you see a man die, you see only yourself; not someone apart whom you once knelt to in your heart and offered up your love to. Revered and dwelt on in your reveries. Or if not, some other man did.

She falls from higher than a man, from over the heads of men, whether they're lovers or husbands or brothers. And whether she was good or she was evil, whatever evil is, she falls with a flash and a fiery trace, like a disintegrating star plunging into the water. A man just falls like a clod; clay back to the clay he came from. That is why judiciaries and law-enforcers so seldom kill women by law, no matter what their crime.

And when it is done by one man alone, personally and individually acting as his own sentencer and his own executioner, as you do now, think how much more affecting and impact-bearing it is.

That face you see before you that has just finished dying will come back palely haunting into every night's sleep for the rest of your life, no matter how much she deserved it, no matter how tough your mind. You know it will, you know. That scene you saw before you that has just ended will come back meshed into every dream you ever dream again, so that you don't just kill her once, you kill her a thousand and one times, and she never stays quite dead. And all the brandy and all the barbiturates can't make it go away.

Those lips that pressed against yours like warm velvet and clung there in soft adhesion, look at them now, twisted into an ellipse, a crevice for a surprise that never finishes coming out. Those eyes that glittered with love and hate and laughter and hate and doubt and hate, and hate and hate and hate, they don't hate now anymore. Those arms that gestured so gracefully in the light, and wound around you so importunately in the dark, paid out on the floor now limp and curlicued, like lengths of wide ribbon that have slipped off their spools. The polish on the fingertips of the one lying facedown looking strangely like five little red seeds burst out of some pod and lying there scattered. A polish that claimed proudly to be long-lasting. I know; I used to see the bottle. This will prove it now: it will outlast her.

The hair your hand strayed through over and over, and found so soft and responsive each time; lying there fanned out and flotsam like a mess of seaweed washed up on the shore.

The body that once was the goal, and the striving, and the will-o'-the-wisp of the act of love . . .

All of this now devastated, distorted, and in death.

No, it isn't good to see a woman . . .

I did a number of banal things that struck me strange, although I had never done this thing before and had no way of knowing whether they were banal or not, strangely out of key or not, or were to be expected to follow anything like that.

I smoothed down the sleeves of my shirt, first of all. They hadn't been rolled up, but I kept smoothing and straightening them down as though they had been. Then I shot my cuffs back into more conforming place, and felt for their fastenings. One had come open in the swift arm-play that had occurred, and I refastened it.

Then I looked at the watch on my wrist, not to tell the time, but to see if it had suffered any surface-harm. I prized it a great deal; some men do. It showed no signs of any harm, but to guard doubly against that, I stem-wound it briefly but briskly. You weren't supposed to have to, it was self-winding. But I figured the little added fillip would benefit it. I'd bought it in 1957 at Lambert Brothers for $150, and I'd never regretted it since.

Meanwhile she was dying there on the floor.

I went into the bathroom, and ran a little warm water, and washed off my hands. (Just like you do after you do almost anything.) Then I changed it to cold and smoothed a little of it on my hair. I don't like warm water on my hair, it opens the pores, I think you catch cold quicker that way.

I was going to use the john, but somehow it seemed indecent, disrespectful, I don't know how to say it. I didn't have to very badly anyway, so I didn't. It had only been a nervous reflex from the killing.

Then I dried off my hands on one of her towels, and came outside again.

By that time she had finished dying on the floor. She was dead now.

I bent down and put my hand to her forehead. It was the last time I ever touched her, out of all the many times I'd touched her before.

Put my hand to her forehead, and said out loud: "You can't think any more now in back of there, can you? It's quiet in back of there now, isn't it?"

What a mysterious thing that is, I thought. How it stops. And once it does, never comes on again.

When I came out into the outside room again, I saw her shoe still lying there, where it had come off in the course of our brief wrestle. It looked so pathetic there by itself without an owner, it looked so lonely, it looked so empty. Something made me pick it up and take it in to her. Like when someone's going away, you help them on with their coat, or their jackboots, or whatever it is they need for going away.

I didn't try to put it back on her, I just set it down there beside her close at hand. You're going to need this, I said to her in my mind. You're starting on a long walk. You're going to keep walking from now on, looking for your home.

I stopped and wondered for a minute if that was what happened to all of us when we crossed over. Just keep walking, keep on walking, with no ahead and no in-back-of; tramps, vagrants in eternity. With our last hope and horizon—death—already taken away.

In the Middle Ages they had lurid colors, a bright red hell, an azure heaven shot with gold stars. They knew where they were, at least. They could tell the difference. We, in the Twentieth, we just have the long walk, the long walk through the wispy backward-stringing mists of eternity, from nowhere to nowhere, never getting there, until you're so tired you almost wish you were—alive again.

The gun I picked up and looked around with, not knowing what to do with it, and finally put it into my own pocket. I don't know why, don't know what made me. It had been hers in the first place. Just some kind of a tidying-up reflex, I guess. Don't leave things lying around. You learn that in your boyhood.

Then I opened the door and went out. And it was over.

Standing outside the reclosed door, I lowered my head thoughtfully for a moment and spit on the floor at my feet. Not the way you spit in anger or in insult, or even in disgust. But simply the way you would spit to rid your mouth of a bad aftertaste, to clear it out.

That television that I had noticed the first time, when I crossed the hall on my way in, was still raging away from behind a door at the far end, set at right (or left) angles to all the rest of them, depending on which side they were on. No wonder the shot hadn't been heard around. It would have been drowned in the torrent of noise like a raindrop falling in an ocean.

The only thing I could figure was that whoever was in there with it had it turned or slanted in such a way that the full impact was away from them and toward the door and the hall beyond it, and they didn't realize what it was doing themselves. Some people are insensitive to television noise anyway; ask a cross-section of average neighbors, they'll always point one out.

It was belting the hall like a hurricane, only its waves were audial instead of wind and water. "What happened to me," it bragged at the top of its thundering tubes, "was a simple little pill called Compoz. Now I work relaxed and I sleep relaxed—"

And no one else does, I thought inattentively with a stray lobe of my mind.

I brought the car up to me—it was an automatic—and on the short, sleek glide down, a momentary impulse occurred to me to go up to Charlie when I got down below. He was the doorman. Go up to Charlie, hand him the gun, and say: "Better ring in to the police. I just killed her up there. I just killed twelve-ten."

But it had started to fade even before I got all the way down. Then when I got out and didn't see him around anywhere, that scotched it entirely. You don't hang around *waiting* to report you've killed someone. You do it with your throttle wide open or not at all.

Then when I emerged into the street, I saw where he was. He was one house length down, in front of the next building, helping some people get into a taxi *there*. It must have dropped a fare off there, and couldn't roll back to his stop-whistle because of the traffic coming on behind, so he and his party had had to go down there after it. They were bulky, and the furs on the women made them even bulkier, and they took a great deal of handling to shoe-horn in. His attention was fully occupied, and his back was to me.

He hadn't seen me going in either. Must have gone around the corner for a quick coffee break.

How strange, I thought, he didn't see me at either of the two points that count. But in between I bet he was killing time hanging around here in front of the entrance with nothing to do. That's the way those things go sometimes: try not to be seen, and everybody spots you; don't give a good damn whether or not you are, and everybody looks right through you just as though you weren't there.

I turned away from him and went on my way, up the street and about my business. The past was dead. The future was resignation, fatality, and could only end one way now. The present was numbness, that could feel nothing. Like Novocaine needled into your heart. What was there in all the dimensions of time for me?

I turned left at the first up-and-down transverse I came to, and went down it for a block, and stopped in for a drink at a place. I needed one bad, I was beginning to feel shaky inside now. I'd been in this place before. It was called Felix's (a close enough approximation, with a change of just one letter). It was three or four steps down, what you might call semi-below-sidewalk-level. It was kept in a state of chronic dimness, a sort of half-light. Some said so you couldn't see how cut and watered your drinks were.

It was just the place for me though. I didn't want a bright light shining on me. That would come quick enough, in some precinct back room.

My invisibility had run out though. I had no sooner sat down than, before my drink had even had time to get in front of me, a girl came over to me. From behind, naturally; that was the only way she could. She tapped me on the shoulder with two fingers.

I didn't know her, but she knew me, at second hand, it seemed. I leaned my ear toward her a little, so if she said anything I could hear what it was.

"Your friend wants to know why you don't recognize him anymore," was what she said, reproachfully. And with that prim propriety that sometimes comes with a certain amount of alcohol—and almost invariably when a feeling of social unsurety goes with it—she added, "You shouldn't be that way. He only wanted you to come over and join us."

"What friend? Where?" I said grudgingly. She pointed with the hand that was holding the change left over from the record player she'd just been to, which impeded the accuracy of her point somewhat because she had to keep three fingers bunched over in order to hang onto the coins. "In the booth. Don't you see him?"

"How can I see anybody from here?" I asked her sullenly. "They're all wearing shadow masks halfway up their faces. All I can see is their foreheads." (The edge of the bar drew a line at about that height all around the room; the lights were below it, on the inside.)

"But he could see *you*," she challenged. "And so could I."

"Well, he's been in here longer than me. I only just now walked in through the door." I thought that would get rid of her and break it up. Instead it brought on a controversy.

She gave the sort of little-girl grimace that goes with the expression "Oo, what you just said," or "Oo, I'm going to tell on you." Rounded her mouth to a big O, and her eyes to match. Which sat strangely on her along with the come-on makeup and the martinis or whatever they had been.

"You've been buzzing around up here for the better part of an hour. First you were sitting in one place, then in another, then you went over to the cigarette machine. Then you were gone for a while—I guess to the telephone or the men's room—and then you came back again. We had our eyes on you the whole time. Every time he hollered your name out, you'd look and then you'd look away again. So it wasn't that you didn't hear, it was you didn't want to h—"

"What is my name then, if he hollered it so many times?" I nearly fell over. She gave me my name; both of them in fact. Not quite accurately, but close enough to do.

Still not convinced, but willing to be, I went over with her to take a look at him. He was in a sour mood by now over the fancied slight. He wouldn't get up. He wouldn't smile. He wouldn't shake hands. He was also more than a little smashed. His head kept going around on his shoulders; the shoulders didn't, just the head.

I didn't know him well at all, but I did know him. But this wasn't the night nor the particular segment of it to become enmeshed with stray one- or two-time acquaintances. All I kept thinking, with inwardly raised eyes, was: Why did I pick this particular place? There's a line of bars all along this avenue. Why did I have to come in here and run into these two?

"I appreciate this no end," he said sarcastically.

"You got your wires crossed," I told him briefly. "I just came in."

"You tell him," he said to the girl.

"Look," she catalogued, "we saw everything you got on. Just like you have it on you now."

("But not on me, on someone else," I put in.)

"This same light-gray shortie coat—" She plucked it with her fingers.

("There's been a rash of them all over New York this season.")

"And a shave-head haircut?"

("Who hasn't one?")

"And even a shiny tie clip that flashed in my eyes from the light every time you turned a certain way?"

("Everyone carries some kind of hardware across the front.")

"But *all three* of them match up," she expostulated. "You're wearing them all."

"So was somebody else. Half an hour ago, or maybe twenty minutes, sitting on the same stool I was, that's all. It was a double-take." And I omitted to add: You're both blurry with booze, anyway.

He turned to address the girl, as a way of showing me what his feelings toward me were. "He's copping a plea. You think you know a guy, and then you're not good enough for him."

"Your knowing me ended right now," I said tersely.

He pushed his underlip out in hostility. "Then stand away from my table. Don't crowd us like that."

He got up in his seat and gave me a stiff-arm back, hand against chest.

I shoved him in return, also hand against chest, and he sat down again.

This time he got up and came out and around from behind the table and swung a roundhouse at me. I can't remember whether it clipped or not. Probably not or I'd be able to.

I swung back at him and could feel it land, but he only gave a little. Maybe a step back with one foot.

His second swing, and the third of the whole capsule fight, and I went sprawling back on my shoulders across the floor. He was springier than he looked in his liquored condition.

The whole thing didn't take a half-minute, but already everyone in the place was around us in a tight little circle, the way they always are at such a time. The bartender came running out from behind, cautioning, "All right, all right," in an excited voice. All-right what he didn't specify.

He helped me up, and then continued the process by arming me all the way over to the door and just beyond it, before I knew what was happening. He didn't throw me out, simply sort of *urged* me out by one arm. There he let go my arm, told me, "Now go away from here. Go someplace else and do that." And closed the door in my face.

I guess I was the one selected to be evicted because the other fellow had had a girl with him, and from where the bartender stood it looked as if I had gone over and accosted them, said something out of the way to her. The pantomime of what he had witnessed alone would have been enough to suggest that to him, without the need of an accompanying soundtrack.

He had turned his back to me, and was walking away from the door, when I reopened it wide enough to insert my head, one foot and one shoulder past it, and to protest indignantly: "I still have a drink coming to me. I paid you for it, and I never got it. Now where is it?"

"You've had enough," he said arbitrarily and quite inaccurately. I hadn't had anything. "You're cut off."

And with that he came back toward me, and this time did push me, gave me a good hearty shove out through the partial aperture I had been standing in. So tempestuous a one in fact that I went all the way back and over, and again sprawled on my shoulder blades in a sort of arrested skid across the sidewalk.

This time he locked the door from the inside (evidently a

temporary measure until I should go away) and pulled down a shade across the grimy glass portion of it in final dismissal.

It was the second time I'd been toppled in about three minutes and I blew a fuse.

I got up into a crouched-over position, like a runner on his mark just before the start of a race. I swung my head around, this way and that, looking for something to throw. There was a fire hydrant, but it was immovable. There was one of those Department of Sanitation wire-lattice litter baskets that stud the sidewalks of New York. I went over to that, still at a crouch, and looked in it for something heavy. All I could see from the top was layers of newspapers. So instead of throwing something from its contents, I threw the whole receptacle itself.

Lifted it clear, hoisted it overhead, took a few running steps with it, scraps of litter raining out of it, and let it fly.

The door responded with an ear-splitting bang like the backfire from a heavy truck's exhaust tube.

But it wasn't strong enough to break the glass, which was what I'd been trying for, or my throw wasn't strong enough, or there was a wire-mesh backing protecting the glass. It just fractured it and rolled off, leaving behind a star-shaped cicatrice that looked like it was made of powdered sugar.

The barman flew out and grabbed me. I never saw anyone come out of anywhere so fast. Everyone else came out too, and some stayed and some skipped out on their drinks.

A couple of patrol cars knifed up in pincers formation, one with the traffic, one against the traffic, dome lights dead for surprise value, and caught me in between them.

The next thing I knew I was standing in front of a police sergeant's desk.

The barkeeper said his door pane was worth fifty-five dollars. I felt like saying his whole place wasn't worth fifty-five dollars, but I wasn't in a position to submit appraisals. The desk sergeant asked him if he would be willing to drop the complaint if I made good on the fifty-five dollars. He said he would. The desk sergeant asked me if I had fifty-five dollars. I checked myself out, and said I didn't have. The desk sergeant asked me if I could *get* fifty-five dollars. I said I'd try. The desk sergeant said I could use his phone.

I called up Stewart Sutphen, my lawyer. I knew it was no use calling his office at that hour of the night, so I called his home instead. He wasn't there either. He was up in the country some-where. He was always up in the country somewhere whenever you tried to reach him, I reflected rather disgruntledly. He had been the last time too, I remembered. He was the out-of-town-ingest attorney I ever heard of. He'd once told me he liked to go over his briefs up where it was quiet and peaceful and there were no dis-tractions, at one of these little country hotels or wayside stopping-off places. I often wondered if anyone went along to help him turn the pages, but that was a loaded question. And none of my business besides. He seemed to be happily enough married. I'd met his wife.

I left my name and where I was, and asked her to tell him to come down in the morning with the fifty-five dollars.

The fifty-five being in default, my pocket-fill was taken away from me, stacked into an oblong manila folder, the flap of this was wetly and sloppily licked by a police property clerk who seemed to be oversalivated, and it was then pummeled into adhesion, and held, to be returned to me on exit. My name and my other details were entered on the blotter, and I was booked and remanded into a cell to be held overnight on a D. and D. charge.

I'd never been in one of them before. Actually, it wasn't so bad. If you closed your eyes a minute and didn't stop to tell yourself what it was, it could have been any barren little room, except that the light was on the outside and never went off all night.

I was alone in it. There were two bunks in it, but the other one was fallow. D. and D., drunk and disorderly (conduct), must have been on the scarce side that night. There are runs on various types of charges at certain times, the cops will tell you that in their line of work. The blanket smelled of creosote, that's the part I remember most. I could hear somebody nearby snoring heavily, but I didn't mind that, it took a little of the alone-ness away.

Even the breakfast wasn't too bad. No worse than you'd get in an average elbow-rest cafeteria. And of course, on the city. They passed it in about six, a little earlier than I usually had mine. Oatmeal, and white bread, and a thick mug of coffee. I skipped the first two, because I don't like soupy oatmeal and because I don't like cottony white bread, but I asked for a refill on the coffee and was given it not only willingly but even (I thought I detected) with a touch of fellow feeling by him outside there in the corridor. I guess I wasn't the usual type he got in there.

And meanwhile I kept thinking: Don't they know yet? Don't they know what I've done? Why is it taking them so long to find out? I thought they were so fast, so infallible.

Sutphen came around ten in the morning and paid out my damages, and in due course they unlocked me and indicated me out. On our way down the front steps of the detention house side by side, he shook his headful of tightly spun pepper-and-salt clinkers at me and gave me a mildly chiding: "A man your age. Breaking bar windows. Brawling. Trying to do, act like a perpetual juvenile?" Beyond that he had nothing else much to say. I suppose to him it was too trifling, and not a legal matter at all but one of loss of temper.

I didn't tell him either what I'd done. I don't know why; I couldn't bring myself to. He was more the one to tell than the cops. My friend and lawyer in one. It would have given him a head start at least on figuring out what was best to do for me. But I was tired and beat. I hadn't closed my eyes all night in the detention cell. I knew once I told I wouldn't be left alone; I'd be dragged here and lugged there and hustled the next place. I wanted time to sleep on it and time to think it out and time to tighten my belt for what was coming to me.

He asked me if he could drop me off, in a perfunctory way. But I knew he was anxious to get back to his office routine and not play anyone's door-to-door driver. And I wanted to be alone too. I had a lot of thinking to catch up on. I didn't want anyone right on top of me for a while. So I told him no and I walked away from him down the street on my own and by my lonesome.

And thus the night finally came to its long-drawn-out end, the memorable unforgettable night that it had been.

I felt rotten, inside and out and all over. Like when you've had a tooth that hurts, and have had it taken out, and then the hole where it was hurts almost as bad as before. You can't tell the diff.

But the paradox of the whole thing was this: on the night that I committed a murder, I was only locked up on disorderly conduct charges.

The next completed chapter, which Woolrich called "Back to the Beginning" and which occupies pp. 18–35 of the typescript, flashes back to Cleve Evans's first meeting with Janet Bartlett, whom he nearly runs over in his sports car one lonely night. This chapter has never been published until now.

CHAPTER 2

I t was one o'clock in the morning and the streets were dead. A fine needle-rain was falling, so fine you could only see it where the beams of the heads caught it and made it seem like silver smudge. And by one or two other side-effects it created: the dark gloss it gave the street-beds, like they'd all just had a shoeshine; a slight distortion to the round outlines of the street light-globes, so that each one seemed pear-shaped and seemed to be "sweating" a single drop of moisture that clung to the bottom of it without ever falling off. It was one of those sneaky saturations that sometimes afflict New York.

I made an incautiously swift right turn-around in the little Simca, bringing me into the side-street of my electing. I had the right to. I had the light. But maybe not quite that fast. And there she was, square in front of me, out in the middle where she had no right to be. I think she'd stepped out there to make it easier to scan the distance for a taxi.

The white raincoat flared up like ignited flashlight-powder as my head-glare leapfrogged over her. I saw two eyes round with nothing at all, not even fright yet.

I had to hit her, there was no time nor room left to do anything else. The only thing there was time enough for was to try to hit her as gently as possible. No, I'm not trying to be funny.

I pounded my leg down so hard I nearly blasted the pedal out through the bottom of the car. She went down without a sound, like a pin in a bowling alley. Well, *that* makes a falling-over sound, she of course didn't even do that. Just went over and down, and wasn't there any more from seat-level view. She flipped from sight, as if she'd turned a handspring of her own free will.

I jacked the door open and hopped out. Her eyes were wide open (accusingly, protestingly, it seemed to me). I crouched and put my head down low next to her, and we spoke our first words to each other.

"I'm sorry," I said contritely. "I'm sorry."

She said, "Oh, why did you have to do that?" Tears were beginning to form in her eyes as the first coating of shock started to thaw out a little.

Neither of us made much sense; people don't at times like that.

I looked around and there was nobody I could call on for help; the area was dead, nobody, nothing, not on foot, not on wheels. I couldn't leave her there on the damp chilling ground while I chased up and down hunting out a police call-box. I palmed my car-horn a couple of times, but that didn't get me a rise. So I picked her up and put her into the car, in spite of the old first-aid precept never to move anyone who's been hurt.

When I had her on the seat, I placed the flat of my hand against her forehead and held it there consolingly for a minute, and we looked at one another. Pain, and sympathy for it, can make partners out of strangers. She smiled at me a little. Wanly maybe, but smiled just a little.

Then I went around to the off-street side and got in. I started tooling slowly along toward the next corner below. I made the corner-turn as cautiously as if I were gliding over eggs, and then I straightened out along that directional there. That one was Lexington, which is south-bound of course. I coasted along for five blocks, hugging the curb-side lane and ready to emergency-brake at every stray leaf of newspaper that cartwheeled past in front of me. I kept looking around, and not a living thing. But this was a residential pocket, insulated and set well below the mid-section of the island. Besides, it was the halfway-mark of a four-day holiday-weekend, half the town had emptied out, and the reverse tide hadn't yet set in. And as any New Yorker can tell you, there is nothing as dead as New York on the 29th of May, the 2nd or 3rd of July, or the first Friday in September.

She moved her head toward me slightly once, and as I quickly turned to find out what she wanted, she murmured "Have you got a handkerchief?" in a muffled, patient little voice.

I took one out of my upper pocket, and first I was going to just give it to her, but when I saw what she wanted it for, I brought the car to a soft stop and did it for her myself: patted it across her eyebrows and just under the line of her hair, wherever there were those tell-tale pore-dots of moisture beginning to peer through.

It wasn't that warm a night; it was painful unease that was bringing them.

I felt lousy.

I shucked off my jacket and spread it across her from shoulder to shoulder, just under the chin, like a great big bib. At least it was better than nothing.

I edged the sole of my foot carefully down to flush again.

I decided I'd have to check her in at the emergency receiving entrance of one of the hospitals myself. I couldn't keep her out on the streets like this any longer. It was unheard of; bad for her and maybe even dangerous.

The nearest one was French, on 30th far over on the West Side, on 10th Avenue. I turned at 29th and went through there, because of the way it was pointed. I made the run across-town without a break, leapfrogging the lights. It's easy to synchronize yourself to them at that hour, with nothing in front of you.

Two guys came over with a stretcher and put it down on the ground. Then they lifted her up and laid her down on it, covered her, and carried her inside to the accident-ward. I went in after them and called 440–1234 and told the police what had happened and where I was. About five or six minutes later a prowl-car, a "micky mouse" as it's known in sidewalkese, came along complete with red roof-flash, picked me up and took me in.

I left my own car behind, in an overnight parking-zone.

Stewart Sutphen my lawyer had gone up to Lake George for that four-day holiday I've spoken of, I knew I couldn't reach him at his home, and it didn't seem important enough to call him all the way upstate about and expect him to come back ahead of time for. Meanwhile the cops were processing me, jotting down prolific notes, and sifting through my credentials and identification papers. They said I'd have to appear at a hearing, and told me when, but for the night or what there was left of it, they let me go home on a fifty-dollar bond, which I posted myself without too much difficulty once I got past the hurdle of convincing them it was all right to accept a couple of Express traveler's checks I happened to have on me. (One of the lameheads among them seemed to think this was before-the-fact evidence I intended to skip the jurisdiction.)

I taxied back to where I'd left my car, switched to that, found a ticket waiting for me on the windshield (I'd overstayed the 6 A.M. legal deadline by about twenty minutes), and finally drove home in it.

It was crowding 7 by this time and the day was peering up pretty pale-blue and gold and white.

I went to sleep, just plain white.

And with that, the pitiful little episode seemed to be over. Or is anything ever really over in this world? Isn't it more likely it has just begun, but we don't know it?

It was after I'd gotten up, and gone down to get into the car, that I found her handbag had been left in it the whole time. All through the overnight-parking period and the next day's sleep. Locked in, of course. It had fallen down into the split between the two seats, probably when the two hospital-jockeys had lifted her out to put her on the stretcher. It had a gilt tassel hanging from one corner of it, and when this started muzzling and tickling my ankle, I looked down and saw it there.

I sat there in the turned-off car with it on my lap, and started going through it. Not larcenously, of course, but the way you get to know someone, build her up, out of the little things that belong to her, that she carries around with her every day on the daily round. I'd seen her face the night before, but that was a mask, it had pain on it and it was in half-light, half-shadow most of the time.

This showed her to me in repose, and in complete candid-snapshot unselfconsciousness, never knowing that a stranger would put these little pieces together—and get to know her by them.

Her name was Janet Bartlett, and she had a room in a furnished-room house on the 200-block of East 25th (for which, she paid twenty-two-fifty a week), her little folded and folded-over and over-folded scrap of a rent-receipt told me.

She weighed an even hundred pounds, a cardboard stub from a coin weight-machine told me.

The only make-up she used apparently (at least once she was dressed for the day and out of her room) was a little flesh-colored powder for the tip of the nose and the cleft of the chin. This was in a little silver container thin as a dime.

She had no problem with perspiration or body-freshness; there were no signs of any corrective for that.

She did part-time work as a demonstrator for some of the department stores. I found vouchers from Gimbel's and Alexander's, among others, but no indication of what the product or merchandise was. The money wasn't good.

She didn't seem to use the subway to get to work. There wasn't a single turnstile-token among the sixty-odd coins ranging from pennies all the way up to quarters I found cached. (Crushable money: eight singles.) But then this was no absolute indication.

She was only a very occasional smoker, and her brand was Marlboro. There was a pack with only about two taken out, but with all its crispness gone from weeks of jogging around with her.

There was someone she wrote to with more or less regularity. I found a sheet of ten five-cent stamps, folded-over to the dimension of one along their perforation-lines. I wondered if it was a man. But it might have been only her mother.

Her favorite color seemed to be yellow. I found a handkerchief with yellow polka-dots running along its edges. I found a choker-collar of yellow milk-beads (off her neck at the time, probably, because the clasp was broken). I found a pair of earrings, each one a—well, an enamel buttercup, I guess you'd call it, on gold backing.

She'd eaten Chinese food somewhere, and the filler from a fortune cookie told her: *Someone is coming into your life who will bring you great happiness but also great sorrow.* (I swear to Christ, I'm not making this up, it really did say that!)

And that was about it. But I knew her pretty well already, you've got to agree. All but what she was really like inside.

I sat there thinking about her—the girl I'd run into. And I asked myself the damnedest question: Would you rather not have hit her, and consequently not known she existed?

And I got the damnedest answer back you've ever heard! No, I'd rather have hit her, and therefore know that she exists.

It was too late to do anything that day, night had come already, the first night following the accident-night. So I slept on the handbag, not literally but as a time-figure. But the first thing the following morning I looked up the information-desk at the hospital and called in to ask about her.

I said: "There was a young woman brought in about two-thirty, three o'clock yesterday morning, a pedestrian-hit-by-car accident-case. Can you tell me how she's coming, please?"

"Have you a name you can give me?" she said. "It would expedite."

Fancy-word user, I thought with tolerant contempt. What's the

matter with, hurry it up? She's so nursy she probably uses a thermometer to shape her lipstick on with when she's off-duty.

"Bartlett," I said. "Miss J. Bartlett or Miss Janet Bartlett."

She came back center-phone again. "We have a Janet Bartlett.
She's on the satisfactory-list."

"That means I can see her?"

"You have to pick up a pass at this desk. Visiting-hours are from
one to three, and again from—"

I chose the earlier slot. I stretched my lunch-hour double, by not
taking any lunch in the first place, and then taking an equal
amount of time all over again to not take any lunch in.

I stopped in at a flower-shop and bought her a mix of jonquils
and roses, and the florist-man made a big sheath around them with
this semi-transparent crisp green paper they use, and then fastened
the open ends at the top down over each other with staples, and the
whole thing looked great. Before doing so he gave me a blank card
and I wrote on it "No hard feelings?"—no name, just that, and
dropped it inside.

She was in a ward on the fifth floor, and when I got up there I
spoke to the nurse-in-charge outside in the hall before I went in.
They'd taken X-rays early the morning before, a few hours after
she'd been admitted, she told me, and fortunately no fractures
showed up. So they'd moved her out of the accident-ward and into
this one. What she did have was a badly wrenched hip-socket,
she'd turned over on it in falling, but this was a matter of the ligaments, they had the leg in traction, and she'd be up and around on
it again in a matter of a week, ten days.

Then she added, apropos of nothing that had gone before as far
as I could see, "She's a cute little thing."

Though I didn't mean to do it, I gave her a quick look without
realizing it that must have said as plain as words: So you think so
too, do you?

I took a hitch in my courage, a gulp in my gullet, and I went on
in. And then I stopped again, just inside the open doorway. There
seemed to be about six beds. Maybe there were only five, I don't

know; I hadn't come there to count beds. But only two of them had occupants. And one of them was she.

And so, for the second time, we met and looked at each other. By the time my eyes found her, though, hers had already found me. She was a beautiful girl. I only saw how beautiful she was right then for the first time. Much more than I remembered from two nights before. She had blue eyes and brown hair. It was the *way* she had them though that made her beautiful. Innocent, clear, little-girl eyes that you could tell had never yet loved any guy, so far until now. And her hair just had a clean, white, soap-and-water-looking part, down low on one side, and after that was allowed to do pretty much what it wanted. No souped-up curls or shellacked contortions; I got the idea she never sandblasted it with any of those sprays they have around. She had on one of those hospital Mother-Hubbard nightshirts, she managed to look lovely even in that, and when you can do that you must be.

"Hello," I said in a husky whisper, "How are you?" from where I was standing over by the doorway.

The damn fool someone in the other bed took her eyes off the Jolly Green Giant commercial on the TV screen, the one where the toy train loaded up with oversized peas runs between his straddled legs, which about matched her moronic mentality I guess, and turned to look at me and tittered. "Come on in," she invited. "Don't be afraid, no one will bite you. We're all friends here." I didn't look at her. I shuffled over the rest of the way until I was standing alongside the bed, and then I handed over the flowers.

When she frittered open the crinkly swathing and saw the yellow inside, of the jonquils and roses both, her face lit up. "How did *you* know!"

Encouraged, I pulled over a straightback chair and sat down beside her.

"But how did you *guess*?" she kept insisting, incredulous.

I told her the only lie I ever did, I guess. Call it a little, not white, but "yellow" lie. Not in the slang sense of the word, but in its original color-adjectival sense. "Just one of those flukes; I must have called the shot without knowing it." I didn't tell her that I'd noticed the touches of yellow here and there on things inside her handbag when I'd opened it the night before; I didn't like her to think I'd been probing into it.

The flowers once past, we were both as constrained and bashful as two kids thrown at each other's heads at a children's dancing-party and told to get along together. She picked at the bedcovers a couple times. I wished I had a cigarette to get behind, but a sign out in the hall had said No Smoking.

I remember, "What's your name?" she came out with at one point.

It's a funny thing to ask a man who's run over you in the street. But then what other way is there to find out but to ask?

"Cleve Evans," I said.

She gave me hers. I already knew it anyway, but she gave it to me as a sort of reflex to my giving her mine.

"I bet your folks are sore at me," I suggested.

"I don't have any."

That was what I'd wanted to find out. Then it wasn't her mother she was writing to and needed all those stamps to do it with.

I looked down at the floor and felt sort of down in the dumps about it for a minute.

Another topic of conversation was the woman in the other bed, who had temporarily absented herself around this time to go to the ladies' room.

"What's the matter with *her*?" I asked resentfully, looking over that way simply because I knew she wasn't there now and the coast was clear. I hadn't liked the braying reception she'd given me before.

She thought I meant symptom-wise and not manner-wise. "Subject to nose-bleeds, from high blood-pressure." But she had a complaint of her own to add, although more in deploration than anger. "She plays that thing the live-long day," she confided, shading her mouth with the edge of her hand.

"I didn't know they allowed it."

"They do in some of the rooms; this is a recuperation-room. I wouldn't mind it so much, but it's *what* she has on. Children's puppet-shows the first thing in the morning."

"Why don't you let me send you in a little radio, that might take some of the curse out of it, give you something else to listen to?"

"All right," she accepted. "Just as a loan-out, while I stay here."

I hadn't meant that, but I didn't crowd my luck by contradicting her.

A bell rang to signal the end of the visiting-period, and I stood up, with an awkward scraping of the chair and of my feet. I didn't offer my hand, afraid it would be turned down. Or worse still, picked up only in unwilling polite compulsion. Instead, she offered me hers.

We both said that word you say when you leave someone. "Goodbye."

It means so little, and yet it means such a lot too. It all depends on how you say it. The way I said it, it meant: I'm coming back again. And again. And again and again and again. For just as long as you'll let me come back.

When I got to the door I turned and looked back. She wasn't looking at me anymore. But she was looking at the yellow flowers now instead, and that was even better.

I went straight from the hospital to the nearest music-store. I bought her a Sony transistor, small but the best one put out, with one of those earphone attachment-cords to it. I paid extra to have it sent over by messenger then and there, instead of waiting for days-after parcel-post delivery.

When I came around next day, she had it put to her ear. (The blood-pressure woman was gone now anyway; I didn't even bother asking if she'd bled to death or been cauterized, I didn't care that much.) "Listen," she beamed, and held it up to my ear for me to share.

They were playing Borodin, bitched into a bossa nova beat, but it was good.

"You like that, hon?" I grinned.

Her face told me.

Inside of a week, I was in love with her. Inside of eight days, she knew it. Inside of ten, she was in love with me. Inside of nine, I knew she was. How did I, so quick? She told me she did. Not in words. What are words anyway? The nestling little curl of her hand around mine, when they clasped. And when we kissed, my lips didn't have to go all the way, hers came halfway to meet them, to make sure they wouldn't lose their way. And in her eyes there was that tender reminiscence, that means you're loved. Reminiscent, because it's thinking of the dream that once was just a dream, and now is a dream that's true. And both match up. And you've found love.

Thirteen days to the day after she and I and my car had met, she left the hospital. I was waiting for her outside to take her home. Sometimes you have a long stand before you get a taxi in New York, and she still wasn't fully footsure. And the tricky down-steps of the subway, where the people are so thick you can't even see the steps, and the even trickier up-steps of the buses, where the pneumatic door folds closed on you and you have to hold it back at arm's length, weren't for her yet for some weeks to come.

So I was waiting there as she came out, whistling "I-found-a-horseshoe-couldn't-go-wrong, And-then-of-course-you-happened-along" in the snappy cloud-scudded Manhattan sunshine. She had the same white raincoat she'd gone in with, but now she had it over her arm, because the day was clear. In her other hand she was holding a small kit, I suppose of personal articles sent on after her by her landlady.

I introduced her to my car. "This is Mamselle. She's a Pujoe. I ought to kick her in the tires for what she did, but then if it hadn't been for her I wouldn't have met you."

She patted a fender by way of answer. (Like you pat a dog that's picked up something and brought it to you.)

I drove as carefully with her as if she were made of spun glass. I glanced at her once and caught her smiling a little to herself about it. I guess it was that; I don't know what else there was.

"This is it, here," she said as we glided up even with it.

I stopped and turned to look at it. Scanning it, I thought with that touch of awe the newly-in-love feel: it holds her in the morning, it holds her in the night. I thought: someday we'll speak of it and say, the rooming-house you lived in when I first met you, that I first brought you home to.

It was clean-looking, it tried to keep itself clean-looking, that was my overall impression about it. But it was old, there wasn't anything as old as it must have been. With those window-embrasures rounded-off at the top, like they used to build them seventy-five years ago. It cried for lace curtains with silver gaslight shining behind them. And the clop-clop of a milkman's horse and wagon to come along and leave a bottle of cream on the doorstep, at ten cents a throw. And if it stood there all day long, still no one would steal it. As out of place among its neighbors as a little bonneted old lady crowding the rail at a speed-car track. And no place for her to live in.

I took her over to the door, and I rang the bell for her, so she wouldn't have to dredge down for her key. I asked if I could call her, she said of course, and I asked for the number. "I don't have one of my own in the room," she said. "But there's one downstairs and you can reach me on that; she'll call up to me."

I didn't have to write it down. I had it memorized before her lips even finished saying it to me. The things you care about, you're a quick-study about.

She went in, and I drove away. I took up whistling again where I'd left off when she came out of the hospital to meet me. "Oh-boy-I'm-lucky-I'll-say-I'm-lucky, This-is-my-lucky-day!"

We saw each other every few nights in the weeks after. Then every few nights became every night. I brought her to the door and left her there each time. We never put it to the test, but the rooming-house manager probably would have frowned if she'd tried taking me up into the room with her. And the lay-out was such anyway, she once told me, that we'd have sat with our knees knocking into each other.

Jack Bojack, a friend of mine, was about to get married, and on top of that was about to be transferred to Chicago. The first was a direct result of the second: salary-hike. He had a funny name, but that has nothing to do with this. French and Indian descent: French trapper, Indian squaw. The ancestor's name had been Beaujacques originally, good-looking Jack, eroded through the generations into Bojack. This Jack of the 1960s was still good-looking. More important, a good solid friend. And more important still, he had a rent-control apartment which was going back on the market.

I set up a three-cornered deal, between Jack, myself, and the renting agent who managed Jack's apartment. I took it over from Jack at the thawed-out rent. A girl was coming around to look at it, a Miss Bartlett. (Take down that name, please; he took down that name please). She was to be told she could have it at the old frozen rent. I agreed to pay the difference each month, but she wasn't to know anything about that, not under any circumstances, understand. It was to be kept strictly inter-office.

The renting agent said: "I think I understand."

"You don't understand," I told him flatly.

"All right, I don't understand," he agreed.

But I knew he still thought he did.

I told her about it casually, gave her the address.

She went around to look at it, she liked it, she took it.

She was almost ecstatic over it. "It's a dream." She dragged me over there to show it to me. (I'd only been in it about two-dozen times before, at all sorts of stags.)

"Look, fluorescent lights. And all that chromium. I could live in this bathroom, alone!"

"You'd get kind of damp," I quieted her down.

Jack had left all his furniture (the bride was going to pick out new stuff in Chicago). There was only one thing she had a dubious comment to make on, and that was Jack's bursting-at-the-seams liquor-cabinet. (He was still in titular occupancy at this point.) "He seems to do a lot of drinking."

"All young unmarried guys do," I generalized incautiously.

"Do you?" she came right back at me.

I side-stepped neatly by acting like I hadn't heard.

Jack left Wednesday, and by Wednesday night she was in.

We had a little house-warming, just for and by and with, the two of us. No noisy noise, no noisy guests, nobody else. Just the two, we two, the me of it and the you. I brought in a bottle of Möet and Chandon, but we only had about one drink apiece of that (and in her case just a lip-wetting) and then, somehow, I don't know how, we started to talk.

"You're not afraid of me, are you?" I said at one point. I indicated the four sides of the room by swinging my upped thumb around them in a twirl. "Of this, and me, and tonight?"

"No," she said quite simply, looking straight at me, untroubled, unevasive. "You're my destiny. I've been coming straight toward you ever since I was born. You, and this room, and this night."

And then she began to tell me. Slowly, and only a little at time.

Whatever incident out of her past Janet was about to tell Cleve we will never know. Next comes an untitled chapter (pp. 38–56 of the type-script) where we learn that Cleve is already married—to a bitchy night-club singer named Adelaide. The action here is all too reminiscent of the sequence in *Into the Night* where Vick Herrick left the Adelaide of *that* novel. The "You and I together all alone" lyrics from the song which Cleve and Janet dance to near the end of this chapter are Woolrich hall-marks, dating all the way to his pre–crime novel *Times Square* (1929). The chapter trails off unfinished, but the last paragraph hints that the new couple's delirious happiness is about to be menaced.

CHAPTER 3

I rang first, I don't know why, before I took out my key. I rang first, to sort of telegraph I was there. I rang first, to make the admittance formal, to show it wasn't a sneak-in. I rang first, but she wasn't in, she didn't come to the door. Then I took out the key and let myself in.

The fellow down on the door had seen me pass, and said a word to me, and I'd said a word to him. "Nice day we're having, isn't it?" was the word he said to me.

"Haven't seen you for a while, been off?" was the word I said to him.

"I been in the hospital for a week with an ulcer. I'm standing here one afternoon and suddenly—"

The elevator-slide, closing between us, cut his ulcer in two. Or at least, cut his ulcer-descriptive in two.

I took out my key and I let myself in.

I went right through into the bedroom. I didn't take in any details. All I had time to notice in passing was a square cut-glass decanter of Scotch that badly needed some Scotch. The only Scotch left in it was four thin dreg-lines running up and down the insides of its seams.

The bedroom smelled. Good, I mean. As if it had to prove: This is a bedroom. This is where people go to bed together. Just take a sniff. Now you *know* it's a bedroom.

I rummaged in the closet looking for that travel-bag one of the air-line companies had once given out to me with its compliments. Good-will and good advertising; lightweight, dark-blue, soft crush-fabric. I'd never used it before. Then, I'd never been going away anyplace for good before.

It was hiding behind a peach silk teaser edged with gray marabou. (Which was a flop, it had never teased me much. Except to make me sneeze.)

I put it on the bed. I started to take my shirts out of the drawers in the chest. I looked up and she was standing there. I hadn't heard her come in.

It started in on a minor-enough key.

She said, "What's this?"

She said, "Charlie told me you were up here."

I said, "Charlie told you right. Ask Charlie, and you'll always know." Something like that.

She was still neutral.

She said, "Back to stay? Or just back to keep your franchise? Or what?"

I gave it to her then, straight but sour. "Back to get the hell out for good."

"That takes two," she said with a sharp cutting-edge starting to show up now along her voice.

"Since when?"

"One to go, and one to let him."

She took my half-packed carryall, knocked it off the edge of the bed, and dumped it upside-down on the floor, with all the shirts and stuff underneath instead of on top of it now.

I opened my hand, brought it out past one shoulder, fanned it around in a half-circle that would have ended out past the other. Her cheek stopped it in the middle, with a sound like an overripe melon dropping and popping open.

"Leave your hands off my things." I picked up my travel-bag, picked up the interred things under it, and started over.

She had turned away with a jumpy little jerk, like when you break off talking to someone, give him your shoulder, and are about to walk away from him. Then she turned back again, but from the other way around, equally hitchy. The whole thing had something of the ludicrous about it, because it wasn't voluntary, it was the impact had done it. Turned her completely around and back again, in two stages, with a leg-stagger in-between to help her brace herself.

A thing like the decalcomania of a poppy showed up on one side of her face, different in shade and intensity from the rouge on the other cheek.

She wasn't sore. Not in any vital spot. Not really where it hurt, not really in her basic pride and dignity. Not the way a man would have been if he was hit like that. I knew her well enough, I knew that. She'd probably known violence like that more than just once, back in her early days, back when she was first starting to go around, back before she could pack enough importance to impress men to respect her. In her catalogue it had probably meant at least the man cared by that much, was that much interested, if he side-swiped her like that.

The slap wasn't the sore-spot, the packing-bit was. The leaving her for someone else.

I could tell by the quiet, dissembled, veiled way her eyes watched me now, with a spray of fine wrinkles at each calculatingly narrowed corner, watched me zip the duffle-bag closed and carry it inside to the other room with me, put it down by the front door, and then come back in again for something. I think it was an outside coat to go over my arm.

Then she asked in a mock-casual demure little voice, seeded with cunning, "Do I know her?"

"Now that's a stupid question. If you knew her, I wouldn't love her, she wouldn't be the type for me."

I changed the coat over from one arm to the other by heaving it up in air off the one arm and catching it onto the other.

"Then you're going to give me a divorce or aren't you, what about it?"

She only bared her teeth at that, as though it was a waste of time. A waste of time to ask, and a waste of time to answer. The bared teeth weren't in a smile or grin, they were in a hate-pattern, vindictive.

She went inside, opened the liquor-cabinet door, and came back holding a bottle of brandy. It wasn't top brandy; it was French but bottled over here. She started to nudge it around the top of the neck where the liquor-stamp was, like she always did, and broke the edge of her nail off, like she always did.

Funny, the little things you do at the unlikeliest times, without even knowing you're doing them sometimes. I took it away from her without a word and nicked it all around the stopper-seam with my tougher, blunter nail, then sprang the cork for her with my thumb joint, and handed it back. "You never could open a bottle." You do the funniest things, at the funniest times. Just a reflex, a carryover, from a dozen times or more before that I'd done it for her.

She drank a little shot. She didn't ask me to drink with her. I wouldn't have if she had. My drinking days with her were over. And hers with me.

She looked down into the little shot-glass, as though the words she was saying, words she was using, were in there, were coming up out of there. Although it was very small to hold that many words. She even circled it around a little in her hand, as if to stir up the words a little, blend them, mix them better. Make them come out better as she said her piece.

"Cleve," she said, strangely quiet, "there's a thing they call the point of no return. Did you ever hear of the point of no return? Once you've passed it, you can't turn back, ever. It's too late."

"Too late for what?" I growled. One kidney leaning against the chest of drawers, the coat furled over my arm waiting to go out with me.

"I'm the woman who loved you, Cleve. Once you reach that point and pass it, you turn love into hate, and me into your enemy. And I stay that way for good, you can never go back and undo it again. Think about it. Pull back. Because I make a bad enemy. I warn you, Cleve, I make a bad enemy."

"Why can't you just let me go?" I asked. Not wanting to know, just for the sake of hearing what she'd say.

"She can't have you. What's mine I keep." She slammed down the empty glass with a shot that gave it its right name; it was a shot-glass all right.

"Just like last year's fur coat. A diamond bracelet from two years back. That's all I've ever been, just someone to wear on your arm. Someone that looks good trailing you into a crowded room, shoving in your chair for you, sitting at the table with you so you don't have to be seen sitting alone. Someone to make the other women turn around and say, 'She's got what it takes.' Someone permanent and legally yours to go to bed with, so that you avoid the wear-and-tear, the risks, and the tarnished reputation you run up going in for nothing but one-night-stands all your live-long life long."

And I asked her solemnly and reproachfully: "How can you expect to hold a guy, when he's just a *belonging*? You're supposed to *love*, not *own*."

"Well, wasn't it worth it? You made out pretty good. Who else gets a shake like that?"

"It was worth it until I fell in love and found out what the real thing was like. Eight years late maybe, but not too late. I still got in under the wire."

I never knew anyone could make a laugh sound like such a dirty thing. You wanted to take a shower and have your clothes deloused. I hung my head, not because I was ashamed, but because it was too filthy to stare at in the face.

"What were *you* when I married you, anyway," she railed, "to have the crust, the guts, to throw up love to me? A stage-hand in a country summer-stock theater—"

"I still had the one thing you've never had though: integrity."

She tipped her thumb into herself and looked off across the room, as though she were talking to a third person. "Me, a topflight singer, at the height of her career. Everyone thought I was crazy. Plenty of people tried to warn me."

"Top-flight my pratt!" I blared out angrily. "There never was any talent in your career, there never even was any music in it. Your career was built on muscle, strong-arm stuff. I know your story backward. You told me most of it yourself, lying in bed together, when people tell each other the truth. A kid of fifteen, that didn't know how to do anything but one thing, but knew how to do that like an expert; you go up to this shady, two-bit operator running this shady, two-bit club. He puts the hose on you and then he puts you on at the club. Every kid of fifteen has a dream, at least every one that's a girl, and it's always the same dream: she wants to be an actress, or a singer (same thing). You were the one out of ten thousand of them that was the exception; you got your dream. It came out. He got it for you. It came out true.

"First at the dinky little club itself, it started to be just the way it was going to be later. If they didn't applaud loud enough their checks were padded. If they showed they didn't like your 'voice' by ignoring you or going on talking, they got mickys. If they were foolish enough to call out anything uncomplimentary, they got thrown out and beaten the hell out of in the alley in back of the stage-door. Even women were pushed around and had their clothes torn by the tough ladies' room attendant.

"Then he branched out from there. When he couldn't get you a recording-date, he formed his own record-company, hired a studio, had you make them on your own and he handled the distributing for you. And he got good distribution. Because any music-store or music-counter that didn't stock up enough or re-order enough, got a Molotov cocktail through its plate-glass store-window in the middle of the night. Once a whole consignment of pianos was hijacked and dumped into the water's edge. Remember? Nobody could figure out why, the cops, nobody. Since when are pianos hot or bootleg? But I bet wherever it was they were going, did plenty of business on your latest release the next few weeks after that. Then there was the case of that disk-jockey on an all-night radio program, out in one of the midwestern cities, I forget where; used to play your records all right, but used to make fun of you night after night each time he did. Turned it into a spoof. 'Gravel Gertie' and 'Buzz-saw Betty.'

"They picked him up out of a ditch one morning way out of town. Something must have sideswiped his car. But they never could figure out how his tongue came to be torn out almost by the roots. Was he driving with his tongue sticking out the side of the car, or what? You were two thousand miles away in New York, but you could, *couldn't* you honey?

"He never said 'Gravel Gertie' again.

"He never said anything again."

"That was a long time ago, and I guess the statute of limitations has covered it up and buried it by this time. But I wonder what he does now, that poor mute disk-jockey?"

She hiccoughed in derision, but a little unsurely. "Danny should hear all this."

"I got some of it right from him himself. What you didn't tell me, he did. I know d'Angelo like I know the back of my hand. We used to sit together over drinks many a time waiting for you to come back from some show or singing-date. When two guys sit like that over drinks, they're bound to get to know each other, particularly when they share an interest in the same woman, the ex-lover and the current husband, and particularly where there's no competitive-angle involved anymore. D'Angelo never pulled any punches with me, why should he have to? The sex-part of it had been over between you long before I came along. He stayed on in your life because he had a good investment going, and because a strong bond of friendship had formed between the two of you by this time. Every man loves his own handiwork. He admired some of that very same glamor that he himself had helped to create. Hooked on his own bait. That's why he didn't object when you took a whim to marry me.

"Most of the rough-stuff was over by then anyway, it wasn't needed anymore. You sell anyone a name long enough, and they begin to know the name, good bad or indifferent doesn't matter. After a while they'll accept it without asking themselves why. *Somebody* must like it, or it wouldn't come up so much; that's good enough for them."

"Why does it bother you now, how I got to the top, if it didn't bother you before?"

She had a point there, a real good point there.

"A guy is a naturally dirty animal, until some woman comes along and cleans him up. What did I care what you were? I didn't have anything else, I didn't know any better. I was getting mine. The only thing I did know, though, was it wasn't love. But I'd never known love, never had it, so I didn't know what I was missing."

Clean language has an infinite variety. But filthy language is extremely narrow in its scope. There are only a limited number of things you can tell someone to do with that well-worn four-letter word. They all point the same way. And after it's been told to you once it's been told to you for good and all.

She quit after a while, and got back to where she could've been quoted again. And now she wasn't just demonic, she was dangerous. She wasn't just loud, she was lethal.

"You've crossed the point of no return. No more love now. Only hate, only hate. And you know something, I already like it much better. It feels good. It feels better than love does." She hugged herself around the middle, arms reversed. "I was made for it, and it was made for me. I should've hated you long ago. All that time I wasted."

There wasn't anything more to say. Too much had been said already.

"I spit on your love," I told her, "and I (something-else-with-the-same-two-terminal-letters) on your hate."

"I'll destroy you, Cleve," she bayed. "And her along with you."

I walked in a straight line across the room to the door, and without breaking stride scooped up the duffle-bag from the floor, opened the door and closed it again in back of me.

An instant later the brandy-bottle detonated against the inside of the door right where my head had just been. (She'd been a pin-girl in a bowling alley, I think she'd told me, when she was a kid.)

I didn't look around. I tipped one shoulder to myself and kept going. Before I could get off the outside floor-landing though the reek of the brandy had leaked through the door-seam. I told you it was raw stuff, cut.

Riding down in the elevator, it came back once more. I'm not talking about the brandy now. "I'll destroy you, Cleve. And her along with you." Then it went away again. For a little while.

Charlie saw me come out and shy the duffle-bag into the car.

"You're leaving us?" he asked me.

"And I'm not coming back," I said.

I turned the key and started to glide off.

Then I remembered I should have given him something. It was the last time I'd see him after all. All those months, twice a day, in and out. It wasn't his fault if they'd been drags.

I didn't want to reverse and go back to him again. I couldn't anyway, there was somebody coming up behind me. So I fished a bill out of my pocket, flagged him with it to catch his eye, and threw it over the side of the car. It spiraled around a couple of times and then settled on the ground. He was very good at retrieving things like that though; you should have seen him dart in and out between me and the car behind and snatch it up, without a fender nicking him.

When I got back, Janet just looked at me, just stood and looked at me, without asking me anything. But I answered her look all the same.

"She won't set me free. We're going to get married anyway."

We left our apartment, our little place we lived in, about eight o'clock one of those New York mornings that are as crisp and sparkling as cornflakes and champagne, and started out on our way to get married. Funny, I thought once or twice on our way across-town to the Midtown Tunnel, the usual way is for a girl and man each living in a different place to come together to get married, and from then on to both live together in the same place. The way we're doing it, we both start out by living together in the same place, we go out and get married, and then we go back where we were living before. That doesn't take anything away from it, that doesn't make it any the less the real, the lifetime thing.

People have been married by proxy, people have been married by captains at sea, and stuck to each other the rest of their lives. What's the difference if the justice talks Spanish or talks English, what's the difference if it's said in Latin in a cathedral, or in deaf and dumb sign-language in the front parlor of an institutional home? What's the difference if it takes five minutes or five weeks from the posting of the banns? You're still hers, she's still yours, you've been made one.

We came out into the Jersey flats, and even they looked good. And fellow, if the Jersey flats look good to you, you've found the right girl, you're doing the right thing.

We ran straight down as far as Jaxville, everybody knows how to get there, and then made a right-turn across the Florida panhandle, followed the Gulf Coast into New Orleans and out again the other side, then hugged the slow curve of the Louisiana and Texas shore-lines down into Brownsville, the southernmost tip of the conti-nental United States land-mass (Key West don't forget is an island). But we didn't cross over there, somebody at one of our Texas stops had given us a steer to a better place. We doubled right again and went back up the Rio Grande as far as a border town called Eagle Pass, crossed over into its Mexican opposite-number, and that was it, that was the place.

I left Janet at the little *parador* or inn, and went out to get my divorce. Even in today's free-wheeling world, it would have looked a little bit out of line to have her standing there right alongside me when it was handed down to me. The whole thing was in Spanish. I sat there on a bench at the back of the court-room and just watched, without knowing what it was all about. But it was about me, I could tell, because once they all turned their heads and looked over at me, and the court-clerk asked me something. I stood up and nodded my head and sat down again.

It must have been my name they'd asked me, because that seemed to satisfy them.

First they had instant coffee and instant tea, I said to myself. Now they have instant divorce. But there's one thing they'll never have: instant love. You can't get that out of a test-tube.

I looked the certificate over, when it had been handed to me after payment of the necessary fees. It sure looked legal all right, nothing could have looked more legal. It had my name (misspelled in at least two places, but still mine: "Cleave Eavans"; but with my domicile and date-of-birth, so there could be no potential later mix-up of identities) and the opposite party's both on it; it had the judge's signature, and the date in Spanish: *20 de marzo*, 1966. And the coat-of-arms of the Mexican Republic stamped in violet ink (an eagle grasping a snake in its talons; the old Aztec mystique: stop here when you come upon this sign and found your nation).

We were married the day after that around sunset, by the same judge who had handed down the divorce the day before. But not in his chambers, out at his home; a signal distinction. He must have taken to Janet, he had a daughter of his own only a year or two younger than she was. We stood up in the open patio, with the oxidizing Mexitex sunshine pelting us like a shower of shiny newly minted copper pennies for good luck. Janet was holding the bridal bouquet the judge's daughter had made up for her and gifted her with; it wasn't exclusively all-yellow, but as close to it as she could get on such short notice: the gardenias in it were a sort of ivory-color, but that was close enough.

We couldn't of course have been married by a priest, but there was one there, as an old family-friend and guest of the judge's. He stayed inside during the actual minutes (see no evil, I suppose) but he joined us all later in a glass of wine and even upped his a little in our direction, though he voiced no actual toast to our welfare (speak no evil). Which is about the next-best thing to a religious ceremony, when you've been married before and can't have one.

Immediately afterward we went back across to our own side of the river and started the long many-legged journey back to New York. About ten-thirty we stopped at a motel somewhere along the line in Texas, and that was our wedding-night. We didn't feel any different than we had on all the other nights before it, how could we? But she had this ring on now.

She said: "Remember that nylon shorty-gown you liked so on me? Wait'll you see what that hurry-up laundry at the last place did to it!"

She said: "Cleve, you've been out of toothpaste two or three days now. I don't mind your using mine, but don't you think you better get some tomorrow on our way out?"

I watched a repeat football-game on the motel TV. screen, but I kept the set slanted aside so the glare wouldn't keep her awake.

If all this sounds cynical and flip, that wasn't the mental attitude we brought to it at all. When a man loves a girl, he doesn't give her up; when a girl is loved by a man, she doesn't give him up. If one or both do, then it wasn't much of a love. It wasn't our fault if the divorce laws were in some cases as out-of-date as a crank-handle on a wall-telephone or in some places as unevenly matched as a mosaic floor after a high-powered seismo has coursed through it.

There can be no hard and fast rules for any human relationships. It's like setting an altitude-limit on flame-tips, or a navigation-course for a wave. Marriage is the most human of human relationships. It shouldn't be kicked around like a football. But neither should it be permitted to die and then to continue to weigh down the living with its dead weight. Dead things should be buried, not left above the ground.

We came back by slow and happy stages, pretty much the way we'd come down, with just a few variations. At Biloxi the water was so green that day you couldn't believe you were looking at it but only at one of those garishly colored postcards of the way the water was at Biloxi that day. You expected somebody to turn the rack and the whole thing to swing around and something else show up in its place. You wanted to paste a four-cent stamp up in the right-hand corner of it and send it to someone back home.

On a rise in North Carolina we stopped at the top and just sat there, an arm hanging down outside each side of the car with a cigarette in it, and talked and told our hopes and made our plans. The moon was full, and it made all North Carolina silver. A snatch of a song winged through my head, and I wished it hadn't, because it was a sad sort of a thing. "On our backs we'd lie, gazing at the sky, till the stars were strung, / Just a dream ago, when the world was young."

Like that skeleton they say the Egyptians propped up at their feasts, to remind them: this will pass.

In Richmond we walked along King Street in all the lights, and another couple came by and smiled as they passed us. It was a tender sort of smile, not making fun but making one with us. He wore white slacks and she a ribbon-band flat across the top of her head. I wonder why they smiled at us? Did they recognize themselves in us? We smiled back, just before it was too late, just before they'd gone on past.

On the DelMarVa ferry, the wind blew downward, down Chesapeake Bay, outward to the ocean, and her hair tried its best to follow after it, streaming and fanning out like an aureole, a halo of shimmering brown gauze. I took her picture, but it didn't come out right. It couldn't catch and hold the shine, the light, the love the her, in her eyes. Only other eyes could do that, mine, not a photographic appliance.

It was spring everywhere, including our hearts.

Then across the Washington Bridge, and back into the one and only town of them all, back into the greatest town of them all, back into New York. We drove up in front of the same apartment-house we'd started out from six or seven days ago, and put on the brakes and sat there a few minutes, each with an arm around the other. We were legally married, husband and wife, at least in the eyes of herself and of me and of Mexico. And screwdrive anybody else.

And then the bad times began.

• • •

At first nothing happened.

Happiness is easy to experience, but hard to put into words, it almost can't be done. You can describe fear and hate a lot easier, they're more violent and more active. But happiness is so limpid and so smooth, when you try to pin it down on paper, the essence runs away from you like quicksilver or the iridescent colors on a soap-bubble. About all you can do is live it.

We lived it, then. We knew it, and we had it.

We shook down into marriage.

I used to come out of the alcove in the morning whipping my tie around by its ends, and find her making coffee in two glass bowls set one over the other, and a funny thought used to run through my mind: You've never lived, you've never been alive at all, until you've had coffee made for you in the morning by someone who loves you.

We went out nearly every night at first, like most young couples do in the secondary stages of a honeymoon. Ate at little Italian places, that New York is so full of; once in a while a Chinese place, or a German one over in Yorkville. One night we went to a place they had dancing, and we stood up together and danced. We'd never danced together before, for some reason; this was the first time we had. We danced well together, we found out; without any effort and almost instinctive. Like we'd been waiting all our lives to dance together, and hadn't known it. Because the essence of true dancing isn't in the following or the guiding in the steps, that's just the mechanics of it. You have to think like one another, and feel like one another, and be so attuned, such affinities to one another, that when you move you're more like one than two. And we did and we were, I guess that's why we found we danced so well together.

With her head nudged against my shoulder, she asked with that drowsiness that comes from perfect contentment, "What is that they're playing?"

I didn't know, but the next time we moved close enough to the little three-piece combo, I asked the man farthest out in front. He was on strings, and had his lips free.

" 'You and I,' " he said.

I hunted it up for her the next day, and found a label of it at that record-mart they have on Fifth, between 42nd and 43rd Street. I brought it home to her and we played it on Jack's ex–hi-fi. I mean the hi-fi we had inherited from Jack, I should say.

We used to play it a lot after that. Sometimes we'd dance to it there by ourselves in the room.

"You and I," it was called. It was for us.

The following 21 pages of unpaginated typescript appeared in a men's magazine a few months before Woolrich's death as a self-standing short story ("Warrant of Arrest," *Escapade*, April 1968) but has never been published in book form until now.

CHAPTER 4

I could almost feel it coming before it came. I could almost feel it on the way. Don't ask me to explain. Don't ask me to try to make this plausible, make this logical. I only know I'm telling it true, the way it was. Not hindsight, but foresight, some sort of sixth sense. I think there can be such things: some sort of personal radar that warns you of something coming, before your eyes can see it or your ears can hear it. Not under normal circumstances of course, but at times of heightened superattenuated crisis.

For two days, for forty-eight hours, ever since the second night back, I'd been expecting it, expecting them to come and take me. That much was true. But I didn't know the exact time it would happen, the exact moment, how could I?

And then suddenly—I knew it was about to happen. Right then, any minute, within the next few, the next five, the next ten.

I was standing holding a cup of coffee in my hand, with saucer and spoon attached. She'd just made us coffee. Why I was standing up with it I don't know. Too uneasy to sit down, I guess. I had my head inclined a little toward it, not much, just slightly, the way you bend a little toward a cup in hand in order to avoid tipping or spilling from it. She was sitting on the couch, one leg to floor the other bent back under her, her favorite sitting position, frittering through some big glossy woman's-type magazine, her own cup in accompaniment alongside on the floor.

There was a tink and my spoon had jumped a little on its saucer. I looked and saw what had done it. A spasm or a sort of flicker had been transmitted from my hand.

And then this prickling feeling ran up my backbone, about like if I didn't have my shirt on, say, and a line of ants went traveling up it single-file. But when the figurative "ants" got to the nape of my neck, it became a cold feeling instead, as if an ice-cube had been rubbed up against me there. Not hard, but very lightly.

I put the cup down, this time with a loud rattle, and I straightened my head and shoulders up to fully alert height, and I knew it was on the way, coming toward the door, that very minute.

It cast its shadow before it, and the shadow lay heavy and cold all over my awareness.

She looked up at me just then and said: "Why're you so white? What's making you so white? All the color's left your face."

I made a stroke with my hand that couldn't be translated because there was no translation for it. Simply a punctuation-mark written on the air, a hyphen or a dash given with the hand.

I went over to the window and looked down, without appearing at it full-face. Obliquely, from the side.

There wasn't anything the matter, anything wrong down there. I could see the roof of a black sedan that was parked squarely in front of our door, but that didn't necessarily have to mean anything. There are a lot of black sedans. It could have belonged to someone who lived in the house.

But my premonition held, and I knew it didn't. I knew it was there on official business, police business. To pick someone up for murder.

I knew, I knew there was someone talking to the doorman right then. One someone or two someones, that much I didn't know. But *someone*. Talking to him about me. And he was answering the curt, clipped, low-voiced questions. Yes, he's up there now. I haven't seen him go out in two days. He hasn't gone to work in two days, far as I know. They've had their meals sent in, too, from the delicatessen around the corner. Sandwiches. They used to go out and eat most nights.

Then they'd step into the elevator and push the control for this floor, mine. They were on the way now, it was bringing them up. Nearer every minute, closer all the time.

I wondered: what do men like that think about, the last moment or two, just before they collar somebody, as they're on their way to do it? What passes through their minds? Who can tell you that?

More to the point, what passes through the mind of the one waiting to be the one who is collared? I can tell you that. For I was he, and that was me.

I wish she wasn't here with me to see it. I wish she wasn't in the room with me to watch it happen. Why didn't I send her out some-place ahead of time, make some excuse, get her out of the way? Then when she came back it would be over and I would be gone; make it a clean break. She probably wouldn't have gone though, and I didn't know when they were coming.

The car's almost up to floor-level now, the slide's about ready to glide open. If I made a fast move, maybe I could still get past them in the hall and down the safety-exit stairs, which are around in the other direction from where they'll come out. And leave her here alone, leave her behind me holding onto the passed buck?

Not on your life. Not by a long shot. No dice. No soap. And every other way of saying No that was ever invented.

I'll try to be brave, though. Maybe I won't fool her heart, but I will fool her eyes. I won't be gruff, and I won't be tough, and I won't act like a hero does in the movies. But at least I won't flinch and I won't quail and I won't cringe. I won't beg off. I won't say "I didn't do it" and "You've made a mistake." Because they know I did and they know they haven't. And I know I did and I know they haven't.

Yes, I'll take it like a man. For if I'm not the greatest of men, or the bravest, or the most admirable, at least I am one. I still am one. Let me keep that little. It was given me at birth. No one can take it from me. Only I myself.

(She once said to me: I don't want a hero. Let the others have a hero. Having muscles around you all day must get tiresome. And with his nose sticking up in the air all the time, about what a lucky girl you are to have him.

(I like all the things you are, but even more so, all the things you aren't. Your strengths, they make me feel: who needs this? Your weaknesses, they make me feel: he needs me.

(Your transparency when you lie, your uncomplicatedness when you're angry, and your unsophistication when you're happy.

(Your brief surges of very real but very temporary courage. And the surprise it always elicits afterward in you yourself, as if to say, "Was that me? Really me?"

(Your innocence of treachery, and envy, and of the malicious remark; and of all real deep-down evil [whatever that may be].

(Your native good-nature when you're sober, and your sheepish amiability when you're drunk.

(Your inability to pass a dog on the street without petting it if the owner permits.

(Your small-boy fears, of dentist-chairs and all-hen groups and swallowing laxative mixtures and the act of washing inside your ears.

(Even the way you sneeze, and that little shake you give your head each time right after.

(Even the mild way you snore, that doesn't grate but simply says, I'm here, you're safe. You may have to wake me first, but still—I'm here, you're safe, you're not alone, no harm will be able to come toward you.

(In other words you're Cleve, and that's why I love you. Repair any failing, take any fault away, and you'd be less Cleve by that much, and by that much less I'd love you.

(I'm glad I came across you, and I'm glad I've been given you to have for my own. My life has fulfilled itself in and with and by you, and when it's over, or almost, I may feel sad but I won't feel cheated.

(You are all three things that make up a woman's life, but all at one time instead of one at a time: you are my lover, and my husband, and my little baby boy. You are Cleve. You are my Cleve. That names it all. That calls it all.)

I won't say anything at all. Not one word, unless I'm asked to, called upon to speak, to answer something. And then all I'll say will be: I'll say my name, if they ask me that. And I'll say: I'm ready to go, if you want me to. And to her just these words: I'm sorry, I didn't mean to bring you pain.

And these are the things that I thought, as they were coming toward my door, to take me in for murder.

I had my head cocked to the seam of the door now, and was listening hard, for all I was worth, to catch any little sound that might filter through.

The magazine had skidded to the floor. She'd turned around and half-climbed the sofa back-to-front, one knee to the seat, the other trailing toward the floor, hands clamped to the top of the sofa, watching me over it. I'd frightened her now. "What's the matter?" she said in an out-of-breath voice.

I knew what the sound was, knew it well, because I'd heard it many times before. Heard it and yet never paid any attention, heard it with half of an ear. It was one of the daily accompaniments to our living there in the building. A slight click of separation, silence while the electrically induced motion along its track was in progress, then a faint cluck of termination. Not bodied enough to even fill out the descriptive just given it. But I knew what it had been:

The slide over the elevator-shaft had just gone back. Opened, is what I mean.

I guided her wide-stretched eyes with a sideward duck of my

head. "Go inside," I said. "Go in there. The bathroom. Wait in there. Somebody's going to knock in a minute. Stay in there until—after it's over."

She wouldn't have moved, she couldn't understand.

I came around to where she was, I took her by the arm, I led her over to the bathroom-entrance, and impelled her inside. Not pushed, just urged her gently.

I tried to close the door after her, but she turned and held it back, to ask:

"But how do you know someone's going to knock? How can you tell—?"

Just then the knock occurred.

It almost surprised me myself, it came so on-cue.

I had no more time for her now. The rest of this was my concern.

Meanwhile the knock had occurred a second time.

There hadn't been any slack between. The second one started where the first one ended. (Two different fists.)

The voice that came with it this time said: "Police Department. Open here."

The tone wasn't blustery or threatening, as I had thought it would be in such cases. As a matter of fact it was flat, mechanical, as though this was so routine to them by now they didn't bother putting any emotion into it anymore.

And strange to tell, somehow it was far more ominous and compelling that way than if it had been blustery and angry. It was like being arrested by an IBM machine. Nothing there to reason with.

And the same went for their faces as I put the door aside and they came up before me.

I'd never seen the faces of men who come to arrest you before, because no one had ever come to arrest me before. I don't know what I expected, thought I'd find. But I thought that at least they would show some indication that this was an important moment.

And the strange thing was—that they were just faces. They showed nothing at all, as far as I could see. They were like linedrawings, outlines. Pinkish-tan or yellowish-pink, whatever skincolor is, ovals, or actually pear-shapes; two eyes, one nose, one mouth, two ears, apiece. Everything there but the spark of animation.

I used to see a commercial for Kent cigarettes on the television, and it reminded me a lot of that. The face of the guy smoking was indicated with such deft rationing of lines that it was beautiful, it was almost sheer power of suggestion alone. Two black dots, like raisins, for the eyes; two joined lines, one down, one under, for the nose; a single slightly tipped-up line for the contented mouth. And there you had it. Whoever the artist was, he was good.

But this wasn't a commercial. There should have been more in their faces than that. This was my destiny, my turning-point.

One showed me a cased badge, but I didn't look. I believed them.

They came in without asking, and they partially reclosed the door, up to seam-contact but without relatching it. I suppose to keep the gist of what was going to be said from becoming common property outside in the hall.

"Evans?"

This was one of the few things I had said I was going to answer. "Yes."

"Your name?"

I thought he had just asked me that. Then I saw where he was looking, and I looked too.

She had come forward out of the bathroom again, where I had tried to efface her. He was looking at her.

I answered for her. "Mrs. Evans."

He ignored me, still waited for her.

"Janet Evans," I heard her say.

"Don't you mean Bartlett?"

"She's my wife. She means Evans."

He wouldn't have any traffic with me. "Are you or are you not Janet Bartlett?"

"I was up until our marriage."

"The warrant we hold says he has a wife already, and that she is, rather was, Adelaide Evans, known professionally as Dell Nelson, and that's what we're here about."

"I have a Mex divorce on that."

He still wouldn't land his eyes on me. I was only background-material. "That's not for us," he said to her. "That's something for the lawyers to decide. We're Homicide Detail."

"Strictly," said his duplicate-number, opening his mouth for the first time to let the one word out.

"I have a warrant here for Janet Bartlett, living with a man named Evans, Apartment Three Section D, Two-Hundred-Such East Three-Nine. That fits you."

I thought that meant they wanted her as some kind of a material witness, against me. If they didn't consider us man and wife, then the old restriction about testifying one against the other wouldn't hold.

There was a sound like ice-cubes hitting bottom in a Collins glass. Or a hard roll of the dice across a cement garage-floor. Or a maraca being chucked aside after a work-out.

I saw one stirrup of a handcuff peering from his hand, like the jaw of a little silver-fanged animal, open and ready to nip, and I closed my eyes in stolid acceptance and offered up my wrists, pulse turned to pulse, to let him pick whichever one he chose.

I heard the click as they went on, but I didn't feel them, feel their weight or feel their coldness.

And my hands were sidewise now, as if someone had shunted them out of the way in passing or in reaching across them to the other side.

I opened my eyes. I saw the terrible whiteness in her face, first. Whiter than any face ever was before. Then I looked down lower. She was handcuffed to another man. Someone else, someone who wasn't me. She was handcuffed to a stranger. But worse than that, oh worse than that, she was handcuffed to a policeman, to a criminal-punisher.

"We're charging you with the murder of Adelaide Evans, known professionally as Dell Nelson, this man's legal wife, in her apartment two nights ago. Now, you're under arrest. Come along without making trouble. You'll be given all your legal rights."

The rest was a nightmarish mix-up of violent body-play. He had her ready to go through the door already before the freeze wore off me. She gave just one little hiccup of forlorn despair. Like an aborted sob. And that was all. I ran in-between them, my hands still together as they'd been, and chopped them down on the handcuff-link uniting him and her, as though they were a cleaver or a hatchet that could sever it.

But this only swung her and flung her against him, her face pressed into his chest, in an odd parody of an intimate position, and frightened her I could see even more than she was already.

He called out in belated warning to the other man, the unprisonered one, "Watch him!" I say belated because he was already doing more than just watch me. He had me from the back in some way, I had no leisure to diagram, I think an arm around my throat in mug-position, my right arm, the swing-arm, held down by his own, also from the back, and with his foot hooked around my ankle, pried that away from the floor, so that I went over and down, he with me and partly under, in a turned-over-caterpillar effect of waving arms and legs.

Meanwhile the absconder had her out, door open behind them, and going down the hall with him. I could hear the quick-tap of her little heels as he forced her down the composition-floored hall beside him at a run which he didn't have to join her in because his leg-spread was far longer.

The fall-down had been to my advantage more than to my tackler's. It had broken the neck-lock, it had broken the arm-hold, and it had broken the foot-hook.

I kicked backward with my heel, gouged backward with the point of my elbow, rolled off and clear of him, scrabbled to my feet, and bellowing pleadingly (if a bellow can plead and a plea can bellow) "No! Not her. Me. It was me! I was the one!" charged after them.

They were at the elevator-opening already. I could tell that by the stripe of brighter light that seemed to come out of the wall from nowhere and light them up.

They both turned and looked at me, with a curious suggestion of normalcy to the little head-turn they both made. As though this were Everyday, and they heard someone yelling down the hall: "Wait! Hold the car for me please."

Then I heard her say "Don't Cleve, you'll only make it worse."

He didn't speak, but he did something I didn't like. He put his free hand to her hip-socket, to guide her in before him. And to the man in me this was worse than the false arrest itself. They should have had a matron bring her in, my mind flashed to me.

He ushered her before him, like in ordinary going-out-for-the-evening etiquette, and then stepped into the elevator after her.

And like in that nightmarish dream-pattern, where the door always closes just before you can get to it and shuts you out, the door just closed before I could get to it and shut me out.

No good, my hands all up and down that smooth satiny sheet of chrome, applauding in an access of imploration, beating time to a heartbreak. It wouldn't open. Only God could make it open now, and He had other things to do, better things to do than interfere with the electric impulse of an automatic elevator.

Then the other one was on top of me again, and this time there was no breaking away.

He got some sort of a double arm-lock around me underarm, from behind of course, and started to haul me backward the whole length of the hallway, toward and in through the apartment-door once more. He knew his job, or at least he knew this particular technique. For he kept my body like a cantilever, only touching floor, only scraping along, with the backs of my heels. So that I couldn't gain leverage to resist. Nothing else was touching, not even my can. And all I could do was twirl around this way and that like a length of rope cut off short.

In an instant's lull, in a break that came in all the noise of our scrimmaging, the bellows-like breaths, the stamping off-balance feet, the loose up-kicking ones, the chewed-off swear-words, in an instant's lull that came in all this when he had to stop to tighten hold on me or to draw a new reserve of breath to see him through some more of the strenuous back-tracking, I heard a voice report to someone behind a fearfully-narrowed-down door-crack: "It's that couple that was so in love, up in the end-apartment. They mustave taken her away from him."

Something deep inside me sang out unheard: They have, oh they have. Oh mister, if you ever were in love yourself, give me a hand.

But no one came near me.

He dragged me all the way back in and over to the window. The carpet softened up the noise we were making a little, but the stupid, mutually liquidating fight went on just the same. It was meaningless now, because I had no breath left to run with even if I'd freed myself, and he had none left to overtake me with even if he'd lost hold of me. A floor-lamp we had went over and knocked itself out. The bulb popped inside the rayon shade, which was the only thing kept me from being bee-stung all over the face with grits of glass, because it was inches away from my straining, floor-level eyes.

I kept trying to reach up and back-over with my hands and get my thumbs into his eye-sockets, but he either tilted his head back beyond reach or slanted it over to the side, because I couldn't get anywhere near. They just dragged sterilely down his cheeks each time, pulling the skin partly with them like stretched rubber. I finally got them, and two accompanying fingers apiece on each hand, hooked in under his collar-band, but that didn't do any good, because though it constricted at the back, the slack my own fingers made kept it from choking him in the front. Finally they let go and dropped off of their own bent-knuckle fatigue.

At some point, I don't know exactly which, he either managed to get the window open backhand behind his back while still holding onto me, or else it had been open from the first. But I suddenly heard his voice ring out with a wider ring, as if it were out in the open, the open air, so he must have thrust his head partly out of the window—a dangerous maneuver, but I wasn't aware of it until it had already occurred and was over, so it didn't foul him up—and I heard him holler down to somebody below, probably a cop left posted outside by the street-entrance: "Hey, hobatta little help up here? Ginneme a hartime."

73

A shout under stress like that is more phonetic than spelled-out, primarily and primitively a basic signal without words.

Moments later a big bruiser of a bull in blues, he was as broad as he was high and seemed to cork-up the whole doorway-opening as he came through it, took me over from him. Like a sackful of flexibly-sidling potatoes or lumps of coal is passed from man to man along a work-gang chain. Its contents may shift a little but by and large it remains inert.

After that there was a sort of intermission or static period with nothing going on but deep breathing. My recent combat-partner doing his standing facing toward the wall, both hands pasted flat against it up over his head, his head hanging down in-between and making noises like an asthmatic or a consumptive or a man choking on a fish-bone. While he kept staring at his own shoecaps as though he'd never seen them before. His shoulders kept going up and down too; I had never noticed before that breathing shows from the back as well. I'd thought only crying does.

I doing mine down on the point of one knee, one arm twisted up behind my back by the new custodian, tilted like the guard-rail at a railroad-crossing after the train has gone safely by. Every time I'd try a move, he'd give it a little adjustment that would send staggers of pain up into my shoulder and make my face screw up as though I'd tasted a lemon and make me breathe in cool, through rounded lips.

He knew how to hold a man.

I was like an insect. Did you ever watch an insect that's caught or hindered in some way, but otherwise not mortally damaged? The insect and I, we struggled each time to test whether the restraint had been removed or not. Then when we found it hadn't, we stopped struggling and fell supine again. Until the next time to test it came.

We couldn't seem, the insect and I, to keep the continuous thought in our head from one time to the next: It's still there.

But then what do you want from an insect? And what do you want from an instinct? The instinct to love and protect, and go there where she is.

The blues-cop broke the silence. After one of my spasms and his resulting tourniquet-twist that scotched it, he solemnly admonished: "We're respecting your rights. Now you respect our duties."

It would have been funny if it wasn't so flagrantly obtuse, so fatally obstructive, in the particular application he was making of it now: the Sunday-schoolish, almost prudish expression of face and inflection of voice he gave it. I mean, with the physical duress that was accompanying it. It was more than just satirical, it was a sight-gag, outright slapstick. But not to him of course.

"You call that respecting my rights?" I blazed. "Tearing my wife away from here as if she was some kind of common ordinary chippy!"

He cut me cold and asked the other one: "Do you want him brought in?"

"I have no orders on that. Only the woman."

"For something she didn't do!" I yelled at top-volume.

The patrol-cop looked at me for a moment with a curious eye. Not sympathetic, not even understanding, just curious.

"He's trying to take the rap for her," he said musingly. "That's that—waddy they call that stuff—?" He nearly said "chevrolet," but that would have been too fortuitous and too pat. It came out about like this: "chillevry."

"You don't see much of it now anymore," reflected the street-clothes man.

"I ain't never seen any," admitted the cop.

I felt like they were discussing someone who was dead already.

The business-suited cop had his wind back now, and after making a few minor adjustments—bringing his necktie around into true again, yanking loose a button that was ready to come off anyway, biting away a fragmented remainder of nail-end, and pacifying his outraged hair (this was the only damage I seemed to have been able to do)—"I gotta report back for the preliminary questioning," he said.

The sight of him turning and casually walking out like that did something to me psychologically. It made me feel as if I was one step farther away from her now. Cut off by that much more. The harness-cop hadn't been involved in her removal.

I held back until he'd gone safely down in the elevator, because if I stood only a slim chance of breaking away from one of them, I stood absolutely none at all of breaking away from both of them at once.

The first melee wasn't in it compared to this second one, when it had started. Within seconds we were staggering and reeling all over the place, like a pair of drunken, berserk, double-arm-locked waltzers. He let go his hydraulic jack arm-grip voluntarily, in order to have me facing him so the blows would travel straight and not have to come around a corner. He was using his club at first, then later on his fist.

I could hear him saying things to me in between. I didn't have time to stop and listen, or figure what they were about. (One time he called me illegitimate. That much I understood.)

He knocked one of my teeth out. But it had been shaky anyway; it used to vacillate everytime I touched it with the tip of my tongue.

I blew it out of my mouth and he thought I meant it as a saliva-salute to him and swung another bomb-burst into me. "Do that to me will you?"

I didn't go down simply because his hold on me kept me up. He was holding me up with one arm, and knocking me down with the other. Between the two I didn't feel good.

"I don't want to kill you," he whispered almost fearfully. "I'm alone here with you, and whatever I would tell them about how it come about, would go. It ain't that, but there's so much paper-work afterward. And yir suspended. And you lose a week or ten days pay."

He seemed to really mean it. It seemed to worry him, as if he knew by experience he had a violent temper and had been in trouble over it before.

Finally he took his hold off, and I fell down of my own accord. Nice and easy, smooth and soft as a bolt of satin-goods unrolling.

He planked down his foot on my rib-cage to hold me pinned

down, and his foot felt as if it weighed a ton, felt like an elephant's hoof cast in concrete. Just below it my poor stomach was swelling up and down like an oxygen-bladder over a patient's face during surgery.

That touch of the ludicrous, which in the case of this particular officer never seemed very far away even in the moments of his sincerest intensities and intensest sincerities, now showed itself again. For he wanted to span the distance to the phone, and he overestimated me and thought that if he took his foot away I'd immediately spring up again. I couldn't have got up even if it wasn't on me, even if only a gnat was settled on me.

But in order to accomplish the reach and still leave the foot, he had to slant his whole leg far over to one side, and then to continue the slant still further along with the whole length of his arm, before his fingers could get to the phone. And strain and stretch for dear life to be able to make it. Which is somehow grotesque if you visualize it.

Then he had to uncap, hold, and dial the phone, all with the one hand. Because he needed the other kept free as a precaution. But even more, as a counterweight stretched back and up the other way to keep him from going over on his ear. Which is a difficult trick, if you've ever tried it. But he had a very large and sinewy hand. And as a policeman he only had to dial once for "O" and then give her the message.

I heard him ask her for Bellevue Hospital, and a shudder went through me, all-in as I was. That meant the psychiatric ward. And the stories you hear about that place—

Until they came the two of us maintained the same frozen, antic, statuary-like position. Me flat as a ruler on the floor, he crouched on his haunches now beside me, but with the one foot still on me staking his claim. Like a pensive watcher gazing at his own image in a still pool.

Every once in a while I'd twitch a little at both ends, shoulders and legs, I couldn't move in the middle. Like a form of the Twist performed lying flat. And by a very tired dancer.

The top of my head was pointed toward the door, so I didn't see them come in.

I heard a man's voice say: "Giving you a bad time, himm?"

"They picked his wife up. He's taking it hard."

I rolled my head over indolently to its opposite side without uttering a word.

Who was there to say it to, who was there to hear it?

Somebody ripped my shirt-sleeve, but all the way up to the shoulder in one clean sweep. It made a sound like the death-squawk of a chicken.

The squeeze on my distended main-line veins tightened so convulsively it almost felt like they were going to spring a leak.

Somthing wet touched me like the muzzle of a miniature friendly pup.

Then a needle jammed into me so far I thought it was going to come out the other side. I roared out "No!" now in protest against imminent helplessness, stupefaction.

"See? Wuddai tell you," said the cop, as if this was the vindication he'd been looking for all along, for what they were all doing to me.

"We know how to treat babies like this," said the attendant with phony soothingness. He chivvied something home with as much finesse as if he were manipulating a cue-stick against a tough side-pocket shot.

The emission hurt much worse than the skin-puncture had itself. It seemed to backfire against my blood-course directional, force its way upstream.

"No!" I rebelled again.

"He's a one," said the cop to the man in the hospital smock.

They were standing on opposite sides, looking down on me the way you look down on the carcass of a dog that's been run over and left lying in the street.

"Going to ride him in with you?" asked the cop, nudging me with the edge of his foot to see if I was still able to move or not.

"He'll keep," opinioned the ambulance-runner. "I put enough into him to hold him for a week. We're packed to the rafters right now. They'd only turn him out again in the morning anyway."

I said "No," in a voice that started loud and came out puny.
Their faces went slowly out, like an iris-out on a tel-screen.
"No," I whispered forlornly to myself, and no one heard me.

What was meant to happen next is anyone's guess. Clearly Janet was to have been convicted of Adelaide's murder, which means we would have been treated to another of the Stupid Trial scenes Woolrich occasionally perpetrated. Following her imprisonment, Cleve obviously was to have left New York in search of the evidence on which his lawyer Sutphen might have gotten the conviction reversed. Perhaps at this point Woolrich would have borrowed from his early short story "Murder in Wax" (*Dime Detective*, March 1, 1935; collected in *Darkness at Dawn*, 1985) and we would have followed Cleve as he hunted for someone to frame for Adelaide's murder. If so, the most likely candidate would seem to have been her former manager d'Angelo. Woolrich never filled in this part of the novel.

The final chapter exists in two versions, but only one of them, published here for the first time, is consistent with the rest of the novel. Cleve returns to New York with the evidence he needs, but too late—except for the wild unbearable grief of the final pages. In the other and clearly later draft Woolrich rearranged some of the plot so that it made a self-standing short story, in which it's Cleve himself who was locked up for Adelaide's murder and, after being pardoned, returns home to the same unbearable grief. A more polished version of this draft was published as "The Release" in the Mystery Writers of America anthology *With Malice Toward All* (Putnam, 1968). Detective novelist Robert L. Fish (1912–1981), who edited the volume, not only made the chapter read more smoothly but even paid Woolrich's MWA dues so that the story would qualify for inclusion. Sadly, before the book came out that wretched recluse was dead.

CHAPTER 5

I left the taxi with a splurge, like a man arching his legs to straddle a sidewalk-puddle though no puddle was there.

He called out something about my change; I showed him the back of my hand.

No elevator ever went so slow as the one that took me up to Sutphen's office. There never were so many floors-between. So many people never got off, never got on. So many late-comers never made it at the last minute, and caused the doors that had already closed to a hair's width to reopen all the way out again. The indicator-sweep up on the inside wall never moved so reluctantly, never stayed on 3 so long before, on 4 so long before, on 5, on 6. Sweat never prickled so, along the pleats in somebody's forehead, and in the crotches below his arms. A heart never went so fast before, except in the hurdle-race finals in the Olympic Games, and everything else around it so slow before, slow before.

Then at last it was 7, and I stepped on someone's toes, knocked someone else's hat askew, carried still someone else's handbag halfway out of the car with me, hooked onto the buttons down at the cuff of my coat-sleeve.

Then I was out running, and no corridor was ever so long before, or had so many people on it getting in your way before. Or playing that simultaneous-impulse game, before, where as you move to the left, they move to the left and block you all over again. To the right, and they do too, and block you all over again.

He'd moved his office. The number on the door hadn't changed, but it was fifty doors further down the line now, and twenty-five more around the turn.

I was in, I was on the other side of it now. There was a receptionist at the desk. She didn't try to stop me, ask me who I was. She saw my face, saw what was on it. (She'd seen it before of course, and must have known what the problem had been. And now this shining light that showed the problem to be gone.) She just pointed, briefed me: "In there, door on your left; and he's by himself."

I pushed it out of the way, knocking was for other times, knocking was for times when there was time: and he was in there walking back and forth.

I caught him doing that. No one with him. Walking back and forth, one hand in his pocket like when you're broke, one hand hooked around the back of his neck like when you're at a loss. Sour in the face. Disturbed, discouraged, disgusted—I couldn't tell what it was. Some other case, not mine. Mine was won, mine was over, mine was squared.

You know how lawyers are. They have dozens of cases. Some of them fizzle, some of them go wrong. Not yours, the other guy's. You know how lawyers are, they have other cases.

He stopped when he saw me come in. He said the funniest thing to himself. I heard him. He said, "Oh merciful God."

Then he asked me, after waiting a minute and watching me: "How'd you come down here?"

"By taxi." I wondered why he'd ask that. I was here, that was all that should have mattered.

"Did it have a radio? Was its radio on?"

"It had a two-way radio, steering it to pick-ups by its despatcher."

"Oh, that kind." He seemed to lose interest. In the radio, not in me.

I whipped the thing d'Angelo had signed out of my inside pocket and pushed it at him. "Don't yawant to see what I've got here?" I jabbered, staccato, jubilant. "Don't yawant to hear what it is? Don't yawant to read what it says? This gives you what you wanted! You can get your reversal—" My voice slowed and started to dwindle. "Doesn't it matter?" was the last thing came out. Then it faltered and died.

It didn't. He didn't say it didn't, but he showed it didn't.

He took the paper the statement was on, pleated one end of it like he was making a paper dart out of it, poised it over his desk-wastebasket, and speared it in.

I jolted. "What'd you do that for?"

He just looked at me. Everything that anyone was ever sorry for was in that look. You could see it there.

"I can't tell you. I'll have to let the radio do it for me. They can do it better." He went over and thumbed it. "I'll see if I can get it on W-I-N-S. They give news all day long. It'll come around again. Sit down a minute."

He took a cigarette out of a gold-tooled desk-box and put it into my mouth; even lit it for me. He put his hand on my shoulder and pressed down hard. As if to say, Brace yourself.

In the background familiar names began to sound off dimly. Names that were far-away though, had nothing to do with me. "Hanoi— / Cape Kennedy— / Hurricane Faith— / Mayor Lindsey— / Stan Koufax— / U-Thant— / Cicero, Illinois— / President Johnson—"

He opened a drawer and took out a bottle of Hanky Bannister.

I hadn't known he kept anything like that there. He didn't drink himself. Oh well—but not in his office, I mean. He kept it there for clients, I guess. And sufferers who needed it for imminent shock, like I was going to (he seemed to think). He passed me a shot-glass-full.

I drank it down, still in happiness, although the happiness was now a little dazed. Not dimmed, but dazed by his peculiarity.

I started to get scared by all this indirection. I felt like a guy waiting for surgery, without knowing what form it was going to take.

It came. It hit. Before you knew it, it was already over. And the slow-spreading after-sting had only just started in.

He brought it up. The sound, I mean. Touched it with his finger. And I noticed as he did so he didn't look at me, he looked the other way, away from me. As if he didn't like to look at me right then, couldn't face my face.

". . . Mrs. Janet Evans took her own life early today in the cell in which she was being held awaiting transfer. Mrs. Evans had been sentenced on August 30th to twenty-years imprison-ment in connection with the death of singer Dell Nelson. Lacking any other means of carrying out her attempt, the young woman had apparently spent the night pulling out her own hair a few strands at a time. These she finally coiled into a noose strong enough to support her body from the top of the cell-grid. The death occurred some time between 4 and 6 A.M., when the body was discovered by the matron making her first rounds of the day. . . ."

The cigarette fell out of my hand. Nothing much else happened. How much has to happen, to show your life just ended, your heart just broke? Nothing shows it, nothing. Your cigarette falls on the carpet. After a while your head goes down lower. Then lower, then lower. You stare, but you don't see. No words, no tears, no any-thing. It's a quiet thing. It's a your-own thing, that no one else can share. You reach up behind you, and turn your coat-collar up, and hold it close to your throat in front with your fingers, though you know the room is warm for anyone else.

You're cold, you're hungry, you're thirsty, you're scared, you're lonely, you're lost. And you're all those things together at one time.

"I saw her only two days ago," I heard him saying. "I was down there and I spoke to her. I think she tried to tell me then what was going to happen, only I didn't catch on. 'It's too late now for both of us,' she said. 'We can't win either way. Win or lose, we've lost. The sentence isn't still to come, the sentence has already been handed out. Wait twenty years and then get together again, two strangers hardly knowing each other, grubbing around in the debris looking for something they once had? Even if I got out tomorrow, what would we be? The shadow of it would hang over us, every minute of every day. Two ghosts sitting in the twilight, with a bottle somewhere between us. Until after a while, we didn't swallow from the bottle, the bottle would swallow us. Both of those are actually worse than the prison I'm due to be sent to.

" 'Tell him to love somebody like he loved me, and that'll be his love for me all over again. I won't be jealous, I'll be a part of it. Tell him this after I go up.

" 'After I go up.' That threw me off-guard. Don't you see, there's a play on words there. I thought she meant, after she was sent up. She really meant, after she strung herself up."

I looked up at him and I complained, "I hurt all over."

But he couldn't help me. He wasn't a bandage.

I stood up finally and turned to the door, and he said, "Where are you going?" and he tried to hold me back.

"Home. I'm going home."

"You can't. You know that, Cleve. There isn't any anymore for you. Stay here in the office a while first. Lie down on the couch. I'll take you with me when I leave. I'll put you into a hotel for a week or two, pay all the expenses, see that you're taken care of, until the worst is over."

"No, I'm going home. Home."

And when he tried to hold me, I shrugged him off. And when

his solicitous hands came back again, I swerved violently and flung them off.

"I'm going home. Don't stop me."

"Or come up with me for a week, to my place. We live up in Bronxville. I have two kids, but we'll keep them away from you, you won't hear them. You don't even have to have your meals with us."

"No," I said doggedly. "I'm going home."

"But you haven't any home anymore, Cleve."

"Everybody has a home—someplace."

The last thing he said to me was: "You'll die out there sooner or later. I hate to see you die, Cleve. It seems such a waste; you loved so well and hard."

"Don't worry," I assured him gravely. "Don't worry about me, Stewe. I have to meet someone. I'm going out tonight. I'm late for it now."

And I closed the door behind me. And he didn't try to come after me anymore, because he knew every man must find his own peace and his own answers. There is a point beyond which no man can accompany another, without intrusion. And no man must do that. It's not allowable. That's about all we're given, our privacy.

As I went hustling down the corridor (which had become very short again now), I heard a curious sound from back inside there where I'd left him. A whack or impact was what it sounded like. I think he must have swung his own fist around, punched it into some leather chair-back with all his might. I wondered why he'd do a thing like that, what its meaning was. But I didn't have time to figure it out. Some lawyers take the loss of a case hard.

In the second taxi, the one that took me away from there, the driver did have his radio going this time. Unlike the one coming over, that Sutphen had asked me about, this one was only playing music though. I guess to take the edge off the traffic-sounds he lived in all day long.

It was burbling away there. I didn't pay much attention. Until suddenly it came to the bridge. The song the man was singing came to its bridge. *"Night covers all, / And though fortune forsake me, / Sweet dreams will ever take me— / Home."*

That's right, I thought. That's exactly right. That's me, all right.

I heard the echo of it again. That thing she'd said once. "I'll destroy you, Cleve. And her along with you."

"You've won, Adelaide," I said out loud. "You've won your victory."

The driver heard me and started to turn his head around. Then sensing that it hadn't been meant for him, whatever it was, checked himself and looked back ahead again.

"Stop at the next flower-shop you come to," I told him. "I think there's one just up ahead."

I bought some yellow roses, barely opened, just past the bud stage, and those little things that look like yellow pom-poms. I think they're called baby chrysanthemums; I don't know, maybe not.

He wrapped them for me like I'd hoped he would, just like he had that other time. First in tissue, then in smooth lustrous green, then folded it flat across the top and stapled it together. (I could still see her looking at them as I glanced back from the door of the hospital-room.) When I came back to the cab with them, I felt like her young lover all over again.

I rang. I wanted her to come to the door. I wanted to make a big splash with the flowers, shake them spread-open in front of her face and say "A guy sent these to you, lady, with his love." But she didn't come, so I put my key in it instead and went in on my own.

I didn't see her, so I knew she must be in the bathroom, doing something to her hair or things like that they do. I'd often found her in there when I came home nights like this.

I called her name. "Jannie, I'm back," like that. I didn't hear her answer, but that was all right, I guess she couldn't at the moment. Maybe shampoo was running down her forehead. I knew she'd heard me, because she had the door open in there.

("How'd it go?" she asked me. I could almost hear her.)

"Arrh," I said with habitual detraction, "same old treadmill, same old grind. Want me to fix you a drink?"

(I could almost hear her. "Not too strong though.")

I built us two martinis, from the serving-pantry and the sundries that used to be Jack Bojack's, we hadn't run out of them yet: one tiger's milk, the other weak as a woman's tears.

First I was going to take hers in to her, but I didn't. The bathroom is no place to drink a drink or toast a toast. All that soap around.

I called out: "Let's go out tonight. Let's go out like we used to at the start. Let's go somewhere and dance, and eat where they have candles on the table. Let's forget the world and all its troubles."

("What's the big occasion?" I could hear her ask.)

"Who knows how long we have?"

("That's a cheerful thought." I could detect the little make-believe shudder that went with it.)

"Stella's, over on Second. Or The Living Room. Or Copain. Or that little Italian place on 48th where they have the bottles of wine in wicker baskets hanging round the walls and the man plays 'Come Prima' for you on his guitar if you ask him. You name it." (I could see her put the tip of her finger against her upper lip, like she always did when making a choice. "All right, the little Italian place on 48th, then.")

"What dress you want? I'll take it out for you, save time."

("Even if I told you, you wouldn't find it.")

"Try me."

("That one you like the best. The one I got at Macy's Little Shop. You know, the one that's all gleamy and dreamy.")

I found it easy and right away, and took it out and off its hanger. The scent of her faint but unforgettable and unforgotten perfume came up to me from it. More like the extract of her personality than any literal blending of alcohol and attar of roses. She had never used much of that, if any.

While I was waiting for her to come out I put on that record we'd often danced to before, back in the first days. It was a favorite of ours. It *expressed* us. It said for us what we wanted to say for ourselves, thought of, and couldn't.

Then she came out, in all her sweetness and desirability. In all her tender understanding and compassion, for a guy and his poor clumsy heart. All the things we live for and dream about and die without: a man's wife and his sweetheart, his mistress and his madonna. All things in one. Woman. *The* woman. The *one* woman.

Rose-petal pink from her showering in there. Sweet and soft, and just a touch of moistness still lingering here and there. The two little strips crossing her in front, the bra and the waistband, both narrow as hair-ribbons, separating revealed beauty from veiled. And the terry-cloth robe slung carelessly over her back at behind-elbow level. As I'd seen her come out so many times.

She infiltrated into the dress I'd been holding ready for her, and I helped her close the back of it, as I had so many times. (Once I'd accidentally nipped her, in sliding the zipper-catch, and I remembered now how she'd turned partly around and pinched the tip of my nose between her fingers and playfully shook it back and forth.)

We started to dance, her dress floating in my arms, fluttering rippling as if it were empty. First in small pivots in the very center of the room. Then expanding into larger but still compact, still tight-knit circles. Then wider all the time, wider and wider still. Wider each moment and wider each move.

I put my head down on her shoulder, then quickly brought it up again before it even had time to touch. I just want your voice in my ear. Just want to hear your voice in my ear. Just say my name then. Just say Cleve, like you used to say Cleve. Just say it once, that'll be my forever, that'll be my all-time, my eternity. I don't want God. This isn't a triangle. There's no room for outsiders in my love for you. Just say it one time more. If you can't say it whole, then say it broken. If you can't say it full, then say it whispered. "Cleve."

Then because it warms you dancing in a stuffy room like that, I broke off just long enough to throw both halves of the window apart as far as they would go. It was a picture-window and nearly wall-wide. The city smiled in on us from out there, friendly, seeming to understand, sharing our joy and sharing our rapture.

Back again to the spinning rounds of the dance, its tempo slowly mounting into a whirl. The lights, the sky, the monoliths in the background, swung now to this side, now to that, then all the way around and back again to where they were before. Like a painted cyclorama around the outside of a merry-go-round.

Then at last, when we were as far as we could get from it, and it was as far as it could get from us, from all the way back at the back wall of the room we turned as one and with one accord started to run, devotedly, determinedly, yet somehow without grimness, toward it, our arms tight around one another, cheek pressed to cheek. Then at the last moment, instead of turning aside, crossed the low sill and the ledge just beyond with a spread-legged leap, a buoyant arc, that never came down again. Never ever came down again.

And as the suction funnelled up around us and life rushed past our heads like the pull of a tornado gone into reverse, I heard someone cry out: "Wait! Let me catch up. Wait for the boy who loves you."

And the empty music playing in an empty room, to a gone love, two gone lives:

> *"You and I together all alone,*
> *In a little country of our own,*
> *Where the population's only two—"*

TALES

FROM LIFE'S TWILIGHT

In the earliest version of this *noir* cop story Woolrich used, for the first time in his work and perhaps for the first time in crime fiction, a motif which ultimately dates back to the most famous Greek tragedy but is best known today from its employment in some *film noir* classics like *So Dark the Night* (1946, directed by Joseph H. Lewis) and *Somewhere in the Night* (1946, directed by Joseph L. Mankiewicz). "Murder on My Mind" (*Detective Fiction Weekly*, August 15, 1936) is one of the many fascinating stories that have never been collected either in Woolrich's lifetime or since. Sixteen years later he completely revised the tale, eliminating most of the crude slang and pointing up the *noir* elements, and included it as an original—which it certainly wasn't—in the paperback collection *Bluebeard's Seventh Wife* (Popular Library pb #743, 1952). That version, never reprinted since, you are about to read.

MORNING AFTER MURDER

The alarm smashed me wide open, like a hand grenade exploding against my solar plexus. I was already into my shoes and pants before my eyes were even open. Funny, I thought dazedly, when I looked down and saw them on me, how you do things like that automatically, without knowing anything about it, just from long force of habit.

The tin clock went into another tantrum, so I chopped my arm at it and clicked it off. "All right, so I'm up!" I groaned. "What more do you want?" I went into the bathroom and shaved. I looked like the morning after a hard night, eyes all bleary and with ridges under them, and I couldn't understand it. Eight hours' sleep ought to be enough for anyone, and I'd gone to bed at eleven. The mattress must be no good, I decided, and I'd better tackle the landlady for a new one. Or maybe I'd been working too hard; I ought to ask the captain for a leave of absence. Of the two of them, I would have much rather tackled him than her.

She was going off like a Roman candle, at Ephie, the colored maid, when I stepped out of my room into the hall. "Wide open!" she was complaining. "I tell you it was standing wide open, anyone could have walked in! You better count the silverware right away, Ephie—and ask the roomers if any of them are missing anything from their rooms. We could have all been murdered in our beds!" Then she saw me and added with a sniff, "Even though there *is* a detective lodging on the ground floor!"

"I'm off-duty when I come back here at nights," I let her know. I took a look on both sides of the lock of the front door, which was what was causing all the commotion. "It hasn't been jimmied or tampered with in any way. Somebody in the house came in or went out, and forgot to close it tight behind them; the draft blew it open again."

"It's probably that no-account little showgirl who has the third-floor-back, traipsing in all hours of the morning!" she decided instantly. "Just let me get my hands on her!"

I took a deep breath to get my courage up, and made the plunge. "Wonder if you could change my mattress. It must be lumpy or something; I don't seem to be getting my right rest."

This time she went into vocal pyrotechnics that would have put a Fourth of July at Palisades Park to shame. It was the newest mattress in her house; she'd bought it only two years ago last fall; nobody else in the house seemed to find anything wrong with their mattresses; funny that a husky young man like me should. She didn't like single young men in her house, anyway, never had; she'd only made an exception in my case. ("It's not my fault if I'm not married," I protested mildly. "Girls have something to say about that, too.") She liked detectives even less; always cleaning their guns in their rooms. ("I don't clean my gun in my room," I contradicted a little more heatedly, "I clean it down at headquarters.")

She was still going strong by the time I was all the way down at the corner, flagging the bus for headquarters. I had sort of waived my request, so to speak, by withdrawing under fire.

A call came in only about an hour after I got in, sent in by a cop on the beat. The captain sent Beecher and me over. "Man found dead under suspicious circumstances. Go to 25 Donnelly Avenue, you two. Second floor, front."

Riding over in the car Beecher remarked, "You look like hell, Mark. Losing your grip?"

I said, "I feel like I've been dragged through a knothole. I'm going to ask the Old Man for a leave of absence. Know what's been happening to me lately? I go home and I dream about this stuff. It must be starting to get me. You ever have dreams like that?"

"No," he said. "It's like a faucet with me, I turn it off and forget about it till the next day. You used to be that way too. Remember when we were both second-graders, the night that messy Scallopini case finally broke, how we both went to see a Donald Duck flicker, and you fell off your seat into the aisle just from laughing so hard? That's the only way to be in this racket. It's just a job like any other, look at it that way. Why don't you slow up a little, take it easy? No use punishing yourself too hard."

I nodded and opened the door as we swerved in to the curb. "Just as soon as we find out what this thing is."

Number 25 Donnelly Avenue was a cheap yellow-brick flat. The patrolman at the door said, "Now, get away from here, you people. Move on. There's nothing to see." There wasn't, either. Not from down there. "Them are the windows, up there," he said to us. Beecher went straight in without bothering. I hung back a minute and looked up at them. Just two milky-glass panes that needed washing pretty badly.

Then I turned and looked across at the opposite side of the street, without exactly knowing why. There was a gimcrack one-story tax-payer on the whole block-front over there, that looked as if it had been put up within the last year or so, much newer than this flat.

"Coming?" Beecher was waiting for me in the automatic elevator. "What were you staring at out there?"

"Search me," I shrugged. I'd expected to see a row of old-fashioned brownstone houses with high stoops, and then when I turned I saw a cheap row of modern shops instead. But I couldn't have told him why. I didn't know why myself. Maybe the neighborhood seemed to call for them; there were so many other rows of brownstone fronts scattered about here and there. Just some sort of optical illusion on my part, I guess. Or rather, to be more exact, some sort of illusory optical expectancy that had been disappointed. There was almost a sense of *loss* derived from that particular facade, as though it had flattened to one-story height, cheated me of extra height (as I had turned to glance).

A second patrolman outside the flat-door let us in. The first room was a living room. Nothing in it seemed to have been disturbed. Yesterday evening's paper was spread out on the sofa, where somebody had last been reading it; yesterday evening's headline was as dead as the reader who had bought it. Beyond was the bedroom. A man lay dead on the bed, in the most grotesque position imaginable.

He was half-in and half-out of it. He died either getting into it or getting out of it. I looked at the pillow; that answered it for me. He'd died getting out of it. The indentation made by his head overlapped a little on one side. Therefore he'd reared his head, been struck, and his head had fallen back again onto the pillow; but not exactly into the same indentation it had been lying in before.

One whole leg was still under the covers, the other was touching the floor, toes stuck into a bedroom-slipper. The covers had been pitched triangularly off him, up at the right shoulder and side; that was the side the leg was out of bed on. The leg that had never carried him again, never walked again. The window was open about an inch from the bottom, and the shade was down half way.

Apart from the fact that he was half-in, half-out of bed (and that did not constitute a sign of struggle, but only of interruption) there were no noticeable signs of a struggle whatever, in here any more than in the outer room.

The man's clothes were draped neatly across a chair, and his shoes were standing under it side by side. There were three one-dollar bills and a palmful of change standing untouched on the dresser, the way most men leave their money when they empty their pockets just before retiring at night. I say "untouched" because the three bills were consecutively atop one another, and the change was atop the topmost one of them in turn, to hold them down as a weight. And although the continuing presence of money does not always obviate a robbery-motive (it may be too small an amount to interest the killer) the presence of money in that formalized position did proclaim it to be untouched; no intruder would have taken the trouble to replace the coins atop the bills, after having dislodged them to examine the small fund.

I'd worked on Homicide five years to be able to tell small things like that. Only, in murder cases, there are no small things. There are only things.

We were in the bedroom one minute and fifty seconds, by my watch, the first time. We would be in there again, and longer, of course; but that was all, the first time. We'd gotten this from it: It was just like a room with somebody sleeping in it, apart from the distorted position of the dead man's right leg and the scowlingly violent look on his face.

The examiner showed up several minutes after we had got there, and while he was busy in the bedroom we questioned the superintendent and a couple of the neighbors in the outside room. The dead man's name was Fairbanks, he clerked in a United Cigar store, and he was a hardworking respectable man as far as they knew, never drank, never chased women, never played the horses. He had a wife and a little girl in the country, and while they were away for a two-weeks' rest he'd kept his nose to the grindstone, had gone ahead batching it here in the flat.

The couple in the flat across the hall had known him and his wife, and while she was away they'd been neighborly enough to have him in for coffee with them each morning, so he wouldn't have to stop for it on his way to work. In the evenings, of course, he shifted for himself.

They were the ones had first found him dead. The woman had sent her husband over to knock on Fairbanks's door and find out why he hadn't shown up for his morning's coffee yet; they knew he opened his store at seven and it was nearly that already. Her husband rang the bell and pounded for fully five minutes and couldn't get an answer. He tried the door and it was locked on the inside. He got worried, and went down and got the superintendent, and the latter opened it up with his passkey. And there he was, just as he was now.

Beecher said, "When was the last time you saw him?"

"Last night," the neighbor said. "We all went to the movies together. We came back at eleven, and we left him outside of his door. He went in, and we went in our own place."

I said, "Sure he didn't go out again afterwards?"

"Pretty sure. We didn't hear his door open anymore, at least not while we were still awake, and that was until after twelve. And it started teeming not long after we got in. I don't think he'd have gone out in that downpour."

I went in the other room and picked up the shoes and looked closely at them. "No," I said when I came back, "he didn't go out, the soles of his shoes are powder-dry with dust. I blew on them and a haze came off." I looked in the hall-closet and he didn't own a pair of rubbers. "If he was murdered—and we'll know for sure in a few minutes—somebody came in here after you people left him outside his door. The position of the body shows he didn't get up to let them in, they got in without his knowledge."

And they hadn't forced their way in, either. The flat-door hadn't been tampered with in any way, the living-room window was latched on the inside, the bedroom window was only open an inch and there was a safety-lock on it—besides there was no fire-escape nor ledge outside of it. A quick survey, quick but not sketchy, had been enough to establish all these points.

"Maybe a master-key was used," Beecher suggested.

I asked the superintendent, "How many keys do you give your tenants, just one or a pair of duplicates?"

"Only one to a flat," he said. "We used to hand out two where there was more than one person to a family, but so many of them moved away without returning them that we quit that."

"Then Fairbanks and his wife only had one, is that right?" I went in and looked; I finally found it. It was in a key case, along with the keys to his store. And this key case was still in his clothing, from the night before. Just to make sure we tried the key on the door, and it was the right key. So he hadn't lost it or mislaid it, and it hadn't been picked up by anybody and made unwarranted use of.

The examiner came out, about now, and we shipped our witnesses outside for the present. "Compound fracture of the skull," he said. "He was hit a terrific blow with some blunt object or instrument. Sometime between midnight and morning. He had an unusually thin skull, and a fragment of it must have pierced his brain, because hardly any blood was shed. A little in each ear, and a slight matting of the hair, that's all."

"Die right away?"

"Not more than a minute or two after. Goodbye."

I called the captain. "All right, you're both on it," he said. "Stay with it."

A minute later the phone rang and it was Fairbanks's company, wanting to know why he hadn't opened his branch store on time.

That saved me the trouble of calling them. "This is Police; he's dead," I said. I asked about his record with them.

"Excellent. He's been working for us the past seven years. He is—I mean he was—a good man."

I asked if any report had ever reached them on his having trouble with anyone, customers or co-workers.

Never, the man on the wire said. Not once. He was well liked by everyone. As a matter of fact he was known by name to a great many customers of that particular store. A couple of years ago they had shifted him to another location, and got so many inquiries for him afterward, that they'd put him right back again where he'd been. "Sounds funny in a chain-store business, but everybody missed him, they wanted him back."

I hung up and turned to Beecher. "Can you get a motive out of this?"

"About as little as you can. No money taken—in fact no money *to* take—no enemies, no bad habits."

"Mistaken identity?"

"Mistaken for who?" he said disgustedly. "Somebody else with no money, no enemies, no had habits?"

"Don't ask me questions on my questions," I pleaded abjectly. "We have to start somewhere. What do you suppose happened to the blunt instrument Doc mentioned?"

"Carried it out with him, I guess."

Fairbanks had been carried out, meanwhile. I'd seen so many of them go, I didn't even turn my head. After all, where they ended, we began. The fingerprint men had powdered everything they could, which wasn't much, and packed up to go, too. I said, "Wait a minute!" and motioned them back in. I pointed to the ceiling.

"You don't want us to go up *there*, do you?" they jeered.

"The lights are lit, aren't they?" I said. "And they have been ever since it happened. I've established that. And the switch is over by the door, and he was killed with only one leg out of his bed. Now tell me you took prints on that little mother-of-pearl push-button over there."

Their faces told they hadn't, only too plainly. "We'll change jobs with you," one of them offered lamely.

"Not until you know how to do your own right," I said, unnecessarily cuttingly.

They left in silent offense.

We continued working. My back ached from that damned mattress at the rooming-house, and my eyelids felt as if they were lined with lead.

"I've got something," Beecher called to me finally. I went out to him. "What time did it rain last night? It ought to be in here." He picked up the morning paper, the one outside the door that Fairbanks had never lived to read. What we wanted took finding. We found it finally by indirection, in connection with something else. "Started at eleven forty-five and continued until after two." He spanked the item with his fingernail. "Whoever it was, came in here between two-thirty and dawn."

"Why not right during the rain?"

"For Pete's sake, use your eyes, Mark! Don't you see the little dab of dried mud here on the carpet? Came off his shoes, of course. Well, do you see any blurs from drops of water around it? No. This nap is a cross between felt and cheap velour; it would show them up in a minute. His clothes were dry; just his soles had mud on them, probably under the arches. So he came in after the rain, but before the ground had fully dried."

"I've got some more mud," I said finally, crouching down chin to my knees. It was right beside the bed, showing where he'd stood when he struck Fairbanks. The pillows were still in position, even though Fairbanks was gone, one showing a little rusty-brown swirl. Much like a knothole in wood-grain. I stood over the tiny dirt-streak on the floor, and swung my arm stiffly in an arc, down on top of the pillow. It landed too far out, made no allowance for the weapon. No matter how stubby that had been, it would have hit him down near the shoulder instead of on top of the head. Then I remembered that he hadn't been flat on his back but had already struggled up to a sitting position, feeling for his slippers with one foot, when he'd been hit.

I kept my eye on an imaginary point where his head would have been, sitting up, and then swung—and there was a space of about only two or three inches left between my clenched fist and the imaginary point. That space stood for the implement that had been used. What, I wondered, could be that short and still do such damage?

I heard Beecher whistling up for me from down below the windows and chased down. "I've got a print, a whole print!" he yelled jubilantly. "A honey. Perfect from heel to toe! Just look at it! I can't swear yet it was made by the same guy that went into the flat, but I'm certainly not passing it up." I phoned in for him and told them to send somebody over with paraffin and take it, while he carefully covered it over with his own pocket-handkerchief to protect it from harm. Then we stood around it guarding it.

It was a peach, all right. There was a cement sidewalk along the whole length of the flat, but between it and the building-line there was a strip of unpaved earth about three yards wide, for decorative purposes originally, although now it didn't even bear grass. The sidewalk bridged this sod across to the front door, and it was in one of the two right-angles thus formed that the footprint was set obliquely, pointed in toward the building.

"He came along the sidewalk," Beecher reconstructed, somewhat obviously, "and turned in toward the door, but instead of staying on the cement he cut the corner short, and one whole foot landed on the soggy ground. Left foot. It wasn't made by any milkman, either; this man was making a half-turn around to go in, a milkman would have come up straight from the curb. I'd like to bet this is for us!"

"I'm with you," I nodded.

"It's got everything but the guy's initials. Rubber heel worn down in a semicircle at the back, steel cleat across the toe."

We hung around until they'd greased it and filled it with paraffin, and we were sure we had it. They also took microscopic specimens of the dried mud from the room upstairs, and some of the soil down here around the print, for the laboratory to work over.

"Tall guy and pretty husky, too," Beecher decided. "It's a ten-and-a-half." He rolled up the tape-measure. "And pushed down good and hard by his weight, even though the ground *was* wet."

"About my height and build, then," I suggested. "I take a ten-and-a-half myself." I started to lift my foot off the cement, to match it against the impression, but he'd gone in without waiting, and there was a straggling line of onlookers strung along the opposite side of the street taking it all in, so I turned and went in after him. After all, I didn't have to make sure at this late day what size shoe I wore.

"Well, we've got a little something, anyway," he said sanguinely on the way back upstairs. "We've got it narrowed to a guy approximately six-one or over and between one-eighty and two-twenty. At least we can skip all shrimps and skinny guys. As soon as the mold's hardened enough to get a cast from it, we can start tracking down those shoes to some repair-shop."

"And then like in the story-books," I said morbidly, "they got their man."

"I don't think you're eating right," he grinned.

I told him about the arm-measurement I'd taken beside the head of the bed. I repeated it for him; he couldn't try it for himself because his arms weren't long enough. "With just two, three inches to spare, what else could it have been but the butt of a gun? Held right up close to the handle."

"Let's go over the place; we haven't half-started yet." He began yanking open drawers in the dresser; I went out into the other room again, suddenly turned off to one side and went toward the steam-radiator. I put my whole arm down between it and the wall and pulled up a wrench.

"Here it is," I called. "You can stop looking."

He came in and saw what it was, and, by my stance, where it had come from. He took it and looked at it. We could both see the tiny tuft of hair imbedded between its tightly clamped jaws, the bone splinters—or were they minute particles of scalp?—adhering to the rough edge of it.

"You're right, Mark, this is it," he said in a low voice. Suddenly he wasn't looking at it anymore but at me. "How did you know it was there? You couldn't have seen it through the radiator. You went straight toward it; I didn't hear your step stop a minute."

I just stared at him helplessly. "I don't know," I said. "I wasn't thinking what I was doing. I just, I just went over to the radiator unconsciously and put down my arm behind it—and there it was."

It slipped out of my hand, the wrench, and hit the carpet with a dull thud. I passed the back of my hand across my forehead, dazedly. "I don't know," I mumbled half to myself.

"Mark, you're all in. For pete's sake, why don't you ask to be relieved of duty, go home, and catch some sleep. The hell with how you happened to find it, you found it, that's all that matters!"

"I've been put on here," I said groggily, "and I stay on here until it's over."

The superintendent unhesitatingly identified the wrench as his own. He had a straightforward enough story to tell, as far as that went. He'd been in here with it one day tinkering with the radiator—that had been months ago, in the spring, before they turned the heat off—and had evidently left it behind and forgotten about it.

"Does that make it look bad for me, gents?" he wanted to know anxiously. When they're scared, they always call you "gents"; I don't know why.

"It could," Beecher said gruffly, "but we're not going to let it." The superintendent was a scrawny little fellow, weighed about a hundred-thirty. Small feet. "Don't worry about it." Beecher jerked his thumb at the door for him to go.

"Wait a minute," I said, stopping him, "I'd like to ask you a question—that has nothing to do with this." I took him over by the window with me and squinted out. "Didn't there used to be a row of old-fashioned brownstone houses with high stoops across the way from here?"

"Yeah, sure, that's right!" he nodded, delighted at the harmless turn the questioning had taken. "They pulled them down about a year ago and put up that taxpayer. You remembered them?"

"No," I said slowly, very slowly. I kept shaking my head from side to side, staring sightlessly out. I could sense, rather than see, Beecher's eyes fastened anxiously on the back of my head. I brushed my hand across my forehead again. "I don't know what made me ask you that," I said sort of helplessly, "How could I remember them, if I never saw them be—?" I broke off suddenly and turned to him. "Was this place, this street out here, always called Donnelly Avenue?"

"No," he said, "you're right about that, too. It used to be Kingsberry Road; they changed the name about five years ago; why I don't know."

The name clicked, burst inside my head like a star-shell, lighting everything up. I hit myself on the crown with my open hand, turned to Beecher across the superintendent's shoulder, let out my breath in relief. "No wonder! I used to live here, right in this same building, right in this same flat—25 Kingsberry Road. Ten years ago, when my mother and dad were still alive, rest their souls, when I was going to training school. It's been bothering me ever since we got out of the car an hour ago. I knew there was something familiar about the place, and yet I couldn't put my finger on it—what with their changing the street-name and tearing down those landmarks across the way."

"They remodeled this building some, too," the superintendent put in sagely. "Took down the outside fire-escapes and modernized the front of it. It don't look the same like it used to."

Beecher didn't act particularly interested in all this side-talk; it had nothing to do with what had brought us here today. He shifted a little to close the subject, and then said, "I suppose this thing's spoiled as far as prints go," indicating the wrench. "You wrapped your hand around it when you hauled it up."

"Yes, but I grabbed it down at the end, not all the way up near the head the way he held it. He must have held it up there, foreshortened; the mud shows where he stood."

"We'll send it over to them anyway. Peculiar coincidence. Fairbanks must have come across it behind there and taken it out, then left it lying around, out in the open intending to return it to our friend here. Then this intruder comes in, whacks him with it, and on his way out drops it right back where it had been originally. Funny place to drop it."

"Funny thing to do altogether," I said. "Walk into a place, strike a man dead, turn around and walk out again without touching a thing. Absolutely no motive that I can make out."

"I'm going to run this wrench over to the print-men," he said. "Come on, there's nothing more we can do around here right now."

In the car he noticed the dismal face I was putting on. "Don't let it get you," he said. "We're coming along beautifully. Like a timetable, almost. Got a complete, intact print. Now the weapon. And it's not even twelve hours yet."

"Also got a headache," I said under my breath, wincing.

"We might get something out of his wife; she'll be in from the country this evening. Everyone I've spoken to so far has praised her to the skies, but there might be some man in the background had his eye on her. That's always an angle. Depends how pretty she is; I'll be able to tell you better after I get a look at her."

"I don't agree," I said. "If it were a triangle motive, the man would have tried to cloak it with a fake robbery motive, anything at all, to throw us off the track. He'd know that leaving it blank this way would point twice as quickly—" I broke off short. "What's the idea?"

We'd pulled up in front of my rooming house.

"Go on, get out and get in there," he said gruffly, unlatching the door and giving me a push. "You've been dead on your feet all day! Grab a half-hour's sleep, and then maybe we'll be able to get someplace on this case. I'll start in on the shoeprint-mold, meanwhile. See you over at headquarters later."

"Won't that look great when the captain hears about it!" I protested. "Going home to sleep right in the middle of a job."

"The case'll still be there, I'm not swiping it from you behind your back. This way you're just holding the two of us up. They'll probably have the prints and the mud-analysis ready for us by the time you come down; we can start out from there."

He drove off and cut my halfhearted arguments short. I turned and went up to the door, fumbled for my key, stuck it wearily in the lock—and the door wouldn't open. I jiggled it and wiggled it and prodded it, and no use, it wouldn't work. "What'd the old girl do," I wondered resentfully, "change the lock without telling anybody, because she found it standing open this morning?" I had to ring the bell, and I knew that meant a run-in with her.

It did. The scene darkened and there was her face in the open doorway. "Well, Mr. Marquis! What did you do, lose your door-key? I haven't got a thing to do, you know, except chase up and down stairs all day opening the door for people when they have perfectly good latchkeys to use!"

"Aw, pipe down," I said irritably. "You went and changed the lock."

"I did no such thing!"

"Well, you try this, then, if you think it's perfectly good."

She did and got the same result I had. Then she took it out, looked at it. Then she glared at me, banged it down into my palm. "*This* isn't the key I gave you! How do you expect to open the door when you're not using the right key at all? I don't know where you got this from, but it's not one of the keys to my house. They're all brand-new, shiny; look how tarnished this is."

I looked at it more closely, and I saw that she was right. If I hadn't been half-asleep just now, I would have noticed the difference myself in the first place.

I started going through my pockets then and there, under her watchful eye, feeling—and looking—very foolish. The right one turned up in one of my vest-pockets. I stuck it in the door and it worked.

My landlady, however, wasn't one to let an advantage like this pass without making the most of it. Not that she needed much encouragement at any time. She closed the front door and trailed me into the hall, while I was still wondering where the devil that strange key had come from. "And—ahem—I believe you had a complaint to make about your mattress this morning. Well, I have one to make to you, young man, that's far more important!"

"What is it?" I asked.

She parked a defiant elbow akimbo. "Is it absolutely necessary for you to go to bed with your shoes on? Especially after you've been walking around out in the mud! I'm trying to keep my laundry bills down, and Ephie tells me the bottom sheet on your bed was a sight this morning, all streaked with dried mud! If it happens again, Mr. Marquis, I'm going to charge you for it. And then you wonder why you don't sleep well! If you'd only take the trouble of undressing the way people are supposed to—"

"She's crazy!" I said hotly. "I never in my life—What are you trying to tell me, I'm not housebroken or something?"

Her reaction, of course, was instantaneous—and loud. "Ephie!"

she squalled up the stairs. "Ephie! Would you mind bringing down that soiled sheet you took off Mr. Marquis's bed this morning? I'd like to show it to him. It hasn't gone out yet, has it?"

"No, ma'm," came back from upstairs.

I kept giving her the oddest kind of look while we stood there waiting. I could tell from her own expression, she couldn't make out what it was. No wonder she couldn't. It was the kind of look you give a person when you're floundering around out of your depth, and you want them to give you a helping hand, and yet you know somehow they can't. You want *them* to give *you* a word of explanation, instead of your giving it to them. You need it badly, even if it's just a single word.

I distinctly recalled pulling off my shoes the night before when I was turning in. I remembered sitting on the edge of the bed, dog-tired and grunting, and doing it. Remembered how a momentarily formed knot in the lace of one had held me up, remembered how I'd struggled with it, remembered how I'd sworn at it while I was struggling (aloud, yet, and extremely bitterly); and then how I'd finally eradicated it, and given the freed shoe a violent fling off my foot. Remembered how the impetus had thrown it a short distance away and it had fallen over on its side and I'd left it there. All that had been real, not imaginary; all that had happened; all that came back clear as a snapshot.

That peculiar feeling I'd had all morning over at Fairbanks's flat returned to me, redoubled. As though there were some kind of knowledge hidden just around the corner from me, waiting to be exposed. And yet I couldn't seem to turn that corner. It kept pivoting out of reach. Or like a revolving door that keeps taking you past the point where you should step out and you miss it each time. Buildings that suddenly flattened from second to first-story level. Monkey wrenches that come up to meet your hand from behind a radiator. Shoes that find their way back onto your feet without your hand touching them, like magic, like with wings, like in a Disney cartoon. Tired nerves, blurred reflexes, a sick detective trying to catch a healthy murderer.

Ephie and the old girl spread out the sheet foursquare between them, as if they were going to catch someone jumping down from upstairs. "Just look at that!" she declaimed. "That was a clean sheet, put on fresh yesterday morning! I suppose you'll stand there and try to tell me—"

I didn't try to tell her anything. What was there to tell her? There were the sidewise-prints of muddied shoes all over it, like elongated horseshoes, and that was that. But I wasn't listening, anyway. I'd just remembered something else, that had nothing to do with this sheet business. Something that hit me sickeningly like that wrench must have hit poor Fairbanks.

I had a flash of myself the previous Sunday night, that was the night before last, rummaging through an old valise for something, finding a lot of junk that had accumulated in my possession for years, discarding most of it, but saving a tarnished door-key, because I couldn't remember where or what it was from, and therefore I figured I'd better hang onto it. I'd slipped it into my vest-pocket, because I'd had that on me at the time, unbuttoned and without any coat over it.

They must have seen my face get deathly white; I could see a little of the fright reflected in both of theirs, like in a couple of mirrors. Or like when you point a pocket-light at a wall, and it gives you back a pale cast of the original.

"I'll be right back," I said, and left the house abruptly, left the street door standing wide open behind me. I sliced my arm at the first cab that came along and got in.

He took me back to 25 Donnelly Avenue. It was still light out, light enough to see by. I got out and went slowly across the sidewalk, as slowly and rigidly as a man walking to his own doom. I stopped there by that footprint Beecher had found. It was pretty well effaced as far as details went, but the proportions were still there, the length and width of it if nothing else. I raised my left foot slowly from the cement and brought it down on top of it.

It matched like a print can only match the foot that originally made it. After a while I turned the bottom of my own foot up toward me and studied it dazedly. The cleat across the toe, the rubber-heel worn down in a semicircle at the back.

The driver must have thought I was going to topple, the way I stood there rocking, and then the way I put out my hand gropingly and tried to find the doorway for support. He made a move to get out and come over to me, but saw that I'd steadied and was starting to go in the house.

I went upstairs to the locked Fairbanks flat and took out the key that I'd found in my valise two nights ago that I'd mistakenly used on the rooming house door a little while ago. It opened the flat; the door fell back without a squeak in front of me.

"Pop's key," came to me then, sadly, "or maybe Mom's from the long ago and far away." I pulled the door toward me, closing it again, without going in. And as it came back close against my eyes, the door's shiny green coat dimmed off it and it became an old-fashioned walnut dye. "This used to be my door," I said to myself. "I used to come in here. On the other side of it was where I came— when I came home." I let my forehead lean against it, and I felt sort of sick all over. Fright-sick, if there is such a thing.

After a while I went downstairs again, still without having gone into the flat. I phoned Beecher from a pay station, on the outside. "Come over to my place," I said, and I hung up again. Just those few words.

"I should never have been a detective," I said out loud, without noticing I was back within earshot of the cabman again.

"What, are you a detective?" he said immediately. "You look awful sick right now. You guys get sick too? I didn't think you ever did."

"Do we," I moaned expressively.

I was waiting for Beecher in my room when he showed up. I had the muddied sheet in there with me (evidence; detective to the bitter end). He found me sitting there staring at the wall, as though I saw things on it. "Was that you?" he said incredulously. "You sounded like the chief mourner at somebody's funer—"

"Beecher," I said hollowly, "I know who killed that guy Fair-banks. It was me."

He nearly yelped with fright. "I knew this was coming! You've finally cracked from overwork, you've gone haywire. I'm going out and get a doctor!"

I showed him the sheet. I told him about the key, about measuring the footprint. My teeth started chattering. "I woke up half-dead this morning and couldn't remember putting my pants on. And they were all wrinkled. I know now that *I'd been sleeping in them.* The street-door here in this house was found standing wide open first thing this morning before anyone was up yet. It was me went out, came in again, in the early hours.

"I used to live in that same flat he did. I went back there last night. Didn't you notice how I found that wrench, went straight toward it without knowing why myself, this morning?" I ducked my face down, away from him. "Poor devil. With a wife and kid. He's never harmed me. I'd never even seen him before. I told you I've been dreaming lately about the cases we've worked on. And this dream *got up and walked.*

"I must have found my way there in my sleep, with crime and criminals on my mind, all because I used to live there long ago. Put on the light in what I thought was my own room, found him there, mistook him for an intruder, and slugged him with a monkey-wrench right in his own bed—all without waking up." I shivered. "I'm the guy we've both been looking for all day. I'm the guy—and I didn't even know it!" I couldn't stop shaking. "I've been chasing myself. I've been on both ends of the case at once!" I covered up my eyes. "I think I'm going crazy."

I had a small-sized bottle there. It was a Christmas gift; I don't use the stuff worth mentioning. He broke the seal and poured me a short drink. He put it away again without taking one himself. On duty, I suppose. He opened the door and looked out into the hall, to see if anyone was around. No one was; he closed it and came back in again.

"Mark," he said gloomily, "I'm not going to tell you to forget it, that you're crazy, that you're talking through your hat. I wish I could; I'd give my eye-teeth if I could. But from me, you're entitled to it straight from the shoulder."

And then he made a face, like every word he was about to say tasted rotten, tasted moldy, ahead of time.

"You did. I think you did. I think you must have."

I didn't answer. I already knew that myself, was sure of it; he wasn't telling *me* anything.

"Here are the findings, as of now. The only prints that would come off the wrench were yours—yours and Fairbanks's. (And he obviously didn't swing it at himself. His were on the mid-section of the stem, where he lifted it from a horizontal position behind the radiator, when he first found it back there.) The ones near the head of the wrench, where by your own calculations the killer actually held it, matched the ones down at the opposite end of the handle. Both yours. From the light push-button, they got one entire thumb-print. Yours. And those lights were already on when we first arrived this morning, I was a witness to that myself.

"Finally, I've already located the shoe repair-shop which did the cleat job matching up with the mold. It wasn't hard; there aren't many people use them; there are even fewer use them on that par-ticular size shoe." He said this slowly, like he hated to have to, "It wasn't hard to find. It was the first shop I walked into, *right on the corner below headquarters*. I didn't expect to find out anything there. I only went in to get an opinion from him. He recognized it at sight. He said, 'That's *my* job.' He said he'd only done one job like that in the past six months. He said, 'I did that for your buddy, you know the one you call Mark, from headquarters.' He even remembered how you had to sit waiting in one of the little stalls in your socks, because you told him you only own one pair of shoes at a time.

"Until I came over here just now, and you told me what you just did, none of this added up. I even cursed you out a little at first, I remember, because I thought you'd simply fouled up the job *after* we got over there this morning, being half-awake like you were all day. Left the footprint *then*, smudged up the wrench and push-button *then*. In spite of the fact that with my own eyes I saw that the lights were already on, that your fingers didn't go near the handle of the wrench, that the ground was too hard and dry to take a footprint anymore by the time we got here."

I held myself by my own throat. "You see how your side of it fits with my side. You see how it must be, *has to be*, the only possible thing that could have happened. You see how we've solved it between us, the way we're paid to, the way we're trained to, and come out with the right answer. I don't remember it even yet, but I have proof now that I did. I walked over there and back in my sleep—with my eyes wide open. What am I going to do?"

"I'll tell you what you're going to do," he suggested in a rough-edged undertone, leaning over toward me and putting his hand down on my shoulder. "You're going to shut up and forget the whole thing. Forget every word you've said to me in here. Get me? I don't know anything, and you haven't told me anything. Case unsolved."

I shifted away from him. "That's what you're trying to talk me into doing because I'm your partner and because it's *me*. Now tell me what you'd do if it was *you*."

He sighed. Then he smiled halfheartedly, and turned away, and gave up trying. "Just about what you're going to do anyway, yourself, so why ask?"

He stood there looking out the window of my room at nothing, brooding, feeling bad. I sat there looking down at the floor, hands pressed to my face, feeling worse.

Finally I got up quietly and put on my hat. "Coming?" I said.

"I'll ride over with you," he agreed. "I've got to go back anyway."

In the car he said, "It's not the first man you've killed"; hesitantly, as though realizing it was a rough thing to say to me, especially right then.

"Yes, but they were criminals, and they were trying to kill me at the time. This man wasn't. He had the law on his side. I killed him in his bed."

"It'll be all right. The Old Man'll know what to do. An inquiry. Sick-leave, maybe, for a while."

"That won't bring him back. I have to sleep with this for the rest of life."

"Nothing lasts that long. The very mayor of New York himself, once—Memory wears out. Sound sleep comes back, one night. A year from now you'll be chasing assignments in the car with me again, and looking at mud and looking at light-switches."

I knew somehow, deep in my heart, that he was right. But that didn't make tonight any easier on me. Tonight was tonight, and a year from now was a year from now, and never the two could meet. It's the year between you have to pay for, each time, and I was ready to do my paying.

He didn't offer to shake hands with me, when he left me outside the Old Man's door, that would have been too theatrical. Just—

"I'll see you, Mark."

"I'll see you, Beecher."

It must be hell not to have a partner, no matter what your job is.

I opened the door and went in. I didn't say anything; I went all the way over to his desk and just stood there.

The captain looked up finally. He said, "Well, Marquis?"

I said, "I've brought the man who killed Fairbanks in to you, Captain."

He looked around, on this side of me and on that, and there was no one standing there but me.

Woolrich's major project of the fifties, and his last sustained effort to break out of crime-suspense fiction and be accepted again as a mainstream author, was *Hotel Room* (Random House, 1958), an episodic novel almost completely devoid of the elements that had made him a legend in his own lifetime. The setting is the Hotel St. Anselm—obviously modeled on the Hotel Marseilles where he and his mother, to whom the book was dedicated, had been living from about 1933 until her death—and the story of the building is told through the stories of the people who checked into Room 923 between 1896 and the Eisenhower era. The next story is the single chapter from *Hotel Room* that appeared first in a magazine ("The Black Bargain," *Justice*, January 1956) and the only one that proclaims loud and clear that its author is the Hitchcock of the written word. It links with Woolrich classics like "Three O'Clock" and "Guillotine," at least in the sense that we are compelled to identify with a hateful and depraved character at the point of his rendezvous with death. This was one of three Woolrich stories adapted for cable TV's short-lived *noir* anthology series *Fallen Angels*. "The Black Bargain" (November 19, 1995) was directed by Keith Gordon from a teleplay by Don Macpherson. The leading roles were played by Miguel Ferrer, Lucinda Jenney, and Grace Zabriskie.

THE NIGHT OF
FEBRUARY 17, 1924

T hree women came first. One was a blonde, one a redhead, one a brunette. As though exemplifying the differing tastes of that many unseen men. They all had one thing in common: They were all extremely tall. As though that, too, had been a determining factor in their present status. Among others. They were dressed as the mode of the moment dictated: shorn hair (in the case of one, it was even shingled at the back of the neck like a man's); cocoon-like wraps, held closed by being interfolded across the body, with the arms kept on the inside; and pencil-straight skirts that fell almost to the tops of their shoes.*

---

*N.B.—For a short period during the highly stylized twenties, a fact which is not generally recalled, women wore skirts almost to the insteps. This was a brief intermission, a sort of breathing spell, between the first onset of knee-length dresses, which had occurred in 1920, and the final capitulation to them, which rode the rest of the decade out. It coincided, roughly, with the years 1923–24.

Behind them walked a man. Very close behind them. Almost giving the impression of a watchful sheep dog, guiding his charges in his master's absence. Although his arms weren't extended out from his body, that was the feeling one had: that if these girls should stray a little too far over, either to one side or the other, he would corral them back to dead-center again.

Unlike women walking together as a rule, no matter how short the distance, they moved in prudent silence. As if having learned that the slightest word, no matter how harmlessly said, might be misconstrued and turned against the speaker at some later summing-up or betrayal, and it was safer therefore not to speak at all.

Close together and yet in this lonely sort of silence, they entered the elevator with their guard and were carried up from sight. It came down again presently, but the girls were no longer on it, only the man was. He was dancing a key up and down in his hand. The sheep were in the fold, and the shepherd's loyal helper had them safely locked in. He went out to the entrance and stood there on the topmost step, as if watching for someone's arrival.

Within moments after, the arrival had occurred. It was the looked-for event. The way the man blocking the entrance quickly took his hand from the doorway, stepped back to give clearance, showed that. It was both multiple and yet strangely compact. It was that of a phalanx of men. One man in the center, one at each side of him, one at his back. Their bodies all swung to the same walking-rhythm: brisk, staccato, purposeful.

The one in the center was rather short. The rest were all a half-head taller. Perhaps because of his shorter height, he gave an impression of plumpness that was not justified by his actual girth. Padding in the shoulders of his coat, almost as oblique as epaulettes, did its part as well.

He was surprisingly young-looking, thirty-three or -four at most. But even here there were qualifying factors. It was not the youthfulness of pre-maturity, when character lines have not yet become deeply enough indented to be permanent attributes of the countenance; it was rather a reverse process, an erasure, of lines and traces that had already *been* there. The face was becoming vapid, a cipher, and tricked the eye at first into mistaking this for juvenility. It wasn't; it was decay, an immeasurably hastened senility. It was erosion, leading toward an ultimate idiocy.

The group compressed itself into the elevator. The man who had been waiting at the doorway entered last and took over the controls, motioning the regular operator out. The latter, taken by surprise, just stood there with his mouth open as the car went up. The impromptu operator overshot the correct floor. He had to check the car jarringly, reverse it with a jerk, and then again he overshot the mark slightly in the opposite direction. He finally adjusted the car-level to the correct height.

When they stepped off, one of them dropped behind long enough to warn the recent operator in an undertone: "What's the matter, you nervous? He didn't like that; I saw him look at you!"

"I never drove one of them before," protested the unhappy amateur.

"Well, you shoulda practiced. He likes everything to run smooth. Now take it down back where it come from."

Meanwhile, ghostly music that had been whispering along the corridor suddenly blared out as a door opened to admit them, and the blonde one of the three girls stood by it waiting to receive them. The hindmost one chucked her under the chin as they entered, and an incandescent smile immediately flashed on, as though he'd turned a switch just below her jaw.

The door was closed, but one of them remained by it, immovable. "Augie's still coming up," he explained. "I sent him down with the car."

Within a few moments a low-pitched voice said, "Augie," just outside; it was reopened briefly, and then it was closed and locked with a finality that meant all further ingress was at an end.

Nobody said anything for several minutes, although there were now eight people in the room. The short man who had been in the center of all of them spoke first. It was as though they had all been waiting to take their cue from him.

A baleful expression flickered across his face. "Who would've ever thought that Abbazzia would find himself holed up in a fleabag hotel like this with the last few of his guys?" he said, as though speaking about some third person of great consequence.

"It'll blow over," the one they called Carmine said.

Abbazzia went over and sank into an easy chair. "My mistake was waiting too long," he said. "I got careless. Now he's taken the town away from me."

"He won't have it long," Sal promised.

Abbazzia looked at him bleakly. "He's got it now, Salvatore, and it's the now that counts, in this deal. There ain't no more than now. There ain't no next time. Every speak from Tenth Avenue over to Third is paying its protection to him now, not us anymore. Every truck that comes down from the border—" He put his hand to his eyes, shading them for a minute.

The redhead began sidling over on a careful diagonal, like someone who watches where she puts her foot at every step, her object evidently consolatory.

Augie caught sight of her and tactfully motioned her back. "He'll call you over when he wants you."

Abbazzia continued to direct his remarks to the men in the room, ignoring the girls. He showed them his open hand, to show them that it was empty. "Seven," he whined in lamentation. "Seven all at one time. Who've I got left? Where'm I gonna get that kind again? They don't come like them anymore. Guys that started out with me in the old days."

"Did you read the papers, about how they found Ruffo?" Sal asked him, with a peculiar glitter in his coffee-bean eyes that might have been latent sadism as much as vengeful group-loyalty.

"How'm I gonna read the papers?" Abbazzia answered impatiently. "I come away from there so fast, when the word come the heat was up—"

Sal moistened his lips. "He was on the top floor of this garage, when they found him. Him, he was the only one didn't have no shoes or socks on. So first they couldn't figure it. Then they noticed these razor blades lying there. The skin on the bottom of his feet was peeled off, real thin, like when you buy ham in a delicatessen. And then on the sea-ment floor was this big burnt place; you know, like when you pour a big puddle of crankcase oil and put a match to it. And then bloody footprints that kept going back and forth, back and forth, over it. I guess they held onto him tight and made him keep walking across it, over and over—maybe with a couple of car engines turning over downstairs, to drown out his screams."

Abbazzia's expression didn't falter, his contemplative eyes never once left the speaker's face as he listened. "That's one I never thought of myself," he mused wistfully when it was over. "I wonder who got it up?"

"I wonder how long he lasted?" Carmine remarked idly.

Sal turned toward him scornfully. "What's the difference how long? He didn't make it, did he?"

"A lot of difference to *him*, I bet," Carmine pointed out, "if it was long or short." A chuckle clucked in his throat.

Abbazzia yawned, hitched his elbows back, straddled his legs still further apart. "I'm tired," he droned languidly. "Getting out of there in such a hurry, like that. My feet cramp me."

At once, as though an esoteric signal had been given her, the redhead sluiced forward from her position in the background, dropped deftly to her knees directly before his chair, began to pick busily at the lace of his shoe with her long magenta-lacquered nails. In a moment she had eased the shoe off. He lordily crossed one leg over the other, so that she could more easily reach the second one. Having taken off the second shoe, she steadied his foot by placing her hand under the arch, lowered her head, and pressed her lips warmly to his instep.

"That's what I think of my Jakie!" she proclaimed, rearing her head again.

Abbazzia reached out and roughed her hair slightly, as one would playfully disarrange a dog's coat. "You stay with me tonight," he vouchsafed indulgently.

The two remaining girls exchanged a quick look of chagrin and frustration.

Whether due to the preceding little by-play or not, Abbazzia had now mellowed into a better humor. "Come on!" he ordered. "What're you guys standing around looking so glum about? There ain't nobody dead here. And when there is, it ain't going to be any of us. Let's liven it up a little!" He turned to Augie. "Got anything on you?"

"Sure, never travel without it." Augie produced a bottle.

"That ain't our own, is it?" Abbazzia cautioned mistrustfully.

"Naw. This is the regular stuff, uncut," was the answer.

The blonde was busily cranking the handle of a little flat-topped portable phonograph. She put a record on the mildly stirring turntable, lowered the needle-arm, and after a brief series of thin, piping discords, a tinny smothered voice began to whine:

"Whaddya do Sunday, Whaddya do Monday, Mai——ry?"

"Dance with Augie," Abbazzia commanded, giving the nestling redhead a slight push to dislodge her from the chair-arm.

The redhead pouted. "I'd rather dance with you."

"Who're you that he should dance with you?" one of the men reminded her.

Abbazzia's eyelids lowered a trifle, dangerously. "I said dance with Augie. And you know how I mean. I get a kick just watching the two of you."

At the repetition of the order, the redhead rose to her feet with a swift immediacy that left no doubt of her intention to fully obey, gave her dress a downward pull, and opened her arms statically toward her enjoined partner.

He remained fixed where he was. "Well, come over where I am, if you want to danst with me," he said churlishly. "I ain't going to you."

She had to cross the better part of the room, until she was standing right up against him. Only then did he exert himself enough to put an arm about her waist.

They began to move together with tiny, almost minuscule steps that barely took them anywhere.

Abbazzia watched for a moment with eye-bulging intentness. Then, with querulous dissatisfaction, "That ain't hotsy enough. Do it like you did it up in my place the other night."

"It takes 'em a minute or two, they gotta get warmed up." Sal chuckled obscenely.

"The music's too slow," the redhead protested defensively, her voice smothered against her partner's shoulder. "You can't do anything with it."

"Here's a better one," the self-appointed custodian of the small phonograph announced, having shuffled a number of records hastily through her hands.

She interrupted the bleats coming from it, and after a brief hiatus, it resumed at a quicker tempo, with a sound like twigs being snapped coursing rhythmically through it.

"Doo wacka-doo, doo wacka-doo,
Doo wacka-doo-wacka-doo-wacka-doo."

The redhead's convolutions became almost serpentine. Her partner remained more rigid, though only by a matter of degrees. She was like a wind-walloping pennant flickering and buffeting back against its flagstaff. Neither moved their feet, except to shift weight upon them. Now Sal, crouching on his haunches, beat his hands together in accompaniment low above the floor, as if fanning the music underneath their feet. The blonde snapped her fingers in time, throwing her hand out first to one side of her, then to the other. She called out, "Hey-hey! Hey-hey!" while she did so.

Abbazzia picked up a shaded reading lamp standing on a small table near him, held it aloft, and tipped the shade, so that all the light flooded out at one side, none at the other. He aimed it so that it fell upon the girl's frenzied figure, making a luminous oval across the mid-section, striking her directly in the posterior.

Apprised of this, perhaps from former occasions, the girl accommodatingly hiked her skirt up to a point at which it revealed the undersides of her thighs.

"Back up more," Abbazzia instructed the pair. "You're getting out of range." He adjusted the lamp meticulously as they did so, like a surveyor correcting his sights.

The girl, who had been snapping her fingers in time during the earlier stages, changed her jargon-calls now that a climax was being reached. She called out at intervals: "Charles-burg! Charles-burg!"

"Where'd you get that one?" the brunette squealed delightedly.

"There was an out-of-town guy at the club the other night," the other explained. "Every time he got up, he wanted to say 'Charleston!' and he couldn't get it straight, it wouldn't come out right."

"I like that," her companion proclaimed zestfully. "It's good."

"Help yourself," the first invited drily. "It's free."

They both chimed in together, parroting "Charles-burg! Charles-burg!" Then doubled over in risible appreciation of this newly coined *bon mot*.

The male participant in the exhibition, meanwhile, had suddenly begun to flag; moisture bedewed his pale face. His partner's gyrations continued without inhibition.

"Hold it a minute," he panted in an urgent, suppressed voice. "Get back from me, will ya?" He wrenched his companion's clutching hands off and thrust her back away from him, so that there was clearance between them for the first time.

He stood as though unable or unwilling to move for a moment, exactly as the last paroxysm of the dance had left him.

The other four men watching gave vent to a roar of spontaneous delight that had something as unclean about it as a geyser of mud.

The brunette commented in an undertone: "Get that. He wore out before she did."

The blonde said something to her in explanation behind the back of her hand.

"Oh," said the first one knowingly, now that she was enlightened. "I forgot to think about that."

"You *what?*" was the tart rebuttal. "How old are you anyway?"

The dancers separated and went their ways. Each in his own manner. She, to throw herself down in a chair, with head lolling back and fanning herself with one hand held limply, but otherwise composed, unconcerned. But he, slinking off with a suggestion of crouched maladroitness in his carriage, as though he were undergoing a private imbalance that she could not by nature be subject to. To seek a corner by himself, hook his fingers into his shirt collar, as if to ease an intolerable constriction, and sit there, head bowed, in a sort of male loneliness.

"That was good," Abbazzia summed it up. "That was the best yet. He ain't got no sense of humor, though," he regretted, dismissing the whole episode.

He yawned cavernously. "I'm beat," he said.

There were immediate preparations for departure by everyone in the room except the redhead. The brunette knuckled the closed bath-door glancingly in passing. "Come on," she said possessively over her shoulder. "Jake's getting sleepy."

Carmine turned and asked Sal, "Which side of him you taking?"

"I'll go over here," Sal decided with a pitch of his thumb at the blank wall behind him. "You get in there. Augie can go downstairs and stick by the switchboard, Nick can go out in the hall and keep the elevator covered."

"Go in there next door first and see if you can hear me," Abbazzia ordered, eyes glittering alertly with the instinct for self-preservation. "We don't want no slips. Both of you. Then come back and let me know."

They nodded, opened the door, went out into the hall, and closed it after them.

Abbazzia got up from the chair, rammed one fist deep down into his pocket, arm held stiffly at his side in tension. "They gotta get in here fast, in case I need them," he explained to the respectfully watching girls. He went over toward the wall on the left-hand side first, coiled his free hand, drew it back, and thumped loudly three times, at spaced intervals.

Within a matter of seconds, not minutes but seconds, the room-door burst backward and Carmine strode in, a snub-nosed revolver held springily down beside his hip-joint.

"Heard je," he said triumphantly. "How was that for speed?"

Abbazzia narrowed his eyes mistrustfully. "How many knocks 'dI give it?" he catechized.

"Three," Carmine answered. He reinserted his gun under his left armpit.

Abbazzia nodded approvingly. "You heard me," he admitted.

He turned to face the other way. "Now we'll try Sal's side." He pummeled the wall heavily. Then a second time. Then a third. "I'll give it four this time," he said, jaw clenched with effort. The impact of the blow coincided with the flaring-open of the door, with the latter just preceding it by some instants.

Sal's revolver was bedded within the side pocket of his coat, but reared perpendicularly so that the whole coat hem rose with it to a squat-nosed projection. "Clear as a bell!" he reported sanguinely.

Again Abbazzia's eyes squinted. "How many times 'dI sound off?" he growled truculently.

Sal looked slightly taken back. "I only caught two," he admitted.

Abbazzia's face twisted into a violent blob of rage, like unbaked dough squeezed between the hands of a pastry cook. "You lyin' ——!" he exploded virulently. "I done it four times! You're going to tell me it's twice, haa?"

He coiled a forearm far back of his own shoulder, swung rabidly with it, caught the bodyguard flat-handed on the side of the face with a sound like wet linen being pounded on a clothesline. Then again on a pendulum-like reverse swing. The third slap only missed contact because Sal veered his head acutely aside, without how-ever moving his body back.

Hand poulticing his stricken cheek, his attitude was one of rueful, misunderstood loyalty. "Hold it, boss," he protested virtu-ously. "Hold it a minute."

"I don't like for nobody to lie to me, see?" Abbazzia shrilled.

"I caught the first one sitting in the chair, waiting for it to come. By the time the second one come, I was halfway through the door already. Naturally, I missed the last two because I wasn't in the room no more by that time. What should I do, sit there counting 'em off on my fingers? If them things was wrong-way bullets, four would be too many to wait for. While I'm waiting to count, you're—" He left it eloquently unfinished.

Abbazzia took a moment to consider this, crinkling his eyes speculatively first, then widening them in elated appreciation. "Yeah!" he concurred with enthusiasm. "That was the smart thing to do! It's the speed what counts when I'm sending for you, not the arithmetic." He turned his head a moment in oblique disparagement. "Whyd'n't you think of that, Carmine?" And to the rest of them, as though he had been the one taking Sal's part all along and they had been in opposite judgment: "See what a smart boy I got here? What're you trying to tell me, he ain't smart?" Again his hand went out toward Sal, but this time to clap him on the shoulder rewardingly, to squeeze his biceps affectionately. Even to pinch the point of his chin and wag it playfully to and fro.

He reached into his pocket, took out a billfold, took something out of that, prodded it down into Sal's breast pocket like a handkerchief. "Blow your nose on that," he instructed jovially.

"Now clear out and lemme get some sleep." He crossed his forearms, fanned them apart, in general room-wide dismissal. They went in pairs for the most part, Carmine with the blonde, Sal with the brunette, the other two to do night-long sentinel duty, one downstairs, one in the hall. No good nights were said. Perhaps good-nights were for people who lived less dangerously; just to survive the night itself, that alone was sufficient well-being.

"Take good care of him for us," the blonde warned, with an undertone of jealousy.

"And I'm the girl that can do it," was the pert answer.

The door closed.

"Lock it up on the inside," Abbazzia ordered.

He looked at her from where he lay sprawled out in the chair. His look was lethargic, even somnolent. Not the somnolence caused by sleep, but the somnolence caused by the dregs of a spent passion that can no longer stir or vivify. His arms and legs seemed to fall away from him of their own accord, so that his sprawl became even looser.

"Undress me," he commanded in a monotone.

The girl quickly advanced, a smile starched on her face. She slid downward onto her knees before him, reached gingerly forward toward the topmost button of his jacket, as quiveringly as though she were afraid of getting an electric shock.

He allowed the lids to close over his eyes, the better to retain whatever distorted images this was about to bring him.

Just as her fingertips touched the button, and almost as though it were an effect generated by her touching of it, there was a single, low knock on the outside of the door.

Her hands scampered back to her own person, like two ashamed things seeking refuge. They all but tried to burrow inside her clothing and hide themselves.

His eyelids went up, furrowed with annoyance. "Go see what they want now," he told her. "One of 'em must have forgot something."

She unlocked the door, but her arm held out across it still blocked the way. A hand flung the arm contemptuously aside.

An old, old woman all in black was standing there. Short and stocky, like he was. Her face long-dead; only the eyes still alive. Bitterly alive.

This black wasn't the black of fashion, the black of Rome and New York, trim and just-so. This was the black the women of Catania wore, in the after-years of their lives, after they had lost their men. Homespun and shapeless, and with no intent to please. To show life was through, and that the wearer was through with life.

"Get out!" she commanded the girl stonily.

Stunned into alertness, his back reared from its supine position against the chair. "How'd *you* get here?" he breathed in amazement.

He became aware of the girl, still cringing there to one side of the two of them. "You heard her. Get out," he repeated. "Wait outside. I'll let you know when I want you back."

She slipped around one side of the door-frame and was gone from sight, as furtively as though she were afraid to come into line with those terrible eyes staring so fixedly into the room at him, like messengers of denunciation.

"*Rifiuto!*" the old woman said balefully. Garbage.

He demanded: "Whaddya doin' here like this? Don'tcha know it's risky to come here?"

She pitched her head interrogatively. "*Che significa,* 'risky'?"

"*Pericoloso,*" he translated unwillingly, as though averse to following her into the language of his former days, the one learned at her lips.

"*Pericoloso per chi?*" She gave a snort of scorn-curdled laughter.

Risky for whom? Risky for you, maybe. Not for me. I have killed no one. I have robbed no one. I go unafraid.

"Now that you're here, whaddya want? Whadja come for? To say good-bye to me?"

She tossed her head impatiently, as when one is bored by having to return to an old subject that was closed long ago. "*Ti dissi addio . . .*"

I said good-bye to you ten long years ago, night after night in the dark, on my knees before the blessed image of Our Lady, drops of water falling from my eyes, drops of blood falling from my heart. She did not smile on me. It was too late then already for anything except good-bye. Then, it was finished. That was my good-bye.

"You're talkin' crazy," he said uncomfortably. He got up from the chair. "Then whaddya here for, to preach to me?"

She grappled beneath the seedy black garb that encased her. A sheaf of banded currency was in her hand when she brought it out again.

"*A ridarti . . .*"

To give back this . . .

She showed it to him first, lying in her palm. Then she spat violently into the middle of it, and flung it away from her. It landed anywhere, she did not look to see, she did not want to know.

"*Danaro insanguinato . . .*"

Money with blood on it! The dead cry out from this kind of money. Their voices are within it.

"You're a fool," he sneered. "You could have had everything in the world, and you live like a rat in a hole—"

"*No, sei tu l'idiota . . .*"

No, you are the fool, not I! She struck her hand sharply against her chest.

"*Io sono onesta . . .*"

I am honest. I am a poor woman, but I am honest, clean. My husband worked hard all his life until he died worn-out, but he too was clean. We were not like you.

He strode toward her furiously, backed his arm in threat.

She didn't flinch. "*Colpiscimi . . .*" Hit me. It will not be the first time.

"You lying old bat!" This time his arm completed the threat, he struck her across the face.

She tottered, regained her balance, only smiled sleepily. The eyes that looked at him held no pity, no softness, not any kind of feeling at all. They were eyes of glass, of agate in a statue.

"*Questo e' il momenta . . .*"

This is the hour I knew would come. I have waited for it many years. Now it is here. In my village there was a saying when I was a young girl. "God punishes without having to use hands or feet." I see the punishment before me now. I feel no pity for you. My heart is as dead as a stone. For *I am one of those you have killed*. The first, perhaps. More slowly than some of the others, but just as completely. I walk around in the grave you have put me in. And in the grave there are not mothers, only corpses.

She turned away abruptly, in leave-taking without farewell.

"It will be finished soon, anyway," he heard her say stonily.

"They'll never get me!" he shouted toward her. "D'ye hear what I'm saying? They'll never—"

She looked back briefly, nearer the door now. "They do not have to. You will go just as surely, without them. Your years are already days, your days are minutes. You have the Bad Sickness in you. The sickness that creeps like a worm, and once it is in, cannot be got out again. No man's hand needs to be raised against you . . ."

He stared at her in almost superstitious fright. "Even that you know—" he breathed in awe. "Who told you? Nobody knows that about me!" Mechanically, as if from some long-forgotten habit interred for years and now brought to the surface again by sudden instinctive fear, he made a sneaking, furtive sign of the cross. "What are you, a witch or something?"

She slitted her eyes at him in contempt. *"Non v'era bisogno di dirlo . . ."*

One does not have to be told. One knows. One sees the signs. This is nothing new. I saw it in my village, small as it was, when I was young. Even there it was not new. One crossed to the other side of the road in passing it by, that was all. I knew it had come into my house already when you were still only a boy of sixteen.

His breath hissed in stunned intake.

"La tazza, la forchetta . . ."

The cup you drank from, the fork you ate with, kept apart, hidden from the rest. They were always missing when I washed the things. Those were the signs that told me. You did not come to me for help. You went to the streets for help, instead. The streets where you already robbed the storekeepers, and roamed at night the leader of a pack, marauding with knives. And the streets gave you back what you had given to them. Now the mark is on you, and it is too late for help anymore.

The arms and the legs die, and you cannot move anymore. Then the tongue dies, and there are no more words, only sounds like the animals make. Childhood comes back, but going the other way, rushing toward you from the grave.

"Shut up!" he squalled, and cupped the heels of his hands tight against his ears.

She turned away with a flick of disgust. The door opened at her grip. He was watching her now with a mixture of disbelief and defiant bravado.

"You walking out on me this way? You too? My own mother? All right, go ahead! Who needs you? *Vecchia.* Just an old woman. You shut up all these years, though, didn't you, when things were going good?" he railed. "And now cuz you think they're going bad, you turn on me like all the rest."

She released a scoffing breath.

He changed suddenly, softened for a moment. "Close the door," he coaxed. "Come on back in. Stay with me awhile. I'm lonely. I ain't got nobody of my own. These others— D'you remember when I was a kid, and you used to make lasagne for Vito and me, and bring 'em hot to the table—?"

"Quella non ero io . . ."

That was not I, that was another woman, long gone now. A woman whose prayers were not answered.

"You're my mother, you can't change that," he told her, between a snicker and a derisive grin, like one who is certain he holds the upper hand.

"Io non sono piu' tua madre . . ." she whispered smolderingly.

Mother, no. Just a woman who bore a devil. The woman who once bore you says good-bye to you.

The door clapped closed and she was gone.

His mouth opened in a gape of disbelief, a disbelief such as one might feel if one stood back and watched one's own self betray one.

Then it clicked shut, and defiance spread over his face once more. He swept his arm out and around before him in contemptuous dismissal. "All right, let 'em all go!" he bellowed. "All of 'em! I don't need nobody! I'll make it alone! I come up by myself, and I'll stay up by myself!"

He went over and looked into the mirror, and straightened the hug of the padding that sloped upon his shoulders.

"It's me for me, all by myself, just like it's always been," he said aloud to the scowling reflection facing him. "If God ain't going to forgive you, if God ain't going to give you a break, then what good is God? They can have God. I'll take Abbazzia. What good is being good? You stay poor all your life, like her and eighty million others. You get run over by a car like my brother Vito did, and they let you lie there in the rain, newspapers from a trash-can spread over you. Then 'cause a priest comes and mumbles over you, that means you're going to heaven. Who wants to go to heaven in the rain, on an empty stomach, soaking newspapers thrown over you, without a dime in your pocket? The hell with heaven. He worked hard, he never stole, he never scrapped, he never pulled a knife on no one. *He* was good, and look what he got. I was smart, and look what *I* got—"

He flourished his own hand toward his reflection's hand, so that his reflection's eyes could see the explosively brilliant diamond on the little finger.

He picked up the money she had flung on the floor. "There ain't no good or bad, anyway," he grunted. "They just tell you that in the church when you're a kid, to keep you from getting wise that everyone else has something, and you ain't got nothing. There's only dumb and smart. And if you don't want to be the one, then you gotta be the other."

He riffled the money back into orderly shape, tucked it into his billfold, put it away.

He summed up his life, content with it, proud of it.

"Abbazzia picked smart for his."

Then he went over to the door, and opened it. He gave a curt summons, without looking. "Hey, you! You can come in now. Whaddya waiting for? Didn't you see her go?"

He turned away without waiting, and took out a cigarette and a pocket lighter. Then before he had brought the two of them together, he stopped again and glanced back at the door in angered disbelief. It was still open just as he had left it. No one had come in through it.

He flung the cigarette down, went over to it a second time, and looked out.

There was no one in sight. The hall was empty.

He stalked across the room to the telephone, wrenched the earpiece off the crotch that held it, and shouted harshly, "Hey, down there! Is that bi—Is that girl around? Tell her to get back up here, and make it snappy, or I'll—"

A man's voice, subdued, almost faint by comparison to the violence in his own, intercepted: "Yes, sir?"

"That girl—" he fairly shrieked. "I want her up here! I don't let nobody make me wait like this!"

"A—a red-headed young lady?" the man at the other end finally hazarded.

"Who remembers what they look like!" thundered Abbazzia. "Yeah! Red-headed."

"I'm sorry, sir. She left the building."

There was a moment of sudden stunned silence. "She *what?* What'd you just say?"

"She's not in the building any longer," the voice repeated. "I saw her leave by the front entrance."

A sudden blue bead of flame winked up from the incessantly manipulated pocket lighter in his free hand, and noticing for the first time what he had been doing with it, he flung it violently away from him, as though it, somehow, were to blame for this unprecedented affront, this laceration to his dignity, offered to boot not even by a subordinate but by a lower form of life altogether.

He picked up at long last the remaining part of the phone, the stem part. His voice was less raucous now, more bated. "That man I left down there. Put him on. Tell him I want to talk to him a minute."

"The man that was posted here by the switchboard?" the voice inquired, to make sure of correct identification.

"Him! Get a move on!"

"I'm sorry. He left with her."

The stunning impact of the news made Abbazzia take a step back on one leg, as though the telephone had suddenly pushed him away.

He was having trouble with his breathing now; it came too full one moment, too scant the next. He didn't answer; he closed off the connection almost furtively. As though afraid to leave even that small orifice leading into his room: an electrical impulse within a sheathed wire.

The pupils of his eyes moved too far over into one corner, then too far back into the opposite corner, then all the way back to the first again, never remaining at calm center. Like pools of quicksilver clinging to a ledge.

He darted a look at the lateral wall. "Wait'll I get Sal in here! Gotta get Sal in here—!"

He scurried toward it on the bias, giving a heedless shove to a chair that nearly overturned it, to get it out of the way rather than go around it, so intent was he on getting over there fast.

He struck at the wall, and it gave back a loud but flat-sounding throbbing, that raced around the room and died again into silence. Then he struck once more, and then once more. Silence came back again each time. He even turned around to face the door, waiting to witness Sal's headlong rush across the threshold, as at the rehearsal. He even took a precautionary step out of the way, to allow him plenty of clearance, so that they wouldn't collide.

Nothing occurred. The door remained lifeless.

This time his arm moved like a triphammer. Its motions blurred, they could no longer be identified individually, so fast it struck, so incessantly. So frightenedly, so despairingly. He even cried out his name: "Sal!" And then again: "Sal! Why don't you come in here?"

His arm suddenly dropped, and swung there fallow.

"Gone," he panted. "Him too."

Then he laced around with the swiftness of a top when a child whisks the wound-up guide cord out from under it, and flung himself at the opposite wall, across from the first. Both his arms were out, as when one runs forward to embrace someone or something, enclose it, draw it to you. Thus his whole body careened into the wall in that position, arms akimbo, hands overhead, chest pressed flat against it.

For a moment he lay that way, like a cardboard cutout of a man pasted flat against a wall-surface; every inert turn of his body expressing the one word "despair." Then his hands began to ripple, beating tattoo with their palms, like a drummer using the plaster for his drumhead. Faster and faster they went, frenzied, battering. And his voice-box, partly stopped up by the wall and made hollow-sounding against it, kept calling out in agonized repetition the second one's name, the one who was supposed to be behind there on this side. And broke and crumbled at last into pleadings and sobbings that could not have carried through to the other side even *had* somebody been there. "Carmine, come in, I need you!

Carmine, you're there, ain't you? Carmine, I'll give you anything you want, only come in! It's empty all around me, I'm by myself in here!"

No one, nothing; no sign, no sound. The door stayed mute.

His hands fell still at last, couldn't strike any more. For a moment they stayed in place against the wall, then like five-pronged stains first one and then the other slowly coursed down it and dropped off.

His cheek remained flat against it, nuzzling it, as if he held it in some kind of crazed affection, because it had once meant protection, even if it didn't anymore.

Then his head turned slowly, and he looked across his shoulder at the door, bulge-eyed, fearful.

Panic. Agoraphobia, with its limitless black horizons and chill, unimpeded death-winds. Nothing at hand to shield, to shelter, to cover one over. His voice whispered its terror. "I'm wide open. They can walk right in off the street and get me! There's nobody in-between anymore!"

He flung himself against it, as he had the two walls, and the impact of his body tossed it closed with a violent clout. His hands, trembling, groped for and turned the lock. And then a last slap against the center of the panel, to hold that fast.

He turned and looked and saw the door of the clothes closet. He opened it, and backed in, and half-crouched there. And drew the door partly to in front of him. For a moment only the four tight-pressed tips of his fingers studded along its edge could be seen, and the brightness of his recessed eyes, glistening with watery animal-istic sparkle. And his breath could be heard, against the cavernous echo-chamber that the closet became for it.

Briefly only, he stayed like this. It brought no palliation. Unrea-soning agoraphobia wanted more: a hole in the ground, a burrow. Something tighter, closer overhead.

He came out again. And like a naked man who plunges into icy water, the open room caused him to draw shivering breaths.

He made for the bed, and dropped down against the edge of it, the way children do when they're about to say their prayers. But he had no gods, he was his own god, and therefore he had nothing to pray to. Then he lowered himself to the floor from there, all but his rump, and padding on the flats of his hands, like some odd, ungainly animal, drew his head and shoulders in under the bed. Then lolled over on his side, and switched his legs in after him, and then drew his knees up close against his stomach. And lay coiled like that, like some unborn foetus pulsing with premature breath.

His dilated eyes were sighted out along a two-dimensional garden patch of scuffed beige carpet-flowers that seemed to climb upward in their symmetrical rows, shutting out the whole rest of the world. Their perfume was dust, and they lay like dead, unstirring. The edge of the bed came down and cut them off short. They had no sedative effect for terror; they were the flowers of delirium, that come back at night in dreams if looked at too closely and too long.

Now swiftly, within the space of breath-choked minutes, his mania blew inside-out, like an umbrella in a gale. Or like a sleight-of-hand performer who draws a length of gauze through his fingers and causes it to change magically from one hue to the next. Confinement, craved just now, suddenly became the form of terror itself. Agoraphobia turned into claustrophobia. Both were still the same terror, with another name.

His hand pounded the floor beside him, "I can't stay here like a rat in a trap, waiting for 'em to come and get me! I gotta get out of here! Gotta get out of here fast!" He lashed his legs out into the open, then padded backward on the flats of his hands until his head was in the clear.

"Gotta get on the outside!" he kept muttering. "Gotta lose myself on the outside! That's the only thing'll save me."

He ran to where the suitcase was standing, tossed the lid up and over. His ravening fingers disemboweled its contents; neckties of tropical brilliance splashed up, like a neon-geyser, to fall back around him and stay that way, in static ripples. Shirts threw up their empty sleeves like struggling ghosts and expired lifeless on the floor.

He was still talking brokenly to his unseen companion: self-preservation. "Who needs neckties, when it's your neck itself you gotta save?"

Then a gun, bedded in layers of undergarments. He inserted it underneath his coat somewhere. "The only one you can trust, anyway; the one that's right on you." Then more money went into the already sausage-plump billfold.

He stood up and turned to go. "That's all you need," he said. "That's all, in this-here world. Money and a gun. A gun and money. Everything else you can get with one or the other of them two." And leered with his own wisdom.

He went over to the closed door once more—for the last time, this was to be—and opened it sparingly to look out.

A man was standing down the hall, where the elevator-shaft door was. Not moving, not doing anything. Just standing motionless, head lowered attentively, newspaper spread open just across his breastbone. The brim of his hat kept the light from the upper part of his face, as though he were wearing an eyeshade.

He didn't turn at the sound of Abbazzia opening his door, though he must have heard it in all that stillness. He didn't even seem to be breathing, he was so still.

Abbazzia's fear-sensitized nerves jerked and recoiled throughout the length and width of his body. He knew. These were the lookouts, these who stood like this. He knew the ways of those who stalk to kill, he knew them well, they'd done his own errands for him too many a time. Sometimes he'd even watched them at a distance, from within the safe anonymity of a parked car. That rigor-mortis-immobility, the down-held head so that the eyes could not be seen to move, the sheltering hat-brim, the newspaper that provided the excuse. Then when the quarry had passed, they made the signal that doomed him. In many ways, in many different ways, they made it. They lowered the newspaper, or blew their nose on a handkerchief, or threw a cigarette away, so that it made a momentary red streak across the dark. All these were the messages of death. Who should know them better than he, he had prearranged so many of them himself.

The ribbon's-width of door-opening had already been effaced, instantly, at first glance. "The window—" came racing down the millway of his thoughts like a bright pebble. "There may be a fire ex-cape—get out through there." He'd first used the word at seven with an *x;* he'd used it that way ever since, and never known in all that time that it was wrong; no one had ever told him so. A wrong word used many times throughout a life; a wrong deed done many times throughout a life; wherein lies the difference?

He didn't draw the shade up, he simply slanted it aside, making a crevice to look through. He saw at once that under the ledge there was nothing, only a sheer drop all the way down to the street.

He was cut off, sealed up in here. The room that had been chosen for a sanctuary because of its inaccessibility, had turned for that very same reason into a tomb.

He lurched with sagging knee-joints back deeper into the room, pushing away an impeding table, propping himself in passing against the top of a chair. Then he stood there a moment, both hands inter-crossed and pressed flat against the center of his forehead. As if there were a pasty-colored star affixed there, with spreading fingers for its many rays.

"I'm finished!" he shuddered deeply. "I'll never get out of here by myself, alive!"

Silence at first, both of voice and of thought. Then that "by myself" began coming back, like an echo, like an afterthought. Louder, more insistent each time, as though he had shouted it out at the top of his voice just now (and he had barely given it breath).

"By myself—" *"By myself—"* "BY MYSELF—"

Ricocheting, playing back to him, glancing off the walls themselves in eerie polyphonic impetus.

His hand dropped from his forehead, suddenly tightened, as if it were grasping an idea, holding onto it for dear life.

"By myself, not a chance. But with somebody else I could make it!"

Then his hand opened a little, almost let the idea go. "Where's the somebody else for me, though? They've all run out. And it would have to be somebody that they're afraid of. Somebody bigger than them. Bigger than them and bigger than me, both—"

His hand tightened again. Far tighter than it had been the time before. The idea was caught fast now, had taken form, had taken body.

"Them!" he breathed, as if in amazement at the idea's simplicity, its logic; in fact, that it had not occurred any sooner than it had. He drove the clenched hand into its opposite now, like a mallet. "Sure! Them! Why not them? I've always laughed at them—They were for the chumps—For the little guys, not the big guys like me—They were for decoration. They turned their backs, when I passed the word. But always with a hand sticking up behind them, like a tail. All I had to do was put something in it, and then they were never around where I didn't want them to be at a certain time. Now I *want* them to be around, that's all. It worked that way, why shouldn't it work this way just as good?"

He hastened to the phone, caught it up.

"I got no bodyguard left?" he breathed above an hysterical, abortive chuckle. "I'll make a bodyguard out of *them!*"

Then he talked into the phone.

"Gimme the police," he ordered.

It was a commanding knock. A double one first, then a single one after. Urgent, demanding. As if to say: "We are the police, and we don't like being kept waiting."

He turned with a grin on his face. "Coming, boys!" he hallelu-jahed. "Ri-i-ight with you!"

The brassware under his fingers was like a caress, as he unfastened it. It was like gold, and he had always loved to touch gold. Just for its own sake alone.

This door that had kept death out all the long night through—he opened it now to let life in.

He saw their faces first. Life had three faces. There were three of them, one on each side of the opening, the third in mid-center. Oh, what beautiful faces they had; oh, what handsome guys they were; never such good-looking faces before. Next his eyes feasted on their uniforms, like moths that gorge themselves on fabric. The blue service-garb of the Police Department of the City of New York. The brass buttons, the visored caps, the pewter-looking badges affixed over the heart.

Their eyes regarded him, and that was all. Eyes that revealed nothing, other than that they saw him. They didn't speak; he was the one did.

"Gee, am I glad to see you fellows! I never was so glad to see anyone in my life before—!"

"You are?" one said, and that was all.

Beside himself, and scarcely knowing what he was doing, he even tried to press the hand of one of them. The man passively let him do so, without making any move of his own. His hand did not return the pressure, and when Abbazzia let it go, it fell back lifeless, boneless, to where it had been before. Thus, there was no handclasp exchanged, for it takes two to produce one.

Two of them came forward now into the room, one turning to the third as they did so and instructing, quiet-voiced: "You wait outside here by the door. We'll be right out."

The door was closed again, locked on the inside, crisply.

Abbazzia had been made almost antic by happiness. He cupped his hands together, leaving an orifice. He blew into it zestfully. He rubbed them together, in anticipation of imminent welcome activity.

"Now I'll get what I'm taking with me," he told them. "Won't take no time at all."

The second officer had crossed to the window, as if to draw the shade. Then seeing that Abbazzia already had it down, he modified his intention, simply stood there with his back to it, in a waiting attitude, hands behind him.

"You won't need that," the other one suggested helpfully to Abbazzia.

"No, I guess you're right," Abbazzia conceded. He cast aside the rejected garment, stooped again to his task.

"Y'got a gun?" the man asked him matter-of-factly.

"Yeah, sure."

"Better let us take it," the patrolman said quietly.

"Okay, if you think it's better that way," Abbazzia assented accommodatingly. He drew it out, offered it to him grip-first.

"Take his gun for him, Charlie," the first one instructed his fellow-patrolman without offering to touch it himself.

The second one uncoupled his hands, came over, accepted it from Abbazzia, and disposed of it somewhere within his uniform jacket, unbuttoning it, rebuttoning it again.

"Thanks a lot," said Abbazzia absently, bending once more.

"You're welcome," answered the first one tonelessly.

Abbazzia straightened again, about to insert something within his own clothing this time.

"You won't need that," he was told, as tonelessly as ever.

Abbazzia stopped long enough to give him a blank look. "Oh, this I will," he contradicted. "This time you're wrong. This is dough. You need that every place you go."

"There's one place you don't," the policeman said expressionlessly. "Not where you're going."

Abbazzia stopped to look at him more fully, more uncomprehendingly than the first time. His look became a stare. "What d'ya mean? I don't get you—"

The other one spoke unexpectedly, from behind them. "Let's get finished, shall we, Mike? This is no fun anymore."

Abbazzia turned sharply to look at him. He had a gun held in his hand. Not the one Abbazzia had just handed over to him, but one that must have come out of his police-holster. He wasn't aiming it, it just lay idle in his hand, sidewise, as if he were testing its weight.

Abbazzia turned back in consternation to the first one. "What does he need that for?" he asked with quickening tension.

"I don't know," was the dispassionate answer. "Ask him."

But even as he answered, he was unlimbering one of his own.

Abbazzia's voice was beginning to throb. "Wait a minute—I don't get it—"

"You don't get it?" said the one before him, meticulously repetitive. "He don't get it," he said to the one behind.

"Something's wrong here—"

This time the policeman gave a slight head-shake. "Nothing's wrong. Everything's just the way it should be."

"No, it isn't! I feel peculiar. You're making me feel peculiar—the way you're looking at me—something about the way you're looking at me—" He could hardly breathe. Suddenly suspicion, seeping into the overheated crannies of his mind all this while like a combustible gas, ignited, exploded into a ghastly white flash of certainty.

"You ain't real cops—" His lower jaw dangled loosely, as though the mental detonation just now had unhinged it. He got it to cleave to its upper part long enough for utterance. "Barney—Maxwell—didn't—send you!"

"What d'ya know?" the one in front of him apprised the one behind him. "Barney Maxwell didn't send us."

The voice in back of Abbazzia said, "Who's Barney Maxwell?"

"Crooked police captain," the first one explained. "Must've been trying to make a deal with him, to get in out of the open."

At this, Abbazzia's eyes flickered closed in expiring confirmation.

The patrolman plucked briefly at his own coat sleeve to indicate it. "So the cop suits worked?" he leered at Abbazzia. "It's new. First time. And when a thing's still new, you can count on it paying off."

Abbazzia sank downward onto his knees between the two of them, into the little cranny their bodies made for him.

("That's smart," the rearward one said approvingly, "less distance for you to fall.")

His face was turned upward. He started to talk for his life. Only, lives can't be put into words. "Fellas. Fellas—"

"We *are* fellas," the face bending over him said.

"Fellas, my money— All my money, fellas— Much more than is in this room—"

"What d'ya think, we came here to rob you?" the face smiled. "We ain't thieves."

His voice came straight from his heart now. Every heartbeat swelled it, thinned it, and they were dynamo-quick. "Two minutes. Just give me two minutes. Two minutes, that ain't long to ask for. Just one minute. Don't give it to me cold. Just let me pull myself together, just let me get ready."

"You're ready now," the overhanging face said. And it said crisply to the other one, "Get a pillow. Use one of them."

He put his hand downward onto Abbazzia's shoulder; not heavily, but lightly, as if just to balance him there in place. As you hold some inanimate thing steady, keep it from toppling over, until you are ready to have to do with it—whatever it is you have to do with it.

Abbazzia made an infantile puking sound, as when a suckling infant regurgitates upon its mother's milk, and lurched sideward onto his shoulder and hip. Then like a bisected snake that still has reflexes of motion left to it, he tried to writhe in underneath the bed, to gain the shelter of its iron frame.

The man in the police uniform made a wide scooping motion with his foot, as when you sweep something back toward you that has eluded you, whether inert refuse or scurrying vermin it matters not; and Abbazzia had to avert his face from the scraping shoe. Then the man recoiled his foot and drove his shoe into Abbazzia's lower face, along the floor.

There was dental pain, and bone pain, and a pale-blue flash, like shattered starlight on a disrupted mill-pond. Sluggish warmth backed against the seams of Abbazzia's mouth, and peered forth, emulsion-thick, a laggard bead at a time.

"Hang onto him a minute, be right with you," one of the voices recommended belatedly, as though its owner had only then just glanced around at what was taking place.

"Got him," the other assured.

Abbazzia's eyes, like circular mosaics embedded in the floor, stared upward, could see only the ceiling now: an edgeless expanse of white. It was like a burial ground suspended upside-down over him, a potter's field with a fill of white clay.

"A minute—Only a minute—" he whispered.

The sole of a shoe came down across his throat, full stamping-power withheld though, and kept him pinned there. He could not raise his head at the one side of it, he could not raise his trunk at the other. His fingers scratched the empty air, his arms jittered upward and back in opposing directions like someone flat on his back playing the strings of an invisible harp. Once his flexing fingertips caught onto trouser-leg fabric, at sheer random, and pulled it back, revealing gnarled pebble-white shank and a triangular banding of elastic garter.

Someone chuckled.

Now from opposite sides of the white ceiling-expanse their faces curved over toward him. There was a gusty impact, as when someone drives a blow into the plumpness of a pillow.

Abbazzia gave a choking whinny, and striving mortally managed to tilt the back of his head a little bit off the floor. At once the entire length of body under one of the faces came into perspective. The man was holding a pillow before his own mid-section, the curve of one arm supporting it. With the other hand, clenched into a fist, he kept walloping the pillow, driving each successive blow deeper into it. Until he had driven a deep hollow into the inner side of it, opposite his own abdomen.

Then neatly and economically he inserted the gun into the pit he had punched within the pillow. His eyes scanned Abbazzia's form steadily for a moment, as though he were taking aim sight-unseen, by dint of finger-feeling alone. Without raising them, he remarked to his fellow-killer, "Get your foot outta the way, I don't want to nick you."

The waist of the shoe suddenly left Abbazzia's throat. His windpipe seemed to unfold, like a rubber tube that has been trodden flat and slowly fills out again.

The shots followed immediately afterward, without any further preliminary.

The pain came first, then the throbbing drumbeats of the sound. There were many pains, and many drumbeats, but they all came unvaryingly in that order. The pain, and then the stifled thumping sound, and then the pain again, and then the sound. Twice, thrice, four times, five, six.

The pain, each time, was like a rabid needle going into him, drawing after it a scarlet thread of fire. The withdrawal-stitch that followed each plunge of the needle into the fabric of his life was equally excruciating. And then it would plunge in again in a new place, to depths he'd never known he'd had until now, drawing its flaming, snaking thread after it, in sutures that never were over and done with. For the old place continued to hurt no less, while the new place quickly matched it in height of agony.

He moved very little, just rocked a little from side to side, with an ebbing motion, like something settling to rest. He didn't cry out. This pain was too deep to be voiced. It lacked the breathing spells in-between, in which to gather voice and eject it.

His eyesight fogged, as when someone breathes too closely on a glass, and then cleared again momentarily, but not to the full expanse it had had before, just a small clear patch in the center, with mist all around its edges.

He saw a feather come wafting sluggishly down, in zigzag graduated volplane glides from side to side, like something suspended on a hidden thread. It looked so enormous, like the lush tail-plume of an ostrich. It landed on his chest someplace, was lost to sight.

High up above he saw a trace of smoke-haze. This went up the other way, as slowly as the feather had come down, erasing itself to nothingness as it went. First it was there, then it was gone.

His eyesight dimmed again, and was no more.

His hearing lingered on, futile, moribund.

An inquiring tap on wood sounded, and a voice answered it, "Yeah, we're through. We're coming."

The hard hub of a shoe pounded against his ribs, like a mallet swung underhand seeking to drive them apart. The pain this time was not of needles, but of splinters. They did not course in and out as the needles had, they remained in his side, crushed, fragmented. As though a huge burr were being held pressed tight up against him.

"Take that with you," a voice said way off in the distance. "That's Big Matt's regards."

A door-latch clicked, many rooms away it seemed.

And in that other, far-off room, that was the world now, that was life now, men exchanged a brief remark or two in passing one another, as he had once himself when he was still among them.

"How'd it sound?"

"Like a guy snapping his fingers at a crap game, that's about all."

And then someone laughed. That was the last time he heard laughter. Only the living can laugh, only the living can hear it. "That was the crap game of death, buster. We cleaned up in there."

Then momentarily a voice came again. "Close the door," it jeered. "Let him die in privacy."

A latch gave a single clocklike tick, and then there was nothing more of other men, their voices nor their stirrings nor the pain they gave. He was alone in a world of his own, a world between two other worlds, a blend of each: one of which he had always known, one of which he was still to know.

It was twilight in this world. A peculiar India-ink sort of twilight, in which long horizontal bands of dark, like brush-strokes on a Japanese print, kept ebbing slowly downward, with alternate bands of light between each one. As though somebody were endlessly unfolding a Venetian blind, a blind which never found bottom.

It was *un dormetto*, but a particular moment of *un dormetto* caught and held static, prolonged beyond time-reckoning. The moment just before full sleep comes, the moment just before awakening sets in. An empty echo-chamber of the things that were, or the things that were about to be. In each sleeping-time, passed through at a single moment; but in this death-sleep, stretched out into a lifetime of nothingness, the nothingness of a lifetime.

Because it was twilight, and once long ago she had used to call him at twilight, a memory came back from somewhere, and found its way into the emptiness.

She was calling him, from the high window of a six-story tenement. Patiently calling, over and over. Never answered, never even acknowledged by an upward turn of the head. Until at last the calling faltered, and wore out, and was gone, defeated until the next time, the next twilight, when it would be defeated again.

"*Giacopo! Giacoppino! vieni a mangiare . . .*"

Jake. Jakie. Come in and eat.

Over and over again, each twilight. Never answered, never obeyed. Until twilight ended, and it was night, and it was too late. Tired, defeated, the call came no more. Until all the twilights ended, and it was too late. Until boyhood ended, and it was forever night, the long dark night of wayward manhood, and it was too late.

"*Giacopo! Giacoppino . . . !*" Fainter and fainter, going away now. Just a memory now, just an echo drifting through eternity.

He stirred restlessly, and his heart answered, muted, twenty years too late. His lips struggled to pronounce the answer, the answer she had waited for so long and never had. His tongue peered forth, drew back. His whole head moved with striving. And then a sighing word stole forth. A single word.

"*Vengo . . .*"

One word, that would have changed his life, and changed his death, had it been given then instead of now.

And then the effort to obey set in, coursing slowly through him like some hypodermically introduced plasma. His struggles now were terrible to watch, they were so very small. A finger quirked, a foot twitched, an eyelid flickered as if the light of life still shone too strongly on it. In a moment, or in forty, one knee had switched up toward his body like a piston-rod and then gone down again; switched up, and then at last stayed up. And then his trunk gave a half-turn over, and his hand caught in the bed-stuff above him, and clawed, and stayed.

Then in a little while the other hand was up there with it. But his head hung down between them of its own weight. He'd raise it, but it would go down again. Until a time came, in the blank space that now was time, when it too stayed up.

The night was getting late, and the supper was getting old, but he'd get there if it took him all eternity. For a spark within him said to heed her call.

The tenement stairs were steep and hard to climb—they always had been, even in those days—and he kept slipping back and slipping back, sometimes only a floor or two, sometimes all the way to the bottom, but without hurt, without bruising hardness.

Until at last he breasted them, he reached the top. There only remained the door now, the door to their tenement flat. He could see it over there from where he was, here.

He picked up his coat. He knew where to go for it. Strange, but he knew where to go for it. The sleeves were white-satin lined, but only before his arms had introduced themselves.

He'd been hurt in some kind of a street fight. It must have been a bad fight. It was starting to run down, now that he was perpendicular. He looked down at the floor, and there were dark polka dots all around him. Like splashes of Marsala wine.

Everything was so hard, even to get the buttons through the buttonholes. The buttons turned sticky after a while, and that made it even harder.

He even took the hat by the brim and gropingly settled it on his head. He had always been nattily dressed, impeccably so, these latter times of affluence and power. He still was, this last time of all. He didn't look in the mirror, though; that was the one thing he didn't do now.

He had difficulty with the door. Getting it open. His own leaning body kept pushing it back again each time. At last he got it to scrape past him all along one side, and that gave it clearance to swing free.

He saw it no more, knew of it no more; he was out in the hall now, up against the wall in the hall, standing very still, face inward, like a pupil being punished by being made to stand there face to wall. On the threshold where he'd just been lay a moistly glittering star, still pulsing with his life-force. Then the pulsing went out of it. A swirl of ruddy shellac remained, like a brush-stroke left by a careless painter.

He began to inch along the wall now, the flats of his hands patting each new place to see if it was there first, then his feet shifting over with a dragging scrape.

Death, pretending to be alive.

Then after a while he'd reached the point at which he'd have to cross in openness, because the elevator was on the other side. Three times he tried it, and three times he came right back to the wall again, to stay up on his feet. And once he kissed it with his lips, as if pleading with it not to abandon him. It seemed to shed a garnet tear over his predicament, which ran down slowly right where he was standing, and then thickened to a stop.

At last he pushed rudely at it, cast it away from him, and on jumbled, stiffly scissoring legs tottered head-low, to come against the matching wall on the opposite side. Journey's end; no more groping, no more staggering, no more fears of leaving the wall. Thick satiny glass was there beside him, and a nubby little push-button, easy to find. He pressed it with his thumb. Within moments warm yellow light climbed behind the glass, filled it to its top like a tank. There was a muffled unlatching, and the glass slid away and there was open space before Abbazzia's penitently down-hanging face.

A man was standing at the back of the car, his face down-turned, too, a newspaper held open just below it as if to catch it should it fall off out of sheer weariness. And midway between the two of them, a youth with a pillbox cap, too somnolent to look closely at Abbazzia.

Three vagrant people, as unaware of each other as a moment before birth, or a moment after death. Or for that matter, a moment in mid-life.

"Going up?" the boy asked sleepily.

"No," Abbazzia whispered, "going down."

The panel slid closed, and darkness slowly came up in it, pushing the light up out of it.

And as it did so, Abbazzia in turn slowly went down, his palms trailing the glass, lingeringly, to the last.

Then he rolled over very briefly just once on the floor.

Then the spark went out.

And then there was death, the great know-nothing part of life. Or had life perhaps been only the brief know-something part of an endless all-encompassing death?

As was the case with "Murder on My Mind," the earliest version of our next tale first appeared in a pulp magazine ("Death Escapes the Eye," *Shadow Mystery Magazine,* April–May 1947; collected in *Angels of Darkness,* Mysterious Press, 1978) and was later revised for a collection (*Violence,* Dodd Mead, 1958) where it was billed as a brand-new Woolrich story. How do the two versions differ? Originally the female narrator was named Lizzie Aintree, not Annie, and worked as the editor of a mystery magazine. As reconfigured in 1958 she seems to have no job at all, and there's no mention of her physical unattractiveness or that she's several years older than the male lead. Dwight Billings is no longer married to his *ange noir* Bernette but just living with her, and Annie no longer tries to maneuver him into marriage but is willing to have uncommitted sex with him. That Woolrich became more enlightened racially as he grew older is indicated by the black houseman Luther, who is given far more dignity here than he had in his 1947 incarnation. This more recent version was another of the three Woolrich tales to serve as basis for an episode of *Fallen Angels:* an exceptionally evocative one, too. Alfonso Cuaron directed from a teleplay by Amanda Silver, and the main characters were portrayed by Laura Dern, Alan Rickman, and Diane Lane.

MURDER, OBLIQUELY

The other night at a party I met my last love again. By last, I don't mean latest, I mean my first and yet my final one. We said the things you say, holding tall glasses in our hands to keep us company.

"Where've you been?"

"Around. And you?"

"Here and there."

Then there wasn't anything more to say. Love is bad for conversation; dead love, I mean. We drifted on. In opposite directions, not together.

It isn't often that I see him anymore. But when I do, I wonder whatever really *did* become of her.

• • •

I first met him through Jean. Jean collects people, as a velvet evening wrap collects lint. People she has no emotional need for. She is very happily married. In an insulting, slurring way. I've never heard her speak a civil word to, or of, him. Example: "Oh, I don't know why." (shrug) "I had a spare twin bed and it seemed a shame to let it go to waste." She is the most gregarious one-man woman I know. Or else she keeps going through brambles, I can't say. Possibly it has to do with her face. She is not beautiful by wide-screen standards. But there is a winsome, elfin quality to her expression of face. I am not beautiful, either. The similarity ends there, right there.

Even when I was young, I was always the fifth wheel on the wagon. The other girl they had to ring in an extra man for, on dates. She never brought one of her own along. Never had one to bring. And these telephone-directory swains never repeated themselves. It was always someone else, the next time around. Once had been enough, for the one before.

Jean and her husband, the Cipher, stopped by for me in a cab at six-thirty, and the three of us went on together from there. The Cipher wore glasses, was beginning to show baldness, and grew on you slowly. You found yourself beginning to like him after a time lag of about six months. The nickname, Jean's creation, was not inappropriate at that. The Cipher was singularly uncommunicative, on any and all subjects, after five o'clock in the afternoon. He was resting from business, she and I supposed. "He *has* a voice," she had once assured me. "I called for him one day, and I heard it through the office door. I wasn't at all certain until then."

He said, on the present occasion, " 'Lo, Annie," in a taciturn growl as I joined them in the cab, and that, we knew, was all we were likely to get for the next hour to come, so it had to do. But " 'Lo, Annie," when it's sincere and sturdy and reliable, isn't bad, either. In fact, it may be better than a lot of facile patter. Jean had settled for it, and Jean was smarter when it came to men than I could ever hope to be.

Number 657 was one of the tall monoliths that run along Park Avenue like a picket fence from 45th to 96th, but a picket fence that doesn't do its job. It doesn't seem to keep anyone out; everyone gets in.

"Mr. Dwight Billings," Jean said to the braided receptionist.

"Sixth floor," he said.

We entered an elevator that was a trifle small. Space, presumably, was so expensive in this building that only a minimum could be spared for its utilities. We stepped out into a foyer, and there was only a single door facing us. A colored man opened it. His accent was pure university. "Good evening, Mrs. Medill, Miss Ainsley, Sir. If you'll allow me." He took the Cipher's hat. "If you ladies would care—" He indicated a feminine guest room to one side.

Jean and I went in and left our wraps there, and looked at our faces in a wide, triple-winged vanity mirror. She unlidded a cut-crystal powder receptacle, being Jean, and sniffed at it. "Quite good," she said. "Coty's, unless I'm slipping. Rachel for brunettes, and"—she unlidded a second one on the opposite side—"flesh for blondes. Evidently there are no redheads on his list."

I didn't answer. I've been red-headed since I was twenty.

We rejoined the Cipher in the central gallery. It ran on for a length of about three rooms, cutting a wide swath through the apartment, and then you stopped, and turned to your left, and came down two steps onto the floor of the drawing room. It was artfully constructed for dramatic entrances, that room.

Overhead hung two rock-crystal chandeliers. One was lighted and sparkled like a rhinestone hornet's nest inhabited by fireflies. The other was unlighted, and showed cool blue with frosty crystalline shadow. A man was sitting behind the upturned ebony lid of a grand piano. Desultory notes of "None but the Lonely Heart," played with one hand alone, stopped short at the bustle of our coming down the two steps. Then he stood up and came forward, one hand out for Jean.

I like to study people. Even people that I think I'm going to see only once.

He was tall, and he was thirty-five; brown eyes and lightish hair, blonde when he was still a boy. He was like—how shall I say it? Everyone's glimpsed someone, just once in her life, that she thought would've been just the right one for her. I say would've, because it always works out the same way. Either it's too late and he's already married, or if he isn't, some other girl gets across the room to him first. But it's a kindly arrangement, because if you *had* got across the room to him first yourself, then you would have found that he wasn't just the right one for you after all. This way, the other girl is the one finds it out, and you yourself don't get any of the pain.

What's the good of trying to describe him? He was—well, how *was* that man that you didn't quite get over to in time?

I like to study people. People that I know I'm going to see lots more than just once. That I want to, that I've got to.

"This is Annie," Jean was saying in that careless way of hers. Nothing could be done about that. I'd given up trying. All the "Anyas" and "Annettes" when I was seventeen and eighteen hadn't helped any. I was back to plain Annie again, this time to stay. Good old Annie, there's a good girl.

We all sat down. He looked well sitting: not too far forward, not too far back. Not too straight, not too sunken. Couldn't he do anything wrong? He should do something wrong. This wasn't good for me.

We talked for a while, as people do, entering on the preliminaries of social intercourse. We said a lot of things; we said nothing. His man brought in a frost-clouded shaker and poured bacardis and offered them to us. The talk that was talk for the sake of making talk went on, at quickened pace now, lubricated by the cocktails.

"How did you happen to get hold of all this?" Jean blurted out in that pseudonaïve way of hers. We were at the table now.

"An aunt," he smiled. "The right kind."

"Old and rich," she quickly supplied.

"Fond of me," he contributed.

"Dead," she topped him.

"It's a co-operative, she owned it, and when she died two years ago, I found it on my hands."

"Why don't I find things like that on my hands?" Jean wondered innocently.

"I didn't know what to do about it, so I moved in here, along with Luthe. He's my man. The estate takes care of the upkeep, so that what it amounts to practically is I'm living here rent-free."

I kept wondering what he did. I didn't know how to go about asking, though. Jean did. It was a great convenience having her along, I couldn't help reflecting.

"Well, what do you do?" she pressed him.

"Nothing," he said bluntly. "Simply—nothing."

She burst out with enthusiasm. "Now, there's a man after my own heart! Let me shake hands with you." And she proceeded vigorously to do so.

"I did have a job until this—this windfall descended upon me," he said. "I even kept it up for a while afterwards—at first. And then I got up too late for work one day after a party, and it felt good not to go to work, so I said to myself, 'Why haven't I done this before?' and I never did go back from then on."

The Cipher made his hourly utterance at this point. "I admire you," he stated emphatically. "That's the way all of us have felt at one time or another. Only, you had spunk enough to go ahead and carry it out."

"Do you always carry out the things you feel like doing, stray impulses that come along?" Jean asked him mischievously. "If you do, I'd hate to be the lady in front of you in a theater seat wearing one of those tall, obliterating hats."

"Pretty nearly always," he said with grim determination. "Pretty nearly always."

And you could tell he wasn't joking.

We left early. He closed the door, and we could hear his step going away down the corridor inside. He had a fine, firm, crisp tread: clean-cut, without any slurring. He even walked right.

She stood there looking at me with her brows raised.

"Why are your brows up?" I asked, finally.

"Are they up?"

"Well, they don't grow that way."

She let them down at length. Presently she remarked, as if to herself, "He's unhappy." She turned back to me for corroboration. "Don't you think so? Couldn't you notice?"

"Women," observed the Cipher, eying the cab ceiling light.

She ignored him. "Some girl, probably." She pondered the matter. Then she nodded confirmation of her own line of reasoning. "He's the broody type, would let it get him."

"I couldn't see anything the matter with him," the Cipher put in. "What did you expect the poor fellow to do, stand on his hands?"

"Men," she said crushingly.

"I think I saw her," I told her.

"What was she like?" she wanted to know eagerly.

"Not good for him," I said somberly. "Or anyone else. She was inside a frame in one of the rooms there. He had the door closed, I guess so we wouldn't look in, but the key was still in it on the outside. It said 'To my Dwight,' down in a lower corner, but her own name wasn't signed. As though," I went on resentfully, "there could be no possible danger of confusion, there was only one of her in his life."

"Ho, you were busy!" she reveled.

"She must use the room sometimes. Stay over," I said bitterly. "It was all in peach and marabou."

"He's a big boy now," Jean drawled extenuatingly. "And he is a bachelor. And they do say there's an awful lot of it going on."

"That will do," said the Cipher with mock primness.

And so we began to know him, the little that you could. The little that he would let you. Or perhaps I should say, the little that we were capable of.

I had him at my place, and then Jean had him at hers. It went better there. Anything always did at Jean's place. Even a funeral would have been lively. We were all even now. I don't know why you have to be, but you have to be. Then he called, in about a week, and invited us to dine with him again, starting the thing over.

Jean, it was obvious, already didn't view the prospect with any great enthusiasm. "I'm not going to stay too late," she remarked. "You come away blue. I don't mind anyone being lovesick, but not if I have to sit and watch it."

I didn't answer. I was trying to decide what I was going to wear.

The dinner was just as good as the first time. He was just as hard to get to know as ever.

After we'd left the table, Luthe kept coming to the door with telephone calls. Effect without cause: you never heard it ring. Dwight just shook his head in refusal each time. I counted about five or six times it happened. It got on Dwight's nerves finally.

"Not anyone, understand?" he said sharply. "Not anyone at all."

Jean looked into her drink as though she were wondering whether it were big enough to drown herself in.

The next thing, Luthe had come back to the door again, in spite of the recent blanket injunction he'd been given.

Dwight turned his head abruptly. "I thought I told you—"

Luthe beamed at him. Wordlessly a message passed between them. I don't know how they did it, but it was sent and it was understood.

"No!" Dwight gasped incredulously. And then I saw his face light up as I'd never seen it light up yet. There was only one way to describe it. It was the face of a man deliriously in love. The face of a man who had thought all along he'd lost something, and now found it was being returned to him. That it was his once more.

It hurt me a little to see that light on his face. Second-degree burns, most likely, from foolishly trying to get too near.

The telepathic currents continued to flow back and forth between the two of them. Luthe was all white teeth. "Sure enough," he grinned.

Dwight choked on some sort of too-turgid happiness brimming up all over him. "Luthe, you're not fooling me? Don't do that."

"Don't I know the right voice?"

"When did she get back?"

"You better find that out for yourself."

He went into a sudden flurry of—I don't know what you'd call it—altruistic ecstasy. "More drinks for everybody! Annie, Jean, another. Champagne this time, Luthe. I'll join you in it, be right back!" And as he zigzagged to get out of the room in the shortest time possible, he passed close by where I was sitting, and in a sudden blind effusion—it must have been blind, it must have been—he bent and elatedly kissed the top of my head.

He didn't walk down the gallery out there. You could hear him running. It was a long thing, and he ran the whole length of it; then his footsteps stopped, and he'd arrived; he was there, he was talking to her.

I sat very still, as though I were afraid of spilling a drop of the champagne Luthe had just poured for me.

Nothing was said.

There was a muffled thud, outside there, about where the footsteps had ended. As when a chair goes over, perhaps. A little less sharply defined than that. Or when you sway unexpectedly and bump your head upon a table or against a doorframe.

Luthe looked up sharply. Then he hastened over and looked out, down the gallery. He hurried from sight, in that direction.

We waited there, holding our champagne.

He took a long time to come back to us.

Jean got up and wandered over to the radio console, and studied it. But then she didn't turn it on. There was more and better drama here, on the outside of it. I'd been hoping she wouldn't. She came back again presently and reseated herself about where she'd been before.

It must have been about ten minutes. Then he came walking in again. A little tiredly, a little inertly. There was a neat little patch of adhesive up on his temple, back from the eye.

"I got a little bump on the head," he smiled. "Luthe insisted on giving me first aid. Sorry I was so long."

His face was too white for that. It was drawn, it was sick. You don't get that look on your face even when you half knock yourself out. It was behind the eyes, mostly, inside them.

"She's said good-bye—whoever she is," I said to myself.

I took a sip of champagne. Funny how quickly it worked through you, making you glow, making you feel happy, even such a small sip.

Luthe had come in with a drink for him. It was straight brandy. It was a giant. It wasn't a drink for conviviality; it was a restorative.

He looked at it dubiously while Luthe stood there holding it for him. Then he looked up into Luthe's face, as though appealing to some superior wisdom, more than he himself had at the moment. "That won't help much, will it?" I heard him say almost inaudibly.

"No, that won't help much," Luthe agreed ruefully.

Luthe turned away with it, set it aside someplace, went out without it.

We tried to pick up the pieces of the conversation. Even Jean chipped in now, her humanitarian instincts aroused.

I kept watching his flayed face. I wondered if we were being cruel or kind.

"Don't you think we'd better be getting along?" I suggested.

"No, don't go yet," he said, almost alarmedly. "Wait a little while longer, can't you? It's good to have you here. I feel sort of—"

He didn't finish it, but I knew the word: lonely.

We stayed on, by common consent. Even the Cipher forbore looking at his watch, that gesture with which he had a habit of harrying Jean, any evening, anywhere—but home.

It would have been a case of leaving just as the curtain was about to go up, though we didn't know it.

Suddenly drama had come fuming in around us, like a flash flood.

Luthe reappeared, went to him, bent down and said something. This time wholly inaudibly.

Dwight looked up at him, first in complete disbelief. Then in consternation. Then he pointed to the floor. I caught the word. *"Here?"*

Luthe nodded.

I caught the next two words too. "*With* him?" I saw him wince, as if in imminence of unendurable pain.

"All right," he said finally, and gave his hand an abrupt little twist of permission. "All right."

I got it then. There's somebody else; that was her first message, the one that floored him. But not only that: She's come right here with the somebody else.

He was a bad actor. No, I shouldn't say that. We were in the wings, watching him; we were backstage. All actors are bad when you watch them from behind-scenes. He was a good actor from out front. And that was from where he was meant to be seen.

He got up and he went over quickly to where Luthe had parked that brandy bombshell. And suddenly the glass was empty. I never saw a drink go down so fast. It must have flowed in a steady stream, without a stop for breath between. He did it with his back to us, but I saw him do it just the same. Then he wagged his head and coughed a little, and it was all down.

It wasn't a restorative now, it was more an anesthetic.

Then he slung himself to the arm of the settee I was on, and lighted a cigarette, not without a little digital difficulty, and he was ready for the curtain to go up. On the last act of something or other.

His timing was good, too.

Luthe showed up at the gallery opening, announced formally: "Mr. and Mrs. Stone."

She came out onto the entrance apron, two steps above the rest of us. She, and a husband tailing her. But what it amounted to was: *She* came out onto the entrance apron. He might just as well not have been there.

She was familiar with the stage management of this particular entryway, knew just how to get the most out of it. Knew just how long to stand motionless, and then resume progress down into the room. Knew how to kill him. Or, since she'd already done that pretty successfully, perhaps I'd better say, knew how to give him the shot of adrenalin that would bring him back to life, so that she could kill him all over again. To be in love with her as he was, I couldn't help thinking, must be a continuous succession of death throes. Without any final release. I imagined I could feel his wrist, hidden behind me, bounce a little, from a quickened pulse.

She stood there like a mannequin at a fashion display modeling a mink coat. Even the price tag was there in full view, if you had keen enough eyes, and mine were. Inscribed *"To the highest bidder, anytime, anywhere."*

She had a lot of advantages over the picture I'd seen of her. She was in color: skin like the underpetals of newly opened June rosebuds, blue eyes, golden-blonde hair. And the picture, for its part, had one advantage over her, in my estimate: It couldn't breathe.

She had on that mink she was modeling, literally. Three-quarters length, flaring, swagger. She was holding it open at just the right place, with one hand. Under it she had on an evening gown of white brocaded satin. The V-incision at the bodice went too low. But evidently not for her; after all, she had to make the most of everything she had, and not leave anything to assumption. She had a double string of pearls close around her neck, and a diamond clip at the tip of each ear.

They have the worst taste in women, all of them. Who is to explain their taste in women?

She came forward, down the steps and into the room. Perfume came with her, and the fact that she had hip sockets. The bodice incision deepened, too, if anything.

I kept protesting inwardly, But there must be something more than just what I can see. There *must* be something more. To make him fall and hit his head at the telephone, to make him down a glass of brandy straight to keep from moaning with pain. To make his pulse rivet the way it is against the back of this settee. As though he had a woodpecker hidden in it.

I kept waiting for it to come out, and it didn't. It wasn't there. It was all there at first glance, and beyond that there was nothing more. And most of it, at that, was the mink, the pearls, the diamonds and the incision.

She was the sort of girl who got whistled at, passing street corners.

Her two hands went out toward him, not just one. A diamond bracelet around one wrist shifted back a little toward the elbow, as they did so.

"Billy!" she crowed. And her two hands caught hold of his two, and spread his arms out wide, then drew them close together, then spread them wide again. In a sort of horizontal handshake.

So she called him Billy. That would be about right for her, too. Probably "Billy-boy" when there were fewer than three total strangers present at one time.

"Well, Bernette!" he said in a deep, slow voice that came through hollow, as from inside a mask.

One pair of hands separated, then the other. His were the ones dropped away first, so the impulse must have come from him.

"What happened?" she said. "We were cut off." I saw her glance at the court plaster. "Billy!" she squealed delightedly. "You didn't *faint*, did you? Was it that much of a shock?" She glanced around toward her oncoming fellow arrival, as if to say: "See? See what an effect I still have on him?" I read the look perfectly; it was a flicker of triumphant self-esteem.

The nonentity who had come in with her was only now reaching us; he'd crossed the room more slowly.

He was a good deal younger than either one of them; particularly Dwight. Twenty-three perhaps, or -five. He had a mane of black hair, a little too oleaginous for my taste, carefully brushed upward and back. It smelled a little of cheap alcoholic tonic when he got too near you. He had thick black brows, and the sort of a beard that leaves a bluish cast on the face even when it is closely shaven. He was good-looking in a juvenile sort of way. His face needed a soda-jerk's white cocked hat to complete it. It was crying for something like that; it was made to go under it. And something told me it had, only very recently.

Her hand slipped possessively back, and landed on his shoulder, and drew him forward the added final pace or two that he hadn't had the social courage to navigate unaided.

"I want you to meet my very new husband. Just breaking in." Then she said, "You two should know each other." And she motioned imperiously. "Go on, shake hands. Don't be bashful. Dwight. Harry. *My* Dwight. *My* Harry."

Dwight's crisp intelligent eyes bored into him like awls; you could almost see the look spiraling around and around and around as it penetrated into the sawdust. You could almost see the saw-dust come spilling out.

It's not the substitution itself, I thought; it's the insult of *such* a substitution.

The wait was just long enough to have a special meaning; you could make of it what you willed. Finally Dwight shook his hand. "You're a very lucky—young fellow, young fellow."

I wondered what word he would have liked to use in place of "young fellow."

"I feel like I know you already," the husband said sheepishly. "I've heard a lot about you."

"That's very kind of Bernette," Dwight said dryly.

I wondered where she'd got him. He had the dark, slicked-back good looks that would hit her type between the eyes.

Then again, why differentiate? They went well together. They belonged together.

The line of distinction didn't run between him and her; it ran between her and Dwight. And part of her, at that, belonged on one side of the line, and part belonged on the other. The mink coat and the pearls and the diamond clips belonged on Dwight's side of the line, and she herself belonged on the other side of it. She wasn't even an integrated personality. The husband, with all his cheapness and callowness, at least was.

Dwight introduced the rest of us, introduced us, after I already knew her better than he ever had or ever would, with a pitiless clarity that he would never have.

Jean might have aroused her antagonistic interest, I could see that, but the married title deflected it as quickly as the introduc-tion was made. Then when it came to myself, one quick compre-hensive look from head to foot, and she decided, you could tell, there was nothing to worry about *there*.

"Drinks for Mr. and Mrs.—" Dwight said to Luthe. He couldn't get the name yet. Or didn't want to.

"Stone," the husband supplied embarrassedly, instead of letting the embarrassment fall on Dwight, where it rightfully belonged.

She at least was perfectly self-possessed, knew her way around in this house. "My usual, Luthe. That hasn't changed. And how are you, anyway?"

Luthe bowed and said coldly that he was all right, but she hadn't waited to hear. The back of her head was to him once more.

Their drinks were brought, and there was a slow maneuvering for position. Not physical position, mental. She lounged back upon the settee as though she owned it, and the whole place with it; as she must have sat there so very many times before. Tasted her drink. Nodded patronizingly to Luthe: "As good as ever."

Dwight, for his part, singled out the husband, stalked him, so to speak, until he had him backed against a wall. You could see the process step by step. And then finally, "By the way, what line are you in, Stone?"

The husband floundered badly. "Well, right now—I'm not—"

She stepped into the breach quickly, leaving Jean, with whom she had been talking, hanging on midword. "Harry's just looking around right now. I want him to take his time." Then she added quickly, just a shade too quickly, "Oh, by the way, remind me; there's something I want to speak to you about before I leave, Billy." And then went back to Jean again.

That told me why she'd dragged him up here with her like this. Not to flaunt him; she had no thought of profitless cruelty. The goose that had laid its golden yolks for one might lay them for two as well. Why discard it entirely?

"Where'd you go for your honeymoon, Bernette?" Dwight asked her.

She took a second, as though this required care. She was right, it did. "We took a run up to Lake Arrow."

He turned to the husband. "Beautiful, isn't it? How'd you like it?" Then back to her again, without waiting for the answer he hadn't wanted anyway. "How *is* the old lodge? Is Emil still there?"

She took a second. "Emil's still there," she said reticently.

"Did you remember me to him?"

She took two seconds this time. "No," she said reluctantly, mostly into the empty upper part of her glass, as though he were in there. "He didn't ask about you."

He shook his head and clicked with mock ruefulness, "Forgetful, isn't he? Has he done anything about changing that godawful wallpaper in the corner bedroom yet?" He explained to me, with magnificent impartiality: "He was always going to. It was yellow, and looked as though somebody had thrown up at two-second intervals all over it." He turned and flicked the punch line at her. "Remember, Bernette?"

It was now she who addressed the husband.

"We were both up there at the same time, once. I went up there on my vacation. And Billy went up there on his vacation. At the same time. And the room that Billy had, had this godawful wallpaper."

"At the same time," I thought I heard Dwight murmur, but it wasn't a general remark.

"I know, you told me," the husband said uneasily.

I saw the way his eyes shifted. It's not that he doesn't know, I translated; it's that he doesn't want to be forced into admitting publicly that he knows.

I watched them at the end, when they were about to go. Watched Dwight and her. When the good-bye had been said and the expressions of pleasure at meeting had been spoken all around—and not meant anywhere. They reversed the order of their entry into the room. The husband left first, and passed from sight down the gallery, like a well-rehearsed actor who clears the stage for a key speech he knows is to be made at this point. While she lingered behind a moment in studied dilatoriness, picking up her twinkling little pouch from where she had left it, pausing an instant to see if her face was right in a mirror on the way.

Then all at once, as if at random afterthought: "Could I see you for a minute, Billy?"

They went over to the side of the room together, and their voices faded from sound. It became a pantomime. You had to read between the attitudes.

I didn't watch. I began talking animatedly to Jean. I didn't miss a gesture, an expression of their faces, a flicker of their eyes. I got everything but the words. I didn't need the words.

She glanced, as she spoke, toward the vacant gallery opening, just once and briefly.

Talking about the husband.

She took a button of Dwight's jacket with her fingers, twined it a little.

Ingratiation. Asking him something, some favor.

She stopped speaking. The burden of the dialogue had been shifted to him. He began.

He shook his head almost imperceptibly. You could scarcely see him do it. But not uncertainly, definitely. Refusal. His hand had strayed toward his billfold pocket. Then it left it again still empty.

No money for the husband.

The dialogue was now dead. Both had stopped speaking. There was nothing more to be said.

She stood there at a complete loss. It was something that had never happened to her, with him, before. She didn't know how to go ahead. She didn't know how to get herself out of it.

He moved finally, and that broke the transfixion.

They came back toward us. Their voices heightened to audibility once more.

"Well—good-night, Billy," she said lamely. She was still out of breath—mentally—from the rebuff.

"You don't mind if I don't see you to the door, do you?" He wanted to avoid that unchaperoned stretch between us and it, wanted to escape having to pass along there alone with her, and being subject to a still more importunate renewal of the plea.

"I can find the way," she said wanly.

She left. I had him all to myself for a moment, at least the exterior of him.

Not for long, just between the acts. It wasn't over yet. Suddenly, over his shoulder, I saw she'd reappeared at the lower end of the room, was standing there.

"Billy, talk to Luthe, will you? What's the matter with him? Has he had a drink or something? I can't get him to give me my coat." And her whole form shook slightly with appreciative risibility.

He called and Luthe appeared almost instantly there beside her in the gallery opening, holding the mink lining-forward in both arms. Like someone who has been waiting in the wings the whole time and takes just a single step forward to appear and play his part.

"Luthe, what are you doing?" he said amiably. "Is that Mrs. Stone's coat you're holding?" And before she could interject "Of course it is!" which it was obvious she was about to do, he added: "Read the label in the pocket lining and see what it says."

Luthe dutifully peered down into the folds of satin and read, "Miss Bernette Brady."

There was a pause, while we all got it, including herself. It was Miss Brady's coat, but not—any longer—Mrs. Stone's. Dwight stepped over to a desk, lowered the slab, and hastily inked something on a card. And then he went to her with it and handed it to her. "Bernette," he said, "take this with you."

It was an ordinary visiting or name card. She held it bracketed by two corners and scanned it diagonally, puzzled.

"What's this for?"

"I'll call him and make an appointment for you," he said quietly. "Go in and talk to him. The whole thing'll be over in no time."

"What do I need a lawyer for?" she blurted out.

I understood then, without the aid of the card. An annulment.

Anger began to smolder in her eyes. She gave him warning, but a warning that was already too late to avert the brewing storm. "That isn't funny."

"I'm not trying to be funny."

Her fingers made two or three quick motions and pieces of cardboard sputtered from them.

"Think it over," he urged, a second too late.

"I just did," she blazed. "Just then." She quirked her head sideward, then back toward him again. "Is Luthe going to give me my coat?"

"Come back for it," he drawled soothingly. "It'll be here—waiting for you—any time you say. . . ."

Her voice was hoarse now, splintered. "Then let's be consistent, shall we? How about it?"

Her hands wrestled furiously at the back of her neck. The pearls sidled down the bodice incision. She trapped them there with a raging slap, balled them up, flung them. They fell short of his face, they were probably too light, but they struck the bosom of his shirt with a click and rustle.

"Bernette, I have people here. They're not interested in our private discussions."

"You should have thought of that sooner." Her hands were at her earlobe now. "You want them to know you gave me things, don't you? You don't have to tell them! *I'll* tell them!" The ear clips fell on the carpet at his feet, one considerably in advance of the other.

"You can't carry that out down to its ultimate. . . ."

"I can't, hunh? You think these people being here is going to stop me, hunh? The hell with them! The hell with you yourself! I'll show you! I'll show you what I think of you!"

She was beside herself with rage. There was a rending of satin, and suddenly the dress peeled off spirally, like a tattered paper wrapper coming off her. Then she kicked with one long silk-cased leg, and it fluttered farther away.

She had a beautiful figure. That registered on my petrified mind, I recall. We sat there frozen.

"Keep your eyes down, ducky," I heard Jean warn the Cipher in a sardonic undertone. "I'll tell you when you can look up."

For a moment she posed there, quivering, a monotoned apparition all in flesh tints, the undraped skin and the pale-pink silk of vestigial garments blending almost indistinguishably.

Then she gave a choked cry of inexpressible aversion, and darted from sight.

Dwight raised his own voice then, but not in rage, only for it to carry to a distance. "Luthe, that raincoat in the hall! Put it over her."

A door slammed viciously somewhere far down the gallery.

None of us said anything. What is there that can be said following such a thing?

Jean was the first one to speak, after the long somewhat numbed silence that followed. And, probably unintentionally, her matter-of-fact minor-keyed remark struck me as the most hilariously malapropos thing I had ever heard. I wanted to burst out laughing at it.

She stirred and said with mincing politeness: "I really think we should be going now."

A six-week interval, then. It must have been fully that; I didn't time it exactly. Oh, why lie? Why write this at all, if not truthfully? I counted every week, every day, every hour. I didn't tally them up, that was all. At least once every day I had to remind myself, unnecessarily, "I haven't seen him since that explosive night. That makes it a day more, that I haven't seen him." It worked out at something like six weeks.

Nothing happened. No word. No sight. No sign.

Was he with her once more? Was he with somebody else entirely different? Was he alone, with nobody at all? Where was he? What was he doing? Was he still in New York? Had he gone somewhere else?

I had it bad. Real bad.

Finally I sent him a little note. Just a little note. Oh, such a very little note. "... *I haven't heard anything from you in some time now—*"

A coward's note. A liar's note, a liar even to myself.

The phone rang the next afternoon. I made a mess of it. I dropped the phone. I burned myself on a cigarette. I had to trample the cigarette out first. Then I hung onto the phone with both hands, when I'd once retrieved it.

He said things. The words didn't matter; it was just the voice they were pitched in.

Then he said: "I don't dare ask you and the Medills to come up here after what happened that last time."

"Dare," I said faintly. "Go on, dare."

"All right, would you?" he said. "Let's all have dinner together and—"

When I told Jean that he had called, about fifteen minutes later, she said the strangest thing. I should have resented it, but she said it so softly, so understandingly, that it never occurred to me until later that I should have resented it.

"I know," Jean said. "I can tell."

She murmured presently, "I think we should. I think it'd be good for us."

How tactful of her, I thought gratefully, to use the plural.

So back we went, the three of us, for another glimpse at this real-life peepshow that went on and on with never an intermission, even though there was not always someone there to watch it.

He was alone. But my heart and my hopes clouded at the very first sight of him as we came in; they knew. He was too happy. His face was too bright and smooth; there was love hovering somewhere close by, even though it wasn't in sight at the moment. Its reflection was all over him. He was animated, he was engaging, he made himself pleasant to be with.

But as for the source of this felicity, the wellspring, you couldn't tell anything. If I hadn't known him as he'd been in the beginning, I might have thought that was his nature. He was alone, just with Luthe. We were only four at the table, one to each side of it, with candles and a hand-carved ship model in the center of it.

Then when we left the table, I remember, we paired off unconventionally. I don't think it was a deliberate maneuver on anyone's part, it just happened that way. Certainly, I didn't scheme it; it was not the sorting of partners I would have preferred. Nor did he. And the Cipher least of all. He never schemed anything. That left only Jean; I hadn't been watching her. . . .

I think I do recall her linking an arm to mine, which held me to her. And then she leaned back to the table a moment and reached for a final grape or mint, which resulted in reversing the order of our departure. At any rate, the two men obliviously preceded us, deep in some weighty conversation; she and I followed after. We gave them a good headstart, too. She walked with deliberate slowness, and I perforce had to follow suit.

She stopped short midway down the gallery, well before we had emerged into view of the drawing room, which the two men had already entered.

"I have premonitions of a run," she said. "I don't trust these sheers." But what she did was jog her elbow into my side, in a sort of wordless message or signal, as she turned aside and went in through the nearest doorway. *That* doorway.

I turned and followed her; that was what her nudge had summoned me to do.

Lights went on, and the big bed leaped into view in the background.

She went toward the full-length mirror in a closet door. She went through the motions of validating her excuse for stepping in here; raised her skirt, cocked her leg askew toward the mirror, dropped her skirt again. Then she reached out and purposefully took hold of the faceted glass knob of the closet door.

"Jean," I said with chaste misgivings. "Don't do that."

I saw she was going to anyway.

She swept it wide, the door, with malignant efficiency, and stood back with it so that I could see, and looked at me, not it, as she did so.

Satins and silks, glistening metallic tissues, flowered prints; and in the middle of all of them, like a queen amidst her ladies in waiting, that regal mink.

Then there was a blinding silvery flash as the electric light flooded across the mirror, and the door swept back into place.

"Back again," she said, brittly. "This time, for keeps." And, I thought, what an apt word.

But for long moments afterward, long after the other things had faded and been effaced, it still seemed as if I could see the rich darkness of that mink, through glass and all, as if shadowed against some X-ray apparatus. Then finally it, too, dimmed and was gone, and there was just clear mirror left. With somebody's woeful, heartsick face on it. My own.

She put out the light as she shepherded me across the threshold; I remember the room was dark as we left it behind. I remember that so well. So very well.

She held her arm around me tight as we walked slowly down the remainder of the gallery.

I needed it.

"Tune in the stadium concert, Luthe," he suggested at one point. "It must be time for it."

I wondered what he wanted that for.

Some very feverish dance band drumming filtered out.

"If that's the stadium concert," Jean said, "they've certainly picked up bad habits."

"Luthe," he said good-naturedly, "what're you doing over there? I said the open-air concert, at the Lewisohn Stadium."

"I can't seem to get it. What station is it on?"

"ABC, I think."

"I'm on ABC now. Doesn't seem to be it."

"Does it?" agreed Jean, pounding her ear and giving her head a shake to clear it, as a particularly virulent trombone snarl assailed us.

"Call up the broadcasting station and find out," he suggested.

Luthe came back.

"No wonder. It's been called off on account of rain. Giving it tomorrow night instead."

"It's not raining down here," Jean said. She returned from the window. "It's bone-dry out. Do you even have special weather arrangements for Park Avenue?" she queried.

"Look who we are," he answered her. A little distraitly, I thought, as though he were thinking of something else. "What time is it now, Luthe?" he asked.

● ● ●

She arrived about an hour and a half later. Perhaps even two hours. I don't know; since I hadn't been expecting her, I wasn't clocking her exactly. If he was, he'd kept it to himself; you couldn't notice it. No more parenthetic requests for the time, after that first one.

There was one thing noticeable about her arrival. I mean, even over and above the usual flashlight-powder brilliance of her arrival anywhere, anytime. It was that she was not announced. She simply entered, as one does where one belongs. Suddenly, from nowhere, she had taken her stance there on the auction block (as I called it after that first time). Then, after flamboyant pause and pose there, she was coming down the steps to join us.

He'd made a few improvements in her. Surface ones only; that was the only part of her he could reach, I suppose. Or maybe he needed more time. Her dress was a little higher at the neck, now, and the phantom price tag had been taken off. You got her value after a while, but not immediately, at first sight.

She'd even acquired an accent. I mean an accent of good, cultivated English; and since it was false, on her it was an accent.

When she walked, she even managed to use the soles of her feet and not her hips so much anymore. I wondered if he'd used telephone directories on her head for that, or just clouted her there each time one of them swayed, until she'd stopped it.

Or maybe she was just a good mimic, was getting it all by suction, by being dunked into the company of the right people more and more often. For my money, she'd had all the other makings of a good sponge right from the start; why not in that way, too?

"You remember Annie and Jean, and Paul," he said.

"Oh yes, of cowass; how are you?" she leered affably. She was very much the lady of the manor, making us at home in her own domain. "Sorry I'm so late. I stayed on to the very end."

"Did you?" he said.

And I thought, Where? Then, No! It can't be! This is too good to be true. . . .

But she rushed on, as though speaking the very lines I would have given her myself. She wanted to make a good impression, avoid the cardinal social sin of falling mute, not having anything to say; all those unsure of themselves are mortally afraid of it. So the fact of saying something was more important than the content of what it was she said.

"Couldn't tear myself away. You should have come with me, Billy. It was heavenly. Simply heavenly." Business of rolling the eyes upward and taking a deep, soulful breath.

"What'd they play first?" he said tightly.

"Shostakovich," she said with an air of vainglory, as when one has newly mastered a difficult word and delights in showing one's prowess with it.

You couldn't tell she'd said anything. His face was a little whiter than before, but it was a slow process; it took long minutes to complete itself. Until finally he was pale, but the cause had long been left behind by that time, would not have been easy to trace anymore.

She caught something, however. She was not dense.

"Didn't I pronounce it well?" she asked, darting him a look.

"Too well," he said.

She was uneasy now.

She didn't like us. She was hampered by our being there, couldn't defend herself properly against whatever the threat was. And although she didn't know what it was herself, as yet, she couldn't even make the attempt to find out, because of our continuing presence.

She sat for a moment with the drink he'd given her, made a knot with her neck pearls about one finger, let it unravel again. Then she stood up, put her drink down over where they originally came from.

"I have a headache," she said and touched two fingers to the side of her head. To show us, I suppose, that that was where it was, in her head.

"Shostakovich always gives me a headache, too," Jean said sweetly to her husband.

She shot Jean a quick look of hostility, but there was nothing she could do about it. There was nothing to get her teeth into. If she'd picked it up, that would have been claiming it for her own.

"If you'll excuse me now," she said.

She was asking him, though, not the rest of us. She was a little bit afraid. She wanted to get out of this false situation. She didn't know what it was, but she wanted to extricate herself.

"You don't have to stand on ceremony with us, Bernette." He didn't even turn to look at her, but went ahead dabbling in drinks.

I thought of the old Spanish saying, *Aquí tiene ústed su casa.* My house is yours. And it probably was as little valid in the present circumstance as in the original flowery exaggeration.

"But you just came," the Cipher said. He was only trying to be cordial, the poor benighted soul. He hadn't stepped aside into that room with us.

Jean and I simply looked at each other. I could almost lip-read what she was about to say before it came out. "She hasn't far to go." I nearly died for a minute as I saw her lips give a preliminary flicker. Then she curbed herself. That would have been going too far. I breathed again.

She made her good nights lamely, and yet with a sort of surly defiance. As if to say, I may have lost this skirmish, but I haven't even begun to fight yet. This was on ground of your choosing; wait till he's without his allies, and must come looking for me on ground of my own choosing. We'll see whose flag runs down then.

She even reached out and shook hands with him. Or at least, sought out his, took it up, then dropped it again, all the volition coming from hers.

Oh, really, I protested inwardly. You don't do that from room to room.

She climbed the steps, she turned galleryward, she passed from view. Tall and voluptuous in her black summer dress, her head held high, her chin out. A little cigarette smoke that had emanated from her on the way lingered behind her for a moment or two. Then that dissolved, too.

And that's all the trace you leave behind in this world, some-times: a little cigarette smoke, quickly blown away.

Presently another figure passed the gallery opening, coming from farther back in the apartment, but going the same way she had. Handsome, well-dressed, almost unrecognizable for a moment in his tactfully cut suit and snap-brim hat. There wasn't a garish detail of attire from head to foot. He would have passed without obtruding himself upon us, but Dwight turned his head.

"Going now?"

"Yes, sir. Good night." He tipped his hat to the rest of us, and left.

This time you could hear the outside apartment door close after him. Not like the time before.

"Luthe goes home out to Long Island one night a week to visit his mother, and this is his night for it." He shook his head. "He's studying law. I wish I lived as quietly and as decently as he does."

We left soon afterward ourselves.

As we moved down the gallery in leisurely deliberation, I looked ahead. That room that Jean and I had been in before was lighted now, not dark as we had left it. The door was partly ajar, and the light coming from it lay on the floor outside in a pale crosswise bar or stripe.

Then as we neared it, some unseen agency pushed it unobtru-sively closed, from the inside. I could see the yellow outshine narrow and snuff out, well before we had reached it.

We were kept waiting for the elevator for some time. Finally, when it appeared, it was being run by a gnarled elderly individual in fireman's overalls, quite *declassé* for this building. There was no night doorman on duty below when we got there, either.

"What happened?" Jean asked curiously. "Where's all the brass?"

"Walked off," he said. "Wildcat strike. The management fired one of the fellows, and so they all quit. Less'n 'n hour ago. They ain't nobody at all to run the back elevator. I'm practic'ly running this whole building single-handed, right now. You'll have to get your own taxi, folks. Can't leave this car."

"She stayed," I breathed desolately, while the Cipher was off in quest of one.

"Just wait till he gets her alone, though," Jean chuckled. "She'll have a lot of explaining to do. I'd give anything to hear what's going on between the two of them right now."

He was waiting for me, the driver. I'd dropped them off first.

"I've lost something. Look, you'll have to take a run back with me a minute."

He meshed gears. "To where the other folks got out?"

"No, the first place. Where we all got in."

I'd lost something. A door-key. Or pride. Or self-respect. Something like that.

"Want me to wait?" he said when we'd arrived.

"No, you'd better let me pay you. I don't want you clocking me the whole time I'm in there."

"You may have a wait for another, lady, at this hour."

He looked me too straight in the eye, I thought. The remark didn't warrant such a piercing gaze. And he had no need to crinkle the corners of his eyes like that; it gave his glance too familiarly knowing an aspect.

I dropped my own eyes primly. "Keep the rest."

The same elderly pinch hitter was still servicing the building's elevators singlehanded. "They ain't nobody at all looking after the back one," he complained unasked.

I felt like saying, "You said that before," but I didn't.

He took me up without announcing me. I got out and I knocked at Dwight's door. The car went down and left me alone there.

No one came. I knocked again, more urgently, less tentatively. I tripped the Louis XVI gilt knocker, finally. That carried somewhat better, since it had a metal sounding board, not a wooden one.

Suddenly his voice said, "Who is it?" Too quickly for this last summons to have been the one that brought him; it must have been the first one after all, and he had been waiting there behind the door.

"Annie," I whispered, as though there were someone else around to overhear.

The door opened, but very grudgingly. Little more than a

crevice at first. Then at sight of me, it widened to more normal width. But not full width of passage, for he stood there in the way; simply full width enough to allow unhampered conversation.

He was in a lounging robe. His shirt was tieless above it, and the collar band was unfastened. It had a peculiar effect on me: not the robe nor the lack of tie, simply the undone collar band; it made me feel like a wife.

"Don't look so stunned. Am I that frightening?" I couldn't resist saying. "Didn't you hear me give you my name through the door?"

"No," he said, "I missed it." Then he changed that to: "I thought I heard someone whisper, but I wasn't sure."

I didn't quite believe him, somehow. If he'd heard the whisper, then he'd heard the name whispered, I felt sure. I didn't resent the implication of a fib; quite the contrary. It was complimentary. It allowed me to believe—if I chose to, and I did—that my name effected the opening of the door, that another name would not have been able to. Castles in a foyer.

"Did I get you out of bed?" I said.

He smiled. It was a sort of vacant smile. The smile with which you wait for someone to go away. The smile that you give at a door when you are waiting to close it. Waiting to be allowed to close it, and held powerless by breeding. It had no real candlepower behind it, that smile. "No," he said, "I was just getting ready, by easy stages."

His face looked very pale, I thought, unnaturally so. I hadn't noticed it the first moment or two, but I gradually became aware of it now. I thought it must be the wretched foyer light, and I hoped I didn't look as pale to him as he did to me. I take pallor easily from unsatisfactory lights. The thing to do was to get inside away from it.

"It's my outside door key," I said. "I can't get into my house."

"It couldn't have been up here," he said. "I would have—I would have found it myself right after you left." He gestured helplessly with one hand, in a sort of rotary way. "It must have been in the taxi. Did you look in the taxi?"

The light was the most uncomplimentary thing I'd ever seen. It made him look almost ghastly.

"It wasn't in the taxi," I insisted. "I looked and looked. We even picked up the seat cushions." I waited for him to shift, but he didn't. "Won't you let me come in a moment and look?"

He was equally insistent. We were both strainedly civil but extremely insistent. "But it isn't up here, I tell you. It couldn't be, Annie, don't you see? If it was, I would have come across it by now myself."

I sighed exasperatedly. "But did you look for it? Did you know it was lost, until I told you so myself just now, here at the door? Then if you didn't look for it, how do you know it isn't there?"

"Well, I—I went over the place, I—" He decided not to say that, whatever it was to have been.

"But if you didn't know *what* it was that was lost, you couldn't have had your eye out for it specifically," I kept on, sugaring my stubbornness with reasonableness. "If you'd only let me step in for a moment and see for myself . . ."

I waited.

He waited, for my waiting to end.

I tried another tack. "Oh," I murmured deprecatingly, turning my head aside, as if to myself, as if in afterthought, "you're not alone. I'm sorry. I didn't mean to . . ."

It worked. I saw a livid flash, like the glancing reflection from a sun-blotted mirror, sweep across his face. Just for an instant. If it was fear, and it must have been of a kind, it was a new fear at this point: fear of being misunderstood, and no longer fear of my entering. He stepped back like magic, drawing the door with him.

"You're mistaken," he said tersely. "Come in."

And then as I did, and as he closed the door after me and pressed it sealed with his palm in one or two places, he added, and still quite tautly, "Whatever gave you that idea?" And turned to look the question at me, as well as ask it.

"After all," I drawled reassuringly, "I'm not anyone's grandmother."

This point, however, was evidently of importance to him, for some intangible reason that escaped me. Certainly I'd never detected any trait of primness in him before. "I never was so alone in my life," he said somewhat crossly. "Even Luthe went out home."

"I know," I reminded him. "He left while we were still here."

I had been thinking mainly of somebody else, not Luthe.

We moved slowly down the gallery, I preceding him.

She was gone, just as Jean had said she would be. The door that I had seen slyly closing before, shutting off its escaping beam of light, was standing starkly open now, and the room was dark. It looked gloomy in there, unutterably depressing, at that hour of the night.

"In here, maybe," I suggested, wickedly. I wasn't supposed to have been in there.

I heard him draw some sort of a crucial breath.

"No," he said quite flatly. "You didn't."

"I may have, just the same." I took a step as though to go in.

"No," he said, tautly, almost shrilly, as though I were getting on his nerves. He reached out before me and drew the door closed in my face.

I glanced at him in mild surprise, at the use of such a sharp tone of voice for such a trifling matter. The look I caught on his face was even more surprising. For a moment, all his good looks were gone. He was ugly in mood and ugly of face.

Then, with an effort, he banished the puckered grimace, let his expression smooth out again. Even tried on a thin smile for size, but it didn't fit very well and soon dropped off again.

Meanwhile, he'd withdrawn the key and the door was now locked fast.

"Why do you do that?" I asked mildly.

"I always keep it that way," he said. "It's not supposed to be left open. Luthe must have done that."

But Luthe had gone home before we had.

"Well, won't you let me go in and look at least?" I coaxed. I thought: I still love him, even when his face is all ugly and wizened like that. How strange; I thought it was largely his looks that had me smitten, and now I see that it isn't.

"But you weren't in there, so how could it get in there?"

"I was. I was in there once earlier tonight. I don't know whether you knew it or not, but I strayed in there one time this evening."

He looked at me, and he looked at the door. "Wasn't that a breach of manners on your part?" he suggested stiffly.

"There are no manners between a man and woman," I said. "There are only manners, good or bad, between a man and a man, or a woman and a woman."

He gave the cryptic answer, "Oh?"

Why do I drive him like this? I wondered. To see how far I can go? To make him fully aware of my being here alone with him? I didn't know, myself.

We stood and looked at each other for a moment, he waiting for me to make the next move.

"Well, I'll have to get along without it," I said. "My key, I mean."
"Sorry."

"He wants me to go," I said, as though speaking ruefully to a third person. "He can't wait until I do."

What could he say then? What could anyone have said, except in overt offense? And that, you see, was why I'd said it. Though it was true, my saying so forced him to deny it, obliged him to act in contradiction to it. Though he didn't want to, and I knew that he didn't want to, and he knew that I knew that he didn't want to.

"No," he said deprecatingly. "No, not at all." And then warmed gradually to his own insistence; picked up speed with it as he went along. "Come inside. Away from that door." (As though my departure from a fixed point was now what he wanted to obtain, and if he could obtain it only by having me all the way in, rather than by having me leave, then he'd have me all the way in.) He motioned the way with his arm and he turned to accompany me. And kept up meanwhile the running fire of his invitation at a considerably accelerated tempo, until it ended up by being almost staccato. "Come inside and we'll have a drink together. Just you and me. Just the two of us alone. As a matter of fact, I need company, this minute."

On the rebound, I thought. On the rebound; I may get him that way. They say you do. Oh, what do I care how, if only I do.

I went down the steps, and he went down close beside me. His swinging arm grazed mine as we did so, and it did something to me. It was like sticking your elbow into an electrical outlet.

That drawing room of his had never looked vaster and more somber. There was something almost funereal about it, as though there were a corpse embalmed somewhere nearby, and we were about to sit up and keep vigil over it. There was only one lamp lighted, and it was the wrong one. It made great bat-wing shadows around the walls, from the upraised piano lid and other immovables, and now added our own two long, willowy emanations.

He saw me look at it, and said, "I'll fix that."

I let him turn on one more, just to take some of the curse off the gruesomeness, but then when I saw him go for the wall switch that would have turned on a blaze overhead I quickly interposed, "Not too many." You don't make very good love under a thousand-watt current.

I sat down on the sofa. He made our drinks for us, and then came over with them, and then sat down in the next state.

"No, here," I said. "My eyesight isn't that good."

He grinned and brought his drink over, and we sat half-turned toward each other, like the arms of a parenthesis. A parenthesis that holds nothing in it but blank space.

I saw to it that it soon collapsed of its own emptiness, and one of the arms was tilted rakishly toward the other.

I tongued my drink.

"It was a pretty bad jolt," I admitted thoughtfully.

"What was?"

"You don't have to pretend with me."

"Oh," he said lamely.

"You're still pretending," I chided him. "You're pretending that you haven't thought of it, that I'm the one just now brought it back to your mind for the first time. When all along it hasn't left your mind, not for a single moment since."

He tried to drown his face in his drink, the way he pushed it down into it. "Please," he said, and made a grimace. "Not now. Do we have to—? Don't let's talk about it now."

"Oh, that much it hurts," I said softly.

The parenthesis had become a double line, touching from top to bottom.

"Why don't you put iodine on it?" I suggested.

He made a ghastly shambles of a smile. "Is there any for such things?"

"Here's the bottle, right beside you," I offered. "And there's no death's head on the label."

That symbol seemed to frighten him for a moment, or at least be highly unwelcome. He screwed up his eyes tight, and I saw him give his head a shake, as though to rid it of that particular thought.

"It stings for a minute, and then you heal," I purred. "You heal clean. No festering. And then you're well again; even the mark goes away. And you have a new love." I dropped my voice to a breath. "Won't you try—iodine?"

So close his face was to mine, so close; all he had to do . . .

Then he turned it a little; oh, a very tactful little. The wrong way, so that the distance had widened a little. And he could breathe without mingling his breath with mine. Which seemed to be what he wanted.

"Don't you understand me, Dwight? I'm making love to you. And if I'm awkward about it, it's because women aren't very good at it. Can't you help me out a little?"

I saw the look on his face. Sick horror. I wish I hadn't, but I did. I never thought just a look on a face could hurt so.

"Would it be that bad? Would it be that unbearable, to be married to me?"

"Married?"

His backbone gave a slight twitch, as though a pin overlooked in his shirt had just pricked him. I caught him at it, slight as it was. That was no compliment, either, any more than the look on his face before had been.

"You've just been proposed to, Dwight. That was a proposal, just then. The first I've ever made."

He tried, first, to carry it off with a sickly grin. The implication:

You're just joking, and I'm supposed to know you are, but you make me a little uncomfortable just the same.

I wouldn't let him; I wouldn't accept the premise.

"You don't laugh when a lady proposes to you," I said gently. "You don't laugh at her. You meet her on her own ground; you give her that much, at least."

He put his hand on my knee for a moment, but it was a touch of apology, of consolation; it wasn't what I wanted.

"I'm not—cut out—" He floundered. "It would be about the dirtiest trick I could play. I couldn't do *that* to you. . . ." And then finally, and more decidedly, like a snap-lock to the subject: "You'd be sorry."

"I want to be. Let me be. I'd rather be sorry—with you—than glad—with anyone else."

He looked down his nose now. He didn't say anything more. A sort of stubborn muteness had set in. That was his best defense; that was his only one. He probably knew it. Their instincts are just as valid as ours.

I had to do the talking. Someone had to. It would have been even worse to sit there in silence.

I took a sip of my drink. I sighed in feigned objectivity. "It's unfair, isn't it? A woman can refuse a man, and she doesn't have to feel any compunction. He's supposed to take it straight, and he does. But if a man refuses a woman, he has to try to spare her feelings at the same time."

He hadn't as a matter of fact made any such attempt until now; he did now, possibly because I had recalled his duty to him.

"You're a swell gal, Annie. It's you I'm thinking of. You don't know what you're asking. You don't want me."

"You're getting your pronouns mixed," I said sadly.

All he could repeat was: "No, I mean it, you're a swell gal, Annie."

"You're a swell gal, Annie," I echoed desolately, "but you don't ring the bell."

He made the mistake of putting his arm around my shoulder, in what was meant as a fraternal embrace, I suppose. He should have left his hands off me; it was hard enough without that.

I let my head go limp against him. I couldn't have kept it up straight if I'd tried. And I didn't try.

"Then on shorter terms," I whispered, closing my eyes. "As short as you wish."

He tried to jerk his arm away, as he realized this new danger, but I caught it from in front with mine, and held it there, around my shoulders, like a precious sable someone's trying to take away from you.

"Even just—for tonight. Just for—an hour. Do I have to speak any plainer than that? *Your* terms. Any terms at all."

He shuddered and hit himself violently in the center of the forehead. As if there were some thought lodged in there that he couldn't bear the contemplation of. "My God," I heard him groan. "My God! Right here and now, in this apartment . . ."

"Is there something wrong with this apartment?" I asked innocently.

"Not with the apartment, with me," he murmured.

"I won't dispute you there," I said cattishly.

I let go of his arm, and he promptly called it back. I stood up. I got ready to go. I'd been rejected. To have prolonged it would have veered over into buffoonery. I had no self-respect left, but at least I still had my external dignity left. The law of diminishing returns would only have set in from this point on.

I turned and looked at him, still sitting there. "Seduction doesn't agree with you," I let him know. "You look positively harassed."

I saw him wince a little, as though he agreed with me; not only looked it, but felt it. He stood now, to do the polite thing as host.

"I'll get over it," I said, speaking out loud to keep my own courage up. "It doesn't kill you."

He blinked at the word, as though it grated a little.

I was ready to go now. He came closer, to accelerate the process.

"Won't you kiss me good-night?" I said.

He did it with his brakes on; used just one arm to support my back. Put his lips to mine, but with a time valve to them. Took them away again as soon as time was up. Mine tried to follow, and lost their way.

We straightened ourselves. "I'll see you out," he said.

"Never mind. Don't rub it in."

He took me at my word, turned back to pour himself another drink. His hand was shaking, and if that's a sign of needing one, he needed one.

I went down the long gallery alone. So safe. Too safe. As safe as when I'd come in. My heart was blushing and my cheeks felt white.

I came opposite that door, the door to his lady-love's room. I stopped and looked at it. And as I did, a creepy feeling all at once came over me. Like a cold, cold wind that comes from nowhere and suddenly knifes you where you stand. As if the room were not empty. As if there were something in there, some terrible revelation, waiting, crying, to be seen. There was almost a pull to it, the feeling was so strong. It seemed to draw me, the way forbidden sights do. Evil sights, sights that are death in themselves and death to behold.

I started to put out my hand toward it. Then I felt his eyes on me, and turned, and saw him standing, watching me, at the end of the gallery, where I'd just come from myself.

"Annie," he said. "Don't." His voice was toneless, strangely quiet. He didn't offer to approach, stayed where he was, but his hands strayed to the cord of his robe and, of their own accord, without his seeming to know what they were doing, fumbled there, until suddenly the knot had disheveled, fallen open. Then each one, holding a loose end of the cord, flicked and played with it, all unconsciously. The way the two ends danced and spun and snaked, suggested the tentative twitching of a cat's tail, when it is about to spring.

He was holding it taut across his back, and out at each side, in a sort of elongated bow-shape. It was just a posture, a stance, a vagary of nervous preoccupation, I suppose. An odd one, but meaningless.

I flexed my wrist slightly, as if to complete the touching of the doorknob.

The cord tightened to almost a straight line, stopped moving.

His eyes met mine and mine met his, the length of the gallery.

The impulse to annoy him died.

Indifferently, I desisted. I dropped my hand slowly, and let the door be.

His hands dropped too. The taut pull of the cord slackened, it softened to a dangling loop.

I went on to the outside door and opened it.

"Good night, Dwight," I murmured wanly.

"Good night, Annie," he echoed.

I saw him reach out with one arm and support himself limply against the wall beside him, he was so tired of me by this time. I closed the outside door.

They tell you wrong when they tell you infatuation dies a sudden death. Infatuation dies a lingering, painful death. Even after all hope is gone the afterglow sometimes stubbornly clings on and on, kidding you, lighting the dark in which you are alone. Infatuation dies as slowly as a slower love; it comes on quicker, that is all.

Twice I went by there in a taxi, in the two weeks following that night. A taxi that didn't have to go by there, that could have taken me another way; but whose way I altered, I interfered with, so that it would take me by there. And each time it stopped a moment at the door. Not of its own accord, either. "Stop here a moment."

But then I didn't get out after all. Just sat there. Perhaps to see if I could sit there like that without getting out, I don't know. Perhaps to see if I was strong enough.

I was. I just barely made it, both times, but I made it.

"Drive on," I said heroically, when the driver turned his head around inquiringly after nothing had happened. It was like leaving your right arm behind, jammed in a door; but I left it.

One of the two times, I had been on my way to a party, and the excuse would have been to ask him if he wanted to come along with me. Had I carried the stop out to its ultimate conclusion. But I don't think we would have gone on to any party, even had I put the invitation to him. It takes two to want to go to any party, when there are two, and one of us wouldn't have wanted to go—even had he said yes.

(I didn't, incidentally, even go on to the party myself, after I drove on from his door; I went home and took off the regalia it had taken me an hour's solid work to array myself in. It hadn't been meant for the general admiration of any party.)

And the second of the two times I stopped, the excuse was even more flimsy. I was supposed to be on my way somewhere else. To friends, I think, for an evening of bridge.

"Drive on," I told the driver.

But I was convalescing; it was only like leaving your hand caught in the door, not your whole arm now.

"Your game isn't what it used to be," my partner told me acidulously later that evening, after we'd gone down for a grand slam.

"No," I agreed, word for word, "my game isn't what it used to be." ("And I'm a dud at the new one," I added to myself.)

But the third time, ah the third time, I stopped down there at the door, there was no excuse at all. None whatever. Not even so fragile a one as a secondhand party or a secondhand game. I did it as a sort of test, and I found out what I wanted to.

I was practically over it. I was cured. I made the discovery for myself sitting there in the taxi, taking my own blood pressure, so to speak, holding my own pulse, listening to my own heart. I could drive away now without a wrench, without feeling that I'd left a part of me behind, caught in his door.

I lighted a cigarette and thought with a sigh of relief: It's passed. It's finished. Now I've got nothing more to worry about. That was the vaccine of love. Now I'm immune. Now I can go on and just work and live and be placid.

"Y'getting out, lady, or what?" the driver asked fretfully.

"Yes," I said coolly, "I think I will. I want to say good-bye to someone in there."

And in perfect safety, in perfect calm, I paid him and got out and went inside to visit my recent, my last, love.

But, as I have often said, they tell you wrong when they tell you infatuation dies a sudden death. It doesn't. *I* know.

I seemed to have picked an inappropriate time for my farewell visit. Or at least, a nonexclusive one.

There'd been somebody else with him. The apartment door was already open, when I stepped off at his foyer, and he was standing there talking to some man in dilatory leave-taking.

The man was heavily built and none too young. In the milder fifties, I should judge. His hair was silvering, his complexion was florid, and there were little skeinlike red blood vessels threading the whites of his eyes. He had a hard-looking face, but he was being excessively amiable at the moment that I came upon the two of them. Almost overdoing it, almost overly amiable, for it didn't blend well with the rest of his characteristics, gave the impression of being a seldom-used, almost rusty attribute; he had to push down hard on the accelerator to get it working at all. And he was keeping his foot pressed down on it for all he was worth so that it couldn't get away from him.

"I hope I haven't troubled you, Mr. Billings," he was apologizing just as the elevator panel opened.

"Not at all," Dwight protested indulgently. There was even something patronizing in his intonation. "I know how those things are. Don't think twice about it. Glad to—" And then they both turned at the slight rustle the panel made, and saw me, and so didn't finish the mutual gallantries they were engaged upon. Or rather, postponed them for a moment.

Dwight's face lighted up at sight of me. I was welcome. There could be no doubt of it. Not like that other night. And yet— How shall I put it? It was not a question of being relieved. I didn't detect that at all. It was rather that he was already so pleased with himself, and with everything else, this evening, that even my arrival pleased him. And I use the adverb "even" advisedly. So that I was welcome by good-humored reflection—anyone would have been at the moment—and not in my own right.

He shook my hand cordially. "Well! Nice of you! Where've you been keeping yourself?" And that sort of thing. But made no move to introduce the departing caller to me.

And his manners were too quick-witted for that to have been an oversight. So what could I infer but that there was a differentiation of status between us that would have made a social introduction inappropriate? In other words, that one call was a personal one and the other was not, so the two were not to be linked.

At the same time, he did not offer to disengage himself from his first caller, conclude the parley, and turn his attention to me. On the contrary, he postponed my playing on his attention and returned to the first matter, as if determined it should run its unhurried course and be completed without any haste, first of all. He even signaled to the car operator not to stand there waiting to take the leavetaker down, as he'd been inclined to do. "We'll ring," he said, and motioned the panel closed with his hand.

And to me: "Go in, Annie. Take your things off. I'll be right with you."

I went in. My last impression of the man standing there with him was that he was slightly ill at ease under my parting scrutiny; call it embarrassed, call it sheepish, call it what you will. He turned his head aside a moment and took a deep draught of an expensive cigar he was holding between his knuckles. As if: Don't look at me so closely. I certainly wasn't staring, so it must have been his own self-consciousness.

I went down the gallery of lost loves. The room door was open now. I went past it without stopping, and down the steps to the drawing-room arena.

I took off my "things," as he'd put it, and primped at my hair, and moved idly around, waiting for him to join me.

I looked at things as I moved. One does, waiting in a room.

He'd left them just as they were, to take his visitor to the door. Probably I hadn't been announced yet, at that moment. I must have been announced after they were both already at the door, and he hadn't come all the way back in here since leaving it the first time.

There were two glasses. Both drained heartily, nothing but ice sweat left in their bottoms; the interview must have been a cordial one.

There were two strips of cellophane shorn from a couple of expensive cigars.

There was a single burned matchstick; one smoker had done that courteous service for both.

His checkbook folder was lying on the corner of the table. He must have taken it out of his pocket at one time, and then forgotten to return it again. Or perhaps thought that could wait until afterward; it was of no moment.

I didn't go near it, or touch it, or examine it in any way. I just saw it lying there.

There was a new blotter lying near it. Almost spotless; it had only been used about once.

That I did pick up, idly, and look at. As if I were a student of Arabic or some other right-to-left scrawl. I looked at it thoughtfully.

He still didn't come in.

Finally I took it over to the mirror with me and fronted it to that, and looked into that.

Part of his signature came out. *"-ilings."* It was the thing he'd written last, so the ink was still freshest when the blotter'd been put to it. Above it were a couple of less distinct tracings, *"-earer."* And three large circles and two smaller ones. Like this: "OOOoo."

I turned swiftly, as though that had shocked me (but it hadn't; why should it?) and pitched it back onto the table from where I stood. Then I fixed my hair a little more, in places where it didn't need it.

He came in, looking sanguine, looking zestful. I don't remember that he rubbed his hands together, but that was the impression his mood conveyed: of rubbing his hands together.

"Who was that man?" I said indifferently.

"You'll laugh," he said. And he set the example by doing so himself. "That's something for you." Then he waited, as a good raconteur always does. Then he gave me the punch line. "He was a detective. A real, honest-to-goodness, life-sized detective. Badge and everything."

I stopped being indifferent, but I didn't get startled. Only politely incredulous, as a guest should be toward her host's surprise climaxes. "Here? What'd he want with you?"

"Asking if I could give him any information," he said cheerfully. Then in the same tone: "You've heard about Bernette, haven't you?"

I said I hadn't.

"I think you met her up here once."

I visioned a pink brassiere and pink drawers. "Yes," I said, "I seem to recall."

"Well, she's disappeared. Hasn't been heard of in weeks."

"Oh," I said. "Is that bad?"

He gave me a wink. "Good," he whispered, as if afraid she'd come in just then and overhear him. And he flung one hand disgustedly toward the doorway, meaning it for her invisible presence. She should stay away.

"Why do they come to you about it?" I asked him.

"Oh," he said impatiently, "some tommyrot or other about her never having been seen again after—after the last time she left here. I dunno, something like that. Just routine. This is the third time this same fellow's been up here. I've been darn good-natured about it." Then he said, more optimistically, "He promised me just now, though, this is the last time; he won't come back anymore."

He was fixing two drinks for us, in two fresh glasses. The first two had been shunted aside. The checkbook and the blotter had both vanished, and I'd been facing him in the mirror the whole time; so maybe I'd been mistaken; they hadn't been there in the first place.

"And then there was something about some clothes of hers," he went on offhandedly. "She left some of her things here with me. . . ." He broke off to ask me: "Are you shocked, Annie?"

"No," I reassured him, "I knew she stopped here now and then."

"I was supposed to send them after her; she said something about letting me know where she could be reached." He shrugged. "But I never heard from her again myself. They're still waiting in there. . . ."

He finished swirling ice with a neat little tap of the glass mixer against the rim.

"Probably ran off with someone," he said contemptuously.

I nodded dispassionately.

"I know who put him up to it," he went on, with a slight tinge of resentment. I had to take it he meant the detective; he offered no explanation to cover the switch in pronouns. "That dirty little ex-husband of hers."

"Oh, is he ex?" I said. That was another thing I hadn't known.

"Certainly. They were annulled almost as soon as they came back from their wedding trip. I even helped her to do it myself, sent her to my lawyer—"

And paid for it, I knew he'd been about to add; but he didn't.

"I told this fellow tonight," he went on, still with that same tinge of vengefulness, "that they'd better look into his motives, while they were about it. He was only out to get money out of her—"

(And she was only out to get money out of you, I thought, but tactfully didn't say so.)

"Do they think something's happened to her?" I asked.

He didn't answer that directly. "She'll probably turn up some-place. They always do." Then he said grimly, "It won't be here. Now let's have one, you and me." And he came toward me with our drinks.

We sat down on the sofa with them. He didn't need any urging tonight.

We had another pair. Then a third. We let the third pair stand and cool off a while.

I was the upright arm of the parenthesis tonight, I noticed presently; he was the toppled-over one.

I didn't move my head aside the way he had his; his lips just didn't affect me. It was like being kissed by cardboard.

"I want you to marry me," he said. "I want—what you wanted that night. I want—someone like you."

(That's not good enough, I thought. You should want just me myself, and not someone like me. That leaves it too wide open. This is the rebound. You want the other kind of woman now. Safety, security, tranquility; not so much fire. Something's shaken you, and you can't stand alone; so if there was a female statue in the room, you'd propose to that.)

"Too late," I said. "I've passed that point, as you arrive at it. You got to it too late. Or I left it too soon."

He wilted and his head went down. He had to go on alone. "I'm sorry," he breathed.

"I am, too." And I was. But it couldn't be helped.

Suddenly I laughed. "Isn't love the damnedest thing?"

He laughed, too, after a moment, ruefully. "A bitch of a thing," he agreed.

And laughing together, we took our leave of each other, parted, never to meet in closeness again. Laughing is a good way to part. As good a way as any.

I read an item about it in the papers a few days afterward, quite by chance. The husband had been picked up and taken in for questioning, in connection with her disappearance. Nothing more than that. There was no other name mentioned.

I read still another item about it in the papers, only a day or two following the first one. The husband had been released again, for lack of evidence.

I never read anything further about it, not another word, from that day on.

The other night at a party I met my last love again. I don't mean my latest; my last, I mean my final one. And he was as taking and as debonair as ever, but not to me anymore; a little older maybe, and we said the things you say, holding tall glasses in our hands to keep from feeling lonely, keep from feeling lost.

"Hello, Annie. How've you been?"

"Hello, Dwight. Where've you been keeping yourself lately?"

"I've been around. And you?"

"I've been around, too."

And then when there wasn't anything more to say, we moved on. In opposite directions.

It isn't often that I see him anymore. But whenever I do, I still think of her. I wonder what really did become of her.

And just the other night, suddenly, for no reason at all, out of nowhere, the strangest thought entered my head for a moment. . . .

But then I promptly dismissed it again, just as quickly as it had occurred to me, as being too fantastic, too utterly improbable. The people you know never do things like that; the people you *read* about may, but never the people you *know*.

Woolrich originally called the following story "A Penny for Your Thoughts" and intended it as a chapter in *Hotel Room,* but the editors removed it so that all the book's episodes except the first and last (which made up the framing material) would be tied, however loosely, to some historic event. Frederic Dannay (1905–1982), who with his cousin Manfred B. Lee co-authored the Ellery Queen novels and who in his own right was the founding editor of *Ellery Queen's Mystery Magazine,* paid Woolrich $250 for the periodical rights and published the tale under its present title in *EQMM'*s September 1958 issue. The situation portrayed here was not uncommon in the frantic world of pulp fiction and apparently happened at least once to Woolrich himself. Limiting himself to a single confined setting and main character, he not only keeps us on the edge of our seats but offers the most vivid picture ever drawn of the insane pressures and feverish energy of the pulpster's life, with the fate of Dan Moody's hackneyed thriller symbolizing the fate of everyone and everything in the world as Woolrich sees it. The story was first collected in *Nightwebs* (Harper & Row, 1971) and has never been reprinted since.

THE PENNY-A-WORDER

The desk clerk received a call early that afternoon, asking if there was a "nice, quiet" room available for about six o'clock that evening. The call was evidently from a business office, for the caller was a young woman who, it developed, wished the intended reservation made in a man's name, whether her employer or one of the firm's clients she did not specify. Told there was a room available, she requested, "Well, will you please hold it for Mr. Edgar Danville Moody, for about six o'clock?" And twice more she reiterated her emphasis on the noiselessness. "It's got to be quiet, though. Make sure it's quiet. He mustn't be disturbed while he's in it."

The desk man assured her with a touch of dryness, "We run a quiet hotel altogether."

"Good," she said warmly. "Because we don't want him to be distracted. It's important that he have complete privacy."

"We can promise that," said the desk clerk.

"Thank you," said the young woman briskly.

"Thank you," answered the desk man.

The designated registrant arrived considerably after six, but not late enough for the reservation to have been voided. He was young—if not under thirty in actuality, still well under it in appearance. He had tried to camouflage his youthful appearance by coaxing a very slim, sandy mustache out along his upper lip. It failed completely in its desired effect. It was like a make-believe mustache ochred on a child's face.

He was a tall lean young man. His attire was eye-catching—it stopped just short of being theatrically flamboyant. Or, depending on the viewer's own taste, just crossed the line. The night being chilly for this early in the season, he was enveloped in a coat of fuzzy sand-colored texture, known generically as camel's-hair, with a belt gathered whiplash-tight around its middle. On the other hand, chilly or not, he had no hat whatever.

His necktie was patterned in regimental stripes, but they were perhaps the wrong regiments, selected from opposing armies. He carried a pipe clenched between his teeth, but with the bowl empty and turned down. A wide band of silver encircled the stem. His shoes were piebald affairs, with saddles of mahogany hue and the remainder almost yellow. They had no eyelets or laces, but were made like moccasins, to be thrust on the foot whole; a fringed leather tongue hung down on the outer side of each vamp.

He was liberally burdened with belongings, but none of these was a conventional, clothes-carrying piece of luggage. Under one arm he held tucked a large flat square, wrapped in brown paper, string-tied, and suggesting a picture-canvas. In that same hand he carried a large wrapped parcel, also brown-paper–bound; in the other, a cased portable typewriter. From one pocket of the coat protruded rakishly a long oblong, once again brown-paper–wrapped.

Although he was alone, and not unduly noisy either in his movements or his speech, his arrival had about it an aura of flurry and to-do, as if something of vast consequence were taking place. This, of course, might have derived from the unsubdued nature of his clothing. In later life he was not going to be the kind of man who is ever retiring or inconspicuous.

He disencumbered himself of all his paraphernalia by dropping some onto the floor and some onto the desk top, and inquired, "Is there a room waiting for Edgar Danville Moody?"

"Yes, sir, there certainly is," said the clerk cordially.

"Good and quiet, now?" he warned intently.

"You won't hear a pin drop," promised the clerk.

The guest signed the registration card with a flourish.

"Are you going to be with us long, Mr. Moody?" the clerk asked.

"It better not be too long," was the enigmatic answer, "or I'm in trouble."

"Take the gentleman up, Joe," hosted the clerk, motioning to a bellboy.

Joe began collecting the articles one by one.

"Wait a minute, not Gertie!" he was suddenly instructed.

Joe looked around, first on one side, then on the other. There was no one else standing there. "Gertie?" he said blankly.

Young Mr. Moody picked up the portable typewriter, patted the lid affectionately. "This is Gertie," he enlightened him. "I'm superstitious. I don't let anyone but me carry her when we're out on a job together."

They entered the elevator together, Moody carrying Gertie.

Joe held his peace for the first two floors, but beyond that he was incapable of remaining silent. "I never heard of a typewriter called Gertie," he remarked mildly, turning his head from the controls.

"I've worn out six," Moody proclaimed proudly. "Gertie's my seventh." He gave the lid a little love-pat. "I call them alphabetically. My first was Alice."

Joe was vastly interested. "How could you wear out six, like that? Mr. Elliot's had the same one in his office for years now, ever since I first came to work here, and he hasn't wore his out yet."

"Who's he?" said Moody.

"The hotel accountant."

"Aw-w-w," said Moody with vast disdain. "No wonder. He just writes figures. I'm a *writer.*"

Joe was all but mesmerized. He'd liked the young fellow at sight, but now he was hypnotically fascinated. "Gee, are you a writer?" he said, almost breathlessly. "I always wanted to be a writer myself."

Moody was too interested in his own being a writer to acknowledge the other's wish to be one too.

"You write under your own name?" hinted Joe, unable to take his eyes off the new guest.

"Pretty much so." He enlarged on the reply. "Dan Moody. Ever read me?"

Joe was too innately naive to prevaricate plausibly. He scratched the back of his head. "Let me see now," he said. "I'm trying to think."

Moody's face dropped, almost into a sulk. However in a moment it had cleared again. "I guess you don't get much time to read, anyway, on a job like this," he explained to the satisfaction of the two of them.

"No, I don't, but I'd sure like to read something of yours," said Joe fervently. "Especially now that I know you." He wrenched at the lever, and the car began to reverse. It had gone up three floors too high, so intense had been his absorption.

Joe showed him into Room 923 and disposed of his encumbrances. Then he lingered there, unable to tear himself away. Nor did this have anything to do with the delay in his receiving a tip; for once, and in complete sincerity, Joe had forgotten all about there being such a thing.

Moody shed his tent-like topcoat, cast it onto a chair with a billowing overhead fling like a person about to immerse in a bath. Then he began to burst open brown paper with explosive sounds all over the room.

From the flat square came an equally flat, equally square cardboard mat, blank on the reverse side, protected by tissues on the front. Moody peeled these off to reveal a startling composition in vivid oil-paints. Its main factors were a plump-breasted girl in a disheveled, lavender-colored dress desperately fleeing from a pursuer, the look on whose face promised her additional dishevelment.

Joe became goggle-eyed, and remained so. Presently he took a step nearer, remaining transfixed. Moody stood the cardboard mat on the floor, against a chair.

"You do that?" Joe breathed in awe.

"No, the artist. It's next month's cover. I have to do a story to match up with it."

Joe said, puzzled, "I thought they did it the other way around. Wrote the story first, and then illustri-ated it."

"That's the usual procedure," Moody said, professionally glib. "They pick a feature story each month, and put that one on the cover. This time they had a little trouble. The fellow that was supposed to do the feature didn't come through on time, got sick or something. So the artist had to start off first, without waiting for him. Now there's no time left, so I have to rustle up a story to fit the cover."

"Gee," said Joe. "Going to be hard, isn't it?"

"Once you get started, it goes by itself. It's just getting started that's hard."

From the bulkier parcel had come, in the interim, two sizable slabs wrapped alike in dark-blue paper. He tore one open to extract a ream of white first-sheets, the other to extract a ream of manila second-sheets.

"I'm going to use this table here," he decided, and planted one stack on one corner of it, the second stack on the opposite corner. Between the two he placed Gertie the typewriter, in a sort of position of honor.

Also from the same parcel had come a pair of soft house-slippers, crushed together toe-to-heel and heel-to-toe. He dropped them under the table. "I can't write with my shoes on," he explained to his new disciple. "Nor with the neck of my shirt buttoned," he added, parting that and flinging his tie onto a chair.

From the slender pocket-slanted oblong, last of the wrapped shapes, came a carton of cigarettes. The pipe, evidently reserved for non-occupational hours, he promptly discarded.

"Now, is there an ashtray?" he queried, like a commander surveying an intended field of action.

Joe darted in and out of several corners of the room. "Gee, no, the last people must have swiped it," he said. "Wait a minute, I'll go get—"

"Never mind, I'll use this instead," decided Moody, bringing over a metal wastebasket. "The amount of ashes I make when I'm working, a tray wouldn't be big enough to hold it all anyway."

The phone gave a very short ring, querulously interrogative. Moody picked it up, then relayed to Joe, "The man downstairs wants to know what's holding you, why you don't come down."

Joe gave a start, then came down to his everyday employment level from the rarefied heights of artistic creation he had been floating about in. He couldn't bear to turn his back, he started going backward to the door instead. "Is there anything else—?" he asked regretfully.

Moody passed a crumpled bill over to him. "Bring me back a— let's see, this is a cover story—you better make it an even dozen bottles of beer. It relaxes me when I'm working. Light, not dark."

"Right away, Mr. Moody," said Joe eagerly, beating a hasty retreat.

While he was gone, Moody made his penultimate preparations: sitting down to remove his shoes and put on the slippers, bringing within range and adjusting the focus of a shaded floor lamp, shifting the horrendous work of art back against the baseboard of the opposite wall so that it faced him squarely just over the table.

Then he went and asked for a number on the phone, without having to look it up.

A young woman answered, "Peerless, good evening."

He said, "Mr. Tartell please."

Another young woman said, "Mr. Tartell's office."

He said, "Hello, Cora. This is Dan Moody. I'm up here and I'm all set. Did Mr. Tartell go home yet?"

"He left half an hour ago," she said. "He left his home number with me, told me to give it to you; he wants you to call him in case you run into any difficulties, have any problems with it. But not later than eleven—they go to bed early out there in East Orange."

"I won't have any trouble," he said self-assuredly. "How long have I been doing this?"

"But this is a cover story. He's very worried. We have to go to the printer by nine tomorrow—we can't hold him up any longer."

"I'll make it, I'll make it," he said. "It'll be on his desk waiting for him at eight-thirty on the dot."

"Oh, and I have good news for you. He's not only giving you Bill Hammond's rate on this one—two cents a word—but he told me to tell you that if you do a good job, he'll see to it that you get that extra additional bonus over and above the word count itself that you were hinting about when he first called you today."

"Swell!" he exclaimed gratefully.

A note of maternal instruction crept into her voice. "Now get down to work and show him what you can do. He really thinks a lot of you, Dan. I'm not supposed to say this. And try to have it down here before he comes in tomorrow. I hate to see him worry so. When he worries, I'm miserable along with him. Good luck." And she hung up.

Joe came back with the beer, six bottles in each of two paper sacks.

"Put them on the floor alongside the table, where I can just reach down," instructed Moody.

"He bawled the heck out of me downstairs, but I don't care, it was worth it. Here's a bottle opener the delicatessen people gave me."

"That about kills what I gave you." Moody calculated, fishing into his pocket. "Here's—"

"No," protested Joe sincerely, with a dissuading gesture. "I don't want to take any tip from *you*, Mr. Moody. You're different from other people that come in here. You're a Writer, and I always wanted to be a writer myself. But if I could ever get to read a story of yours—" he added wistfully.

Moody promptly rummaged in the remnants of the brown

paper, came up with a magazine which had been entombed there. "Here—here's last month's," he said. "I was taking it home with me, but I can get another at the office."

Its title was *Startling Stories!*—complete with exclamation point. Joe wiped his fingertips reverently against his uniform before touching it, as though afraid of defiling it.

Moody opened it for him, offered it to him that way. "Here I am, here," he said. "Second story. Next month I'm going to be the lead story, going to open the book on account of doing the cover story." He harked back to his humble beginnings for an indulgent moment. "When I first began, I used to be all the way in the back of the book. You know, where the muscle-building ads are."

" 'Killing Time, by Dan Moody,' " Joe mouthed softly, like someone pronouncing a litany.

"They always change your titles on them, I don't know why," Moody complained fretfully. "My own title for that one was 'Out of the Mouths of Guns.' Don't you think that's better?"

"Wouldje—?" Joe was fumbling with a pencil, half afraid to offer it.

Moody took the pencil from Joe's fingers, wrote on the margin alongside the story title: "The best of luck to you, Joe—Dan Moody," Joe the while supporting the magazine from underneath with the flaps of both hands, like an acolyte making an offering at some altar.

"Gee," Joe breathed, "I'm going to keep this forever. I'm going to paste transparent paper over it, so it won't get rubbed off, where you wrote."

"I would have done it in ink for you," Moody said benevolently, "only the pulp paper won't take it—it soaks it up like a blotter."

The phone gave another of its irritable, foreshortened blats.

Joe jumped guiltily, hastily backed toward the door. "I better get back on duty, or he'll be raising cain down there." He half-closed the door, reopened it to add, "If there's anything you want, Mr. Moody, just call down for me. I'll drop anything I'm doing and beat it right up here."

"Thanks, I will, Joe," Moody promised, with the warm, comfortable smile of someone whose ego has just been talcumed and cuddled in cotton-wool.

"And good luck to you on the story. I'll be rooting for you!"

"Thanks again, Joe."

Joe closed the door deferentially, holding the knob to the end, so that it should make a minimum of noise and not disturb the mystic creative process about to begin inside.

Before it did, however, Moody went to the phone and asked for a nearby Long Island number. A soprano that sounded like a schoolgirl's got on.

"It's me, honeybunch," Moody said.

The voice had been breathless already, so it couldn't get any more breathless; what it did do was not get any less breathless. "What happened? Ooh, hurry up, tell me! I can't wait. Did you get the assignment on the cover story?"

"Yes, I got it! I'm in the hotel room right now, and they're paying all the charges. And listen to this: I'm getting double word-rate, two cents—"

A squeal of sheer joy answered him.

"And wait a minute, you didn't let me finish. If he likes the job, I'm even getting an extra additional bonus on top of all that. Now what do you have to say to that?"

The squeals became multiple this time—a series of them instead of just one. When they subsided, he heard her almost gasp: "Oh, I'm so proud of you!"

"Is Sonny-bun awake yet?"

"Yes. I knew you'd want to say good-night to him, so I kept him up. Wait a minute, I'll go and get him."

The voice faded, then came back again. However, it seemed to be as unaccompanied as before. "Say something to Daddy. Daddy's right here. Daddy wants to hear you say something to him."

Silence.

"Hello, Sonny-bun. How's my little Snooky?" Moody coaxed.

More silence.

The soprano almost sang, "Daddy's going to do a big important job. Aren't you going to wish him luck?"

There was a suspenseful pause, then a startled cluck like that of a little barnyard fowl, "Lock!"

The squeals of delight this time came from both ends of the line, and in both timbres, soprano and tenor. "He wished me luck! Did you hear that? He wished me luck! That's a good omen. Now it's bound to be a lulu of a story!"

The soprano voice was too taken up distributing smothered kisses over what seemed to be a considerable surface-area to be able to answer.

"Well," he said, "guess I better get down to business. I'll be home before noon—I'll take the ten forty-five, after I turn the story in at Tartell's office."

The parting became breathless, flurried, and tripartite.

"Do a bang-up job now"/"I'll make it a smasheroo"/"Remember, Sonny-bun and I are rooting for you"/"Miss me"/"And you miss us, too"/"*Smack, smack*"/"*Smack, smack, smack*"/"*Gluck!*"

He hung up smiling, sighed deeply to express his utter satisfaction with his domestic lot. Then he turned away, lathered his hands briskly, and rolled up his shirt sleeves.

The preliminaries were out of the way, the creative process was about to begin. The creative process, that mystic life force, that splurge out of which has come the Venus de Milo, the Mona Lisa, the Fantasie Impromptu, the Bayeux tapestries, *Romeo and Juliet*, the windows of Chartres Cathedral, *Paradise Lost*—and a pulp murder story by Dan Moody. The process is the same in all; if the results are a little uneven, that doesn't invalidate the basic similarity of origin.

He sat down before Gertie and, noting that the oval of light from the lamp fell on the machine, to the neglect of the polychrome cardboard mat which slanted in comparative shade against the wall, he adjusted the pliable lamp-socket so that the luminous egg was cast almost completely on the drawing instead, with the typewriter now in the shadow. Actually he didn't need the light on his typewriter. He never looked at the keys when he wrote, nor at the sheet of paper in the machine. He was an expert typist, and if in the hectic pace of his fingering he sometimes struck the wrong letter, they took care of that down at the office, Tartell had special proofreaders for that. That wasn't Moody's job—he was the creator, he couldn't be bothered with picayune details like a few typographic errors. By the same token, he never went back over what he had written to reread it; he couldn't afford to, not at one cent a word (his regular rate) and at the pressure under which he worked. Besides, it was his experience that it always came out best the first time; if you went back and reread and fiddled around with it, you only spoiled it.

He palmed a sheet of white paper off the top of the stack and inserted it smoothly into the roller—an automatic movement to him. Ordinarily he made a sandwich of sheets—a white on top, a carbon in the middle, and a yellow at the bottom; that was in case the story should go astray in the mail, or be mislaid at the magazine office before the cashier had issued a check for it. But it was totally unnecessary in this case; he was delivering the story personally to Tartell's desk, it was a rush order, and it was to be sent to press immediately. Several extra moments would be wasted between manuscript pages if he took the time to make up "sandwiches," and besides, those yellow second-sheets cost forty-five cents a ream at Goldsmith's (fifty-five elsewhere). You had to watch your costs in this line of work.

He lit a cigarette, the first of the many that were inevitably to follow, that always accompanied the writing of every story—the cigarette-to-begin-on. He blew a blue pinwheel of smoke, craned his neck slightly, and stared hard at the master plan before him, standing there against the wall. And now for the first line. That was always the gimmick in every one of his stories. Until he had it, he couldn't get into it; but once he had it, the story started to unravel by itself—it was easy going after that, clear sailing. It was like plucking the edge of the gauze up from an enormous criss-crossed bandage.

The first line, the first line.

He stared intently, almost hypnotically.

Better begin with the girl—she was very prominent on the cover, and then bring the hero in later. Let's see, she was wearing a violet evening dress—

The little lady in the violet evening dress came hurrying terrifiedly down the street, looking back in terror. Behind her

His hands poised avariciously, then drew back again. No, wait a minute, she wouldn't be wearing an evening dress on the street, violet or any other color. Well, she'd have to change into it later in the story, that was all. In a 20,000-word novelette there would be plenty of room for her to change into an evening dress. Just a single line would do it, anywhere along.

She went home and changed her dress, and then came back again.

Now, let's try it again—

The beautiful redhead came hurrying down the street, looking back in terror. Behind her

Again he got stuck. Yes, but who was after her, and what had she done for them to be after her for? That was the problem.

I started in too soon, he decided. I better go back to where she does something that gets somebody after her. Then the chase can come in after that.

The cigarette was at an end, without having ignited anything other than itself. He started another one.

Now, let's see. What would a beautiful, innocent, *good* girl do that would be likely to get somebody after her? She had to be good—Tartell was very strict about that. "I don't want any lady-bums in my stories. If you have to introduce a lady-bum into one of my stories, see that you kill her off as soon as you can. And whatever you do, don't let her get next to the hero too much. Keep her away from the hero. If he falls for her, he's a sap. And if he doesn't fall for her, he's too much of a goody-goody. Keep her in the background—just let her open the door in a negligée when the big-shot gangster drops in for a visit. And close the door again—fast!"

He swirled a hand around in his hair, in a massage-like motion, dropped it to the table, pummeled the edge of the table with it twice, the way a person does when he's trying to start a balky drawer open. Let's see, let's see . . . She could find out something that she's not supposed to, and then *they* find out that she has found out, and they start after her to shut her up—good enough, that's it! Now *how* did she find it out? She could go to a beauty parlor, and overhear in the next booth—no, beauty parlors were too feminine; Tartell wouldn't allow one of them in his stories. Besides, Moody had never been in one, wouldn't have known how to describe it on the inside. She could be in a phone booth and through the partition—No, he'd used that gambit in the July issue—in *Death Drops a Slug.*

A little lubrication was indicated here—something to help make the wheels go around, soften up the kinks. Absently, he picked up the bottle opener that Joe had left for him, reached down to the floor, brought up a bottle and uncapped it, still with that same one hand, using the edge of the table for leverage. He poured a very little into the tumbler and did no more than chastely moisten his lips with it.

Now. She could get a package at her house, and it was meant for someone else, and—

He had that peculiar instinctive feeling that comes when someone is looking at you intently, steadfastly. He shook it off with a slight quirk of his head. It remained in abeyance for a moment or two, then slowly settled on him again.

The story thread suddenly dropped in a hopeless snarl, just as he was about to get it through the needle's eye of the first line.

He turned his head, to dissipate the feeling by glancing in the direction from which it seemed to assail him. And then he saw it. A pigeon was standing utterly motionless on the ledge just outside the pane of the window. Its head was cocked inquiringly, it was turned profileward toward him, and it was staring in at him with just the one eye. But the eye was almost leaning over toward the glass, it was so intent—less than an inch or two away from it.

As he stared back, the eye solemnly blinked. Just once, otherwise giving no indication of life. He ignored it and turned back to his task. There's a ring at the bell, she goes to the door, and a man hands her a package—

His eyes crept uncontrollably over to their extreme outer corners, as if trying to take a peek without his knowledge. He brought them back with a reprimanding knitting of the brows. But almost at once they started over that way again. Just knowing the pigeon was standing out there seemed to attract his eyes almost magnetically.

He turned his head toward it again. This time he gave it a heavy baleful scowl. "Get off of there," he mouthed at it. "Go somewhere else." He spoke by lip motion alone, because the glass between prevented hearing.

It blinked. More slowly than the first time, if a pigeon's blink can be measured. Scorn, contempt seemed to be expressed by the deliberateness of its blink.

Never slow to be affronted, he kindled at once. He swung his arm violently around toward it, in a complete half circle of riddance. Its wing feathers erupted a little, subsided again, as if the faintest of breezes had caressed them. Then with stately pomp it waddled around in a half-circle, brought the other side of its head around toward the glass, and stared at him with the eye on that side.

Heatedly, he jumped from his chair, strode to the window, and flung it up. "I told you to get off of there!" he said threateningly. He gave the air immediately over the surface of the ledge a thrashing swipe with his arm.

It eluded the gesture with no more difficulty than a child jumping rope. Only, instead of coming down again as the rope passed underneath, it stayed up! It made a little looping journey with scarcely stirring wings, and as soon as his arm was drawn in again, it descended almost to the precise spot where it had stood before.

Once more they repeated this passage between them, with identical results. The pigeon expended far less energy coasting around at a safe height than he did flinging his arm hectically about, and he realized that a law of diminishing returns would soon set in on this point. Moreover, he over-aimed the second time and crashed the back of his hand into the stone coping alongside the window, so that he had to suck at his knuckles and breathe on them to alleviate the sting.

He had never hated a bird so before. In fact, he had never hated a bird before.

He slammed the window down furiously. Thereupon, as though it realized it had that much more advance warning against possible armstrikes, the pigeon began to strut from one side to the other of the window ledge. Like a picket, enjoining him from working. Each time he made a turn, it cocked that beady eye at him.

He picked up the metal wastebasket and tested it in his hand for solidity. Then he put it down again, regretfully. He'd need it during the course of the story; he couldn't just drop the cigarette butts on the floor, he'd be kept too busy stamping them out to avoid starting a fire. And even if the basket knocked the damned bird off the ledge, it would probably go over with it.

He picked up the phone, demanded the desk clerk so that he could vent his indignation on something human.

"Do I have to have pigeons on my window sill?" he shouted accusingly. "Why didn't you tell me there were going to be pigeons on my window sill?"

The clerk was more than taken aback; he was stunned by the onslaught. "I—ah—ah—never had a complaint like this before," he finally managed to stammer.

"Well, you've got one now!" Moody let him know with firm disapproval.

"Yes, sir, but—but what's it doing?" the clerk floundered. "Is it making any noise?"

"It doesn't have to," Moody flared. "I just don't want it there!"

There was a momentary pause, during which it was to be surmised the clerk was baffled, scrubbing the side of his jaw, or perhaps his temple or forehead. Then he came back again, completely at a loss. "I'm sorry, sir—but I don't see what you expect *me* to do about it. You're up there with it, and I'm down here. Haven't—haven't you tried chasing it?"

"Haven't I tried?" choked Moody exasperatedly. "That's all I've been doing! It free-wheels out and around and comes right back again!"

"Well, about the only thing I can suggest," the clerk said helplessly, "is to send up a boy with a mop or broom, and have him stand there by the window and—"

"I can't work with a bellboy in here doing sentinel duty with a mop or broom slung over his shoulder!" Moody exploded. "That'd be worse than the pigeon!"

The clerk breathed deeply, with bottomless patience. "Well, I'm sorry, sir, but—"

Moody got it out first. " 'I don't see what I can do about it.' 'I don't see what I can do about it'!" he mimicked ferociously. "Thanks! You've been a big help," he said with ponderous sarcasm. "I don't know what I would have done without you!"—and hung up.

He looked around at it, a resigned expression in his eyes that those energetic, enthusiastic irises seldom showed.

The pigeon had its neck craned at an acute angle, almost down to the stone sill, but still looking in at him from that oblique perspective, as if to say, "Was that about me? Did it have to do with me?"

He went over and jerked the window up. That didn't even make it stir anymore.

He turned and went back to his writing chair. He addressed the pigeon coldly from there. Aloud, but coldly, and with the condescension of the superior forms of life toward the inferior ones. "Look. You want to come in? Is that what it's all about? You're dying to come in? You won't be happy till you do come in? Then for the love of Mike come in and get it over with, and let me get back to work! There's a nice comfortable chair, there's a nice plumpy sofa, there's a nice wide bed-rail for a perch. The whole room is yours. Come in and have yourself a ball!"

Its head came up, from that sneaky way of regarding him under-wing. It contemplated the invitation. Then its twig-like little vermilion legs dipped and it threw him a derogatory chuck of the head, as if to say "That for you and your room!"—and unexpectedly took off, this time in a straight, unerring line of final departure.

His feet detonated in such a burst of choleric anger that the chair went over. He snatched up the wastebasket, rushed to the window, and swung it violently—without any hope, of course, of overtaking his already vanished target.

"Dirty damn squab!" he railed bitterly. "Come back here and I'll—! Doing that to me, after I'm just about to get rolling! I hope you run into a high-tension wire headfirst. I hope you run into a hawk—"

His anger, however, settled as rapidly as a spent Seidlitz powder. He closed the window without violence. A smothered chuckle had already begun to sound in him on his way back to the chair, and he was grinning sheepishly as he reached it.

"Feuding with a pigeon yet," he murmured deprecatingly to himself. "I'd better get a grip on myself."

Another cigarette, two good hearty gulps of beer, and now, let's see—where was I? The opening line. He stared up at the ceiling.

His fingers spread, poised, and then suddenly began to splatter all over the dark keyboard like heavy drops of rain.

"For me?" the young woman said, staring unbelievably at the shifty-eyed man holding the package.

"You're

One hand paused, then two of its fingers snapped, demanding inspiration. "Got to get a name for her," he muttered. He stared fruitlessly at the ceiling for a moment, then glanced over at the window. The hand resumed.

"You're Pearl Dove, ain't ya?"

"Why, yes, but I wasn't expecting anything."

("Not too much dialogue," Tartell always cautioned. "Get them moving, get them doing something. Dialogue leaves big blanks on the pages, and the reader doesn't get as much reading for his money.")

He thrust it at her, turned, and disappeared as suddenly as he appeared

Two "appeareds" in one line—too many. He triphammered the x-key eight times.

and disappeared as suddenly as he had showed up. She tried to call him back but he was no longer in sight. Somewhere out in the night the whine of an expensive car taking off came to her ears

He frowned, closed his eyes briefly, then began typing automatically again.

She looked at the package she had been left holding

He never bothered to consult what he had written so far—such fussy niceties were for smooth-paper writers and poets. In stories like the one he was writing, it was almost impossible to break the thread of the action, anyway. Just so long as he kept going, that was all that mattered. If there was an occasional gap, Tartell's proofreaders would knit it together with a couple of words.

He drained the beer in the glass, refilled it, gazed dreamily at the ceiling. The wide, blank expanse of the ceiling gave his characters more room to move around in as his mind's eye conjured them up.

"She has a boyfriend who's on the Homicide Squad," he murmured confidentially. "Not really a boyfriend, just sort of a brotherly protector." ("Don't give 'em sweethearts," was Tartell's constant admonishment, "just give 'em pals. You might want to kill the girl off, and if she's already his sweetheart you can't very well do that, or he loses face with the readers.") "She calls him up to tell him she has received a mysterious package. He tells her not to open it, he'll be right over—" The rest was mechanical fingerwork. Fast and furious. The keys dipped and rose like a canopy of leaves shot through by an autumn wind.

The page jumped up out of the roller by itself, and he knew he'd struck off the last line there was room for. He pitched it aside to the floor without even glancing at it, slipped in a new sheet, all in one accustomed, fluid motion. Then, with the same almost unconscious ease, he reached down for a new bottle, uncapped it, and poured until a cream puff of a head burgeoned at the top of it.

They were at the business of opening the package now. He stalled for two lines, to give himself time to improvise what was going to be inside the package, which he hadn't had an opportunity to do until now—

He stared down at it. Then his eyes narrowed and he nodded grimly.

"What do you make of it?" she breathed, clutching her throat.

Then he was smack up against it, and the improvisation had to be here and now. The keys coasted to a reluctant but full stop. There was almost smoke coming from them by now, or else it was from his ever-present cigarette riding the edge of the table, drifting the long way around by way of the machine.

There were always certain staples that were good for the contents of mysterious packages. Opium pellets—but that meant bringing in a Chinese villain, and the menace on the cover drawing certainly wasn't Chinese—

He got up abruptly, swung his chair out away from the table, and shifted it farther over, directly under the phantom tableau on the ceiling that had come to a halt simultaneously with the keys—the way the figures on a motion picture screen freeze into immobility when something goes wrong with the projector.

He got up on the chair seat with both feet, craned his neck, peered intently and with complete sincerity. He was only about two feet away from the visualization on the ceiling. His little bit of fetishism, or idiosyncrasy, had worked for him before in similar stoppages, and it did now. He could *see* the inside of the package, he could see—

He jumped lithely down again, looped the chair back into place, speared avidly at the keys.

Uncut diamonds!

"Aren't they beautiful?" she said, clutching her pulsing throat.

(Well, if there were too many clutches in there, Tartell's hirelings could take one or two of them out. It was always hard to know what to have your female characters do with their hands. Clutching the throat and holding the heart were his own favorite standbys. The male characters could always be fingering a gun or swinging a punch at someone, but it wasn't refined for women to do that in *Startling Stories!*)

"Beautiful but hot," he growled.

Her eyes widened. "How do you know?"

"They're the Espinoza consignment, they've been missing for a week." He unlimbered his gun. "This spells trouble for someone."

That was enough dialogue for a few pages—he had to get into some fast, red-hot action.

There weren't any more hitches now. The story flowed like a torrent. The margin bell chimed almost staccato, the roller turned with almost piston-like continuity, the pages sprang up almost like blobs of batter from a pancake skillet. The beer kept rising in the glass and, contradictorily, steadily falling lower. The cigarettes gave up their ghosts, long thin gray ghosts, in a good cause; the mortality rate was terrible.

His train of thought, the story's lifeline, beer-lubricated but no whit impeded, flashed and sputtered and coursed ahead like lightning in a topaz mist, and the loose fingers and hiccuping keys followed as fast as they could. Only once more, just before the end, was there a near hitch, and that wasn't in the sense of a stoppage of thought, but rather of an error in memory—what he mistakenly took to be a duplication. The line:

Hands clutching her throat, Pearl tore down the street in her violet evening dress streamed off the keys, and he came to a lumbering, uneasy halt.

Wait a minute, I had that in in the beginning. She can't keep running down the street all the time in a violet evening dress; the readers'll get fed up. How'd she get into a violet evening dress anyway? A minute ago the guy *tore her white blouse and revealed her quivering white shoulder.*

He half-turned in the chair (and none too steadily), about to essay the almost hopeless task of winnowing through the blanket of white pages that lay all around him on the floor, and then recollection came to his aid in the nick of time.

I remember now! I moved the beginning around to the middle, and began with the package at the door instead. (It seemed like a long, long time ago, even to him, that the package had arrived at the door; weeks and weeks ago; another story ago.) This is the first time she's run down the street in a violet evening dress; she hasn't done it before. Okay, let her run.

However, logically enough, in order to get her into it in the first place, he X-ed out the line anyway, and put in for groundwork:

"If it hadn't been for your quick thinking, that guy would have got me sure. I'm taking you to dinner tonight, and that's an order."

"I'll run home and change. I've got a new dress I'm dying to break in."

And that took care of that.

Ten minutes later (according to story time, not his), due to the unfortunate contretemps of having arrived at the wrong cafe at the wrong time, the line reappeared, now legitimatized, and she was duly *tearing down the street, screaming, clutching her throat with her violet evening dress.* (The "with" he had intended for an "in.") The line had even gained something by waiting. This time she was screaming as well, which she hadn't been doing the first time.

And then finally, somewhere in the malt-drenched mists ahead, maybe an hour or maybe two hours, maybe a dozen cigarettes or maybe a pack and a half, maybe two bottles of beer or maybe four, a page popped up out of the roller onto which he had just ground the words *The End*, and the story was done.

He blew out a deep breath, a vacuum-cleaner-deep breath. He let his head go over and rest for a few moments against the edge of the table. Then he got up from the chair, very unsteadily, and wavered over toward the bed, treading on the litter of fallen pages. But he had his shoes off, so that didn't hurt them much.

He didn't hear the springs creak as he flattened out. His ears were already asleep. . . .

Sometime in the early morning, the very early early-morning (just like at home), that six-year-old of the neighbors started with that velocipede of his, racing it up and down in front of the house and trilling the bell incessantly. He stirred and mumbled disconsolately to his wife, "Can't you call out the window and make that brat stay in front of his own house with that damn contraption?"

Moody struggled up tormentedly on one elbow, and at that point the kid characteristically went back into the house for good, and the ringing stopped. But when Moody opened his blurred eyes, he wasn't sitting up at home at all; he was in a hotel room.

"Take your time," a voice said sarcastically. "I've got all day."

Moody swiveled his head, stunned, and Joe was holding the room door open to permit Tartell, his magazine editor, to glare in at him. Tartell was short, but impressive. He was of a great age, as Moody's measurements of time went, a redwood-tree age, around forty-five or forty-eight or somewhere up there. And right now Tartell wasn't in good humor.

"Twice the printers have called," he barked, "asking if they get that story today or not!"

Moody's body gave a convulsive jerk and his heels braked against the floor. "Gee, is it that late—?"

"No, not at all!" Tartell shouted. "The magazine can come out anytime! Don't let a little thing like that worry you! If Cora hadn't had the presence of mind to call me at my house before I left for the office, I wouldn't have stopped by here like this, and we'd all be waiting around another hour down at the office. Now where is it? Let me have it. I'll take it down with me." Moody gestured helplessly toward the floor, which looked as though a political rally, with pamphlets, had taken place on it the night before.

"Very systematic," Tartell commented acridly. He surged forward into the room, doubling over into a sort of cushiony right-angle as he did so, and began to zigzag, picking up papers without let-up, like a diligent, near-sighted park attendant spearing leaves at close range. "This is fine right after a heavy breakfast," he added. "The best thing I could do!"

Joe looked pained, but on Moody's behalf, not Tartell's. "I'll help you, sir," he offered placatingly, and started bobbing in turn.

Tartell stopped suddenly, and without rising, seemed to be trying to read, from the unconventional position of looking straight down from up above. "They're blank," he accused. "Where does it begin?"

"Turn them over," Moody said, wearied with so much fussiness. "They must have fallen on their faces."

"They're that way on both sides, Mr. Moody," Joe faltered.

"What've you been doing?" Tartell demanded wrathfully. "Wait a minute—!" His head came up to full height, he swerved, went over to Gertie, and examined the unlidded machine closely.

Then he brought both fists up in the air, each still clutching pin-wheels of the sterile pages, and pounded them down with maniacal fury on both ends of the writing table. The noise of the concussion was only less than the noise of his unbridled voice. "You damn-fool idiot!" he roared insanely, looking up at the ceiling as if in quest of aid with which to curb his assault-tempted emotions. "You've been pounding thin air all night! You've been beating the hell out of blank paper! *You forgot to put a ribbon in your typewriter!*"

Joe, looking beyond Tartell, took a quick step forward, arms raised in support of somebody or something.

Tartell slashed his hand at him forbiddingly, keeping him where he was. "Don't catch him, let him land," he ordered, wormwood-bitter. "Maybe a good clunk against the floor will knock some sense into his stupid—talented—head."

In April 1959 Woolrich received an advance of $1,000 to put together a collection of his tales of occult horror, published a few months later as *Beyond the Night* (Avon pb #T–354, 1959). As usual during the 1950s, Woolrich lied to the publisher about the provenance of what he was selling. The collection's copyright page claims that three of its six stories were brand-new, but in fact two of the supposedly original trio were resurrected pulpers from the 1930s. The only genuine new tale in the book was the one you are about to read, a gem of *noir* set in 1929 and, if we are not reading too much into its setting, perhaps originally conceived as yet another chapter for *Hotel Room.* The plot device which propels the young couple on their road to perdition was borrowed by Woolrich from his never-collected pulp story "Wake Up with Death" (*Detective Fiction Weekly,* June 5, 1937) but, the second time around, he integrated it into his vision of the world's random senselessness. The only hardcover appearance of "The Number's Up" until now was in my *Nightwebs* collection of 1971. Is it possible that one of the people who read it there was Steven Spielberg? The exact same plot device pops up in his futuristic *noir* thriller *Minority Report* (2002).

THE NUMBER'S UP

I t was a sort of car that seemed to have a faculty for motion with an absolute lack of any accompanying sound whatsoever. This was probably illusory; it must have been, internal combustion engines being what they are, tires being what they are, brakes and gears being what they are, even raspy street-surfacing being what it is. Yet the illusion outside the hotel entrance was a complete one. Just as there are silencers that, when affixed to automatic hand-weapons, deaden their reports, so it was as if this whole massive car body were encased in something of that sort. For, first, there was nothing out there, nothing in sight there. Then, as though the street-bed were water and this bulky black shape were a grotesque gondola, it came floating up out of the darkness from nowhere. And then suddenly, still with no sound whatsoever, there it was at a halt, in position.

It was like a ghost-car in every attribute but the visual one. In its trancelike approach and halt, in its lightlessness, in its enshrouded interior, which made it impossible to determine (at least without lowering one's head directly outside the windows and peering in at nose-tip range) if it were even occupied at all, and if so by whom and by how many.

You could visualize it scuttling fleetly along some overshadowed country lane at dead of night, lightless, inscrutable, unidentifiable, to halt perhaps beside some inky grove of trees, linger there a while undetected, then glide on again, its unaccountable errand accomplished without witness, without aftermath. A goblin-car that in an earlier age would have fed folklore and rural legend. Or, in the city, you could visualize it sliding stealthily along some warehouse-blacked back alley, curving and squirming in its terrible silence, then, as it neared the mouth and would have emerged, creeping to a stop and lying there in wait, unguessed in the gloom. Lying there in wait for long hours, like some huge metal-cased predatory animal, waiting to pounce on its prey.

Sudden, sharp yellow spurts of fangs, and then to whirl and slink back into anonymity the way it came, leaving the carcass of its prey huddled there and dead.

Who was there to know? Who was there to tell?

And even now, before this particular hotel entrance. It was already in position, it had already stopped.

Then nothing happened.

Ordinarily, when cars stop someone gets out. That is what they have stopped for. In this case it just stood there, as though there were no one in it and had been no one in it all along.

Then the pale, blurry shape of a human hand, as when seen through thick dark glass, appeared inside the window and descended slowly to the bottom, like a pale-colored mussel foundering in a murky tank of water. And with it went the invisible line of a shade. The hand stopped a little above the lower rim and faded from sight again. The shade-line remained where it had been left.

The watch had begun. The death-watch.

In a little while a young man came walking along the street, untroubled of gait, unaware of it. The particular hotel that the ghost-car had made its rendezvous had a seamy glass canopy jutting out over the sidewalk with open bulbs set around the inside of it. But they only shone inward because its outer rim was opaque. Thus, as the young man stepped from the darkness of the street's back reaches under this pane of light it was as though a curtain had been jerked up in front of his face, and he was suddenly revealed from head to foot as in a spotlight.

In the car the darkness found breath and whispered, "That him?"

And the darkness whispered back to the darkness, "Yeah, same type build. Same light hair. Wears gray a lot. And this is the hotel that was fingered."

Then the darkness quickly stirred, but the other darkness quelled it, hissing: "Wait, he wants the girl, too. The girl, too, he said. Let him get up there to her first."

The young man had turned off and gone inside. The four glass leaves of the revolving door blurred and made him disappear.

For a moment more the evil darkness held its collective breath. Then, no longer in a whisper but sharp as the edge of a stiletto, "Now. Go in and get the number of the room. Do it smart."

The man behind the desk looked up from his racing form, and there was a jaunty young man wearing a snap-brim felt hat leaning there on one elbow. How long he'd been there it was impossible to determine. He might have just come. He might have been there three or four minutes already. Ghost-cars, ghost-arrivals, ghost-departures.

"Do something for you?" said the man behind the desk.

The leaner on his elbow nodded his head languidly, but didn't say. "What?"

The leaner considered his bent-back fingernails, blew on them and rubbed them against his coat-lapel a little. "Guy that just came in. Got any idea what his room number would be?"

"Is he expecting—"

"No." He opened his hand and a compressed five-dollar bill dribbled out onto the desk and slowly began to expand. "He dropped this in front of the door just now. I seen him do it. Thought he might want it back."

"You taking it up to him?"

"No. You take care of it for me. I ain't particular." The elbow-leaner was fiddling with one of his cuff links now.

A conniving look appeared on the clerk's yeast-pasty face. He said, through immobile lips that made the words sound furtive, "I'll take it up to One-one-six for you in a little while."

"Try Streakaway in the third race tomorrow."

The five-dollar bill was gone now.

So was the jaunty young man in the snap-brim felt hat.

He knocked because they only had one key between them. The tarnished numerals 116 slanted inward as she opened the door for him. They kissed first, and then she said, "Oh God, I've been so frightened, waiting all alone here like this. I thought you'd never come back!"

She had sleek bobbed hair with a part on the side, and was wearing a waistless dress that came to her knees. The waist was down at the bottom.

"Everything's taken care of," he said soothingly. "The reservation's made—"

"You don't think anything will happen tonight, do you?" she faltered. "You don't think anything will happen tonight?"

"Nothing will happen. Don't be afraid. I'm right here with you."

"We should have gone home to my mother. I would have felt safer there. When something like this comes along, a woman wants another woman to cling to, one of her own kind. A man can't understand that."

"Don't be afraid," was all he kept saying. "Don't be afraid."

The knock on the door was craftily casual. It wasn't too loud, it wasn't too long, it wasn't too rapid. It was just like any knock on the door should be.

Their embrace split open down the middle, and they both turned their heads to look that way.

"Wonder who that is," he said matter-of-factly.

"I can't imagine," she said placidly.

He went over to the door and opened it, and suddenly two men were in the room and the door was closed again. All without noise.

"Come on, Jack," one said. "Nice and easy now."

"Nice and easy now," the other said.

"You must have the wrong party."

"No, we haven't got the wrong party. We made sure of that."

"Made sure of that," the other one said.

"Well I don't know you. I never saw you before in my life."

"Same goes for us. We never saw you before neither. But we know someone that *does* know you."

"Who?"

"We'll tell you downstairs. Come on now. Take your hat. Looks better that way."

The girl's head kept turning from one to the other, like a frightened spectator watching a ball pass to and fro at a deadly tennis match that is not being played for sport.

"You're frightening my wife. Won't you tell us what you—"

"His wife. Did you get that? 'The-lay-of-the-land,' they used to call her, and now this guy claims she's his wife. As that Guinan dame is always saying, 'Hello, sucker!' "

The girl quickly held the man back, her man. "Don't. I don't like their looks. Please, for my sake, don't."

"You got good sense, wife," one of them told her.

"Look, if it's money you want—we don't have much, but—here. Now please go and leave us alone."

One of them chopped the extended hand down viciously, and the bills sprayed like an exploded bouquet. His voice thickened to a muddy growl. "Come a-a-an," he said threateningly. "Outside."

He backed a forearm up over his own shoulder in menace. "Walk," he said. "Don'tcha hear good?"

"Hear good?" said the other.

"This says you do." And there was a gun. Not much of it showing, just a sliver of the harmless end, peering above the lip of his pocket. But with one finger hooked down below in position.

"Don't scream," the other one warned the girl tonelessly. "Don't scream, or you'll wish you hadn't."

She shuddered like someone dancing. "I won't."

"Now come on," the first one said to the man. "You're going to walk with me, like this. Up against me, real close and chummy. Buddy-buddies."

They went out two by two. Slopping fondly against each other, from shoulder down to hip, like a quartet of drunks coming out of a speak at seven in the morning.

"Where you taking us?" he said in the elevator, going down.

"Just for a little ride." The expression had no sinister meaning yet in 1929. It meant only what it seemed to say.

"But why at this hour?"

"Don't talk."

As they made the brief passage from elevator to street, with a minimum of conspicuousness, the desk man carefully avoided looking up. He was busy, extremely busy, looking down into his racing form at that moment.

They walked her around to the outside of the car and put her in from there, next to a man who was already at the wheel. Him they put in from the near side, and then each one got in on opposite sides of him and pinned him down between them on the back seat. It was all done with almost fluid-drive sleekness, not a hitch, not a catch, not a break in its flow.

And suddenly, like in a dream, the street outside that particular hotel entrance was empty again, as empty as it had been earlier that night. The car was gone. It had departed as soundlessly, as ghostlike, as it had first appeared. A true phantom of the night.

But it had been there. It had brought three people and taken five away. That much was no illusion.

The ride had begun.

The theater and club spectaculars seemed to stick up into the sky at all sorts of crazy angles, probably because most of them were planted diagonally on rooftops. *Follow Thru, Whoopee, Show Boat,* El Fay Club, Club Richman, Texas Guinan's. It gave the town the appearance of standing on its ear.

The car slid through rows of brownstones (each one housing a speakeasy on its lower floors) over as far as Eleventh, which had no traffic lights yet. Its only traffic was an occasional milk or railroad-yards freight truck, since no highway connected with it, and it came to a dead end at Seventy-second without even a ramp to its name. They ran down it the other way, to Canal Street and the two-year-old Holland Tunnel, engineering marvel of the decade.

The girl spoke suddenly, as they glided past endless strings of stalled New York Central freight cars. "Don't. Please don't. Please leave me alone."

"What's he doing to you?" came quickly from the back seat.

The man at the wheel answered for her. "Just straightening her skirt a little."

The other two laughed. But it wasn't even bawdy laughter. It was too cold and cruel for that.

When they reached the tunnel-mouth, the driver slowed. As he rolled the window down to pay the toll, she suddenly stripped off her wrist watch and flung it so that it struck the tunnel cop flat on the chest.

He caught it easily with one hand, so that it didn't even have a chance to fall. "Hey, what's that for?" he asked, but laughing good-naturedly.

"My girlfriend here just now said she don't want to know the time anymore from now on, and I guess that's her way of proving it."

The girl writhed a little, as though her arm were caught in a vise behind her back, but said nothing.

The cop pitched the watch lightly back into the car. "Just coming home from a party, folks?"

"No, we're going to one."

"Have fun."

"That's what we intend."

As they picked up speed, and the white tiles flashed blindingly by, the driver gave her a savage backhand swipe with his knuckles across her mouth.

She cried out piercingly, but it was lost in the roar of the onrushing tunnel. The man who called himself her husband made some sort of spasmodic move on the back seat, but the two guns pressing into his intestines from opposite sides almost met inside him, they dug in so far.

They came out into the open, and it was the grimy backwaters of Jersey City now. Tall factory stacks, and fires burning, and spreads of stagnant stinking water.

On and on the ride went. On and on and on.

They turned north soon and left the big city and all its little satellites behind them, and after a while even the rusty glow on the horizon died down and was gone. Then trees began, and little lumpy hills, and there was nothing but the darkness and the night and the fear.

"Don," she shuddered, and suddenly flung one hand up over her shoulder and back, trying to find his.

"Please let me hold her hand," he begged. "She's frightened."

"Let 'em hold hands," one of them snickered.

They held onto each other like that, in a hand-link of fear, two against the night.

"Don, she called me," he said. "Didn't you hear her? Don, that's my name. Don Ackerman."

"Yeah, and I'm Ricardo Cortez," countered one of them, with the flipness so characteristic of the period that it even came into play on a death ride.

On went the ride.

At one point his control slipped away from him for a minute. "God," he burst out, "how far are you taking us?"

"Don't be in a hurry to get there," the one on his left advised him dryly. "I wouldn't, if I was you."

And then again, a little later, "Won't you tell me the name of the fellow you think I am? Can't I convince you—"

"What's the matter, you don't know your own name?"

"Well, what've I done?"

"We don't know from nothing. You were just marked lousy, that's all. We only carry out the orders."

"Yes, but what orders?" he exclaimed in his innocence.

And the answer, grim, foreboding, was: "Oh, broth-urr!"

Then without any warning the car stopped. They were there.

"The ride's over," someone said. "End of the ride."

For a moment nobody got out. They just sat there. The driver cut the ignition, and after that there was silence. Complete, uncanny silence, more frightening than the most threatening noise or violence could have been. Night silence. A silence that had death in it.

Then one of them opened the door, got out, and started to walk slowly away from the car, through ankle-high grass that hissed and spit as he toiled through it. The others just stayed where they were.

There was some sort of an old dilapidated farm building with a slanted roof in the middle distance. It was obviously abandoned, because its windows were black glassless gaps. Behind it was a smaller shanty looking like a tool shed or lean-to, so close to collapse it was almost down flat. He didn't approach either one of them, he went around to the rear in a big wide circle.

They sat in silence, the four of them that were left. One of them was smoking a cigarette. But that didn't make any noise, just a red blink whenever he drew on it.

Finally the driver reached out and tapped the button. A single, lonely, guttural horn-blat sounded. Briefer than a question mark in the air, staccato as the span of a second split in two, yet unfolding into a streamer of meaning through the night air: Come on, what's taking you so long, we're getting tired of waiting.

The walker-in-the-grass came back to the car again.

"Yeah, it's there," he said briefly.

"He told us it would be," was the sardonic answer. "Didn't you believe him?"

There was a general stir of activity as the other two got out, each with a prisoner.

"All right, you and me go this way," the one with the girl said.

"No! Don!" she started to scream harrowingly. "Don-n-n-n!"

His smile was thin as a knife-cut across his face. "Don'll be taken care. Don't worry about Don."

He grasped her brutally by the upper arms, tightened his hold to a crushing vise and drew his lips back whitely, as though the constrictive force came from them and not his hands. He thrust her drunkenly lurching form from side to side before him. Her hair swayed and danced with the struggle, as though it were something alive in its own right. The darkness swallowed them soon enough, but not the sounds they made.

Now Don began to shout himself, frightened, crazed, straining forward like a thing possessed. "Let her go! Let her go! Oh, if there's a God above, why doesn't He look down and stop this!" His voice was willowy with too much vibrancy. The movements of weeping appeared upon his face, the distortion without the delivery. Skin-weeping, without tears.

When the man who had been with her came back he was brushing twigs and leaves off his clothing, almost casually.

"Where is she?" they asked him.

"Where I left her." Then he added, "Wanna take a look?"

"I think I will take a look," the other assented, grinning with suggestive meaning.

But he turned up again almost at once, and his manner had changed. He acted disgruntled, like someone who's been given a false scent and gone on a fool's errand.

"Where is she now?"

"Still there."

"What's up?"

He said something low-voiced that the man she'd called Don

wasn't able to catch. His fright-soaked senses let it float past on the tide of terror submerging him.

"A kid!" the other one brayed outright in his surprise. His face flicked around for an instant toward the prisoner, then back again. "Say, maybe he *was* telling the truth. Maybe she *was* his—"

"Couldn't you tell?" the third man demanded of the girl's original escort, a trace of contempt in his voice.

"Whaddya expect me to do, feel her pulse in the dark?"

"She gone or ain't she?" he wanted to know bluntly, unmoved by any thought of sparing the prisoner's sensibilities.

"Sure. What do I know about those things? I only know her eyes are wide open and she ain't looking."

The man who was being held thrashed rabidly until he almost seemed to oscillate like the bent wing of an electric fan when its spin is dwindling. "Let me go to her! Let me go to her!"

"Pipe down, Jack," one of them admonished, giving him a perfunctory slantwise clip along the jawline, but without any real heave behind it. "Nothing there to go to anymore."

He threw his head back, stared unseeingly straight up overhead, and from the furrowed scalp, the ridged pate that his face had thus become, emitted a full-fledged scream, high-pitched as a woman's, unreasoning as a crushed animal's.

Then his hands rose, fingers hooked wide, and scissored in from opposite sides, clawing at his own cheeks, digging into them, as if trying to tear them off, pull them out by their very ligaments.

"No!" he shrieked, then "No!" he cried, then "No!" he moaned, on a descending tonal scale.

They had taken their hands off him, knowing he was no longer capable of much movement.

His head fell forward again, like something trying to loosen itself from his shoulders, and now he blindly, snufflingly faced the ground as if he were looking closely for something he'd dropped there. His feet carried him around in an intoxicated, reeling little half-circle, and he collapsed breast-first against the fender of the car, head burrowed down against its hood, clasped hands clamped tight across the back of it as if to keep his skull from exploding. His legs, stretched inertly outward along the ground behind him, twitched spasmodically now and then, as if trying to draw themselves in after the rest of him, and always slipped back again each time.

In his travail, words of pain filtered through, suffocated by the pressure of the car-hood against his nose and mouth.

"Mine! She was mine! Mine! Mine!" Over and endlessly over again. "My girl. She was my girl. It was going to be my little baby. I was waiting for it to be my little baby. All my hopes and dreams are gone. . . . Oh, I want to leave this rotten world! I want to get out of this rotten world!"

"You will. You're gonna." The eyes that looked down upon him held no pity, no softness, no feeling at all. They were eyes of stone.

"I don't care what you do to me now," he said. "I want to die."

"That's good," they told him. "We'll oblige."

"Kill me quick," he said. "The quicker the better."

"You're going to get it how we want it, not how you want it." He wouldn't walk, or couldn't. Probably couldn't—emotional shock. Each took him by a shoulder, and his legs dragged along behind him out at full length, giving little jerks and bumps when they hit stones and other obstacles.

They brought him to the edge of a squared-off pit in the ground and let him fall flat on his face and lie there a minute. A dried-out well shaft.

"You start the digging, Playback." It was the first time a name had been exchanged between any of them.

"Yeah, I always get the hard work."

Playback brought a shovel from the toppled-down tool shed, marked off an oblong of surface soil and started to break it up into clods ready for throwing down into the well-shaft.

The other man was saying to the third one: "These pocket-flashes ain't going to be enough to see all the way down there. How about one of the heads from the car?"

"Whaddya have to have light for, anyway?"

"You want to see him die, don'tcha? That's half the kick.

Another thing, there might be space left between those chunks the air could get to him through."

"I have some extension wiring I can rig it up on."

"I don't care what you do now," the man on the ground droned. "I want to die."

"Always get the hard work," said Playback.

The detached headlight was set up on the lip of the well-shaft. The man who had brought it returned to the car to control it from the dashboard.

"Why don't you hurry?" said the man on the ground. "For God's sake, why don't you hurry? Why can't I die, when I want to so badly?"

The one nearest aimed a kick at him along the ground. "You will," he promised.

The headlight was deflected downward into the aperture. "Give her the juice," the one beside it called back guardedly in the direction of the car.

A ghostly pallor came up from below, making the darkness aboveground seem even more impenetrable. Their faces, however, were now bathed in the reflection, like hideous devil-masks with slits for eyes and mouths.

The other one came back from the car.

"There's got to be a lot more fill than that," the one standing beside Playback criticized dissatisfiedly, measuring the results of his efforts.

"I always get the hard work."

The other one grabbed the shovel from him and went at it in his place. "If there's one thing that gets my goat," he muttered disgustedly, "it's to have a guy along on a thing like this that's always bellyaching, the way you do. Just one guy like that is enough to spoil everyone else's good time."

The man on the ground had grasped hold of a small rock lying near him. He closed his hand around it, swung his arm up, and tried to smash it into his own skull.

The nearest one of the three saw it just in time and aimed a swift kick that averted it. The rock bounced out and the hand fell down limp. It lay there, oddly twisted inside out, as though the wrist had been broken.

After that there was silence for a while, only the sound of the shovel biting into the earth and the hissing splatter of the loose dirt.

They stood him up, his back to the well.

In the dark, desperate sky, just above the scalloped line the tree-tops made, three stars formed a pleading little constellation. No one looked at them, no one cared. This was the time for death, not the time for mercy.

The last thing he said was, "Helen, sweetheart. Wait for me. I'm coming to you." The last thing in the whole world.

Then they pushed him down. Took their hands off him, rather, and he went down by himself, for he couldn't stand up anymore.

He went over backward, and in, and down. The sound of the hit wasn't too much. It was soggy at the bottom yet, from the long-ago water. Probably he didn't feel it too much. He was all limp from lack of wanting to live, anyway.

He lay there nestled up, like in a foursquare clayey coffin.

He stirred a little, sighed a little, like someone trying to get comfortable in bed.

Playback tipped the shovel over, and a drench of earth granules spewed down on top of him.

One bent leg got covered up. But his face still breasted the terrestrial wave, like a motionless swimmer caught in the upturn stroke of the Australian crawl and held fast that way, face over shoulder.

Playback brought another shovelful, and the face was gone.

One hand crept through, tentatively, like something feeling its way in the dark.

Playback brought another shovelful and erased the hand.

Three fingers wormed through this time, like a staggered insect that has been stepped on. They only made it as far as the second joint.

"If he said he wants to die, then why does he keep trying to break through to the surface and breathe for?" Playback asked, engrossed.

"That's nature," the one beside him answered learnedly. "His mind wants to die, but his body don't know any better, it wants to live no matter what he says to it."

The stirring fill had fallen motionless at last.

"It's got him, he's quit now," he decided after a further moment or two of judicious observation. "Throw her in on top of him, fill it up the rest of the way, and let's get out of here. I haven't had so much fresh air since—"

A girl opened the door first, looked cautiously up and down the deserted hotel corridor. Then she hitched her head at someone behind her, picked up a small valise from the floor and came on outside.

She was a blonde, good-looking and mean-looking, both at the same time.

"C'mon," she said huskily. "Let's go while the going's good."

A man came out after her. His eyes were the eyes of a poker player. A poker player in a game where the pot is life and death. He had a certain build, a certain way of walking. He was in gray.

He closed the door after him with practiced stealth. Then he stopped and raised his hand to the outside of it.

The girl looked around at him impatiently. "Can that, will you?" she snapped. "This is no time to play games. Every time you go in or out you take time off and fool with that."

"I'm a gambler, remember?"

"You're a gambler is right," she agreed tartly. "That's why the heat's on you right now. You should pay up your losses—"

"I'm superstitious. This little number's been awful good to me. All my big wins come from something with a six in it."

On the 9 at the end of 119 the bottom rivet was gone; only the top one remained. He swung it around loosely upward, made it into a 6 and patted it affectionately. "Keep on bringing me good luck like you always have," he told it softly.

"Didn't you hear me ask for 116 when we first holed up here?" he added. "Only somebody else was already in it. . . ."

The last collection of Woolrich's stories published in his lifetime was *The Dark Side of Love* (Walker, 1965), which was an abysmal failure commercially but gives us a concentrated dose of how the world looked to him as he approached his own death. The last story in that book, "Too Nice a Day to Die," is a faultless gem of *noir* whose facets perfectly reflect a world in which chance is god and beams fall—which is why, more than a third of a century ago, I included it in my 1971 collection *Nightwebs*. That was a long time ago in a galaxy far away, so I take leave to include it again here.

TOO NICE A DAY
TO DIE

Then she went back to where the cushions were, and quite simply and unstudiedly she lay down there, resting the back of her head on them.

There were no symptoms yet. To take her mind off it, she pulled a cigarette out of the package and lit it. Then, as was invariably the case whenever she smoked one, she took no more than two or three slow, thoughtful draws before putting it down on the ashtray and not going back to it again.

She thought of home. "Back home" she always called it whenever she thought of it. But there was no one there to go back to anymore. Her mother had died since she'd left. Her father and she had never been very close. He had a housekeeper now, she understood. In any case, she had an idea he much preferred the unfettered company of his cronies to having her back with him again. Her sister was married and had a houseful of kids (three by actual count, but they seemed to fill the place to spilling-over point). Her brother was doing his military hitch in West Germany, and he wasn't much more than a kid anyway.

No, there was no one for her to go to, anywhere.

It was beginning now. This was it. She wasn't drowsy yet, but she had entered that lulled state just preceding drowsiness. There was a slight hum in her ears, as if a tiny mosquito were jazzing around outside her head. It was too much effort to go ahead thinking things out any longer. She wouldn't beg the masked faces in the crowd for a friendly look anymore. She wouldn't hope for the slot in the letterbox to show white anymore. She wouldn't wish for the telephone to ring anymore. Let the world have its wakefulness—she'd have her sleep. She turned her face to one side, pressed her cheek against the cushions. Her eyes drooped closed. She reached for the soaked cloth, to put it across them, so that they would stay that way.

Then she heard the bell ringing. First she thought it was part of the symptoms. It was like a railroad-crossing signal-bell, far down a distant track, warning when a train is coming. She contorted her body to try to get away from it, and found herself sitting up dazedly, propped backward on her hands. Consciousness peeled all the way back to its outermost limits like the tattered paper opening up on some circus-hoop that has just been jumped through.

It burst into sudden, crashing clarity then. It was right in the room with her. It was over there in the corner. It was the bell on the telephone.

She managed to get up onto her feet. The room swirled about her, then steadied itself. She felt like being sick for a moment. She wanted to breathe, even more than she did just to live, as though they were two separate processes and one could go on without the other. She threw the two windows open one after the other. The fresh air suddenly swept into her stagnant mind, tingling like pine-needles in a stuffy place. She remembered to close off the key under the gas-burner in the kitchen-alcove. It had never stopped ringing all this while. She stood by it, stood looking at it. Finally, to end the nerve-rack of waiting for it to stop by itself, she picked it up.

The voice was that of a woman. It was slightly accented, but more in sentence-arrangement than in actual pronunciation.

"Hello? It is Schultz's Delicatessen, yes?"

In a lifeless monotone Laurel Hammond repeated the question word for word, just changing it to the negative. "It is not Schultz's Delicatessen, no."

The voice, hard to convince, now repeated the repetition in turn. "It is not Schultz's Delicatessen?"

"I said no, it is not."

The voice made one last try, as if hoping persistence alone might yet result in righting the error. "This is not Exmount 3-8448?"

"This is Exmount 3-8844," Laurel said, with a touch of asperity now at being held there so long.

Unarguably refuted at last, the voice became properly contrite. "I must have put the finger in the slot the wrong way around. I'm sorry, I hope you weren't asleep."

"I wasn't, yet," Laurel said briefly. And even if I had been, she thought, it wouldn't have been the kind you could have awakened me from.

Still coughing a little, but more from previous reflex now than present impetus, she hung up.

It took a moment for it to sink in. Then she began to laugh. Quietly, simmeringly, at first. Saved by Schultz's Delicatessen. She wondered why there was something funny about it because of its being a delicatessen. If it had been a wrong-number on a personal call, or on a call to almost any other kind of establishment, there wouldn't have been anything funny in it. Why was there something ludicrous about a delicatessen? She couldn't have said. Something to do with the kind of food they sold, probably. Comedy-food: bolognas and salamis and pigs' knuckles.

She was laughing uncontrollably now, almost in fullblown hysteria. Tottering with it, tears peering in her eyes, now holding her hand flat across her forehead, now over her ribs to support the strain of the laughter. No joke had ever been so funny before, no near-tragedy had ever ended in such hilarity. She only stopped at last because of physical exhaustion, because she was on the verge of prostration.

You couldn't go back and resume such a thing, not after that kind of a farcical interruption. Your sense of fitness, your sense of proportion, alone—any life, even the most deprecated one, deserved more dignity than that in its finish. She turned on the key under the burner again, but this time she lit a match to it. She put on water, to make a cup of tea. (The old maid's solace, she thought wryly: Trade your hopes of escape for a cup of tea.)

I'll see it through for one more day, she said to herself. That much I can stand. Just one more. Maybe something will happen, that hasn't happened on all the empty, barren ones that went before (but she knew it wouldn't). Maybe it will be different (but she knew better). But if it isn't, then tomorrow night—she gave a shrug, and the ghost of a retrospective smile flitted across her face—and this time there'll be no Schultz's Delicatessen.

She spent the vestigial hours of the night huddled in a large wing-chair, looking too small for it, her little harmonica-sized transistor radio purring away at her elbow. She kept it on the Paterson station, WPAT, which stayed on all night. There were others that did too, but they were crawling with commercials; this one wasn't. It kept murmuring the melodies of *Roberta* and *Can-Can* and *My Fair Lady*, while the night went by and the world, out there beyond its dial, went by with it. She dozed off finally, her head lolling over like a little girl's propped up asleep in a grown-up's chair.

When the sun made her open her eyes at last, she gave a guilty start at first, thinking this was like other days and she had to be at the office. But it wasn't. It was the day of grace she'd given herself.

When she was good and ready, and not before, she called the office and told Hattie on the reception-desk: "Tell Mr. Barnes I won't be in today." It was after ten by this time.

Hattie was sympathetic at first. "Not feeling too good, nn?"

Laurel Hammond said, "As a matter of fact, I don't feel too bad. I feel better than yesterday." As a matter of fact, she did.

The girl on the reception-desk still tried to be loyal to a fellow-employee. "You want me to tell him you're not feeling good though, don't you?" she asked anxiously.

"No," said Laurel, "I don't. I don't care what you tell him."

The girl on the reception-desk stopped being sympathetic. She was up against something she couldn't grasp. She became offended. "Oh," she said, "just like that you take a day off?"

"Just like that I take a day off," Laurel said, and hung up.

A day off, a lifetime off, forever off, what difference did it make?

Shortly before noon, with a small-sized summer hat on her head and a lightweight summer dress buoyant around her, she closed the door behind her, put the key in her handbag, and stepped out to meet the new day. It was a fine day too, all yellow and blue. The sky was blue, the building-faces were yellow in the sunlight, and the shady sides of the streets were indigo by contrast. Even the cars going by seemed to sparkle, their windshields sending out blinding flashes as they caught the sun.

Where did you go on your last day in New York? That is, on your *last day* in New York? You didn't walk Fifth Avenue and window-shop, that was for sure. Window-shopping was a form of appraisal for the future, for a tomorrow when you might really buy. You didn't go to a show. A show was an appraisal of the past, other people's lives in the past, dramatized. A walk in the park? That would be pleasant, pastoral. The trees in leaf, the grass, the winding paths, the children playing. But somehow that wasn't for today either. Its very tranquility, its apartness, its *lostness* in the center of the buzzing, throbbing city, she had a feeling would make her feel even more apart, more lost, than she felt already, and she didn't want that. She wanted people around her; she was frightened of tonight.

She got on a bus finally, at random, and let it take her on its hairpin crosstown route, first west along Seventy-second, then east along Fifty-seventh. Then when it reached Fifth and doubled back north to start the whole thing over, she got off and strolled a few blocks down the other way until suddenly the fountain and flower-borders of Rockefeller Center opened out alongside her. She knew then that was where she had wanted to come all along, and wondered why she hadn't thought of it in the first place.

It was like a little oasis, a breathing-spell, in the rush of the city, and yet it was lively, it wasn't lonely in the way the park would have been. It was filled with a brightly dressed luncheon-break crowd, so thick they almost seemed to swarm like bees, and yet in spite of that it was restful, it was almost lulling.

She went back toward the private street that cuts across behind it, which for some highly technical reason is closed to traffic one day in each year in order to maintain its non-public status, and sat on the edge of the sunwarmed coping that runs around the sunken plaza, as dozens of others were doing. She'd come here once or twice in the winter to watch them ice-skate below, but now the ice was gone and they were lunching at tables down there, under vivid garden-umbrellas. Above, a long line of national flags stirred shyly in a breeze mellow as warm golden honey. She tried to make out what countries some of them belonged to, but she was sure of only two, the Union Jack and the tricolor. The rest were strange to her, there were so many new countries in the world today.

And in every one of them perhaps, at this very moment, there was some girl like herself, contemplating doing what she was contemplating doing. In Paris, and in London, yes and even in Tokyo. Loneliness is all the same, the world over.

Her handbag was plastic, and not a very good plastic at that, apparently. The direct sunlight began to heat it up to a point where it became uncomfortable to keep her hand on it and she could even feel it against her thigh through the thin summer dress she had on. She put it down on the coping alongside of her. Or rather a little to the rear, since she was sitting slightly on the bias in order to be able to take in the scene below her. Then later, in unconsciously shifting still further around, she turned her back on it altogether, without noticing.

Sometime after that she heard a curt shout of remonstrance somewhere behind her. She turned to look, as did everyone else. A man who up to that point seemed to have been striding along rather more rapidly than those around him now broke into a fleet run. A second man sprang up from where he'd been sitting on the coping, about three or four persons to the rear of her, and shot after him. In a moment, as people stopped and turned to look, the view became obstructed and they both disappeared from sight.

It was only then she discovered her handbag to be missing.

While she was standing there trying to decide what to do about it, they both came back toward her again. One of them, the one who had given chase, was holding her handbag under one arm and was holding the second man by the scruff of the coat-collar with the other. What made this more feasible than it might otherwise have been was that the captive was offering only a token resistance, handicapped perhaps by his own guilty conscience.

"Whattaya trying to do? Take your hands off. Who do you think *you* are?" he was jabbering with offended virtue as they came to a halt in front of Laurel.

"Is this yours?" the rescuer asked, showing her the handbag.

"Yes, it is," she said, taking it from him.

"You should be more careful," he said in protective reproof. "Putting it down like that is an open invitation for someone to come along and make off with it."

The nimble-fingered one was quick to take the cue. "I thought somebody had lost it," he said artlessly. "I was on'y trying to find out who it belonged to, so I could give it back to them."

"Oh, sure," his apprehender said drily.

A policeman materialized, belying the traditional New York adage "They're never around when you want them." He was a young cop, and still had all his police training-school ideals intact, it appeared. Right was right and white was white, and there was nothing in-between. "Your name and address, please?" he said to Laurel, when he'd been told what had happened.

"Why?" she asked.

"You're going to press charges against him, aren't you?"

"No," she demurred. "I'm not."

His poised pencil flattened out in his hand. He looked at her, first with surprise then with stern disapproval. "He snatched your handbag, and yet you're not going to file a complaint?"

"No," she said quietly. "I'm not."

"You realize," he said severely, "you're only encouraging people like this. If he thinks he can get away with it, he'll only go back and do it some more. Before you know it, this city wouldn't be worth living in."

"You shouldn't be so good-natured, lady," another woman rebuked her from the crowd. "Believe me, if it was me, I'd teach him a lesson."

Yes, I guess you would, thought Laurel. But then, you have a whole lifetime ahead of you to show your rancor in. I haven't enough time left for that.

The prisoner had begun to fidget tentatively now that this unexpected reprieve had been granted him. "If the lady don't want to make a complaint, whaddye holding me for?" he complained querulously. "You got no grounds."

The quixotic young cop turned on him ferociously. "No? Then I'll find some, even if I have to make it loitering!"

"How could I be loitering when I was running full steam ah—" the culprit started to say, not illogically. Then he shut up abruptly, as if realizing this admission might not altogether help his case.

"Oh, won't somebody get me out of this, please!" she suddenly heard herself say, half in wearied sufferance, half in rebellious discontent. She didn't want to spend the little time there was left to spend standing in the center of a root-fast, cow-eyed crowd. Above all, she didn't want to spend it making arrangements to have some fellow-wayfarer held in a detention-cell overnight until he could be brought before a magistrate in the morning. She hadn't meant it for anyone to hear; she'd only meant it for herself. A plea to her own particular private fortunes of the day and of the moment.

But the man who had salvaged her handbag must have caught

it and thought it was meant for him. He put a hand lightly under her elbow in guidance and opened a way for her through the ever-thickening crowd.

"Sure you won't change your mind, lady?" the cop called after her.

"I'm sure," she said without turning her head.

Once detached from the focus of attention, they continued to walk parallel to one another along the flower-studded, humanity-studded promenade or mall that led out to the avenue. Past and past.

"You let him off lightly," he remarked. "Not even a lecture."

She nodded meditatively, without answering. It's so easy to be severe, she thought, when you're safe and intact and sure of your-self, as you probably are. But me, I feel sorry for the whole world and everyone in it today, even that poor cuss back there.

"I remember, in Chicago once," he was saying, "I had my wallet lifted out of my back pocket right while I was standing in line out-side the ticket-window in Union Station—"

They'd reached the avenue. With one accord, without even a fractional hesitancy or break in stroll, they turned and continued on northward, back along the way she'd originally come. It was done as un–self-consciously as though they'd known each other long and walked along here often. As naturally as though they had a common destination agreed upon beforehand.

She noticed it after a moment, but didn't do anything to disrupt it. On any other day, she realized, she would have been alerted, taut to separate herself from him. Not today. Until he said some-thing, or did something, that was out of order—not today. It was better to walk with somebody than to walk with nobody at all.

"—Things like that happen in all large cities, far more than they do in smaller places. I guess the huge crowds give them better cover."

"Aren't you from a large city yourself?"

"We like to think of ourselves as a medium-large city, but we're willing to admit we're no Chicago or New York. Indianapolis."

"Oh, where the speedway races are."

"Our only claim to fame," he said mournfully.

"I suppose you used to go to them regularly."

"I never missed a year until this year, and then I couldn't go because I was here. I saw it on TV, but it wasn't the same. Like a midget-race around a twenty-one-inch oblong."

Suddenly and quite belatedly—for if she'd had any actual objections they would have manifested themselves long before now— he turned to ask: "I'm not bothering you by tagging along like this, am I? I never realized I was until this very—"

"That's quite all right," she said levelly. "It's not a pick-up. And if it were, I'd be the one who did the picking."

"Nothing of the sort," he asserted stoutly.

That was the conventional, the expected answer, she recognized. But in this case it also happened to be true. A pick-up was a planned selection. This had been anything but that: unplanned, un–sought-after, by both of them. "Been here long?" she asked him, to get off the prickly topic.

"About six months now. I was transferred here to the company's New York office."

She asked him a question out of her own melancholy experience. "Did you find it hard to adjust?"

"Very. I was king, back home. The only fellow in a houseful of women. I got the royal treatment. They spoiled me rotten."

That, she decided, was not apparent on the surface, at least.

"My mother spoiled me because I was the only son in a family of girls. (My eldest sister's married and lives in Japan.) My elder sister spoiled me because she looked on me as her kid brother, and the younger one looked up to me as her big brother. I couldn't lose."

"And what did you do to entitle you to all this?"

"Brought home money, and could always be depended on to fix the car or the TV. without calling in costly repairmen, I suppose."

"That's fair enough value received," she laughed. They'd reached Fifty-seventh Street. This time they did stop, but not to part, to decide what next to do, where next to go, together. They both seemed to have tacitly agreed to spend the balance of the afternoon together.

"Have lunch with me," he suggested. "I haven't had any yet, have you?"

"It's late; don't you have to go back to the office?"

"I have the day off. The company's founder died, an old man of eighty. He hasn't been active in years, but out of respect to his memory all our offices everywhere were closed down for one day." He repeated his invitation.

"I'm not hungry," she said. "But I am thirsty, after that stroll in the sun. I'll take you up on an ice-cream soda."

They turned west for a short distance and stopped in at Hicks, at her suggestion. She waived a table, and they sat down at the counter.

"I stop in here every Christmas—or at least, the day before— and buy myself a box of candy," she told him.

His brows rose slightly, but he didn't say anything.

"I have to," she added simply. "Nobody else does."

"Maybe next time around," he said very softly, "you won't have to."

She had a chocolate malted and he a toasted-ham and coffee.

They walked on from there and entered the park at the Sixth Avenue entrance, and drifted almost at a somnambulistic gait along the slow curving walk that paces the main driveway there, then finally straightens out and strikes directly up into the heart of the park itself, toward the mall and the lake and the series of transverses.

Now they were becoming more personal. They spoke less of outside things, of things around them and things on the surface of their lives, and more of things lying below and within themselves. Not steadily, in a continuous stream, but by allowing occasional insights to open up, like chinks in the armor that was each one's privacy and apartness. Thus she learned many of the things he liked, and a few he didn't, and he learned them too about her. And surprisingly many of the things they liked were the same, and not a few of the things they didn't, also.

We're remarkably compatible, the thought occurred to her. Isn't it too bad we had to meet—so late.

It's not so late, she said to herself then, unless you will it to be so. And a daring thought barely ventured to peer forth around the corner of her mind, then quickly vanished again: It needn't be late at all, it can be early, if you want it to be. Early love, first love.

"What were you doing six months ago today, exactly to the day?" she asked him suddenly.

"It's difficult to pin-point it that closely. Let's see, six months ago I was still back in 'napolis. If it was a weekday, then I was slaving over a hot draught-board until five; after five I was driving back to the harem. If it was a Sunday I was probably out driving in the crate with some seat-mate."

Anyone special? she wondered, but didn't say it.

"Why did you ask that?"

She upped a shoulder slightly. "I don't know."

She did, though. How different my life might have been, she couldn't help reflecting, if I'd met you—as you seem to be—six months ago instead of today.

"Do you get lonely at times, since you've come to New York?"

"Sure I do." Then he reiterated, "I sure do. Anyone would."

"It's easier for a man, though, isn't it?"

"No it isn't," he told her quietly. "Not really. Oh, I know, girls think that a man can go a lot of places they can't, by themselves. And he can. But what does he find when he goes to those places? Loud, laughing companionship for an hour—or for an evening. Did you ever know you can be lonely with someone's loud laughter ringing right into your ear? Did you ever know?"

She had a complete picture, a vignette, of his life now, of that one aspect of it, without his having to say anything further.

"No," he said, "we're in the same boat, all of us."

They sat down on a bench overlooking the lake. They didn't talk any more for a while. After a time an indigent squirrel spotted them, made toward them by fits and starts, looked them over from a propitiatingly erect position, then scrambled up to the top-slat of the bench-back and ran nimbly across it. She could feel the fuzz of its tail brush lightly across the back of her neck. It stopped by his shoulder and sniffed at it inquiringly. "Sorry, son," he said to it. They both looked at it and smiled, then smiled to each other.

Completely matter-of-fact, and far too venal to waste time allowing itself to be petted empty-handed, it dropped down to the ground again and went lumbering off bushy-tailed across the grass.

The irregular picket-fence of tall building-tops around them on three sides in the distance looked trim and spruce and spotless as new paint in the sunshine. Much better than when you were up close to them. It was a brave city, she decided, eyeing them. Brave in its other sense; not courageous, so much as outstanding, commanding. It was too nice a town to die in. Though it had no honeysuckle vines and no balconies and no guitars, it was meant for love. For living and for love, and the two were inseparable; one didn't come without the other.

By about four in the afternoon they were already using "Laurel" and "Duane" when they said things to each other. Sparingly at first, a little self-consciously. As though not wanting to abuse the privilege each one had granted to the other. The first time she heard him say it, a warm, sunny feeling ran through her, that she couldn't contradict or deny. It was like belonging to someone a little, belonging to someone at last. While at the same time you at last had someone who belonged a little to you.

There is no hard and fast line that can be drawn that says: Up to here there was no love; from here on there is now love. Love is a gradual thing, it may take a moment, a month, or a year to come on, and in each two its gradations are different. With some it comes fast, with some it comes slowly. Sometimes one kindles from the other, sometimes both kindle spontaneously. And once in a tragic while one kindles only after the other has already dimmed and gone out, and has to burn forlornly alone.

By the time they left that consequential bench overlooking the tranquil little lake tucked away inside the park and started walking slowly onward in the general direction of her place, she was already well on the verge of being in love with him. And she sensed that he was too, with her. It couldn't be mistaken. There was a certain shyness now, like a catch, she heard somewhere behind his voice every time he spoke to her. The midway stage, the falter, between the assuredness of companionability and the assuredness of openly declared love. And when their hands accidentally brushed once or twice as they walked slowly side by side, he didn't have to turn his head to look at her, nor she to look at him, for them both to be aware of it. It was like a kiss of the hands, their first kiss. The heart knows these things. The heart is smart. Even the unpracticed heart.

They were beginning to be in love. The very air transmitted it, carried it to and fro from one to the other and back again. It had perhaps happened to them so quickly, she was ready to admit, because they both came to it fresh, wholehearted, without ever having known it before.

The June day was slowly ebbing away at last, in velvety beauty. The twin towers of the Majestic Apartments were two-toned now, coral where they faced the glowing river-sky, a sort of misty heliotrope where they faced the imminent starting-point of night. The first star was already in the sky. It was like a young couple's diamond engagement-ring. Very small, but bright and clear with promise and with hope.

New York. This was New York, on the evening of what was to have been the last day in the world—but wouldn't be now anymore. It had been a lovely day, a nice day, too nice a day to die.

They emerged at the Seventy-second Street pedestrian outlet, and sauntered north along Central Park West for a few blocks, until they'd arrived opposite the side-street her apartment was on. There they waited for a light, and crossed over to the residential side of the great artery, on which the headlights of cars in the deepening dusk were like a continuous stream of tracer-bullets aimed at anyone with temerity enough to cross their trajectory. There they stopped and stood again, a little in from the corner— in what they both hoped was to be only a very temporary parting—for she had to cross once more, to the north side of the street, to reach her door.

For a moment he didn't seem to know what to say, and for a moment she couldn't help him. They both turned their heads and looked up one way together. Then they both turned the opposite way and looked that way together. Then they looked at each other and they both smiled. Then the muteness broke suddenly, and they both spoke at once.

"I guess this is where—"

"I suppose this is where—"

Then they laughed and there was no more constraint.

She knew he was going to ask her to dinner—the first of all the many that they'd most likely share together—and he did. First she was going to agree with ready willingness, and then she remembered the things that were waiting upstairs. Waiting just as she'd left them, from last night. Waiting dark and brooding all through the sunny, glorious day—for tonight. The pillow on the floor, the cigarette-dish. The little bowl of water with the handkerchief still soaking in it, the blindfold that was to have shut out the sight of death. She shuddered to think of them now. But more than that, she didn't want them to still be there if she brought him up with her. She wanted to go up ahead and quickly disperse them, do away with them.

"Look, I'll tell you what," she said animatedly. "The next time—the very next—we'll go to a restaurant, if you want to. But tonight let's do this: Let's eat in. It's a good night for cold-cuts." She knew he wouldn't misunderstand if she had him up so soon after meeting him; she already knew him well enough to know that. "I want you to go to Schultz's Delicatessen, and pick up whatever appeals to you—I'll leave that to you—and bring it up to the apartment. I'll make the coffee."

"Schultz's," he said dutifully. "Where is it?"

"I don't know," she admitted with a chuckle and a hand-spread. "But I know you can find it in the directory. I can give you the number. It's Exmount 3-8448. It's the same as my own number, just twisted around a little. Promise me you won't go anywhere else. Only Schultz's. I have a very special reason for it. I don't want to tell you what it is right tonight, but someday I will."

"I promise. Schultz's and nobody but Schultz's."

They separated. She started across the street on a long diagonal. She turned and called back: "Don't take too long."

"I won't," he answered.

Then she turned unexpectedly a second time.

"I forgot to give you the apartment-number. It's Three—"

It was a big black shape. It was less like a car than an animal leaping at its kill. It was feline in its stealth, and lupine in its ferocity, big malevolent eyes blindingly aglow. Whether its occupants were drunk, or crazed with their own speed, or fleeing from some misdeed, it gave her no warning. It came slashing around the corner like the curved swing of a scimitar.

She was caught dead-center in front of it. Had she been a little to one side, she might have leaped back toward her companion; a little to the other, she might have leaped forward to the safety of the empty roadway alongside it. She tried to, but at the same moment it swerved that way, also trying to avoid her, and they remained fixed dead-center to one another. Then there was no more time for a second try.

She didn't go down under it. It cast her aside in a long, low parabola. Then it slowed, then it stopped, with a crazy shriek that sounded like remorse. Too late.

She lay flat along the ground, but with her head propped up by the sharp-edged curbstone it had crashed against. The sound it had made striking was terminal. There could be no possibility of life after such an impact.

And it had been too nice a day to die.

Ellery Queen's Mystery Magazine has been the genre's premier periodical since the day it was launched, not long before Pearl Harbor. During the fifties and sixties, however, one of its keenest competitors was the periodical variously known as *The Saint Detective Magazine, The Saint Mystery Magazine,* and *The Saint Magazine.* The Saint, of course, was created by Leslie Charteris (1907–1993) but the guiding genius behind these magazines was Hans Stefan Santesson (1914–1975), whom I was privileged to know in his last years. About a year before the enterprise folded, Santesson paid Woolrich $175 for periodical rights to "Mannequin" (*The Saint Magazine,* October 1966), which begins with several thousand words of pulsating terror-in-the-everyday and ends with the kind of bitter tragic ending that Woolrich could no more avoid than he could the bottle. The spirit of this never before collected gem is so close to that of the French forerunners of *film noir* like *Le Quai des Brumes* and *Le Jour Se Leve* that I half-suspect Woolrich saw those films, wrote the story back in the late thirties, and kept it buried in his files until almost three decades later.

MANNEQUIN

A s usual Leone was well in advance of the nightly seven o'clock stampede to quit work and go home. She was the first of them all to reach the bronze statuette with its spray of flesh-colored light-bulbs at the foot of the stairs on the main floor, while the rest of the girls were still only working their way down from the upper floors. Their clamor could be heard coming down the staircase ahead of them, they were like a bunch of noisy school-children when the dismissal-bell has rung.

"Take it easy there!" a voice ordered with phony severity as her feet came off the last step onto the marble floor with a flat, slapping impact.

Startled, she turned her head around, but without stopping, for seven o'clock was seven o'clock. It was only the lift-boy, grinning at her. "Who for? You?" she called back with arrogant unconcern as she rushed on ahead to meet the evening.

Then she remembered just in time, and stopped short while still shielded by the projecting stone-trim framing the street-entrance. Cautiously, she extended just the tip of her nose and the width of one eye out beyond it for a moment's precautionary look before-hand out where she intended going.

There he was again, big as life, waiting a few yards down the sidewalk from her, shoulders leaning back up against the building-wall. She had an unappealing (to her, anyway) glimpse of a loose-fitting knee-short olive gabardine topcoat, of a yeast-pallid complexion with a cigarette stuck into it, like a thermometer taking its owner's temperature.

Every night now for—how long? More than a week, wasn't it? And maybe even longer, for most likely she hadn't noticed him right away from the start.

She'd had men hang around and follow her before—every girl does—but not like this. They'd close in after a short distance, a few yards, a block or two, tip their hats, make an opening remark—and promptly get brushed off good and solid. He didn't do anything like this: never came any closer, never spoke or tried to speak to her. And most significant, and most unsalubrious, of all, after one or two long, hard, almost-paralyzing stares on the earlier nights, now he pretended not to be looking at her at all. She could never catch his eyes, even though she knew they had been on her only a second before, making her own respond in automatic reflex. It was this part of it that was the scariest and creepiest part of the whole thing. Being stalked is one thing, but this turned it from an amatory into a jungle-kind of thing.

In other words, he didn't give her any chance to defend her-self. How can you defend yourself when no offense has been committed—yet?

What did he want with her? What was it all about? Was he one of these screws, these oddballs, that get their kicks just looking at girls from a distance without going near them at all, and then go home and dream their dirty little dreams?

Whatever he was and whatever it was he was after, he kept gaining ground, encroaching on her more and more as night followed night, while still keeping the distance between them fixed and unbridged, as it was now. The first couple of nights, for example, she'd managed to disengage herself from him at the crowded bus-stop where she took her bus, simply by waiting until the last possible moment before she jumped on, and thus leaving him stranded back there in the crowd. After that he knew which bus she took, so it wouldn't work anymore. Then she shook him off by a reverse twist, maneuvering so that she succeeded in keeping him *on* the bus while she bolted off it without warning at her rightful getting-off place, and he was sent riding on foolishly past her to a destination that hadn't even been his in the first place. But it was a hard thing to do, and now he knew her right departure-point this wouldn't work a second time either. From there on in, it was a case of following her along the street at a carefully held-back distance, just enough to keep her in sight the whole time, and seeing which house she went in. She knew he was back there somewhere every step of the way, even though she couldn't see him at all times. All that remained now was for him to come up openly to the door and try to get into the house after her. And the moment he did that, the tables swung all the way around and the law was suddenly over on her side.

But for tonight at least the problem remained, there before her, a few yards away.

She had to get the bus to go home down that way, past him. If she turned and went up the other way, she stood a good chance of slipping away unnoticed, he might not recognize her from the back. But this meant walking around all four sides of a very long block, in order to get back to where the bus-stop was. And after a hard day, on her feet most of the time since early that morning, she couldn't face the thought. A better idea suddenly occurred to her. She turned and went back in again, almost as quickly as she had come out just now. She had to fight her way upstream against the surging tide of girls who were now pouring out the front entrance.

"Forget something, Leone?" a passing voice asked.

She didn't bother to answer.

She accosted the lift-boy whom she'd passed a moment ago on her way out. "Emile, are you finished with that newspaper you have stuck in your back-pocket?"

"Not quite," he said reluctantly. "I don't get much chance—"

She reached out and pulled it away from him anyway. "Don't be so stingy. I've shared parts of my lunch with you often enough, haven't I?"

"All right, keep it," he consented grudgingly. "Since when are you getting so studious? Next thing, you'll be reading a book."

She went back to the outer edge of the doorway again, keeping herself in just far enough out of sight of the waiter staked-out out there. She folded the paper over three times, so that it had bulk enough to stand upright by itself without sagging over at the top. Then she raised it to the approximate level of her face, covering the side of it that would have to pass closest to him, and held it that way with one hand. As if she was reading with her head turned aside to the paper, while she was walking along. It looked a little grotesque, but not to the point of conspicuousness.

She looked behind her and waited until a group of three had come out together, all going the same way obviously because they had their arms linked in comradely relaxation after the long hard working-day. She attached herself to them with a long swing around to their outermost side, and the four of them passed him abreast. Looking under the bottom of the newspaper, she could see his shoes standing there up against the building.

Curious, how you could read shoes, what they could tell you. She had never thought of this before. And in this particular instance, it was a shivery kind of lore. Shoes could indicate a whole bodily movement, could even indicate thoughts, even though you couldn't see any of the rest of the person, from the insteps up.

Black shoes, these were. Not expensive, plenty rundown. They'd been around a lot, today and every day. They had a patina of dust all over them. The hubs had a line of perforations running around them and in the center a design like a musical clef-sign, she wasn't sure what it was called.

One was flat on the ground toe-to-heel, the way any shoe usually is. The other, crossed over in front of the first, was balanced on its toe, the heel lifted clear. The fixed waiting position, waiting for her to show up, waiting for her to pass by. And as she did so, it went back to where it belonged, on the opposite side of its mate, and flattened out. The readying position: He sees someone. Is it me? Sure. Who else would it be? Now she was past. Looking backward, but still from under the newspaper's bottom, the hubs of both had swiveled, pointing themselves after her. The alerted, about-to-start-out position.

It hadn't worked. She hadn't really expected it to. It was just, she hadn't known what else to do, what other way to try to cover up.

Oh God, she thought with a sickish sinking sensation in her stomach, do I have to have *that* all over again now for the rest of the evening, until I can pull my flat street-door closed after me?

She couldn't look back anymore, not without turning her whole head around, which would have given her away (she was already given away, to him anyway: he had singled her out, he had isolated her from the rest of the crowd; what she didn't want to give away was the fact that she was on to this, knew that he had spotted her; she wanted to hang onto this one last flimsy buffer for whatever slight advantage there might possibly be in it). She didn't have to look back anyway, to know that if he hadn't already started on the prowl after her, he was going to from one minute to the next.

I may live a long time, I may live only a short one, she told herself with a bitter inward shudder, but somehow I'll never be able to look at a pair of men's shoes and not have a little bit of recollection of tonight come back to me.

At the corner she diverged from the other three. They kept going straight ahead, and she turned aside and went over to where the bus-stop was, just a little past the intersection. It was packed, this was the time for it to be that, and she wedged herself into the bee-swarm of people standing there all clustered together. Then later-comers, who kept coming every moment, closed her in and soon she was in the very core of the mass. You couldn't see anyone's shoes, there wasn't spread enough above to look down.

The first one wasn't hers, and then the next one was. She debated whether to hang back and let it go by. But this wouldn't fool him, he'd already been on it with her, he'd only hang back himself and let it go by. And of the two evils, she didn't want to be left there with him in a smaller crowd, or in no crowd at all. Which would soon happen if she let too many go by.

It was so packed you couldn't get inside it anymore, but she managed to get onto the round back-apron, which was left open except for a guard-rail, so that people actually bulged out over its sides. She put her newspaper up alongside her face again, this time with a weary, disheartened gesture, as if to say, what good is this doing me? Her head inclined a little, as part of the same mood.

Alongside her were a pair of snub-toed mouse-colored pumps. And over right next to them—hubs with a design like a musical clef-sign. Like a handwritten capital S with a slanting line through it.

The stops came and the stops went past, and they all quivered and jittered a little in unison, like in a toned-down version of that dance that once was called the Twist. Electricity turned the sidewalks into a dazzling beach, so that even the particles of sand mixed into the cement glittered like spilled sugar. Red, blue, green, white neons warred and clashed in a long perspective that finally ended with a blurred, flashing, spinning Catherine-wheel-effect as its focal point. Inside lighted show-windows wax figures engaged in Leone's own profession, that of modeling clothes, stared down their noses haughtily at the real people going by. Most of the show-windows were oblongs, but a few were ovals with the excess space left over outside their frames blacked-out, as if you were looking into a magnified peephole. Then as they left the more affluent section of the city behind and gradually worked their way into a lower-income district, these status-symbols became fewer and finally disappeared altogether. A movie-theater marquee blazed up like a real, live fire licking up the walls in back of it, proclaimed GIGI for an instant, and then was gone again as suddenly as it had appeared.

A teen-ager on a bicycle caught hold of something on the back end of the bus, lifted both legs to a near-horizontal position, and let it do her work for her and tow her along, blonde pigtailed hair slapping up and down behind her. The man sitting beside the nearest window to her turned his head her way and cautioned her with a typical middle-aged mildness. She gave a wild yell of derision for an answer, let go, and began to pedal madly and to actually outpace the bus and pull ahead of it. It was starting to slow for a stop ahead, anyway.

People had to get off, and this dispersed the pattern of the feet arranged around Leone as they pushed their way through and past them. Then when it had re-formed itself again, she saw that he had taken advantage of the wider amount of space now offered to move—not closer to her still, but further away, all the way over beside the opposite platform-railing. He was holding onto one of the upright stanchions and staring studiedly out and away from her on that side of the bus. All she could see was the back of one ear-rim and the nape of his neck. And a very thin sliver of profile, thin as the peel of an onion.

This was his technique for throwing her off-guard, for trying to keep her from noticing him, for seeming not to be doing the very thing he was doing. And it was a poor, pitifully poor technique indeed, she said to herself scornfully. What kind of a fool did he take her for, to expect her not to be aware of him, when he was always somewhere in the background, wherever she went, whichever way she turned. He must be a dope, among all the other things he was. But in this kind of situation, she reminded herself apprehensively, dopes can be a real danger, rather than not.

He had the inevitable cigarette fixed in his mouth, that he never seemed without, as though it were a part of it, like a malformed tooth projecting. Smoking wasn't permitted, even on the open, back parts of the buses, and for a moment she wondered half hope-fully if this mightn't be a means of having him thrown off. Then she saw that it wasn't burning, it was dry, and the conductor noticed it too at the same time. She could tell that by the way he craned his neck out a little, to get a look around to the front of the offender's face, then went back to his own affairs again without saying any-thing. But what it indicated was an implicit breaking of the rules and disregard for restraints, an outlaw type of attitude. And that, too, wasn't a good factor to involve in a situation like this.

Her face was white and stony-hard with a mixture of fear and hostility, the fear of the pursued, the hostility of the put-upon, that marred and muddied all its usual good looks. Her nerves were being drawn more taut all the time. Each evening she felt less con-fidence than the evening before, felt more of a desire for no reason at all to run and hide away. At times she could feel approaching panic lapping over her feet like a cold slowly rising tide that had to be held back, fought down. One of these times, if it kept up too much longer, control would burst and she would suddenly scream out in the middle of everyone and everything and go all to pieces.

And so the bus swept along, like a majestic ocean-liner, scat-tering the shoals of taxis and lesser cars before it as though they were tugs, while he looked out on his side at the buildings streaming endlessly by, and she looked down on her side at the platform-floor and brooded, eyes intent and furtive.

Her stop was coming up, there were only fixed stops on the buses, not improvised bell-signaled ones like in some other large cities, and the usual cat and mouse play was about to begin. Each one waiting to see the other move first. He didn't turn his head around, she didn't lift hers up from looking at the floor, and yet there was an electrical current of awareness going back and forth between them that almost prickled the skin and made stray hairs stand up singly.

She could feel the bus come to a stop under her feet with a soft slurring sensation and then a final shudder, and she heard the con-ductor call out the name of the stop.

She didn't move a muscle, didn't blink an eye. The shoes with the clef-signs were inert over there, too.

It was no use trying to pin him onto the bus by waiting to the last minute and then jumping for it. He could do that far easier than she could, with her stiletto-heels. She might fall and turn her ankle or something.

She suddenly came to life and gave herself a push away from the railing by main force, almost like a violent fling around the other way, like when you cannot tear yourself away from something, have to exert every ounce of will-power to do so. And sprang down to the ground just as the bus got started once more.

She didn't have to turn around to see if he had followed her off; she knew he had. She knew what he was doing now, because he had done it each time before. He would stand there at first, kill time there, so that she could get far enough up the street, put enough distance between them, to make his coming after her less conspicuous. In other words, so that he wouldn't be treading right at her heels. Her street was straight and sloped slightly upward, so that it was perfect for his purpose: He could keep her in sight without any difficulty from a distance of a whole block behind her.

His ways of marking time until she had gained enough of a lead were various. She had seen him do each one in turn, so she knew what they were. One was to gaze steadfastly in the direction in which the bus had gone, as if he intended walking along that way himself. Only he never did. Another was to actually start out in the reverse direction from her, going down the other way. Only to turn and retrace his steps once she was far enough off. One time he had gone behind a kiosk with a circular outer shell papered with colored three-sheets that stood on the twin corner to the bus-stop. From below the protective outer-rim, she could see his shoes standing there motionless, as she made her way up the sidewalk on the other side of the street. But they were pointed the opposite way. They were pointed outward. That told her it was a sham, in itself.

At the head of the second block to her flat—there were only two between it and the bus-stop—there was a neighborhood place where she always stopped in to eat when she came home from work. It couldn't be dignified by being called a restaurant, although it did have three or four little round white pedestal tables ranged along one wall. But these were mainly for reading your paper over a beer, or playing checkers, or honking your concertina for a quiet evening's relaxation. Everybody sat at the counter. It was run by a husband-and-wife team; she did the cooking, and he did the carrying and setting-out. The prices were sensible, for people who didn't have money to throw around.

Leone always sat on the third stool from where you came in. For no reason, just one of those little human habits that soon become fixed and firm. It became known as "Leone's stool." If it was taken when she came in, and she had to sit somewhere else, as soon as it was vacant she would move herself and her food back over to it again.

I shouldn't have to put up with it, she kept telling herself while she sat there waiting for her order to be prepared. But if she went up to a policeman and complained, *That man keeps following me everywhere I go*, she knew what the outcome would be. Has he come up to you and spoken to you? No. Has he stopped you in any way? No. And even if he were halted and questioned, she knew what the answer there would be, after he gave his side of it. He has a right to take the same bus you do. The buses are free for anyone to ride on. He has a right to walk along the same street you do. The streets are free for anyone to walk on. And the policeman would stroll off with a rebuking shake of his head.

If he would only *do* something, that I could get my teeth into! she whimpered inwardly. But he was just like a shadow. And like a shadow, he left no mark.

When she had eaten, she opened her handbag to pay for the inexpensive little meal, which had been fish, because it was a Friday. (She didn't claim to be a *good* Catholic, but she did claim to *try* to be one as far as possible, without going overboard.) What was left over in the bottle of the wine that had come with it, he put away for her for the next night. She wasn't a drinker.

While she was waiting for her change to come back, she held

the top flap of her handbag propped up and looked at her face in the mirror that was pasted to the underside of the flap. It was more a reflex of habit than a conscious act, an inattentive idle manipulation without any real meaning. And then suddenly she looked more closely, a second time. For, in the mirror, she saw not one face but two. Her own and—her persecutor's. Hers was in the foreground, enlarged, so that just a cross-section of one eye and cheek showed. His was in the background, a small-scale, peering in through the eating-place window. Yellow in the face of the light and shaped like an inverted pear. Or like a child's toy balloon beginning to sag because of losing some of its air. She couldn't see any of the rest of him, his face seemed to hang there disembodied against the night, to one side of the reversed letters E F A. Perhaps this was because he was bending over sideward to look in, and the rest of his body was offside to the plate-glass. It made him look like an apparition, a hallucination. Then suddenly, as he sensed that he had caught her eye, his face vanished.

She drew a deep breath of helpless frustration. Every move she made, watched. Every mouthful she swallowed. And she couldn't fight back, shake him off, there was no way. "He has a right to glance into a restaurant-window as he's passing by outside, anyone does," they would say.

He had a right to go here, he had a right to go there, he had a right to do this, he had a right to do that. He had a right to do everything, it seemed. But he didn't have a right to make her life miserable like this and put such fear into her like he was doing now!

She banged her empty coffee-cup down into its saucer so angrily that the owner of the place heard the sound and came over to her.

"What's the matter, coffee no good?" he queried solicitously. She was a good, steady, nearly everynight customer, and he didn't want her to be displeased.

"It's not the coffee that's the matter, it's something else that's the matter," she answered gloomily. "I was just thinking to myself, that's all."

He shrugged and spread his hands out, much as to say: Well, we each have a right to our own problems, after all.

She got up and went over to the door, and looked around from there, before stepping outside. Gone. There was no sign of him. Or more likely he was covered up in some doorway, and she couldn't distinguish him from here.

There was very little distance left to cover now, but she liked this last lap least of all. On the bus, there were people. In the eating-place, there was the proprietor. But the street was not an overly populous one, and this last had to be made all by herself, strictly on her own.

She almost ran the final few yards until she got safely to her own door. She blew a breath of relief. "Made it once more," was the thought in her mind. And the inevitable corrollary to it was, But some night I won't. The pitcher goes to the well once too often.

One foot safely within the open door, she leaned back far enough to turn her head and scan the street, down along the way she had just come from. Nothing, no one. But in a black door-embrasure a few houses down she thought she saw a wavy line that ran up and down one side of it, instead of being clear-cut and straight-edged like the other side was. That must be him, right there. She didn't hang back to investigate. The door closed after her, and the street kept what it knew to itself.

Winded from the long climb, it was a walk-up of course, she let herself into her own individual flat, and went over to the window to investigate before putting on the lights. She'd been doing this for the last few nights, now. She didn't need the lights to guide her, she knew the place so well, where everything was and how to go around it to avoid it.

The one thing he still might not know was which floor she was on and which window was hers, and she wanted to keep that final protective margin of error for as long as she could.

She went over to the side of the curtain and looked through from there, instead of dividing it in the middle, which might have been noticeable from the street.

She could see him down there, standing still down there. The olive topcoat stood out palely against the dinginess of the night. He wasn't moving. Only one thing moved about him, and that moved while remaining in a still position. That is to say, it pulsed or throbbed; it glowed and dimmed and glowed again. It had a beat to it. The little ember-dab at the end of his immovable cigarette. There was something freezing and horrid about the way that nothing moved about him but that. It had in it a suggestion of leashed ferocity. Of hot-breathing, crouched bated-ness. Of a mauler snuffing and scenting its prey-to-be.

She put her hands up to the sides of her head and pressed them hard. She told herself: I'm walled-in here. If only there were another way out of here, a back way, a side way, any way at all. I'd like to run and run, and never stop. To the ends of the night. To the ends of the earth.

Then she said to herself: Stop thinking things like that. This is your place. You belong in it. Nobody has the right to drive you out of it. He can't come in here. He can't come any nearer than he is now.

She bunched a fist and pounded it down against the top of a chair-back in helpless remonstrance. Why couldn't it have been any of the other girls I work with? Why did it just have to be me? That's not a very charitable thought, I know, but being in a fix like this doesn't give you time to be very charitable.

That's not love, down there. It can't be. Love sends you different kinds of messages. Love begins with talking first, with smiling. Love turns its face toward you, soft and shining, not hides it away from you. Love wants you to know it, not skulks in doorways in the dark.

It's not just ordinary everyday sex, either. *That* sends you different kinds of messages too. Blunt maybe, but honest and open in their crude way. A hard meaningful body-stare. A look that asks you, How about it? You willing? A jostling in the crowd. A brushing of the elbows, a nudging of the foot. Maybe an opening remark in a slurred undertone for no one else to catch.

No, this isn't that, either. This is something clammier than that.

He's sick inside his head. What else could he be but that? Some kind of a maniac. And if people like that once ever get their hands on you—She winced with superstitious horror.

After some time had passed she finally closed the door, which she had left slightly ajar so that its slender wand of outside hall-light would somewhat alleviate the total darkness of the room, and put on the lights. Enough of a time-lapse had now occurred for him not to necessarily connect her entry into the building with the going-on of the lights behind these particular windows. Or so she felt. And the dark held its own nervous terrors, anyway.

She had a little radio there, not much of a thing, but at least it worked. It coughed a lot, and it spit when you turned on any nearby light-switch, but at least it banished the silence of alone-ness. In a croupy, asthmatic, but better-than-nothing way.

She thought maybe a little soft music would take the edge off her nerves, she liked Viennese waltzes in particular, but a news-break was winding up just as she turned it on.

". . . meanwhile the war continues, no immediate end to it in sight.

"Back here at home, the second of three men who broke out of the penitentiary at (cra-a-ack, cra-a-ack, *cra-a-ack*), the so-called escape-proof jail, almost ten days ago has now been recaptured. His condition is serious from a gunshot wound suffered at the time of the break-out, during which two guards were also wounded. The third man, who is still at large, is considered especially dangerous, as he is believed to be armed. An all-out alert has been sounded. . . .

"The weather for the metropolitan area for tonight and tomorrow promises to be fair and . . ."

Her eyes had started to widen even before she reached out to the knob and closed it off. Her fingers remained on the knob long after the sound had died, while without realizing it she turned her head slowly toward the window and stared at it, her eyes now following the direction her thoughts had already taken swift minutes ago.

She took her hand away from the radio at last and started to go over toward the window. And without knowing it she was holding one hand clasped around her own throat, in the immemorial gesture of feminine fear and trepidation.

It couldn't be. There could be no connection. The one thing had nothing to do with the other. How could a runaway, a wanted man, to whom every moment counted, for whom cover-up was essential, how would he have the nerve to hang around a bus-stop night after night in full view of dozens of people, then ride the crowded bus with any number of faces pressed close to his?

And yet, who knows? A man in prison for any length of time becomes sex-starved, which is the same thing as insanity, if only temporarily. She happened to cross his path, his eyes fastened themselves on her and couldn't let go, his thoughts fastened themselves on her and wouldn't let go. And the rest of the sequence followed from there on in natural order. He started to follow her around. Since the sex-drive is stronger than thirst and stronger than hunger, perhaps, at least in his case, it was stronger also than his fear of being recognized, being recaptured, and being taken back to jail. A man in his condition has no sense of precaution, he loses it, it is blotted out, inevitably.

But all this was no solace. This was an explanation only but not a solution.

She had the edge of the curtain back a little now, and was looking down into the street.

He wasn't there, he'd gone, he'd moved on. Maybe he was still watching her from someplace else where she couldn't see him now, but there was no sign of him where he'd been before. The street was empty, and showed up in two shades of gray: a silvery-gray where the street-light washed over it in a wide ellipse that climbed partly up the walls of the nearer buildings, and a dark pewter-gray elsewhere. Then a taxi vibrated through it, making looming yellow moons that went out again after it had passed, but that was another matter.

No, he wasn't down there any longer. It was over for tonight. She phrased a little prayer to her guardian star, her destiny, her luck, whatever it was. Someone, something: "Oh, don't let it happen again tomorrow night. I can't stand any more of it. I'm ready to—*Please*, not tomorrow night. No more . . . No more . . ."

She started to cry. She hadn't cried since she was a little girl. Twelve, eleven maybe. Or if she had, not like this, not ever like this before. All of a week's accumulated and compounded terror started to pour out of her, like when a sluice-gate is suddenly pulled open, in gushes that ran down her cheeks, and when her hands went up as if to stem them, in trickles that still crept through the crevices between her fingers, while her body writhed and twisted with her own sobs and suppressed, stuttering breaths, her head supine on the seat of a chair and her legs drawn out on the floor.

And with that, as if in direct and vengeful rejection of her prayer, as if her pleas had cabalistically produced the very thing she wanted to avert, came the stealthy indicating-signal of someone there out-side the door. It wasn't a knock, or even a tap; it was like someone stroking the door with the nails of two fingers, trying to make as little sound as possible and yet attract her attention.

"Are you in there?" a hushed voice wanted to know, mouth pressed up close against the door-seam.

She jumped erect so swiftly that the whole thing was like a coil shooting free; one single motion and she was up and straight and quivering like the feelers of an insect caught under somebody's palm.

She didn't answer, she couldn't have, but maybe the stunned silence betrayed her. Such things can happen. There is a silence that vibrates, that speaks, that tells things.

It came again, the rasp, about like a match flicking sandpaper. And then a hiss to punctuate it, to attract.

"*Sst.* Are you in there?"

She went over by it on hushed tipped feet and stood there close to it, face lowered intently, her balance in flux but afraid to touch it for support even from the inside.

Then it breathed a name, the door, it spoke a name.

"*Gerard.*"

And suddenly no door had ever opened so fast. Suddenly there *was* no door anymore. Just two in love, trying to make themselves one. Suddenly all the world was heaven, noon-bright, and there was no such thing as fear, even its very definition had faded away from the language-books and left just a blank space where it once had been.

She didn't even wait to see if it was he. There was no time to look at him, scan his face. It didn't matter, her heart knew. Her arms went around him like the back-fling of a cracked whip. Her head was on his shoulder, her face was beside his face, and all she saw was blank wall opposite, but her heart knew him just the same.

His voice was low and cautioning in her ear, and a slight move his head made told her he had looked over his shoulder guardedly. "Not out here. Hurry up, let me get inside first!"

She reclosed the door after them. He went over to a chair, fixed the top of it with his hand first as if afraid it would get away from him, and then sank into it loose as a puddle of water. She thought she never had seen such exhaustion before. It was a collapse.

She couldn't take her eyes off him. She moved first to one side of him, then to the other, then directly before him, slightly crouched, her hands to her knees. "I can't believe it, I can't, I can't! When did you get out?"

He raised his head, which had sunk low almost to his chest with weariness, and looked at her. "I didn't. I broke out."

She gave a quick head-turn across the room, then back again. "God in heaven! You're one of those three, on that broadcast I heard—? I never dreamed—They didn't give any names."

"They never do," he said dully. "We're just people without names. That's so anyone on the outside who might know us, want to help us or hide us, won't hear about it."

"I didn't even know where they'd sent you."

"I didn't want you mixed up in it at all. Did you get that note I smuggled out to you, after I was picked up and being held for trial?"

"A woman I didn't know sat down next to me one night, at that little place I eat down the street. She folded her arms on the counter, and with the outside one slipped it to me underneath the one that was next to me. Then she got up and walked out without a word."

"That was Malin's wife," he said without emotion. "He was the one killed a week ago Monday. Three little kids."

"It wasn't in your handwriting, but I knew it must be—"

"He passed her the message on from me, and had her write it down."

"I can still remember every word of it by heart," she said devoutly, like when you recite your rosary. " *'Stay out of it. Keep away from the trial. And if I'm sent up don't come down and try to say good-bye to me before I go. If they question you, you don't know me.'*

"I kept it for two whole days, and then I did away with it," she said tenderly, as if she were speaking of a love-poem.

"That was the thing to do," he approved.

Outside in the hall before, without looking at him at all, she had known him. Now, inside *and* looking at him, she almost *didn't* know him anymore. The terrible changes the thing had brought to him. The dust of the wayside and the soot of the box-car that were no longer just surface grime anymore but gave the appearance of having gotten under his skin and made him look permanently dingy. The deep sweat-etched lines of intolerable strain and tiredness that would never quite go away again. The hunger of the indrawn cheeks and the out-staring eyes.

He'd been so young once and been so spruce and eye-pleasing. He wasn't now. And strange is the way of the heart: She loved him now more than she ever had then.

She saw him dipping two fingers into the patch-pocket of the caked, bedraggled blue denim shirt he had on, trying to locate a cigarette. All he could find was a charred butt, put out short to save for the next time.

"Wait," she said, and got hold of a box of them she had in the place there, took one out and lit it for him. Then she passed it to him from her own mouth.

"You didn't used to smoke," he remembered.

"I still don't, much. I've had these, I don't know how long. One of the girls at the place gave them to me once, in a fit of generosity. They weren't her brand, or something."

He took the cigarette out of his mouth and looked it over, and it seemed to suggest some other train of thought to him.

"You haven't been going with anybody while I've been away?"

She looked him quietly and simply in the eye. "*Is* there anybody but you—to go with? I didn't know, you'll have to tell me."

She thought of that man on the street and on the bus—and he already seemed so long ago and half-forgotten, like something in a last week's dream—and she decided not to tell him about it. Men were a little peculiar about some things, even the best of them, you had to understand that. He might think, even if he didn't come out with it, that she must have given him some slight encouragement in the very beginning to trigger the thing off like that, and she didn't want him to. It was all over now, anyway. She wasn't alone anymore.

"How'd you get into the house here? Did *she* see you, downstairs?"

"I've been in it since early this afternoon. I came along intending to take just a quick look and see if I could figure out from down below whether you still lived up here or not. Then I saw this junk-cart standing out at the door, and two men were unloading somebody's furniture and taking it into the house—"

"That's the flat on the floor below," she explained. "The old lady there died last week. And it's been rented over."

"So on the spur of the moment, while they were inside, I picked up a chair from the sidewalk and went in after them. I walked right by her. She thought I was with them, I guess. Then when I got up to the floor they were on, I put it down outside the door while their backs were turned, and came on up here to your floor. I found a closet at the back of the hall for keeping rags and pails, and I crouched down inside it. She came to it once and tried to get the door open, but I held onto the inside of the knob with both hands, and she gave up finally and went away again mumbling something about getting a carpenter to come and plane it down.

"I knew if you still had your modeling-job, you wouldn't be back until much later. Then when the people started coming home from work, I had to try to translate their footsteps on the stairs. A man came up first. Then a woman; I knew it wasn't you, because I heard her call out to some kid on the inside, 'Open the door for me, I have my arms full of bundles.' Then I heard a young step, a girl's step, and it seemed to go in right about where your door was, so I waited a couple minutes more and then I took a chance and came out."

"When did you eat last?" she asked him.

"So long ago I can't remember," he said dully. "While I was still out in the open country, it was easier. Farm-women would give me handouts sometimes, if I was careful how I came up to them. But once I'd worked my way into the city, that stopped. In the city they don't give you anything without money. And how could I stand still long enough to earn any? I snatched an orange, I think yesterday morning. I ate the skin and all."

She closed her eyes for a moment, appalled.

"I have to get these things off," he said, bending down to his ravaged shoes. "My feet are like hamburgers."

Then when she saw the stains of the old blood that was already black and the newer blood that was still rusty-colored, "Oh those *feet!*" she moaned in unutterable compassion, clapping her hands together.

She got a basin of water and some cloths, and getting down on her knees before him gently tried to treat and soothe them. And when she had, wrapping a towel around one, held it up and pressed the side of her face against it. "Cut it out," he said embarrassedly. "What am I, a baby?"

"I'll have to go to the pharmacy and get some kind of a salve."

She heated up and brought him coffee-and-milk, and some bread and other stuff that she always kept there for her own use in the mornings, and sat opposite him at the little pushed-over-to-the-wall table, watching him eat. Once she reached over and stroked back a tendril of hair that had come down before his eye.

"What are you going to do?" she murmured finally, low, as if afraid to hear the answer.

He blew out the match he was holding. "One thing I'm *not* going to do, is ever go back there again alive. For me, that's over."

"But how—?" The worry on her face finished it without words.

"All I need is a breathing-spell, one day or two, to rest up and clean myself up."

"You'll stay here with me," she said briefly, as if there were no sense in even discussing that part of it. "We'll manage it somehow. But then—?"

"I know a guy who'll fix me up some fake papers. With them, I can get some job on a ship, outbound. Jump it at the other end, and start all over again clean. It doesn't matter where. Then as soon as I get my bearings, you—you'll come, won't you?"

"*Any*where," she said fiercely. "The minute you say the word."

"It's asking a lot," he admitted, as if telling it to himself.

"What is a lot?" she said. "And what is a little? There are no measurements when you—care. It is all one, one-size."

He sat staring into the distance, hunched over his own lap, hands folded together across his knees. She wondered what he saw there—their future?

After a while she told him about it. This was the time to, to make them more one. When he needed somebody to be close the most.

"I'm going to have your baby. Our baby."

"You fool," was what he said to that at first. "You could have gotten out of that. You've been around." And then he took the hardness out of the words by putting the flat of his hand on top of her head and rumpling her hair in a rough-neck and yet an almost tender sort of way, and scraped his knuckle past her chin.

"I didn't want to," she said softly. And left the "get out of it" part unsaid.

He was testing it in his mind. "A guy likes a kid of his own. To show that he passed through this world at least once. Imagine, *me*. Me of all people. A kid of my own. How the old crowd would laugh. Lejeune, that was too fast for any cop. And too slick for any woman. Well, the cops got me first. And a woman's got me now."

He looked grimly up at her from under his thick black lashes, which were the only thing left of his old looks. "You take good care of it, hear? You watch over it careful. If anything happens to it, I'll break your loving jaw."

She framed his face with her hands and kissed him, laughing but with a softness in her eyes that was more than just the light in the room shining back from them.

"You haven't even got it yet, and you're already growling like an old, experienced father."

When she put out the light, they lay close to one another for a while, quiet and happy just to be together. Then in the darkness, his soft murmur sounded in her ear.

"Let's make doubly sure, shall we?"

Tomorrow was the big opening, the most trying day of the year for a fashion-house mannequin. Like an opening-night is for an actress. She had to be there early, she had to be on her toes. And she'd been rehearsing all day, today just past. But—he was Gerard, her Gerard and nobody else's.

"Let's," she whispered back to him in the dark.

Later, he was asleep but she was still awake, thinking about them and what their chances were. Something from the radio broadcast came back to her: "This man is believed to be armed." And then something that he had said himself. "I'm never going back there again alive." She wondered if he really had a gun on him or not. She hadn't thought about it the whole time until now. Now that she recalled, she hadn't been able to see one anywhere on him. But if he did have one on him, it might cost him his life. Men were so quick about using things like that, and he in particular was so hot-headed, she knew that well.

He was sleeping with his shirt on, turned toward her, lying on his side. She reached out carefully and felt his shoulder, the upper-most one, through the wide-spread gap of his shirt-front. There were several bands of tape spliced around it and going through his armpit. She reached around to the back, to his shoulder-blade, and the gun was there, bedded in some kind of a makeshift holster. She couldn't tell what it was (canvas perhaps or gunnysack fiber, hurriedly put together along the way) except that it held it there, so that he could swing his opposite arm up overshoulder and pull it out with one swift move.

She started to ease it slyly out, a millimeter at a time. There was nothing to impede it, the impromptu holder or sac had no top to it, there was no lid to snap up as a leather one would have had. Then when it was halfway out, she stopped and began going over the possible consequences of what she was about to do.

No, it wasn't fair to do this, disarm him in his sleep this way like a thief in the night, leave him vulnerable to his enemy. It wasn't fair; he had to have his chance to defend himself. Right or wrong, she wouldn't be the one to do this to him. If their positions had been reversed, she couldn't see him doing this to her, she knew his attitudes too well.

She let the gun slide back in again, and he went on sleeping, never knowing.

In the morning she dressed swiftly and quietly, and left him there still sleeping in the pale-blue early morning light, his face looking like a pale-blue terra cotta, with a little scribble alongside the bed for him to find in case he awoke.

"I've only gone down the street a minute to get some foodstuffs. If you hear someone at the door, don't jump at them, it's only me. L."

On her way back inside, burdened with bags and bundles like an overladen coolie, she ran into the fat woman who was in charge of the house.

The latter grinned with a wizened monkey-like expression as she saw her go by. "It pays to buy in large quantities like that, it's more economical," she observed. "You almost have enough there for two people."

Leone halted and whirled around to face her. "Have I?" she challenged.

"One shouldn't be alone too much," the woman went on.

Now what does that mean? Leone wondered, beginning to tighten up inside. She said, "If you mean me, haven't I always been? What about it?"

"After a while you—you know, you start talking to yourself."

She overheard us, last night, Leone told herself, with a cold stricken sensation taking hold of her around the heart. "What do *you* do, come up and listen outside my door?" she flared up angrily. "Well, the next time, let me know what I say to myself! I want to know how good I sound!" And she swung around and continued on up the stairs, but with a chipper indifference she was far from feeling.

He was still asleep; he'd never even heard her leave. She put her things down, and then went over to where he was lying and stood looking at him for a moment. One of those gravely sweet, inscrutable looks that love can give at times. Then she bent over and kissed him, soft as a petal dropping, on the forehead.

His lids flickered and started to go up several times, then lost their battle and settled down once more. But a spark of consciousness had been ignited that was slower in dying down again. He went "Mm," and his head stirred a little, and she knew that he could understand her, even though he seemed not to. Or he would remember what she had said when he fully woke up.

"Listen, I have to go now. I'll be late getting back, this is our big day. Are you listening? When you get up, lock the door on the inside. I'm going to try to fix it with the old woman downstairs, to keep her from coming up here, if I can. And keep away from the windows, don't go near them and try to look out. There are some cigarettes in there, I put them where you can find them, and everything else you need. I brought you in a couple of magazines, too, to help pass the time with. On my way home I'll try to stop off and buy you a clean shirt and underwear, if I can find a place that's still open. Now rest, rest all you can. I only hope God keeps His eye on you for me."

She bent and kissed him twice more, this time once on each cheek.

From the open door she looked back. His arm, which had been

too near the edge of the bed, over-balanced and fell loosely down and dangled there limply over-edge.

She went back a moment, lifted it, and put it back under the cover. Then she tucked it a little to hold it.

Then she went out and closed the door behind her. At the head of the stairs, before starting down she opened her handbag and took out some money. About all she had, all she could afford, leaving just a little over for the bus and to buy him a shirt. She folded it tactfully out of sight under her palm and went down the stairs.

"Here," she said going over to the fat woman, and held out her hand.

"What's this for?" the fat woman said, looking at it. "You're all paid up until the first."

Leone said off-handedly: "You don't need to go up to my place to look after anything today. In fact I wish you wouldn't. It'll hold. Some other time. I'll let you know."

The superintendent pinned her with a look that was undecided between being shrewd and sympathetic.

Leone suddenly threw discretion aside. It seemed the only thing to do. "Look, you're a woman. There's a time in life when—well, someone means a lot to you. You had the time come to you once too, yourself. Try to remember it now and—make an allowance, will you?"

This unkempt, heavily-fleshed hostile, with a shadowed upper lip and a mole on one cheek, who could be so shrill about disturbing noises and so steely about an overdue rent, showed a surprising streak of empathy that Leone hadn't known she'd even had in her until now.

"We're all sisters, all of us," she said. She prodded money back down into the slashed hand-pocket of Leone's raincoat. "All in one big family." She chopped the edge of her hand reassuringly against Leone's upper arm.

As she went on out to the street Leone knew, at least, that she had her on her side.

When she got to the job, Leone raced up the stairs to the dressing-rooms as though she were pursued by devils. Those same stairs she had come bounding down so buoyantly at seven the night before. So much had happened to her in-between, her whole life had been altered. Here too, the place had changed almost beyond recognition from its workaday look. The huge alabaster vase at the back of the ground-floor corridor was filled with fat, puffy chrysan-themums in deftly blended tones of orange, rust, and copper. The glass doors leading into the display-room stood wide open, with a uniformed attendant stationed outside to collect invitations, and a discordant buzz of voices coming from inside, punctuated intermit-tently by the chirpy, twittering sounds of a small stringed orchestra tuning up. On the stairs and in the lower hall, there was a long roll of blue-velour carpeting that began on the floor above and stretched like a rivulet of escaping fountain-pen ink right down to the front door-sill. It stopped there so abruptly you almost expected it to continue out into the street beyond, but it didn't.

There was no one in sight at the moment who could clock her lateness, only the impudent lift-boy, at Prussian-stiff attention before his cage and not at all impudent today. On the stairs she narrowly missed running head-on into a butler or caterer of some sort carrying a hamper of champagne-bottles, who was coming down them just as she hurled herself up. An agile swerve, and the collision was averted.

Everybody was already in the dressing-room and in their places when she came hustling in. The "daytime-wear" group were all dressed already and ready to parade on out. Leone's own group, the "evening-wear" group, were all undressed already and having their faces made-up by a man in shirt-sleeves with a portable kit on his lap, untroubled by all the nudity about him. Renard did nothing by halves. He had it all jotted down on a chart with which she had supplied him; each triangular combination of mannequin's complexion, color of gown, and make-up required to go with them, had been worked out days before.

Paradoxically though, while he gave each face that came before him the expert touch it needed and passed it on improved, a bluish growth showed on the lower part of his own, hairs sprouted at right angles out from his eyebrows and from the pits of his ears, and the creases ridging his forehead were emphasized by grime that looked as if soap had not disturbed it for weeks. But then he wasn't to go on public view, in one of the greatest selling competitions in the world.

One arm recurrently out to the wall to help her keep her balance in the jostling crowd around her, Leone stripped, literally down to the skin—for a Paris original always carries along its own indicated foundations—stuffed her personal things into her locker, pinned a towel around her waist, for the sake of comfort on the hard-surfaced wooden bench if not modesty, and sat down to wait her turn, elbow resting on the mirror-shelf in back of her and head propped in her upraised hand.

When the make-up man had finished work on her, he brushed off some excess powder that had fallen over her breasts with a completely impersonal swipe of the hand that set them dancing for a second or two.

A moment later the hairdresser took over, began switching her head this way and that as if her hair was taffy that he was pulling.

Suddenly the head of the establishment, Renard herself, stood behind her, studying her face and hair-do in the mirror before them both. Leone's that is. She nodded approval, gave an upward hitch with one finger. Leone stood up. A brassiere was brought, attached.

"She's too hefty," Renard complained. "This number calls for a moderate bosom, not a pair of ostrich-eggs like that. Tighten it up a little."

Leone's eyes crossed briefly and inadvertently as the already tourniquet-like constriction was redoubled around her.

"Hold it in. Hold it in. *Breathe in!*" Renard said sternly, giving her a slap across it.

Leone went "ifffff" like the up-swing of a bicycle-pump handle.

Then finally, like the rains of April it was named for, the creation, the original, descended on her and drenched her in slanting streaks of bead-raindrops and fuming mists of silver-gray tissue.

And the magic that Renard always wrought had come to pass. A bewildered, skinny, dead-for-sleep girl became a thing of mystic allure. Every man's dream of Woman, that dream he never overtakes. Every woman's dream of herself, that she never achieves.

Everyone's hand was on her. They backed away, they closed in, they pulled, they pushed, they tucked, they tugged, they smoothed, they crimped. They could do nothing with it. It had been perfect to begin with.

Surrounded by a cluster of people still busily fussing at her, she was led out to the top of the stairs and poised there, as though they were about to throw her headlong down to the bottom.

The customary time-table, or pace, was that as one girl completed two entire circuits of the show-room, the next started down the stairs. They usually met and passed on the lower steps. This gave the briefest pause between numbers, just long enough for the viewers to adjust their minds for the new selection but not long enough to create an awkward delay or gap.

The go-ahead signal was given, and Leone took her first, baptismal step down, with the hypnotic, pavane-like slow-motion of the professional mannequin, feeling her way with the tip of her foot as though she were blindfolded.

There was an urgent, surreptitious follow-up footfall on the stairs behind her, someone thrust a catastrophically forgotten show-handkerchief into her hand, and then whoever it was retreated again into safe anonymity.

She and the other mannequin passed one another. They didn't look at each other, they weren't supposed to.

She reached the foot of the stairs, her course leveled off, and the display-room was now hers alone.

There were some people standing out here, in the space between the stairs and the display-room entrance, all men, who either had shown up late and found all the seats taken, or who wanted to hold private discussions of their own out here, or whatever the reason was.

Those who had their backs to her, and some did, turned around to face her as she started to glide past them. All but one; he kept himself turned away from her. But the man he was standing in front of, looked at her hard and steadily. They all were doing that of course, but there was this difference: The rest were looking at the gown she was merchandising, *he* was looking at her face and only her face. Then the corner of his mouth moved a little, saying something secretive to the man with his back to her. And she saw the latter nod his head, she could see him do that from the back. And right after that, *he* turned, too.

And they were looking at each other again, she and that face from the crowd, that was always there, wherever she went, each night now the whole week past. Outside the door here where she worked, and on the bus, and peering into the cafe, and under the windows of her flat.

She faltered in her stride, she couldn't help doing so, and gave a sagging little knee-dip for a moment, then picked up her swing again and went at a stylized stroll into the packed salon behind, but with a feeling as if there was a knife in back of her poised between her shoulder blades.

She heard a voice introduce: "April Rain, for the important moments of your life," and thought, This is one of mine, but it isn't a good one.

All she was conscious of was tiers of pinkish-beige ovals looking her over from all sides. Even when she felt secure and at ease, she never looked directly into their faces, she had been taught not to. It would have injected a personal note that would have been out of place; more to the point, it would have distracted attention from the very thing she was trying to draw attention to. And now, after seeing him standing out there, she wouldn't have dared look into their faces, it would have broken her up in no time. So she fixed her eyes on an imaginary guide-line along the walls just high enough to miss the tops of their heads, and kept them on it whichever way she turned. And all the while she kept thinking, I have to pass him a second time, on my way out, to get back to the stairs: oh, my God!

There were murmurs of admiration and interest as she moved

around the room, which swelled now and then to a sustained buzz or a spattering of applause. Individual remarks stood out here and there. "*Very* good!" "A natural!" "She always comes up with something!"

In the meantime she kept trying not to swallow (which would have been noticeable along her throat-line), and her tongue felt as if it were drowning in her own fears.

Every now and then she had to make a complete turnaround, to show off the back of the gown as well. The whole routine or technique was a simple one, that could be picked up in fifteen minutes. She had. What your job depended on more than that was word-of-mouth reputation, of having been known to work at one of the other big houses previously. In other words, once you were in, you were in. *Until* you were in, you couldn't get in.

One corner was past, now the second. There remained only one more and then she would be back to the door, that dreaded door, again. And he was waiting out there beyond it. Whoever he was and whatever he was, one thing was sure, he wasn't good. He wasn't good news. Maybe if she—just went by fast, without stopping to think about it and without looking at him, he wouldn't have a chance to—do whatever it was he was going to do. And the other one with him, who was he? Birds of a feather? Maybe he was just some fellow-standee he'd struck up a conversation with. There was a certain freemasonry among men of that kind.

She was out through the door now and about to break into a headlong spurt. And then she suddenly had to slow it down again. Renard was standing there, come to drink in her own triumph. People all around her showering congratulations, but her eye didn't miss a trick. Her behind-the-hand whisper reached Leone as she was about to go past her. "Don't hurry so. You may catch that on something and damage it."

The voice of authority, that could not be disregarded. She tapered to a gracious walk, and one of the two men immediately made a signal to her. Not *him*. The other one.

She didn't stop for it, so they came over to her instead, stood alongside her one on each side, peering closely with professional interest and professional pitilessness. *Not* at the gown this time, but at her. Only at her. She halted, with fear-glazing eyes.

"Your name Leone Aubry?" said one, pointing with a slim putty-green cigar he was holding between his fingers.

"What do you want?"

"*Is* your name Leone Aubry?"

"*Yes*, but what do you want?"

"You're coming with us, is what we want."

Then he showed her something, in a sort of wallet-carrying-case that split open across the top and uplidded, instead of opening along its edge like the usual money-carrying wallet does. She could make out the city's coat-of-arms, then he squeezed it closed, with the same hand he was holding it in.

The police. She knew now who they were. She clapped both hands to her mouth, and held them there, at cross-angles to one another. People started to turn and look curiously at her. Finally she let her hands drop again, so that she could speak without impediment. "What for? What have I done?" she asked them, in a sort of piteous, passive, boxed-in panic.

"We don't stand and talk to you here, in a place like this."

And the other one, the one who had been at her heels for a week, surly: "We didn't come here to buy our wives dresses, you know."

"Can't I go upstairs and change for a minute?" Just a minute more, anything for a minute more. You don't value freedom when you have unlimited lengths and stretches of it. Then when you don't have it anymore, how sweet just one extra minute of it is.

"No delays, you're coming right as you are. Put a coat on over you."

"But I can't take it out of here. It belongs to the house. I'm not allowed to."

Renard intervened. "What's the trouble? Is this an arrest?"

"An interrogation."

"Then please, gentlemen, no commotion. We've all worked too long and too hard for this, to have it spoiled." And with that typical logic which had made her the successful business woman she was, she pointed out: "The dress is my property. You can't take it out of here unless you have an order for its confiscation. Which you don't have. Therefore the dress and the girl must be separated first before you can take the girl."

One of them scratched his head and mumbled in an aside to his partner something about "not only designs clothes but she's a lawyer in the bargain."

"Go upstairs, Leone," Renard said with a sort of localized sympathy. That is to say, a sympathy that was given freely and for the asking, until it collided with or obstructed her own one and only concern, the making and selling of dresses. Then it stopped and didn't go any further. "Maybe it'll work itself out all right. Let me hear from you, if you can."

The three of them stood and stared after her, watching her heels flicker up the stairs like little flesh-toned mallets tacking down a carpet.

Upstairs in the hall, where there were no longer guests to be reckoned with, she made a bee-line for the dressing-room door, elbowing everyone aside and almost stumbling in her haste to get in there. The door clapped shut after her.

"Somebody help me to get out of here, quick!" she gasped.

They all turned on the long dressing-bench and stared at her with one accord.

"There're two men down there—"

"Two?" one girl said. "There must be twenty-five."

"This isn't anything to joke about. These two are cops. They're standing right down at the foot of the stairs. They're waiting to take me with them."

"How do you know it's you?"

"They said so right in front of Renard."

She had the dress off now. She was shivering from head to foot, and not from the cold, either.

"By why you? What've you been up to?"

She summed the whole tragic little story up in just two words. "My fellow."

"What is he, a loser with the cops? I had one like that once. Funny, how those guys always make the best kind of—"

Somebody gave a scream of synthetic modesty, of protest actually more than modesty, and one of the two from downstairs was standing in the open doorway motioning to her with his head. "Are you going to come out of there, or do you want me to come in and get you?"

The inescapability of the thing made her lose her nerve for a minute; the brief reprieve to get out of the dress was now over, there was no chance of any further out, and she was right up face to face with the most precarious of all prospects: apprehension by the police on a provable and grounded charge. Anyone would have quailed.

She looked around at each of the other girls in turn, in a last-minute appeal for aid that was sunk even before it was spoken. "Marthe!—Desi!—Nico!—We all work here together. I see your faces day-in day-out, and you see mine. Isn't there one of you will stand up beside me now and help me, when I need it the most? I don't want them to take me, I don't want to go!"

They just looked at her helplessly. One of them lamented: "What can *we* do?" And another advised with sorrowful resignation: "Go with them, Leone. You have to anyway, and it takes all the fortitude out of it if you welsh."

The ghost of a mannequin, a few minutes ago so radiant and chic and lovely, came out of the dressing-room door and stood there looking at the two men who were waiting for her outside it. Not fashion-show johnnies though, by any means.

She was immediately boxed-in between them and trundled along. They were not gentle, not gentle men, because it was not their business to be. "All right, hup, downstairs we go."

"What is it?" someone asked as she went past the crowd on the lower floor.

"She's being arrested. First time in the history of a fashion show that's ever happened, I'd like to bet."

They took her in an unmarked police car back to the street where she lived. It knifed along glossy-black and somber, and above the jurisdiction of the stop-and-go lights, its siren moaning a dirge that fitted this terrible death-ride. Hope and love and freedom all in one going to their funerals.

And when they turned in there the street was jammed, packed with people, she'd never seen it like that before. Not even on the Fourteenth of July. Not even when another country's President came on a visit.

But they were all on one side of the street only, they were kept back there, by a rope and by some policemen on foot, in a long black line, shoulder-to-shoulder and faces peering overshoulder, all looking over at the opposite side of the street. And on the opposite side of the street there was nothing by comparison. Two or three policemen standing around, looking very small and lonely in all that emptiness. And something covered on the ground, like when you throw something away.

The drone of the crowd hushed temporarily as the new arrival drove up and stopped, and in the momentary silence the crack of the car-door rang out like a shot, as Leone was taken out and they closed it behind her.

They took her over to the quieter side of the street on a long diagonal walk, for the car that had brought her couldn't get in any closer, and long before she had reached there the crowd had started up its rolling, surf-like surge of sound again.

"There she is! That's her. She's the one the flat belongs to."

And a woman began again, for the twentieth time, to anyone around her who would listen: "They were creeping up the stairs, hoping to surprise him. Suddenly he came out of the flat and started firing at them, right there on the stairs. They backed down a little, and he ran up onto the roof. You could see him up there, from the street. I saw him up there myself. They were firing up at him from the street, and he was firing down into the street at them. Then everything stopped, and you could tell someone had hit him.

"First he did a slow lean-over, like he was never going to fall, and then a somersault and then all the way down to the sidewalk—*Blapp!*"

Leone's escort tipped one edge of the covering back. "You know this man?" And then, "You know the penalty for harboring a fugitive?"

She freed her arm from him and sank slowly to her knees, with a peculiar, little-girl forlornness suggested by the attitude.

"How does a nice kid like you," he said, "come to get mixed up with such a type? You see what it's brought you to. It's too late now. You're in for it now. You can't go back and undo the damage now."

And kneeling there, sitting back on her own heels there, on that gritty Paris sidewalk, holding the dead head on her lap that had once kissed her, breathed against her breast, framing it gently with a hand against each side of it and rocking back and forth with it in aloneness and desertion and cold, she looked up at him and cried out in a bitter, defiant, and yet somehow almost exultant voice that rang up and down the packed street and hushed the jabbering crowd:

"And if I *could* go back, if I were given the chance, I'd do it exactly all over again! Because he was a *real* man. What would you understand about that? A *real* man. Just to know him, just to be loved by him, makes it all worthwhile. Go ahead, arrest me! Throw away the key forever! I still come out ahead . . .

"Still come out ahead."

One issue before his periodical folded, Hans Santesson published "Intent to Kill" (*The Saint Magazine,* September 1967), for which he'd paid a paltry $85. It's strikingly reminiscent of Woolrich's classic "The Light in the Window" (*Mystery Book Magazine,* April 1946; collected in *The Dancing Detective,* as by William Irish, Lippincott, 1946) except that this time it's a psychotic veteran of Vietnam, perhaps the first of his kind in fiction, who returns to New York and moves though the nightscape like a zombie, bent on ritually murdering his wife for one transgression while he was overseas. No one but Woolrich could pack so many coincidences into such a tissue-thin storyline, but the *noir* overtones are genuine and the first-person narration believably over the edge.

INTENT TO KILL

It started to get dark, and as nature's generator went dead, the town turned on its auxiliary ones and went ahead working on its own juice. A sort of blazing neon moon came up all around that made the real one of six hours or so before seem as if it had been dim and dingy by contrast.

I kept right on standing there where I was while the changeover took place around me. I'd been standing there like that without moving for some little time now, as if I'd taken root on the spot. As if the impulse to keep on going had run down and needed winding up again. Or as though I'd forgotten what had brought me that far. But I hadn't.

I was right at the edge of the intersection, my toes almost

overlapping the curb-lip. Across the way from me, one flange of a street-directional sign spelled out "Lexington Ave." Abbreviated like that, with no room to take in the whole designation. The second wing, at right-angles, was telescoped by perspective so that it narrowed-down and couldn't be read.

But I knew which street it was. It was the right one, it was the one I wanted. It had been the street she lived on; now it was going to be the street she died on.

A pedestrian cross-walk sign facing me bloomed a warning red, but only the WALK part of it came on, in palsied letters. The wiring loose. Then DONT showed up beside it after it was nearly time for the whole thing to go off again. But nobody had mistaken it for a go-ahead anyway. They went by the color and not the capitals. (Parenthetically the thought occurred to me: A color-blind person could've got knocked down right then, in those few seconds.)

Then it made the switch-back to green, and the whole process repeated itself. But I still didn't go over to the other side.

It wasn't because I was undecided; if I was undecided, I wouldn't have come this far. It wasn't because I was afraid; if I was afraid, I wouldn't have come at all. It wasn't because I wanted to back out; if I wanted to back out, all I had to do was turn around and go away.

It isn't as easy to kill someone as they tell you it is. It isn't as easy to kill someone as you think.

People were going by in droves, but none of them looked at me. They wouldn't have believed it if someone had said: See that man standing where you just went past? He's on his way right now to kill someone, someone who lives down on the next block.

Here's what they might have said, various ones of them: How can you report it *before* he's done it? You have to wait till he does it first, and *then* report it. You can't arrest him just for carrying a thought around in his head.

Or: *You* report it. I have to meet my wife and pick up my car. I'm late now.

Or: Not me. I have an appointment at the beauty-parlor. If I miss it by even ten minutes, they won't hold it for me, I might have to wait a whole week before I can get one again.

Or: I have my own troubles. I just got a ticket. Why should I cooperate with those guys? It's their baby, not mine.

If you looked straight up overhead, the buildings made a picket-fence around the sky that only left a little well of it open in the middle. The rest was all converging lines of aluminum lashed together with gleaming zircons. Like railroad-tracks tilted up into the sky, with tiers and tiers and tiers of twinkling ties spanning them, growing smaller, smaller, smaller as they climbed . . . Until your eyes got tired and dropped off, and you lost them near that end-of-the-line called heaven. That subway-station in the sky.

This was New York, beautiful but cold.

And not for little men and little women and their grudge-matches.

Billowing life all around, and imminent death standing there, still, in the middle of all of it. Elbowed a little bit over this way, edged a little bit over that, nudged a little bit back the first way again. A bus overshot its yellow-stenciled unloading-slot, came a little too far forward, and opened its steaming door right in front of my face. A woman in rubber jack-boots got down heavily side-ways, and one of them landed right on the toes of my left foot. I pulled them out from under, and she glared at me for having my toes there right where her foot was going to come down.

I reached to feel for the gun, not to use it but to see if it had become dislodged, the way you touch your hat to straighten it after a slight collision.

It was all right, it hadn't been disturbed.

The bus paled into an azure silhouette for a moment behind a parting gush of exhaust-fumes and then went on its way. CINZANO stared back from its rear end, in a diagonal, in big block-capitals. Then they contracted into lower-case. Then they contracted into italics. Then into undecipherable molecules. Then the traffic coming behind blotted them out altogether. But the world had read their message.

The deep-freeze or whatever it was that had held me, thawed

and dissolved, and I'd broken stance and was starting to go across at last. I almost wouldn't have noticed it myself, but the ground seemed to be slowly moving backward under me like some sort of conveyor-belt, or a flattened-out escalator-tread going the other way. And now that I'd started, I didn't stop anymore after that. That had been the last time.

I moved slowly, but I kept moving. Going down the street, just going down the street. Like I had no reason, had no purpose, had no thought in mind. I touched the gun once, it was still there.

It felt heavier than it had in the old days, but I'd been in the hospital meantime and had lost weight. It was Government Issue, I'd brought it back with me from Saigon. You're supposed to turn them in when you're separated, but I hadn't.

I looked up at an ascending angle and recognized the building where I'd used to live. I even saw the windows which had once been mine. I counted up to them, that's how I knew them, but I didn't use my finger, I didn't want anyone to notice me do that. I just counted with my eyes instead.

I didn't see the man on door-duty outside, when I turned and went in. Then when I entered, he was in there but he didn't see me. He had his back to me, he was on the house-phone and he was talking to someone in the building, and he seemed very engrossed. More than engrossed, he seemed very excited. Or they were, which amounted to the same. "Now take it easy," I heard him say. "Now pull yourself together and try to talk more slowly so I can understand you."

I went around the turn to the elevator-bank, off-side to the front entrance, and pushed for the car. It came gliding down silent as a pin-drop, all glossy chrome and all empty. I got in and pushed the six-button and it closed and started to take me up.

It had been so easy to get in here unobserved, I almost couldn't believe it. I'd never been able to pass him like that in the old days when I'd still lived here. But maybe it wasn't the same guy, I hadn't seen his face, and they all looked alike in the uniform.

The minute I got out, somebody unseen called it away from me, and it went on further up somewhere else, so it didn't even leave a trace of which floor I was on.

And then I came to the door, the door that had been our door, but wasn't anymore.

I remembered how many times I'd come to it before, cold from being outside, overheated from being outside, tired from being outside. Now I was bringing a gun to shoot and kill with, in from being outside.

Once we'd hung a Christmas-wreath on it.

I remembered the last time, how it had slammed. And I'd thought of a line from a song I used to know: *"And as the door of love between us closes—"*

I got out the key I'd still kept, and opened it, and went in.

I saw the chairs I knew, the lamps I knew, the windows, the walls, the doors I knew. That same water-color in its same white-leather frame, of a Montmartre street-scene signed by someone named either Cobelle or Cubelle (I'd never been able to make sure) was still on the wall up there. A book on the table said: *Tom Jones.* We'd had that one *then.* A record on the player said: *Once Upon a Time, Never Comes Again.* We hadn't had that one *then.*

She must have just come in. Her coat was over a chair-seat dribbling downward to the floor. A glass with half a highball in it that she was coming back to in a minute was on a stand beside the chair. She'd never drunk before. Not by herself I mean. At parties, out with friends. Maybe she had something now to drink by herself about.

I knew she was in the bedroom, must be, although I couldn't hear her making any sound.

I called her name, not loudly, routinely as though we both still lived there in those rooms together, and she came in to me.

She wasn't frightened. She was surprised but she wasn't frightened. She must have been changing her clothes: to rest, to be more comfortable, maybe to get ready for a bath. When she came in she had on just a light-blue corduroy wrap-around over her foundation pieces.

I saw her pull it more closely closed across her when she looked at me. It couldn't have been modesty. We'd been married. It must have been apprehension. Must have been apprehension; she sensed.

"What'd you come back for?" she said. "You said you never were, you never would."

"For this," I said. I took out the gun. "I came back for this."

She stared at it with an odd look of fascination, as though she'd never seen one before. I knew that wasn't it, I knew that was a misreading. It was fear, but it looked like hypnotic fascination.

"Will that," she asked me vaguely, the pupils of her eyes a thousand miles away, on the gun, "undo anything that's been done? Will that rub out the past?"

"It'll rub out the future," I said, "and that's even better."

"There is no future," she said. "It doesn't need a gun to tell us both that."

"No, but it says it awful well."

"You're like all men," she said. "Like they always have been. Like they always will be. Kill, when you're hurt. Kill. Hurt someone else when you're hurt. Two hurts are better than one. Two hurts hurt more than one hurt."

She crossed her arms in front of her breast (with an odd suggestion of chastity, I don't know where I got it from) and lowered her head, waiting.

"Go ahead, kill," she said.

"Look at me then. Look up at me. I want to see your eyes."

She lifted her face. "Here are my eyes," she said.

"Traitor's eyes," I hissed, "that looked at someone else. Softened then closed, for someone else."

"Time never ended, you never came back. Then *he* came. You told me he would, you wrote me to look for him. He came from Saigon, and brought me love from you. He brought me messages. He brought me little snapshots, of a grubby face, unshaven beard, unkempt fatigues, that filled my heart with heaven and filled my eyes with tears. You'd eaten together side by side, drunk together side by side, fought together side by side and almost died together side by side. It was the closest I could get to you. It was as much of you as I could have or hope for. He was your proxy. The kiss was still your kiss, though it came from someone else. The hug was still your hug, though it came from someone else. The possession was still your possession, though it came from someone else. How can you explain these things? I was faithful to you, to only you and only you, through someone else's body.

"It wasn't not-enough love for you that betrayed me, it was too much love for you. That one night, the only night there ever was, ask him, ask him if you ever see him again, ask him whose name he heard me whisper in the night."

"Another man's son," I said bitterly. "Not mine, but another man's. Out of my wife's body, but another man's. Another! Another! Another man's!

"I wanted to dangle him on my knee when he was five. I wanted to play baseball with him when he was fifteen. I wanted to stand beside him and drink with him when he was twenty-five and married his girl.

"Gone now, all that gone now. Another man's eyes, looking out at me from his little-boy's face. Another man's hand, holding mine when he trots along beside me. Another man's tears, when he falls and barks his knee. Another man's blood, peering through the scrape.

"And when I die, and find out all the answers that I missed along the way, another man's son will stand by the grave with his head bowed down. Another man's, not my own."

My voice cracked, forlornly.

"Thief. Give me back the son you gypped me out of. You robbed me of my little hunk of eternity. It's like dying twice and dying for good, when you die without leaving a son."

She kept looking at me, like I'd told her to. She kept letting me see her eyes, like I'd told her to. Her eyelids flickered, though; they kept wanting to blink, and her eyes to shrink away from me. She wasn't brave. Her skin was whiter than the paper you write on. But, here are my eyes, she'd said. She kept letting me see them. She kept holding them as steady as she could. So she *was* brave, after all.

"I walked up the aisle with you," I remembered in a revery. "Away from the altar and away from the priest in his lace surplice. Your wedding-veil folded back clear of your face. The marriage-kiss from me still freshly pledged on your cheek, orange-blossoms, lilies-of-the-valley spraying in your arms."

A sob that I hadn't known was there blurted in my throat.

"No, I can't kill you, I can't shoot to kill you. No matter what you've done to me, you were the girl in my marriage-bed."

I looked down at the outpointed gun as my mind told my fingers to lower it, but my heart already had, and it was down.

"When we first opened our eyes and looked at each other. The self-consciousness, the concern. That first searchingly shy look. (Did I do everything right? Was I the man for her?)"

She supplemented: "(Was he disappointed in me? I wasn't too scared, I wasn't too dainty?)"

"I wanted you to go to the bathroom first, you wanted me to go first. In the end we compromised. Neither of us went. Neither of us spoke, because neither of us knew what way to put it in.

"I went down to a public pay-place in the lobby, when I 'stepped out a minute to get cigarettes.' Where you went, I don't know—

"Then the coffee came we'd asked them to send up. Remember that first coffee together, looking at each other over the tops of our cups? Couldn't even take our eyes off long enough to swallow. Everything was so new, so first, so just-starting. Everything was ahead, nothing behind. Even the sun didn't cast us any shadows in back when we walked.

"Children, making believe they're grown-ups. Grown-ups, acting like the children they are and always will be. Children of God. Poor us."

I swung from the shoulder and flung the gun with all the force that I had in me, against the wall over to the side and back of me. It struck with such violence the impact alone should have been enough to detonate it. I don't know why it didn't. The guard must have still been on. It fell down there in the corner, black and bulky and boding ill, its ugly intention inhibited.

She walked slowly and spent toward a small table there was against the wall, and first leaned over it pressing her hands down on it as though she weighed more than she could hold up. Then sank down upon a chair beside it and let her head roll on the table and clutched her arms around it.

She didn't make much sound. Only the shaking told what it was. But how she shook. As if every hope and every happiness were coming loose.

I looked at her. What was there to say? What do you say, what can you say?

"Cry," I said with sad accord. "Cry for you, for me, for the two of us."

"Cry," she agreed in a smothered voice, "for the whole world, and everyone that's in it."

"Cry and good-bye." I turned slowly and went to the door. There wasn't hate in my heart anymore, there wasn't wanting to get even, there wasn't will to kill.

"Good-bye," she echoed faintly after me. And she said my name, and put that with it. My private name, my given name, my first name. Never mind what it was. It was still her right to use it, only she and no one else.

I opened the door with a strange sort of care, as when you don't want to disturb someone, and let myself out. Then I closed it and looked at it from there.

Once I'd said, this is the door that love has come away from. Once I'd said, just a little while ago, this is the door I'm bringing death into. Now death had been there and had come away again without striking. A door that doesn't hold love, and doesn't hold death either. Oh what an aching empty barren place lies behind there.

The elevator was somewhere else, so I went down the safety-stairs. It was quicker than waiting for it to come. Down and around, then down and around again, five times, from the sixth floor down, at a jogging trot that sounded a little bit like a tap-dancer's time-step, because the steps had steel rims that clicked under me. Then gave the springed end-door at the bottom a sweep aside that opened up the lobby. And as it did so, there was a sudden flare-up of excitement. It had been there all the while but the soundproof door had kept it muffled.

Outside the building-entrance were two, not one but two, police patrol-cars, sometimes called Mickey Mouses in the vernacular, their red roof-reflectors swinging away and spattering all the walls opposite with blood—or red paint or mercurochrome, as your fancy sees and calls it. A cop was posted just inside the street-door, obviously to keep anyone from leaving the building. He'd already kept two people, a man and a woman; I could tell that by the way they were standing awkwardly to one side. Whether they were together or not I couldn't make out. There was a second cop acting as a sort of liaison between the lobby and the cars outside, going back and forth all the time. In the lobby were several more nonuniformed men who were very much of the police, it stood out all over them. The doorman, on the house-phone, was saying to someone: "Keep your door locked, please. Don't open it." Then he was saying it to someone else. Then to still a third.

They pounced as soon as I appeared, one of them on each side of me like magic. I never knew people could move so fast. I couldn't use my arms anymore, before I'd even felt anything.

"Where'd you just come from? Identify yourself."

"From 6-B. I was up there to see someone."

"How'd you happen to use the stairs?"

"Thought I'd save time. I didn't know there was an ordinance against it."

I started skittishly. One of them had had his hands going up and down me without my being aware of it until it was over.

They interrupted the doorman's relay of warning calls to ask: "He live in the house?"

"No, I never saw him before."

He hadn't, and I hadn't either.

"What's it about? I asked, not indignant—because you don't get indignant when they mean business like they did, not if you're sensible—as much as uncomprehending. And let's say, resolutely clear both of eye and inner knowledge and determined to show it. "What's up?"

They didn't answer. The attitude: You don't ask us questions. We do it.

When I turned to the doorman in an unvoiced repetition, he didn't, either. Apparently unsure he had their approval and not wanting to risk disfavor.

But the man over by the door whom I have said it was my impression was being kept in on a stand-by basis, being a civilian answered as one civilian sometimes will to another, police or no police. And notably when they're being inconvenienced.

"There's been an armed hold-up, and the man's still at large somewhere upstairs, he never got out. They're combing the building for him floor by floor."

They gave him a curt look of aside (spelling: never mind talking so much) but nothing was said I noticed to contradict him. So the story stood up.

They took me back up to where I'd just come from, using the car this time.

They rang the bell, and waited, and there wasn't any answer, no one came.

"6-B'd, you say?" they asked, beetling their brows at me in menacing distrust.

"6-B's what I said," I said.

They rang again.

My God, I thought, suddenly cold and constricted at the throat, I left my gun in there. I never took it out with me again. I remember now.

One of them had his hand up pummeling now—the hand that wasn't holding my arm in a twist. And nobody answered.

"Police Department," they kept saying, taking turns at it. And still nobody answered.

Finally they sent a call down for the building-superintendent; he came up in response and he opened it up with his master pass-key.

She'd gone back again to where I'd last seen her (I say back again for she must have got up from there in the meantime, in-between, and then gone back again; she'd have had to, there was no other way about it, no other explanation). She was lying just as before, only not shaking, not crying now. Through with crying. Her head down on the little table against the wall, one arm curved around it. The other though was hanging straight down now toward the floor, inert. Like a pendulum that has stopped.

And the gun, as if a feat of magic levitation had been performed, or as if it had been jerked by a wire suspended from a pulley, had leaped clear across the room, in a straight diagonal from the corner into which I'd thrown it over to the side she was on, and lay under her dangling hand. Not right under, out a few inches.

All that was said was: "No wonder you took the stairs coming down."

There might be her fingerprints on the gun now where mine had been before, but they wouldn't matter much. (Fingerprints can be manipulated by somebody else after the fingers' owner is already dead; they knew that, and I did, too.) Erasing them of all importance was the fact it was my gun, and I had been in there with it.

What strange turns life takes, I thought, gazing down hypnotized into the gloomy pool of my own future. I came here to kill her, I changed my mind, and now they've nailed me for it anyway. As though it were the intention that counted, and not the act. The thought leading up to the deed, and not the deed itself.

And maybe it does. Who can say? Maybe it does.

The last of his stories that Woolrich lived to see published was "For the Rest of Her life" (*Ellery Queen's Mystery Magazine,* May 1968; first collected in *Nightwebs,* Harper & Row, 1971), which Fred Dannay had bought for $350 back in the summer of 1966. It's a grim nightmare of a tale in which every move the doomed couple makes is precisely the wrong thing to do, and Woolrich keeps tightening the screws until we're screaming at Linda and Garry to change their course before it's too late. At the climax, wrote Harlan Ellison, "you hear your spine crack with tension." The distinguished German director Rainer Werner Fassbinder adapted this tale into his film *Martha* (1973), one of many European films based on Woolrich material.

FOR THE REST
OF HER LIFE

Their eyes met in Rome. On a street in Rome—the Via Piemonte. He was coming down it, coming along toward her, when she first saw him. She didn't know it but he was also coming into her life, into her destiny—bringing what was meant to be.

Every life is a mystery. And every story of every life is a mystery. But it is not what *happens* that is the mystery. It is whether it *has* to happen no matter what, whether it is ordered and ordained, fixed and fated, or whether it can be missed, avoided, circumvented, passed by; *that* is the mystery.

If she had not come along the Via Piemonte that day, would it still have happened? If she had come along the Via Piemonte that day, but ten minutes later than she did, would it *still* have happened? Therein lies the real mystery. And no one ever knows, and no one ever will.

As their eyes met, they held. For just a heartbeat.

He wasn't cheap. He wasn't sidewalk riffraff. His clothes were good clothes, and his air was a good air.

He was a personable-looking man. First your eye said: He's not young anymore, he's not a boy anymore. Then your eye said: But he's not old. There was something of youth hovering over and about him, and yet refusing to land in any one particular place. As though it were about to take off and leave him. Yet not quite that, either. More as though it had never fully been there in the first place. In short, the impression it was was agelessness. Not young, not old, not callow, not mature—but ageless. Thirty-six looking fifty-six, or fifty-six looking thirty-six, but which it was you could not say.

Their eyes met—and held. For just a heartbeat.

Then they passed one another by, on the Via Piemonte, but without any turn of their heads to prolong the look.

"I wonder who that was," she thought.

What he thought couldn't be known—at least, not by her.

Three nights later they met again, at a party the friend she was staying with took her to.

He came over to her, and she said, "I've seen you before. I passed you on Monday on the Via Piemonte. At about four in the afternoon."

"I remember you, too," he said. "I noticed you that day, going by."

I wonder why we remember each other like that, she mused; I've passed dozens, hundreds of other people since, and he must have too. I don't remember any of *them*.

"I'm Mark Ramsey," he said.

"I'm Linda Harris."

An attachment grew up. What is an attachment? It is the most difficult of all the human interrelationships to explain, because it is the vaguest, the most impalpable. It has all the good points of love, and none of its drawbacks. No jealousy, no quarrels, no greed to possess, no fear of losing possession, no hatred (which is very much a part of love), no surge of passion and no hangover afterward. It never reaches the heights, and it never reaches the depths.

As a rule it comes on subtly. As theirs did. As a rule the two involved are not even aware of it at first. As they were not. As a rule it only becomes noticeable when it is interrupted in some way, or broken off by circumstances. As theirs was. In other words, its presence only becomes known in its absence. It is only missed after it stops. While it is still going on, little thought is given to it, because little thought needs to be.

It is pleasant to meet, it is pleasant to be together. To put your shopping packages down on a little wire-backed chair at a little table at a sidewalk cafe, and sit down and have a vermouth with someone who has been waiting there for you. And will be waiting there again tomorrow afternoon. Same time, same table, same sidewalk cafe. Or to watch Italian youth going through the gyrations of the latest dance craze in some inexpensive indigenous night-place—while you, who come from the country where the dance originated, only get up to do a sedate fox trot. It is even pleasant to part, because this simply means preparing the way for the next meeting.

One long continuous being-together, even in a love affair, might make the thing wilt. In an attachment it would surely kill the thing off altogether. But to meet, to part, then to meet again in a few days, keeps the thing going, encourages it to flower.

And yet it requires a certain amount of vanity, as love does: a desire to please, to look one's best, to elicit compliments. It inspires a certain amount of flirtation, for the two are of opposite sex. A wink of understanding over the rim of a raised glass, a low-voiced confidential aside about something and the smile of intimacy that answers it, a small impromptu gift—a necktie on the one part because of an accidental spill on the one he was wearing, or of a small bunch of flowers on the other part because of the color of the dress she has on.

So it goes.

And suddenly they part, and suddenly there's a void, and suddenly they discover they have had an attachment.

Rome passed into the past, and became New York.

Now, if they had never come together again, or only after a long time and in different circumstances, then the attachment would have faded and died. But if they suddenly do come together again—while the sharp sting of missing one another is still smarting—then the attachment will revive full force, full strength. But never again as merely an attachment. It has to go on from there, it has to build, to pick up speed. And sometimes it is so glad to be brought back again that it makes the mistake of thinking it is love.

She was thinking of him at the moment the phone rang. And that helped, too, by its immediacy, by its telephonic answer to her wistful wish of remembrance. Memory is a mirage that fools the heart. . . .

"You'll never guess what I'm holding in my hand, right while I'm talking to you . . .

"I picked it up only a moment ago, and just as I was standing and looking at it, the phone rang. Isn't that the strangest thing! . . .

"Do you remember the day we stopped in and you bought it . . .

"I have a little one-room apartment on East 70th Street. I'm by myself now, Dorothy stayed on in Rome . . ."

A couple of months later, they were married. . . .

They call this love, she said to herself. I know what it is now. I never thought I would know, but I do now.

But she failed to add: If you can step back and identify it, is it really there? Shouldn't you be unable to know what the whole thing's about? Just blindly clutch and hold and fear that it will get away. But unable to stop, to think, to give it any name.

Just two more people sharing a common human experience. Infinite in its complexity, tricky at times, but almost always successfully surmounted in one of two ways: either blandly content with the results as they are, or else vaguely discontent but chained by habit. Most women don't marry a man, they marry a habit. Even when a habit is good, it can become monotonous; most do.

When it is bad in just the average degree it usually becomes no more than a nuisance and an irritant; and most do.

But when it is darkly, starkly evil in the deepest sense of the word, then it can truly become a hell on earth.

Theirs seemed to fall midway between the first two, for just a little while. Then it started veering over slowly toward the last. Very slowly, at the start, but very steadily . . .

They spent their honeymoon at a New Hampshire lakeshore resort. This lake had an Indian name which, though grantedly barbaric in sound to the average English-speaker, in her special case presented such an impassable block both in speech and in mental pre-speech imagery (for some obscure reason, Freudian perhaps, or else simply an instinctive retreat from something with distressful connotations) that she gave up trying to say it and it became simply "the lake." Then as time drew it backward, not into forgetfulness but into distance, it became "that lake."

Here the first of the things that happened, happened. The first of the things important enough to notice and to remember afterward, among a great many trifling but kindred ones that were not. Some so slight they were not more than gloating, zestful glints of eye or curt hurtful gestures. (Once he accidentally poured a spurt of scalding tea on the back of a waitress's wrist, by not waiting long enough for the waitress to withdraw her hand in setting the cup down, and by turning his head momentarily the other way. The waitress yelped, and he apologized, but he showed his teeth as he did so, and you don't show your teeth in remorse.)

One morning when she woke up, he had already dressed and gone out of the room. They had a beautifully situated front-view of rooms which overlooked the lake itself (the bridal suite, as a matter of fact), and when she went to the window she saw him out there on the white-painted little pier which jutted out into the water on knock-kneed piles. He'd put on a turtleneck sweater instead of a coat and shirt, and that, over his spare figure, with the shoreward breeze alternately lifting and then flattening his hair, made him look younger than when he was close by. A ripple of the old attraction, of the old attachment, coursed through her and then was quickly gone. Just like the breeze out there. The little sidewalk-cafe chairs of Rome with the braided-wire backs and the piles of parcels on them, where were they now? Gone forever; they couldn't enchant anymore.

The lake water was dark blue, pebbly-surfaced by the insistent breeze that kept sweeping it like the strokes of invisible broom-straws, and mottled with gold flecks that were like floating freckles in the nine o'clock September sunshine.

There was a little boy in bathing trunks, tanned as a caramel, sitting on the side of the pier, dangling his legs above the water. She'd noticed him about in recent days. And there was his dog, a noisy, friendly, ungainly little mite, a Scotch terrier that was under everyone's feet all the time.

The boy was throwing a stick in, and the dog was splashing after it, retrieving it, and paddling back. Over and over, with that tire-lessness and simplicity of interest peculiar to all small boys and their dogs. Off to one side a man was bringing up one of the motorboats that were for rent, for Mark to take out.

She could hear him in it for a while after that, making a long slashing ellipse around the lake, the din of its vibration alternately soaring and lulling as it passed from the far side to the near and then back to the far side again.

Then it cut off suddenly, and when she went back to look it was rocking there sheepishly engineless. The boy was weeping and the dog lay huddled dead on the lake rim, strangled by the boiling backwash of the boat that had dragged it—how many times?—around and around in its sweep of the lake. The dog's collar had become snagged some way in a line with a grappling hook attached, left carelessly loose over the side of the boat. (Or aimed and pitched over as the boat went slashing by?) The line trailed limp now, and the lifeless dog had been detached from it.

"If you'd only looked back," the boy's mother said ruefully to Mark. "He was a good swimmer, but I guess the strain was too much and his little heart gave out."

"He did look! He did! He did! I saw him!" the boy screamed agonized, peering accusingly from in back of her skirt.

"The spray was in the way," Mark refuted instantly. But she wondered why he said it so quickly. Shouldn't he have taken a moment's time to think about it first, and then say, "The spray must have been—" or "I guess maybe the spray—" But he said it as quickly as though he'd been ready to say it even before the need had arisen.

Everyone for some reason acted furtively ashamed, as if something unclean had happened. Everyone but the boy of course. There were no adult nuances to his pain.

The boy would eventually forget his dog.

But would she? Would she?

They left the lake—the farewells to Mark were a bit on the cool side, she noticed—and moved into a large rambling country house in the Berkshire region of Massachusetts, not far from Pittsfield, which he told her had been in his family for almost seventy-five years. They had a car, an Alfa Romeo, which he had brought over from Italy, and, at least in all its outward aspects, they had a not too unpleasant life together. He was an art importer, and financially a highly successful one; he used to commute back and forth to Boston, where he had a gallery with a small-size apartment above it. As a rule he would stay over in the city, and then drive out Friday night and spend the week-end in the country with her.

(She always slept so well on Mondays, Tuesdays, and Wednesdays. Thursdays she always lay awake half the night reminding herself that the following night was Friday. She never stopped to analyze this; if she had, what would it have told her? What *could* it have, if she didn't realize it already?)

As far as the house was concerned, let it be said at once that it was not a depressing house in itself. People can take their moods from a house, but by the same token a house can take its mood from the people who live in it. If it became what it became, it was due to him—or rather, her reaction to him.

The interior of the house had crystallized into a very seldom evoked period, the pre–World War I era of rococo and gimcrack elegance. Either its last occupant before them (an unmarried older sister of his) had had a penchant for this out of some girlhood memory of a war-blighted romance and had deliberately tried to recreate it, or what was more likely, all renovations had stopped around that time and it had just stayed that way by default.

Linda discovered things she had heard about but never seen before. Claw legs on the bathtub, nacre in-and-out push-buttons for the lights, a hanging stained-glass dome lamp over the dining-room table, a gramophone with a crank handle—she wondered if they'd first rolled back the rug and then danced the hesitation or the one-step to it. The whole house, inside and out, cried out to have women in the straight-up-and-down endlessly long tunics of 1913, with side-puffs of hair over their ears, in patent-leather shoes with beige suede tops up to the middle of the calf, suddenly step out of some of the rooms; and in front of the door, instead of his slender-bodied, bullet-fast Italian compact, perhaps a four-cornered Chalmers or Pierce-Arrow or Hupmobile shaking all over to the beat of its motor.

Sometimes she felt like an interloper, catching herself in some full-length mirror as she passed it, in her over-the-kneetop skirt and short free down-blown hair. Sometimes she felt as if she were under a magic spell, waiting to be disenchanted. But it wasn't a good kind of spell, and it didn't come wholly from the house or its furnishings. . . .

One day at the home of some people Mark knew who lived in the area, where he had taken her on a New Year's Day drop-in visit, she met a young man named Garrett Hill. He was branch head for a company in Pittsfield.

It was as simple as that—they met. As simple as only beautiful things can be simple, as only life-changing things, turning-point things, can be simple.

Then she met him a second time, by accident. Then a third, by coincidence. A fourth, by chance . . . Or directed by unseen forces?

Then she started to see him on a regular basis, without meaning anything, certainly without meaning any harm. The first night he brought her home they chatted on the way in his car; and then at the door, as he held out his hand, she quickly put hers out of sight behind her back.

"Why are you afraid to shake my hand?"

"I thought you'd hurt me."

"How can anyone hurt you by just shaking your hand?"

When he tried to kiss her, she turned and fled into the house, as frightened as though he'd brandished a whip at her.

When he tried it again, on a later night, again she recoiled sharply—as if she were flinching from some sort of punishment.

He looked at her, and his eyes widened, both in sudden understanding and in disbelief. "You're afraid *physically*," he said, almost whispering. "I thought it was some wifely scruple the other night. But you're physically afraid of being kissed! As if there were pain attached to it."

Before she could stop herself or think twice she blurted out, "Well, there is, isn't there?"

He said, his voice deadly serious, "*What* kind of kissing have you been used to?"

She hung her head. And almost the whole story had been told.

His face was white as a sheet. He didn't say another word. But one man understands another well; all are born with that particular insight.

The next week she went into the town to do some small shopping —shopping she could have done as easily over the phone. Did she hope to run across him during the course of it? Is that why she attended to it in person? And after it was taken care of she stepped into a restaurant to sit down over a cup of coffee while waiting for her bus. He came into the place almost immediately afterward; he must have been sitting in his car outside watching for her.

He didn't ask to sit down; he simply leaned over with his knuckles resting on the table, across the way from her, and with a quick back glance toward the door by which he had just entered, took a book out from under his jacket and put it down in front of her, its title visible.

"I sent down to New York to get this for you," he said. "I'm trying to help you in the only way I know how."

She glanced down at it. The title was: *The Marquis de Sade. The Complete Writings*.

"Who was he?" she asked, looking up. She pronounced it with the long A, as if it were an English name. "Sayd."

"Sod," he instructed. "He was a Frenchman. Just read the book," was all he would say. "Just read the book."

He turned to leave her, and then he came back for a moment and added, "Don't let anyone else see—" Then he changed it to, "Don't let *him* see you with it. Put a piece of brown wrapping paper around it so the title won't be conspicuous. As soon as you've finished, bring it back; don't leave it lying around the house."

After he'd gone she kept staring at it. Just kept staring.

They met again three days later at the same little coffee shop off the main business street. It had become their regular meeting place by now. No fixed arrangement to it; he would go in and find her there, or she would go in and find him there.

"Was he the first one?" she asked when she returned the book.

"No, of course not. This is as old as man—this getting pleasure by giving pain. There are some of them born in every generation. Fortunately not too many. He simply was the first one to write it up and so when the world became more specialized and needed a separate tag for everything, they used his name. It became a word—sadism, meaning sexual pleasure got by causing pain, the sheer pleasure of being cruel."

She started shaking all over as if the place were drafty. "It is that." She had to whisper it, she was so heartsick with the discovery. "Oh, God, yes, it is that."

"You had to know the truth. That was the first thing. You had to know, you had to be told. It isn't just a vagary or a whim on his part. It isn't just a—well, a clumsiness or roughness in making love. This is a frightful thing, a deviation, an affliction, and—a terrible danger to you. You had to understand the truth first."

"Sometimes he takes his electric shaver—" She stared with

frozen eyes at nowhere out before her. "He doesn't use the shaver itself, just the cord—connects it and—"

She backed her hand into her mouth, sealing it up.

Garrett did something she'd never seen a man do before. He lowered his head, all the way over. Not just onto his chest, but all the way down until his chin was resting on the tabletop. And his eyes, looking up at her, were smoldering red with anger. But literally red, the whites all suffused. Then something wet came along and quenched the burning in them.

"Now you know what you're up against," he said, straightening finally. "Now what do you want to do?"

"I don't know." She started to sob very gently, in pantomime, without a sound. He got up and stood beside her and held her head pressed against him. "I only know one thing," she said. "I want to see the stars at night again, and not just the blackness and the shadows. I want to wake up in the morning as if it was my right, and not have to say a prayer of thanks that I lived through the night. I want to be able to tell myself there won't be another night like the last one."

The fear Mark had put into her had seeped and oozed into all parts of her; she not only feared fear, she even feared rescue from fear.

"I don't want to make a move that's too sudden," she said in a smothered voice.

"I'll be standing by, when you want to and when you do."

And on that note they left each other. For one more time.

On Friday he was sitting there waiting for her at their regular table, smoking a cigarette. And another lay out in the ashtray, finished. And another. And another.

She came up behind him and touched him briefly but warmly on the shoulder, as if she were afraid to trust herself to speak.

He turned and greeted her animatedly. "Don't tell me you've been in there that long! I thought you hadn't come in yet. I've been sitting out here twenty minutes, watching the door for you."

Then when she sat down opposite him and he got a good look at her face, he quickly sobered.

"I couldn't help it. I broke down in there. I couldn't come out any sooner. I didn't want everyone in the place to see me, the way I was."

She was still shaking irrepressibly from the aftermath of long-continued sobs.

"Here, have one of these," he offered soothingly. "May make you feel better—" He held out his cigarettes toward her.

"No!" she protested sharply, when she looked down and saw what it was. She recoiled so violently that her whole chair bounced a little across the floor. He saw the back of her hand go to the upper part of her breast in an unconscious gesture of protection, of warding off.

His face turned white when he understood the implication. White with anger, with revulsion. "So that's it," he breathed softly. "My God, oh, my God."

They sat on for a long while after that, both looking down without saying anything. What was there to say? Two little cups of black coffee had arrived by now—just as an excuse for them to stay there.

Finally he raised his head, looked at her, and put words to what he'd been thinking. "You can't go back anymore, not even once. You're out of the house and away from it now, so you've got to stay out. You can't go near it again, not even one more time. One more night may be one night too many. He'll kill you one of these nights—he will even if he doesn't mean to. What to him is just a thrill, an excitement, will take away your life. Think about that— you've *got* to think about that."

"I have already," she admitted. "Often."

"You don't want to go to the police?"

"I'm ashamed." She covered her eyes reluctantly with her hand for a moment. "I know I'm not the one who should be, he's the one. But I am nevertheless. I couldn't bear to tell it to an outsider, to put it on record, to file a complaint—it's so intimate. Like taking off all your clothes in public. I can hardly bring myself even to have you know about it. And I haven't told you everything—not everything."

He gave her a shake of the head, as though he knew.

"If I try to hide out in Pittsfield, he'll find me sooner or later—it's not that big a place—and come after me and force me to come back, and either way there'll be a scandal. And I don't want that. I couldn't stand that. The newspapers . . ."

All at once, before they quite knew how it had come about, or even realized that it had come about, they were deep in the final plans, the final strategy and staging that they had been drawing slowly nearer and nearer to all these months. Nearer to with every meeting, with every look and with every word. The plans for her liberation and her salvation.

He took her hands across the table.

"No, listen. This is the way, this is how. New York. It has to be New York; he won't be able to get you back; it's too big; he won't even be able to find you. The company's holding a business conference there on Tuesday, with each of the regional offices sending a representative the way they always do. I was slated to go, long before this came up. I was going to call you on Monday before I left. But what I'm going to do now is to leave ahead of time, tonight, and take you with me."

He raised one of her hands and patted it encouragingly.

"You wait for me here in the restaurant. I have to go back to the office, wind up a few things, then I'll come back and pick you up—shouldn't take me more than half an hour."

She looked around her uneasily. "I don't want to sit here alone. They're already giving me knowing looks each time they pass, the waitresses, as if they sense something's wrong."

"Let them, the hell with them," he said shortly, with the defiance of a man in the opening stages of love.

"Can't you call your office from here? Do it over the phone?"

"No, there are some papers that have to be signed—they're waiting for me on my desk."

"Then you run me back to the house and while you're doing what you have to at the office I'll pick up a few things; then you can stop by for me and we'll start out from there."

"Isn't that cutting it a little close?" he said doubtfully. "I don't want you to go back there." He pivoted his wrist watch closer to him. "What time does he usually come home on Fridays?"

"Never before ten at night."

He said the first critical thing he'd ever said to her. "Just like a girl. All for the sake of a hairbrush and a cuddly negligée you're willing to stick your head back into that house."

"It's more than just a hairbrush," she pointed out. "I have some money there. It's not his, it's mine. Even if this friend from my days in Rome—the one I've spoken to you about—even if she takes me in with her at the start, I'll need some money to tide me over until I can get a job and find a place of my own. And there are other things, like my birth certificate, that I may need later on; he'll never give them up willingly once I leave."

"All right," he gave in. "We'll do it your way."

Then just before they got up from the table that had witnessed such a change in both their lives, they gave each other a last look. A last, and yet a first one. And they understood each other.

She didn't wait for him to say it, to ask it. There is no decorum in desperation, no coyness in a crisis. She knew it had been asked unsaid, anyway. "I want to rediscover the meaning of gentle love. I want to lie in your bed, in your arms. I want to be your wife."

He took hold of her left hand, raised the third finger, stripped off the wedding band and in its place firmly guided downward a massive fraternity ring that had been on his own hand until that very moment. Heavy, ungainly, much too large for her—and yet everything that love should be.

She put it to her lips and kissed it.

They were married, now.

The emptied ring rolled off the table and fell on the floor, and as they moved away his foot stepped on it, not on purpose, and distorted it into something warped, misshapen, no longer round, no longer true. Like what it had stood for.

He drove her back out to the house and dropped her off at the door, and they parted almost in silence, so complete was their understanding by now, just three muted words between them: "About thirty minutes."

It was dark now, and broodingly sluggish. Like something supine waiting to spring, with just the tip of its tail twitching. Leaves stood still on the trees. An evil green star glinted in the black sky like a hostile eye, like an evil spying eye.

His car had hummed off; she'd finished and brought down a small packed bag to the ground floor when the phone rang. It would be Garry, naturally, telling her he'd finished at the office and was about to leave.

"Hello—" she began, urgently and vitally and confidentially, the way you share a secret with just one person and this was the one.

Mark's voice was at the other end.

"You sound more chipper than you usually do when I call up to tell you I'm on the way home."

Her expectancy stopped. And everything else with it. She didn't know what to say. "Do I?" And then, "Oh, I see."

"Did you have a good day? You must have had a *very* good day."

She knew what he meant, she knew what he was implying.

"I—I—oh, I did nothing, really. I haven't been out of the house all day."

"That's strange," she heard him say. "I called you earlier—about an hour ago?" It was a question, a pitfall of a question. "You didn't come to the phone."

"I didn't hear it ring," she said hastily, too hastily. "I might have been out front for a few minutes. I remember I went out there to broom the gravel in the drivew—"

Too late she realized he hadn't called at all. But now he knew that she hadn't been in the house all day, that she'd been out somewhere during part of it.

"I'll be a little late." And then something that sounded like "That's what you want to hear, isn't it?"

"What?" she said quickly. "What?"

"I said I'll be a little late."

"What was it you said after that?"

"What was it you said after that?" he quoted studiedly, giving her back her own words.

She knew he wasn't going to repeat it, but by that very token she knew she'd heard it right the first time.

He *knows*, she told herself with a shudder of premonition as she got off the phone and finally away from him. (His voice could hold fast to you and enthrall you, too; his very voice could torture you, as well as his wicked, cruel fingers.) He knows there's someone; he may not know who yet, but he knows there is someone.

A remark from one of the nightmare nights came back to her: "There's somebody else who wouldn't do this, isn't there? There's somebody else who wouldn't make you cry."

She should have told Garry about it long before this. Because now she had to get away from Mark at all cost, even more than she had had to ever before. Now there would be a terrible vindictiveness, a violent jealousy sparking the horrors where before there had sometimes been just an irrational impulse, sometimes dying as quickly as it was born. Turned aside by a tear or a prayer or a run around a chair.

And then another thing occurred to her, and it frightened her even more immediately, here and now. What assurance was there that he was where he'd said he was, still in the city waiting to start out for here? He might have been much closer, ready to jump out at her unexpectedly, hoping to throw her offguard and catch her away from the house with someone, or (as if she could have possibly been that sort of person) with that someone right here in the very house with her. He'd lied about calling the first time; why wouldn't he lie about where he was?

And now that she thought of it, there was a filling station with a public telephone less than five minutes drive from here, on the main thruway that came up from Boston. An eddy of fear swirled around her, like dust rising off the floor in some barren drafty place. She had to do one of two things immediately— there was no time to do both. Either call Garry at his office and warn him to hurry, that their time limit had shrunk. Or try to trace Mark's call and find out just how much margin of safety was still left to them.

She chose the latter course, which was the mistaken one to choose.

Long before she'd been able to identify the filling station exactly for the information operator to get its number, the whole thing had become academic. There was a slither and shuffle on the gravel outside and a car, someone's car, had come to a stop in front of the house.

Her first impulse, carried out immediately without thinking why, was to snap off all the room lights. Probably so she could see out without being seen from out there.

She sprang over to the window, and then stood there rigidly motionless, leaning a little to peer intently out. The car had stopped at an unlucky angle of perspective—unlucky for her. They had a trellis with tendrils of wisteria twining all over it like bunches of dangling grapes. It blanked out the mid-section of the car, its body shape, completely. The beams of the acetylene-bright headlights shone out past one side, but they told her nothing; they could have come from any car. The little glimmer of color on the driveway, at the other side, told her no more.

She heard the door crack open and clump closed. Someone's feet, obviously a man's, chopped up the wooden steps to the entrance veranda, and she saw a figure cross it, but it was too dark to make out who he was.

She had turned now to face the other way, and without knowing it her hand was holding the place where her heart was. This was Mark's house, he had the front-door key. Garry would have to ring. She waited to hear the doorbell clarinet out and tell her she was safe, she would be loved, she would live.

Instead there was a double click, back then forth, the knob twined around, and the door opened. A spurt of cool air told her it had opened.

Frightened back into childhood fears, she turned and scurried, like some little girl with pigtails flying out behind her, scurried back along the shadowed hall, around behind the stairs, and into a closet that lay back there, remote as any place in the house could be. She pushed herself as far to the back as she could, and crouched down, pulling hanging things in front of her to screen and to protect her, to make her invisible. Sweaters and mackintoshes and old forgotten coveralls. And she hid her head down between her knees—the way children do when a goblin or an ogre is after them, thinking that if they can't see it, that fact alone will make the terror go away.

The steps went up the stairs, on over her, up past her head. She could feel the shake if not hear the sound. Then she heard her name called out, but the voice was blurred by the many partitions and separations between—as if she were listening to it from underwater. Then the step came down again, and the man stood there at the foot of the stairs, uncertain. She tried to teach herself how to forget to breathe, but she learned badly.

There was a little *tick!* of a sound, and he'd given himself more light. Then each step started to sound clearer than the one before, as the distance to her thinned away. Her heart began to stutter and turn over, and say: Here he comes, here he comes. Light cracked into the closet around three sides of the door, and two arms reached in and started to make swimming motions among the hanging things, trying to find her.

Then they found her, one at each shoulder, and lifted her and drew her outside to him. (With surprising gentleness.) And pressed her to his breast. And her tears made a new pattern of little wet polka dots all over what had been Garry's solid-colored necktie until now.

All she could say was, "Hurry, hurry, get me out of here!"

"You must have left the door open in your hurry when you came back here. I tried it, found it unlocked, and just walked right in. When I looked back here, I saw that the sleeve of that old smock had got caught in the closet door and was sticking out. Almost like an arm, beckoning me on to show me where you were hiding. It was uncanny. Your guardian angel must love you very much, Linda."

But will he always, she wondered? Will he always?

He took her to the front door, detoured for a moment to pick up the bag, then led her outside and closed the door behind them for good and all.

"Just a minute," she said, and stopped, one foot on the ground, one still on the wooden front steps.

She opened her handbag and took out her key—the key to what had been her home and her marriage. She flung it back at the door, and it hit and fell, with a cheap shabby little *clop!*—like something of not much value.

Once they were in the car they just drove; they didn't say anything more for a long time.

All the old things had been said. All the new things to be said were still to come.

In her mind's eye she could see the sawtoothed towers of New York climbing slowly up above the horizon before her at the end of the long road. Shimmering there, iridescent, opalescent, rainbows of chrome and glass and hope. Like Jerusalem, like Mecca, or some other holy spot. Beckoning, offering heaven. And of all the things New York has meant to various people at various times—fame, success, fulfillment— it probably never meant as much before as it meant to her tonight: a place of refuge, a sanctuary, a place to be safe in.

"How long does the trip take?" she asked him wistful-eyed.

"I usually make it in less than four hours. Tonight I'll make it less than three."

I'll never stray out of New York again, she promised herself. Once I'm safely there, I'll never go out in the country again. I never want to see a tree again, except way down below me in Central Park from a window high up.

"Oh, get me there, Garry, get me there."

"I'll get you there," Garry promised, like any new bridegroom, and bent to kiss the hand she had placed over his on the wheel.

Two car headlights from the opposite direction hissed by them—like parallel tracer bullets going so fast they seemed to swirl around rather than undulate with the road's flaws.

She purposely waited a moment, then said in a curiously surreptitious voice, as though it shouldn't be mentioned too loudly, "Did
you see that?"

All he answered, noncommitally, was, "Mmm."

"That was the Italian compact."

"You couldn't tell what it was," he said, trying to distract her
from her fear. "Went by too fast."

"I know it too well. I recognized it."

Again she waited a moment, as though afraid to make the
movement she was about to. Then she turned and looked back,
staring hard and steadily into the funneling darkness behind them.

Two back lights had flattened out into a bar, an ingot. Suddenly
this flashed to the other side of the road, then reversed. Then, like
a ghastly scimitar chopping down all the tree trunks in sight, the
headlights reappeared, rounded out into two spheres, gleaming,
small—but coming back after them.

"I told you. It's turned and doubled back."

He was still trying to keep her from panic. "May have nothing
to do with us. May not be the same car we saw go by just now."

"It is. Why would he make a complete about-turn like that in
the middle of nowhere? There's no intersection or side road back
there—we haven't passed one for miles."

She looked again.

"They keep coming. And they already look bigger than when
they started back. I think they're gaining on us."

He said, with an unconcern that he didn't feel, "Then we'll have
to put a stop to that."

They burst into greater velocity, with a surge like a forward
billow of air.

She looked, and she looked again. Finally to keep from turning
so constantly, she got up on the seat on the point of one knee and
faced backward, her hair pouring forward all around her, jumping
with an electricity that was really speed.

"Stay down," he warned. "You're liable to get thrown that way.
We're up to 65 now." He gave her a quick tug for additional
emphasis, and she subsided into the seat once more.

"How is it now?" he checked presently. The rear-view mirror couldn't reflect that far back.

"They haven't grown smaller, but they haven't grown larger."

"We've stabilized, then," he translated. "Dead heat."

Then after another while and another look, "Wait a minute!" she said suddenly on a note of breath-holding hope. Then, "No," she mourned quickly afterward. "For a minute I thought—but they're back again. It was only a dip in the road."

"They hang on like leeches, can't seem to shake them off," she complained in a fretful voice, as though talking to herself. "Why don't they go away? Why *don't* they?"

Another look, and he could sense the sudden stiffening of her body.

"They're getting bigger. I know I'm not mistaken."

He could see that, too. They were finally peering into the rear-view mirror for the first time. They'd go offside, then they'd come back in again. In his irritation he took one hand off the wheel long enough to give the mirror a backhand slap that moved it out of focus altogether.

"Suppose I stop, get out and face him when he comes up, and we have it out here and now. What can he do? I'm younger, I can outslug him."

Her refusal to consent was an outright scream of protest. All her fears and all her aversion were in it.

"All right," he said. "Then we'll run him into the ground if we have to."

She covered her face with both hands—not at the speed they were making, but at the futility of it.

"They sure build good cars in Torino, damn them to hell!" he swore in angry frustration.

She uncovered and looked. The headlights were closer than before. She began to lose control of herself.

"Oh, this is like every nightmare I ever had when I was a little girl! When something was chasing me, and I couldn't get away from it. Only now there'll be no waking up in the nick of time."

"Stop that," he shouted at her. "Stop it. It only makes it worse, it doesn't help."

"I think I can feel his breath blowing down the back of my neck."

He looked at her briefly, but she could tell by the look on his face he hadn't been able to make out what she'd said.

Streaks of wet that were not tears were coursing down his face in uneven lengths. "My necktie," he called out to her suddenly, and raised his chin to show her what he meant. She reached over, careful not to place herself in front of him, and pulled the knot down until it was loose. Then she freed the buttonhole from the top button of his shirt.

A long curve in the road cut them off for a while, from those eyes, those unrelenting eyes behind them. Then the curve ended, and the eyes came back again. It was worse somehow, after they'd been gone like that, than when they remained steadily in sight the whole time.

"He holds on and holds on and *holds on*—like a mad dog with his teeth locked into you."

"He's a mad dog all right." All pretense of composure had long since left him. He was lividly angry at not being able to win the race, to shake the pursuer off. She was mortally frightened. The long-sustained tension of the speed duel, which seemed to have been going on for hours, compounded her fears, raised them at last to the pitch of hysteria.

Their car swerved erratically, the two outer wheels jogged briefly over marginal stones and roots that felt as if they were as big as boulders and logs. He flung his chest forward across the wheel as if it were something alive that he was desperately trying to hold down; then the car recovered, came back to the road, straightened out safely again with a catarrhal shudder of its rear axle.

"Don't," he warned her tautly in the short-lived lull before they picked up hissing momentum again. "Don't grab me like that again. It went right through the shoulder of my jacket. I can't manage the car, can't hold it, if you do that. I'll get you away. Don't worry, I'll get you away from him."

She threw her head back in despair, looking straight up overhead. "We seem to be standing still. The road has petrified. The trees aren't moving backwards anymore. The stars don't either. Neither do the rocks along the side. Oh, faster, Garry, faster!"

"You're hallucinated. Your senses are being tricked by fear."

"Faster, Garry, faster!"

"85, 86. We're on two wheels most of the time—two are off the ground. I can't even breathe, my breath's being pulled out of me."

She started to beat her two clenched fists against her forehead in a tattoo of hypnotic inability to escape. "I don't care, Garry! Faster, faster! If I've got to die, let it be with you, not with him!"

"I'll get you away from him. If it kills me."

That was the last thing he said.

If it kills me.

And as though it had overheard, and snatched at the collateral offered it, that unpropitious sickly greenish star up there—surely Mark's star, not theirs—at that very moment a huge tremendous thing came into view around a turn in the road. A skyscraper of a long-haul van, its multiple tiers beaded with red warning lights. But what good were they that high up, except to warn off planes?

It couldn't maneuver. It would have required a turntable. And they had no time or room.

There was a soft crunchy sound, like someone shearing the top off a soft-boiled egg with a knife. At just one quick slice. Then a brief straight-into-the face blizzard effect, but with tiny particles of glass instead of frozen flakes. Just a one-gust blizzard—and then over with. Then an immense whirl of light started to spin, like a huge Ferris wheel all lit up and going around and around, with parabolas of light streaking off in every direction and dimming. Like shooting stars, or the tails of comets.

Then the whole thing died down and went out, like a blazing amusement park sinking to earth. Or the spouts of illuminated fountains settling back into their basins . . .

She could tell the side of her face was resting against the ground, because blades of grass were brushing against it with a feathery tickling feeling. And some inquisitive little insect kept flitting about just inside the rim of her ear. She tried to raise her hand to brush it away, but then forgot where it was and what it was.

But then forgot . . .

When they picked her up at last, more out of this world than in it, all her senses gone except for reflex-actions, her lips were still quivering with the unspoken sounds of "Faster, Garry, faster! Take me away—"

Then the long nights, that were also days, in the hospital. And the long blanks, that were also nights. Needles, and angled glass rods to suck water through. Needles, and curious enamel wedges slid under your middle. Needles, and—needles and needles and needles. Like swarms of persistent mosquitoes with unbreakable drills. The way a pincushion feels, if it could feel. Or the target of a porcupine. Or a case of not just momentary but permanently endured static electricity after you scuff across a woolen rug and then put your finger on a light switch. Even food was a needle—a jab into a vein . . .

Then at last her head cleared, her eyes cleared, her mind and voice came back from where they'd been. Each day she became a little stronger, and each day became a little longer. Until they were back for good, good as ever before. Life came back into her lungs and heart. She could feel it there, the swift current of it. Moving again, eager again. Sun again, sky again, rain and pain and love and hope again. Life again—the beautiful thing called life.

Each day they propped her up in a chair for a little while. Close beside the bed, for each day for a little while longer.

Then at last she asked, after many starts that she could never finish, "Why doesn't Garry come to me? Doesn't he know I've been hurt?"

"Garry can't come to you," the nurse answered. And then, in the way that you whip off a bandage that has adhered to a wound fast, in order to make the pain that much shorter than it would be if you lingeringly edged it off a little at a time, then the nurse quickly told her, "Garry won't come to you anymore."

The black tears, so many of them, such a rain of them, blotted out the light and brought on the darkness . . .

Then the light was back again, and no more tears. Just—Garry won't come to you anymore.

Now the silent words were: Not so fast, Garry, not so fast; you've left me behind and I've lost my way.

Then in a little while she asked the nurse, "Why don't you ever let me get up from this chair? I'm better now, I eat well, the strength has come back to my arms, my hands, my fingers, my whole body feels strong. Shouldn't I be allowed to move around and exercise a little? To stand up and take a few steps?"

"The doctor will tell you about that," the nurse said evasively.

The doctor came in later and he told her about it. Bluntly, in the modern way, without subterfuges and without false hopes. The kind, the sensible, the straight-from-the-shoulder modern way.

"Now listen to me. The world is a beautiful world, and life is a beautiful life. In this beautiful world everything is comparative; luck is comparative. You could have come out of it stone-blind from the shattered glass, with both your eyes gone. You could have come out of it minus an arm, crushed and having to be taken off. You could have come out of it with your face hideously scarred, wearing a repulsive mask for the rest of your life that would make people sicken and turn away. You could have come out of it dead, as—as someone else did. Who is to say you are lucky, who is to say you are not? You have come out of it beautiful of face. You have come out of it keen and sensitive of mind, a mind with all the precision and delicate adjustment of the works inside a fine Swiss watch. A mind that not only *thinks*, but *feels*. You have come out of it with a strong brave youthful heart that will carry you through for half a century yet, come what may."

"*But—*"

She looked at him with eyes that didn't fear.

"You will never again take a single step for all the rest of your life. You are hopelessly, irreparably paralyzed from the waist down.

Surgery, everything, has been tried. Accept this . . . Now you know—and so now be brave."

"I am. I will be," she said trustfully. "I'll learn a craft of some kind, that will occupy my days and earn me a living. Perhaps you can find a nursing home for me at the start until I get adjusted, and then maybe later I can find a little place all to myself and manage there on my own. There are such places, with ramps instead of stairs—"

He smiled deprecatingly at her oversight.

"All that won't be necessary. You're forgetting. There is someone who will look after you. Look after you well. You'll be in good capable hands. Your husband is coming to take you home with him today."

Her scream was like the death cry of a wounded animal. So strident, so unbelievable, that in the stillness of its aftermath could be heard the slithering and rustling of people looking out the other ward-room doors along the corridor, nurses and ambulatory patients, asking one another what that terrified cry had been and where it had come from.

"Two cc's of M, and hurry," the doctor instructed the nurse tautly. "It's just the reaction from what she's been through. This sometimes happens—going-home happiness becomes hysteria."

The wet kiss of alcohol on her arm. Then the needle again—the needle meant to be kind.

One of them patted her on the head and said, "You'll be all right now."

A tear came to the corner of her eyes, and just lay there, unable to retreat, unable to fall. . . .

Myopically she watched them dress her and put her in her chair. Her mind remained awake, but everything was downgraded in intensity—the will to struggle had become reluctance, fear had become unease. She still knew there was cause to scream, but the distance had become too great, the message had too far to travel.

Through lazy, contracting pupils she looked over and saw Mark standing in the doorway, talking to the doctor, shaking the nurse's hand and leaving something behind in it for which she smiled her thanks. Then he went around in back of her wheelchair, with a phantom breath for a kiss to the top of her head, and started to sidle it toward the door that was being held open for the two of them. He tipped the front of the chair ever so slightly, careful to avoid the least jar or impact or roughness, as if determined that she reach her destination with him in impeccable condition, unmarked and unmarred.

And as she craned her neck and looked up overhead, and then around and into his face, backward, the unspoken message was so plain, in his shining eyes and in the grim grin he showed his teeth in, that though he didn't say it aloud, there was no need to; it reached from his mind into hers without sound or the need of sound just as surely as though he had said it aloud.

Now I've got you.

Now he had her—for the rest of her life.

TALES FROM
MEMORY'S MISTS

During the 1960s Woolrich worked sporadically on an autobiographical manuscript he called *Blues of a Lifetime.* How accurately he describes events is anyone's guess since almost nothing he says can be checked against an external source, and the vast majority of the things he said or wrote elsewhere about his life have turned out to be false. I believe he would have done well to have prefaced his manuscript with something similar to the way Carl Jung prefaced his *Memories, Dreams, Reflections* (1962): "I have undertaken today . . . to relate the myth of my life. I can . . . only 'tell stories.' Whether they are true is no problem. . . ." The manuscript, carefully edited by Professor Mark Bassett, was published by Bowling Green University Popular Press in 1990 but has long been unavailable— which is why the two most intriguing chapters are included here.

"I never loved women much, I guess," he says in the first chapter of the manuscript. "The first time it was just puppy-love, but it ended disastrously for at least one of us. . . ." The sixty-nine typed pages of "The Poor Girl" vibrate with the emotional power he'd built up over forty years as a storyteller, and the narrative structure resonates with motifs that will be familiar to readers of his suspense fiction. Was he projecting his literary themes back into his life, or did personal experience hand him those themes on a dark platter? Certainly the chapter doesn't tell the whole tale. His maternal grandfather, in whose house he was living at the time, is never mentioned, and Woolrich seems to want us to believe that he'd spent his entire childhood and adolescence in New York. On the other hand he isn't writing pure fiction here, either. Whoever Vera Gaffney was, her fate recurs in various forms throughout Woolrich's creative life, notably in his novel *The Black Angel* (1943) where Ladd Mason tells the female protagonist-narrator about a woman he once loved. Her name is Patsy but the story Mason tells the woman who will destroy him is very much the same story Woolrich tells us here.

THE POOR GIRL

E veryone has a first-time love, and remembers it afterward, always, forever. I had a first-time love too, and I remember mine:

There was a fellow named Frank Van Craig, a year or possibly two years older than I, who lived a few doors up the street from me. I called him Frankie, as might be expected at that time of our lives, and we were more or less inseparable, although we had only got to know each other a fairly short while before this.

His father was a retired detective of police, who lived on his pension, and the mother had died some years before, leaving this forlorn little masculine menage of three (there was a younger brother, still of school age) to get along as best they could. Frankie used to speak of his father patronizingly as "the old man." But gruff and taciturn as the father was, embittered by his loss and withdrawn into his shell, there must have been some deep-felt if unspoken bond between the two of them, for more than once, when I'd stop by for Frankie, I used to see him kiss his father respectfully and filially on the forehead before leaving. It touched me oddly, and I used to think about it afterward each time I saw it happen, for I had no father, and even if I had had, I couldn't visualize myself kissing him like that; it didn't seem right between two men. But Frankie was my friend, and I was too loyal to entertain even a secret disapproval of him.

Frankie had a job in a machine- or tool-shop, but that was merely his way of earning a living. His real avocation was amateur boxing. He spent every spare moment at it that he could: evenings after his job, Saturdays, holidays. And he was good. I used to go down with him sometimes to the gym where he trained and watch him work out: spar with partners, punch the bag, chin the parallel bars, skip rope, and all the rest. Then when we'd come away afterward, I used to walk along beside him with a feeling almost akin to adulation, proud to have him for a friend.

It was this feeling that had first brought us together, in what amounted on my part, at least in the beginning, to a mild but unmistakable case of hero-worship. He had the athletic prowess and the rough-and-readiness of disposition that I would have given anything to have had myself, and that I could tell was going to be lacking in me for the rest of my life; otherwise, it would already have appeared by this time. Then when this preliminary phase blew over as I became habituated to him, we became fast friends on a more evenly reciprocal basis, for there were things about me that I could sense he, in his turn, looked up to and wished he had.

At any rate, we were strolling along Eighth Avenue one evening side by side, under the lattice-work of the El, when a very pretty girl of about my age, who was coming from the opposite direction, gave him a smile of recognition, stopped beside us and said hello to him. She was blonde, with a fair, milk-and-roses Irish complexion and hazel eyes lively as spinning pinwheels. Her pale hair was smooth and cut evenly all around at ear-tip level, with just a clean, fresh-looking part running up one side of it to break the monotony of its evenness.

After a few words had been exchanged, he introduced us with a characteristically gruff amiability. "Con, meet Vera," he said. "Vera, meet Con." But our eyes had already become very well acquainted by this time.

"Hello Con," she said, and smiled.

"Hello Vera," I said, and smiled back.

Now that I'd met her I remember becoming more diffident than before I'd met her, and having less to say. (I'd already been talking to her before the introduction.) But she didn't seem to notice, and he on his part, obviously unattached, showed no constraint.

We stood and chatted for a while and then we parted and went our ways, on a note of laughter at something that he'd said at the end.

But I looked back toward her several times, and once, I saw her do it, too, and somehow I knew it was meant for me and not for him.

"You know her well?" was the first thing I asked him.

"She lives around here," he answered indifferently, implying, I think, that she was too familiar a part of his surroundings to be of any great interest to him.

Then he turned around and pointed out the house. "Right over there. That one on the corner. See it?"

It was a six-story, old-law, tenement building, one of an almost unbroken line that stretched along both sides of Eighth, from the top of the park well up into the Hundred-and-forties. Its top-floor windows were flush with the quadruple trackbeds of the Elevated, two for locals, two for expresses—two for downtown, two for up.

"She lives on the top floor," he went on. "I been up there. I went up and met her family once, when I first started to know her. Her family are nice 'nd friendly."

"Didn't you ever go back again?"

"Na," he said, blasé. "What for?"

I wondered about this. There just wasn't any amatory attraction there, that was obvious. I couldn't understand it, with a girl as appealing and magnetic as she'd seemed to me. But each one to his own inclinations I suppose, even at that age.

"What's her last name?" I asked. "You didn't give it."

"Her old man's name is Gaffney," he said. "I know, because I've met him." I didn't know what he meant by that at first. Then he went on to explain: "She likes to call herself Hamilton, though; she says it was her grandmother's name and she's entitled to use it if she wants."

"Why?" I wondered.

"I danno; maybe she thinks it's classier."

I could understand that discontent with a name. I'd experienced it a little myself. I'd been fiercely proud of my surname always. Only, all through my boyhood I'd kept wishing they'd given me a curt and sturdier first name, something like the other boys had, "Jim" or "Tom" or "Jack," not "Cornell," a family name, originally). But it was too late to do anything about it now. The only improvement possible was by abbreviation. And even there I was handicapped. "Corny" was unappealing, even though the slang descriptive for "stale" hadn't yet come into use. "Connie" was unthinkable. All that was left was "Con," which always sounded flat to me for some reason.

"Hey!" he jeered explosively, belatedly becoming aware, I suppose, of the number of questions I'd been asking. "What happened? Did you get stuck on her already?"

"How could I have got stuck on her?" I protested uncomfortably. "I only just now met her."

But I knew I was lying; I knew I had.

The next evening, for the first time in a long time, I didn't stop by Frankie's place to have him come out with me. His company had suddenly become unwanted. Instead, I went around to Eighth Avenue by myself. As if to get my courage up sufficiently, I passed and repassed the doorway I had seen her go into, and finally took up my post in a closed-up store inset, across the way, and hopefully and watchfully began my first love-wait.

The love-wait—that sweet, and sometimes bittersweet, preliminary to each new meeting, which can be sanguine, sad, jealous, impatient, hurtful, angry, or even end in a heated quarrel; and which I
have sometimes thought has more in it of the true essence of the
love affair—is the better part by far of the two, than the actual
meeting itself that follows and ends it. For the latter is often hum-
drum, a let-down by comparison. Its opening remarks are certainly
never brilliant, or even worth the making, most of the time. And the
little things they say, and the little things they do, are quite commonplace after all, after the anticipatory reveries of the love-wait.

This love-wait can be carried out only by the boy or the man,
for if the girl or the woman carries it out, she somehow detracts by
just so much from it and from herself: from the desirability of
meeting her, from the uncertainty as to whether she will appear or
not, turning a mystic wistful expectancy, the borderline between
absence and presence, into a flat, casual, commonplace meeting.
Like the difference between a kiss and a handshake.

El trains would trundle by at intervals with a noise like low-
volume thunder and cast strange parallelograms and Grecian-key
friezes of light along the upper faces of the shrouded buildings, like
the burning tatters of a kite's tail, streaming evenly along in the
breezeless night. A little more often, one of the squared-off high-
topped autos of the early twenties would skirt over the gutters and
through the enfilading iron girders that supported the structure
above, with only an imminent collision to stop for, since there were
no traffic lights yet this far uptown.

And on the sidewalks, more numerous still than either of the others,
people on foot passed back and forth, as they'd always done on sidewalks, I suppose, since cities were first built, and as they'd continue to
do long after the elevated trains and the high-topped cars were gone.

Once another girl showed up unexpectedly, and scurried up the
few entrance-steps that led into the doorway, and I thought it was
she, and almost started forward from where I was standing to sprint
across the street and catch her before she went in. But then she
stopped and turned for a moment, to say something to someone on

the sidewalk behind her, and I saw her face and saw it wasn't, and sank back again upon my heels.

As the evening grew later, a sharp-edged wind sprang up, with the feel of cold rain in it. One of these supple, sinuous winds, able to round corners and make circles and eddies along the ground. It made me miserable, made me stamp my feet continuously and duck my chin down into the upturned collar of my coat, but I still wouldn't give up and go away. Until at last it was so late that I knew she wouldn't appear, or be able to linger with me if she did. Finally I turned and trudged off disconsolately, hands in pockets and downcast eyes on the sidewalk before me.

The following night the rain-threat of the night before had become an actuality, but that didn't keep me from my vigil. When you're eighteen and newly in love, what's rain? It didn't bother me as much as the wind had the night before, since it couldn't get into the niche of the store-entrance I had made my own, and the protective shed of the elevated-structure even kept the roadway of the street comparatively dry, though not the sidewalks, for there was an open canal above each one. The rain made the street seem gayer, not more dismal than it was at other times, for all these wet surfaces caught the lights more vividly and held them longer, as they went by. The rain was like an artist's palette, and these blobs of color, these smears of red and green and white and yellow and orange, hid the sooty grayness the street had in the light of day.

But at last I could see that, whatever the reason the night before, the weather would keep her in tonight. I had to turn and go away again, after standing a good deal less time.

The night after that, I reverted to my old habit and sought out Frankie. I wanted his advice. Or at least his reassurance that she actually did live there.

"Remember that girl you introduced me to couple days ago?" I blurted out almost as soon as we'd come out of his place.

"Vera? Sure," he said. "What about her?"

"Does she really live there, where you showed me?"

"Of course she does," he assured me. "Why would I lie about it?"

"Well, I hung around there all last night, and she never showed up, and I hung around all the night before—" I started to say it before I'd thought twice. I hadn't intended to tell him that part of it, but simply to find out if he'd seen her himself or knew her whereabouts. But once it was out, it was out, and too late to do anything about it. You're not anxious to tell even your closest friends about frustrations like that.

"In all that rain?" he chuckled, a wide grin overspreading his face.

"What's rain?" I said negligently.

This comment struck him as very funny, for some reason that I failed to see. He began to laugh uproariously, even bending over to slap himself on the kneecap, and he kept repeating incessantly: "Holy mackerel! Are *you* stuck on her! Waiting in the rain. No, you're not stuck on her, not much! Waiting in the rain."

"I wasn't *in* the rain," I corrected with cold dignity. "Maybe it was raining, but I wasn't *in* it."

I waited sullenly until his fit of (what I considered) tactless amusement had passed, then I suggested: "Let's go around there now, and see if we can see her. Maybe she's around there now." Why I would have been more likely to encounter her with him than alone, I wouldn't have been able to say. I think it was a case of misery wanting company.

When we'd reached the stepped-up entrance to her flat-building, we slung ourselves down onto the green-painted iron railing that bordered it, and perched there. We waited there like that for a while, I uneasily, he stolidly. Finally, craning his neck and looking up the face of the building toward its topmost windows, which were impossible to make out at such a perspective, he stirred restlessly and complained: "This ain't going' get us nowhere. She may not come down all night. Go up and knock right on the door. That's the only way you'll get her to come down." He repeated the story of having once been up there himself, and what kindly disposed people he'd found her family to be.

But this did nothing to overcome my timidity. "Not me," I kept repeating. "Nothing doing."

"Want me to come with you?" he finally offered, tired, I suppose, of being unable to get me to budge.

In one way I did, and in one way I didn't. I wanted his moral support, his backing, desperately, but I didn't want him hanging around us afterward, turning it into a walking-party of three.

"Come part of the way," I finally compromised. "But stay back; if she comes to the door, don't let her see you."

So we walked inside the ground-floor hallway and started to trudge up the stairs, I in the lead, but of necessity rather than choice. We got to the fifth floor, and started up the last flight. He stopped eight or nine steps from the top. I had to go on up the short remaining distance alone, quailingly and queasily.

When I made the turn of the landing and reached the door, I stopped, and just stood there looking at it.

"Go on, knock," he urged me in a hoarse whisper. "Don't just stand there."

I raised my hand as if measuring the distance it had to go, and then let it fall again.

"Go ahead. What's the matter with y'?" he hissed, hoarser and fiercer than before. He flung his arm up and then down again at me in utmost deprecation.

Again I raised my hand, touched the woodwork with it, let it fall back without striking. My knuckles had stage-fright; I couldn't get them to move.

Suddenly, before I knew what had happened, he bounded swiftly up the few remaining steps, whisked around the turn, and gave the door two heavy, massive thumps that (to my petrified ears, at least) sounded like cannon shots, the very opposite of what any signal of mine would be upon that particular door. Then he bounded back onto the stairs again, jolting down each flight with a sprightly but concussion-like jump that shook the whole stairwell. Before I had time to trace his defection (and perhaps turn around and go after him, as I was longing to do), the door had already opened and it was too late.

Vera's father stood there. Or at least, a middle-aged man did, and

I assumed he was her father. He had on a gray woolen undershirt and a pair of trousers secured over it by suspenders. He must have been relaxing in a chair *en deshabille* when the knock disturbed him, for he was reslinging one of them over his shoulder as he stood there. He had a ruddy-complexioned face, and although he was by no means a good-looking man, he was a good-natured–looking one.

If he protruded somewhat in the middle, it was not excessively so, not more than to be expected in a man of his (to my young mind) multiplicity of years. He certainly was not corpulent. I would have stood there indefinitely, without being able to open my mouth, if he hadn't spoken first.

Frankie's bombastic retreat was still in progress, and the sound of it reached his ears.

"What's that going on down there?" he wanted to know. Stepping to the railing, he bent over and tried to peer down the well.

"It must be somebody on one of the lower floors in a hurry to go out," I said meekly. It was technically the truth anyway, even if a subterfuge of it.

Then Frankie gained the street, and silence descended once more.

Coming back to the door and turning to me, the man asked, with a sort of jovial severity, "Well, young fellow, and what can I do for you?"

After a swallow to wet my throat first, I managed to get out: "Excuse me, is Vera in?" And then added, somewhat redundantly: "I'm a friend of hers."

"Oh, are you now?" he said with a chuckle. "Well, come on in, then. Glad to see you."

And before I realized it, I was on the inside, guided by his hand. The door had closed, and hundreds of her family seemed to be staring at me from all directions. Then the motes of momentary panic subsided in front of my eyes, and they condensed into no more than three or four people.

She wasn't there; I found that out almost at once. For the first moment or two I kept hoping she was merely out of sight in one of the other rooms, and would come in when she heard the

increased tempo of their voices, but since she didn't, and they
didn't call in to her, I finally had to resign myself to the fact that
she wasn't in the flat at all. I'd have to face the music by myself as
best I could.

In addition to her father, there were two other members of the
family present; one was her mother, and the other presumably an
aunt, but it took me some little time to differentiate between
them. There was also a little girl in the room, of about nine or ten,
whom they neglected to identify. I couldn't make out whether she
was a smaller sister of Vera's, or the aunt's child, or just some
neighbor's youngster given the freedom of the flat. In any case, at
my advanced age I considered her beneath notice.

My impressions of her mother are not nearly as clear as they are
of her father, possibly because he was the one who came to the
door and who I saw first, and without anyone else to distract my
attention. I have a vague recollection of a tall but spare woman,
with dark hair quite unlike Vera's, with an overtone of gray already
about it at the outside, where it had a tendency to fuzz and fly up
in gauzy little swatches that you could see the light through (the
grayness therefore might have been only an illusion), and she
would frequently put her hand to it and try to bring it back down
to order, but it would never obey for long. Of the aunt, I have no
surviving impressions whatever.

I sat down in the middle of all of them. They were probably actually spread about at random the way people usually are in a room,
but it felt as if they were sitting around me in a complete circle,
eyeing me critically and weighing me in the balance. I felt very constrained and ill at ease, and kept wishing I could sink through the
floor, chair and all. It had been the worst possible timing on my part,
too, I kept telling myself. If I'd just waited a few minutes longer and
not listened to Frankie, I could have met Vera by herself, intercepted
her when she came back and kept out of all this.

I'd already been smoking, sparingly but steadily, for some
months past, and I'd already found it to be good as a bracer in
moments of difficulty or stress. There was a package in my pocket

right as I sat there, but I was afraid to take it out in front of them. I wanted to make a good impression, and I cannily told myself that if they thought me too knowing or advanced for my years they might discourage my trying to see any more of her.

As soon as I'd given my name, her father said: "Oh, sure. Con, is that you? We've heard about you from Veronica."

(He called her Veronica, I noticed, never Vera. I couldn't, if I'd wanted to; there was something too stiff and distant about the name.)

And her mother, nodding approvingly, added: "Yes, she told us about meeting you."

Hearing this made me feel quite good, though it did nothing to alleviate my present misery. It showed she was interested, if nothing else, and it augured well for the future.

The next and natural question from her father was, what did I do, what sort of work?

I told him, with a slight touch of contrition, that I was going to college. This seemed to impress him, to my surprise. I had thought they might turn up their noses at me for not being an honest working-man. "Are you, now?" he said. "A college sthudent."

"I'm just a first-year man," I explained, again a little penitently. I had had impressed on my mind only too well the low opinion held about us by upperclassmen. "Freshman class, Frosh they call us. Then after that come sophomores. Then juniors. Then you're a senior."

Vera's mother clucked her tongue at this, and I wasn't quite sure how to translate the little sound accurately. I think it was intended as sympathy for all that hard work ahead.

"And what are you taking up?" her father asked. "What are you going to be after you get out?"

"Journalism," I said. "I want to be a writer."

"That's a hard job," he said forebodingly.

I tried to explain that I meant free-lance writing and not newspaper writing, that I was just majoring in journalism because that was the closest thing to it. But he didn't seem to follow that too well; he seemed content to remain with his original conception. And turning to Vera's mother, he said, "I think that's the first college sthudent Veronica's ever known, isn't it?"

She tactfully interposed: "Well, she's very young yet."

In the meantime, in spite of the conversation having been an easy one to carry on, since it had dealt exclusively with me, I kept wondering what there would be to talk about next, once this topic was over, and hoping that another elevated train would go clattering by momentarily and bring me a brief respite. It would be impossible to continue a conversation until after the front windows had stopped rattling. But none did. It seemed as though, just when you wanted them, they became few and far between.

At this point there was a twitching-about of the doorknob from the outside, the door was pushed open, and Vera came in. She'd evidently been to the store for groceries. She hugged two very large brown paper bags in one arm, and since these came up past one side of her face and hid it, she did not see me at first.

She rounded her cheeks, blew out her breath, and said something about the stairs. That they were enough to kill you, I think it was. But in a good-natured, not ill-humored way. She closed the door by pushing a heel back against it, without turning.

I remember thinking how graceful and debonair was the little flirt and swirl this movement created in the loose-hanging checked coat she had on, as I watched her do it. Then she turned her head suddenly, so that the obscuring bags were swept to one side, and saw me.

"Con!" she said, in a high-pitched voice that was almost a little scream. She nearly dropped the columnar bags, but reclasped them just in time. "How did you get up here?"

"I walked up," I answered in perfect seriousness, without stopping to think, and they all laughed at that, herself included, as though I'd intended it to be very funny.

"I never thought I'd find *you* up here," she said next. "You're the last one!"

I wasn't sure what she meant by that; and afraid that, if I asked her, the answer might turn out to be unwelcome, I didn't ask.

"How did you know where it was?" she went on. "How did you know this was the right place?"

My instinct told me it might not be in my own best interest to bring Frankie's name into this, or recall him to her mind any more than was strictly necessary. She'd known him before she had me, after all. So I simply and untruthfully said: "I asked somebody in the house," and that seemed to content her.

I had a fleeting impression, as I watched her expression and listened to the intonation of what she was saying to me, that she was enjoying, rather than otherwise, having her entire family as spectators to this little meeting of ours, and auditors to its accompanying dialogue, liked having their attention fixed on her the way it was. But if *she* enjoyed it, I didn't, quite the opposite, and this nerved me to summon up courage to come out with what had brought me up there in the first place.

"Vera," I said nervously, "would you like to come for a walk with me?"

She didn't answer directly, but said "Wait'll I take these back where they belong first," and picking up the two cumbersome bags, which she had set down upon a table, she left the room with them. She was gone for some time, longer than would have been necessary simply to carry them back to the kitchen and set them down there, so I began to imagine she had stopped off in her own room on the way, to tidy her hair or something of the sort. Then when she came back, I saw that she had removed both the checked coat and the tamoshanter she had been wearing, and my hopes were dashed.

After a lame pause, I finally asked her a second time: "Vera, wouldn't you like to come for a walk?"

"I don't know if I can," she said, and I saw her exchange a look with her mother.

The latter remarked cryptically, "You run along. I'll do them for you tonight, and you can do them tomorrow night instead."

Whereupon Vera hurried back inside again, throwing me an auspicious "I'll be ready in a minute, Con," over her shoulder, and this time, when she returned, was once more in coat and tamoshanter, and ready to leave.

I said the required polite and stilted good-byes, she opened the door, and a minute later we were free and by ourselves on the other side of it.

"It was my turn to do the dishes tonight," she told me as we went scrabbling down the stairs, she running her hand along the banister railing, I on the outside with her other hand in mine.

The moment we were by ourselves, the moment the door had closed behind us, perfect ease and naturalness came back to me again, and to Vera too, though she hadn't felt herself to be on exhibition as I had: One didn't have to weigh one's words, they just came flowing out in any kind of order, and yet inevitably they were the right words, without the trouble of trying to make them so beforehand. One didn't have to execute each smallest move or gesture twice, once in the mind and once in the actuality, they too flowed unchecked in perfect unstudiedness. There were no questions that required answers, none were put and none were given, there were just confidences streaming out and blending.

And I remember wondering at the time why this should be, for they had been amiable enough, her people, hadn't been unfriendly, had tried to make me feel at ease, and yet they hadn't been able to. I think I know now: It wasn't because we were a boy and girl who were interested in each other that we felt this lack of constraint the moment we were away from them, it was because we were both of the same generation, and they were not.

There is an insurmountable wall, a barrier, between each generation, especially in the earlier stages of life. Children are so cut off from the grown-up world they are almost a species apart, a different breed of creature than the rest of the race. Very young people of our age, hers and mine, have no interests whatever in common with those who are in the next age group. Then as we progress up through the thirties, the barrier becomes less and less, until finally it has melted away altogether, and everyone is middle-aged alike. Twenty-five and forty-five seem alike to us now. But by that time a new barrier has formed, at the back instead of the front, and new very young are once more walled off from those who, only yesterday, were the very young themselves.

I asked her if she wanted to see a movie.

"No," she said. "Let's just walk instead. I saw the one at the Morningside a couple of days ago, and they haven't changed it yet."

We stopped in first at an ice-cream parlor on the corner of 116th Street. This had little tables separated from each other by lattices, up which clambered waxed-linen leaves and cretonne flowers. It also had an electric player piano at the back, forerunner of the later jukeboxes, and arched festoons of small, gaily colored light bulbs, curved like arabesques across the ceiling. There was a marble-topped soda fountain running the length of it at one side, but we sat down opposite one another at one of the little tables.

She made a selection, and I followed suit and ordered what she had.

These were called banana splits, as far as I can recall. They were served in oblong glass receptacles with stems on them, for no ordinary-size dish could have held everything that went into them. The holder was lined first with two half bananas, sliced lengthwise. On top of these were placed three mounds of ice cream in a row, green, white, and pink. Over these in turn was poured a chocolate syrup. Next were added chunks of pineapple and a sprinkling of chopped or grated nuts. The whole thing was surmounted by a feathery puff of whipped cream, and into this was stuck a maraschino cherry, dyeing the whipped cream red around it.

Beside each of these, for obvious reasons, was placed a glass of plain water.

That we found this concoction not only edible but even immensely enjoyable is only another illustration of the differences there are between the generations.

When we got up I left a tip on the table, more to impress her than for the sake of the waiter. I saw her eyes rest on it for a moment, as I had hoped they would.

After we left there, we walked over to Morningside Park, and through it along a softly lamplit pathway. It is a long but narrow park, no more than a block in depth at any point. That part of New York is built on two levels, and Morningside Heights, which runs along the western edge of the park, is perched high above Morningside Drive, which runs along the eastern edge. From it you can overlook all that part of the city which lies to the eastward, its rooftops and its lights.

We walked along slowly, our hands lightly linked and swinging low between us. I began to whistle "Kalua," which had just come out a little while before, and after a while she accompanied me by humming it along with me. For years, whenever I heard "Kalua," it brought back that first walk I took with her, and I could feel her fingers lightly twined in mine again, and see the lamplight falling over us again in blurry patches like slowly sifted, softly falling cornmeal.

She asked me where I lived, myself. I told her One-hundred-thirteenth Street.

"We're just a block apart," she noted. "Only, on different sides of the park."

But New York then, in its residential zoning, was a snobbish, stratified sort of town, and the park did more than divide it physically, it divided it economically as well. That, however, was of no concern to us. That applied only to our elders.

We climbed the wide, easily sloping stairs that led to the upper level and came out at 116th Street, at that little rotunda with its bas-reliefs and circular stone seat-rest, and stood there a while, taking in the spread of the city's lights below and outward from us, until the eye couldn't follow them anymore, and lost them in the reaches of the night. But the young haven't too much time to spend on mere inanimate beauty, they're too immediately interested in each other.

We turned away and walked down Morningside Heights a block or two, and opposite, where there was a little French church standing, called Notre Dame de Lourdes, I think. We sat down together on a bench without saying a word, and moved close.

And from that night on, whenever we met, we always met at that one particular bench and never any other. I used to wonder at times, later, who had been sitting there after we did, who had met there once we stopped going to it, and if they were young like we were, and if they were happy: what *their* stories were, and how they turned out in the end. They never knew about us, we never knew about them. For park benches can't talk.

We kissed, and nestled close, and (I suppose) laughed together about something now and then. The pattern never changes throughout time. Then presently and very tentatively I crossed the line from the innocuous to the more innate.

The first time she let it pass unnoticed, either not wanting to seem too edgy and ready to take offense, or else mistakenly thinking it had been unintentional and the wiser thing to do was not to call attention to it, and I, misconstruing, repeated it. This time she caught my hand and held it fast, but in such a minor-keyed way that it is difficult to put it into exact words. For she didn't brush it off or fling it aside peremptorily, but held it still with hers, almost where it had been but not quite, so that her gesture couldn't be mistaken for collaboration, only for the deterrent it was.

"Don't do that," she said in a low-spoken voice that was all the more inflexible for that reason. "I'll get up from here if you do.

"And I don't want to," she went on after a moment. "I like you, and I like being here with you."

I kept quiet, feeling that it was not up to me to do the talking. And even if it had been, not knowing what there would have been to say, the thing was so self-explanatory. In my own mind I unjustly put her into the position of having to excuse or at least explain herself, when it should have been the other way around. But she seemed to accept the role without questioning its fairness.

"I know how some girls feel about it," she said thoughtfully. " 'Oh, it's just this once, with this one boy. Then it'll never happen again.' But it does happen again. If you didn't stop the first time, then you never will the second. And before you know, it's with another boy. And then another boy. And pretty soon, with *any* boy at all."

Made uncomfortable, I gave a slight pull to my hand, and she released it, and I drew it away.

"I want to get married someday," she explained. "And when I do, I don't want to have anything to hide." And tracing the point of her shoe thoughtfully along the ground in little patterns and watching it as she did so, she went on: "I wouldn't want to stand up in a church, and know that somewhere some other man was laughing at my husband behind his back. I wouldn't be entitled to wear a bridal veil, it would be a lie before God." Then she asked me point blank: "Would you want to marry somebody that had been with everybody else before that?"

She stopped and waited for my answer.

I hated to have to give her the answer, because it vindicated her own argument so.

"No," I said grudgingly, at last.

I wondered if her mother had instilled this into her, if they had had a talk about it, for it must have come from somewhere to be so strong and clear-sighted in her, but I didn't think it was right to openly ask her.

But almost as if she had read my mind, she added: "I don't need anybody else to tell me. I've had it all thought out from the time I was fourteen, already. From the time I first knew about things like that. Or knew a little about them, anyway. I made up my mind that when I got older, no matter how much I cared for a fellow, it wasn't going to be that way."

"It don't have to be that way," she reiterated, unshakably. "No matter how much in love a girl and a fellow are, it still don't have to be that way."

I remember thinking that, as she spoke, the slight dent in the grammar only added to, didn't detract from, the beautiful sincerity of her conviction.

I looked at her in a new way now, commending her, esteeming her, for the values she adhered to. Nineteen is basically idealistic, far more than the after-years are, and in spite of its young blood would rather have an ideal it can look up to, that keeps itself just beyond reach of the everyday grubbing fingers.

She probably translated the look. I saw her smile with quiet contentment, as if that were the way she had hoped to be looked at. Then, as if to make up for any crestfallenness I might have felt, she stroked me lightly but affectionately along the side of the face with the tips of her fingers. And bunching her lips and poising them, commanded me winningly, "Now let me have a kiss."

After I'd taken her back to her own door and then gone home myself, I thought about it. I'd been very intent in the first place: I could tell that easily enough, as I took off my clothing piece by piece to get ready for bed. But that wasn't the important thing, that was just a reflex, little better than a muscle-spasm. I sat down in a chair first, to quiet down before I tried to sleep, and I turned the whole thing over in my mind.

The important thing about her refusal was the vastly longer term of life and the far more indelible imprint it gave to our relationship. It changed what would have been an overnight thing into a more or less permanent affinity, at least as far as the foreseeable future was concerned. On the one hand there would have been a few short weeks of furtive, overheated meetings, and then oblivion. No name to remember, no face to recall. On the other hand, there was an uncurtailed succession of joyous, daily encounters, sprightly, open and unashamed, and though immature perhaps, in every sense a budding love affair. And an imperishable print on the memory. She stayed with me ever since. I still remember her name, and some of the things she said, and some of the clothes she wore, and some of the ways she looked. There's a sort of inverse ratio at work there.

Women, even very young girl-women (which amounts to the same thing), must walk a precarious tightrope. If they fall off, into somebody's waiting arms, they almost always lose him in the end. If they stay on, even though he's been kept at a distance, they capture some part of him.

I think I dimly sensed this to some extent, even that very first night as I sat there and thought it over. But if I didn't then, I certainly realize it now, as I look back from forty years away. For I must have had some girl fully, must have had my first girl fully, then or not long after. But not a trace of recollection remains. Yet Vera still stays in my mind. The very fact that I'm writing this is proof enough of that.

That first-night incident on the bench set the whole pattern from then on for our little sentimental interlude. (And I suppose it was little, but it was a valid one nevertheless; seventeen and nineteen can't have a bravura romance.) It was understood between us without speaking about it any further, it was crystallized, that that was the way it was going to be. And that was the way it was. And I myself wanted it that way now just as much as she did. She personified that to me now, she was its identification. She wore a halo, as far as I was concerned. Youthful and jaunty and informal, but a halo just the same.

We met every day from then on, without missing one. But not always at the same time. For my schedule of classes was zigzag, no two days alike, and since it was all Greek to her anyway, no matter how often I tried to have her memorize it, she always got to the bench before I did in order to be sure to be on time.

I'd see her doll-sized figure from a distance. As I came closer she'd jump to her feet and fling her arms wide in pantomimic welcome, while I'd break into a headlong run, and as I reached her, I tossed my books carelessly over to the side in order to have both arms free for the hug that would follow.

There was something of the antic in this. We both recognized it and we both would have been willing to admit it. But the underlying emotion was bona fide enough; it was just that we didn't know how to handle it, so we parodied it. If we were too young to actually be in love, to know how to be in love, then we were certainly smitten with one another, infatuated with one another, that much was sure.

We'd sit there for hours sometimes, oblivious of the needling cold, huddled closely together, sometimes my coat around the two of us, our breaths forming bladder-shapes of vapor like the dialogue-balloons cartoonists draw coming out of their characters' mouths.

We talked a lot. I don't remember about what; the language of the young. You forget that language very quickly; within a few short years it's a foreign tongue, the knack for it is completely gone. Sometimes, though, we were quiet and tenderly pensive.

I used to get home at all hours. I ate alone almost every night now; everyone else had usually finished by the time I showed up. But I'd find something put aside and kept warm for me. What it was I never knew half the time, I was so wrapped up in retrospect repetitions of what had just taken place. I don't recall that my family ever voiced any remonstrances about it. They seem to have been very lenient in this respect. Maybe being the only male, even though a very unseasoned one, in a household of two doting women had something to do with it.

This routine went on daily for about two or three months, as the season began its final climb to the holidays at the top of the year and 1922 slowly blended into 1923. Then a fly landed in the honey, from a totally unexpected quarter. I came home one evening and my mother remarked: "Hetty Lambert called up today while you were out."

This was a life-long friend of my mother's. They had been schoolgirl chums, and the intimacy had continued uninterrupted into the married lives of both. Hetty had been well-to-do in her own right even as a youngster (my mother had told me), and she had married a man in the silk-import business who was in turn exceedingly well off, so she must have been a very wealthy woman.

For my part, from my pre-twenty point of view, I found her musty and dowdy. When she wasn't spending whole mornings clipping coupons in a bank vault, she was spending afternoons visiting with her dead in the family mausoleum. Their one recreation, she and her husband, was a lifetime box at the Metropolitan Opera, but since he invariably fell asleep in it, even that was wasted. She used to do her own marketing for the table personally, squeezing produce, with an elderly chauffeur following her around with a basket to put them in, and if she thought the weight was a bit short or the price a few cents too high she would fume to the high heavens, until they let her have it her way for the sake of peace and quiet.

"What'd she have to say?" I said, totally uninterested but dutifully willing to appear to listen for the sake of the high regard my mother seemed to hold her in.

"Thursday of next week is her daughter's birthday. Janet's giving a little party for her friends, and she wants you to come."

"Oh, no I'm not!" I promptly burst out. "That's the last place I'm going. You don't get me there, not on your life!" And so on, at great length.

"I don't see why you feel that way," my mother remonstrated mildly, when I had finally come to a stop. "You've gone every year, since you were both children. You went last year."

"Last year was different." Meaning I'd been a year younger then. And mainly, I hadn't known Vera then.

Then, perhaps thinking this might be an added inducement, she went on reassuringly: "Hetty and her husband aren't going to be there. They're going out for the evening, and turning over the whole apartment to Janet and her friends."

But this was no inducement whatever as far as I was concerned. I found Janet about as appealing—romantically speaking—as an overstuffed chair with broken-down springs, whether her mother was present or not. No mutual dislike felt by two boys toward one another (or by two girls toward one another, for that matter) can ever quite equal in wholehearted intensity the very occasional and very rare dislike felt toward one another by a boy *and* girl, when it does happen to come along. And that was the case with us. We had a beautiful, inbred ill will toward one another, due most likely to having been thrown so constantly at each other's heads when we were both small children.

There wasn't a thing about her that suited me. Her laugh resembled a sneer. Her most inconsequential remark had a cutting edge, but you only realized it sometime after the cuticle had slowly started peeling back. Her clothes were probably costly, but she always managed to do something to them that spoiled the looks of them. Just by being in them, I guess. Her manners weren't bad, for only one reason. She didn't have any at all. She was the only young girl I had ever seen who crumbled her rolls up into pieces at a dinner-party table and then threw them at every boy around her. Not just momentarily, but throughout each and every course, until they became miserable trying to eat without getting hit.

Even the way she kissed was a form of snobbish superiority. She didn't kiss with her mouth at all. She tilted her nose in the air and pushed her cheek up against the recipient somewhere just below the eardrum. I hadn't kissed her since we were twelve, but I had watched her kiss her mother and her older married sister, and she did it that way even with them.

All in all, though it was difficult for me then (and now) to find an exact verbal synonym for the word "brat," a pictorial one was easy to come by. It was simply Janet. She was the perfect spoiled rich brat.

"You'll have to call her up, one way or the other," my mother said, still trying to persuade me. "You can't just ignore it. Even if you're not fond of Janet," she pointed out, "you may have a good time. There may be somebody there you'll like."

A sudden inspiration hit me. You bet there will be somebody there I like, I promised myself. I'll see to it that there is!

I made the courtesy call back, as required. The maid answered first, and then called Janet to the phone.

" 'lo," Janet said, in that sulky voice that was a characteristic of hers.

" 'lo," I answered, equally uncordial.

Neither of us ever used our given names to one another any more than was strictly necessary: another sign of fondness.

"Are you coming?" she asked briefly.

"Yeah," I answered. Then my voice took on an added degree of animation. "Listen," I said.

"What?" she asked, as lifeless as ever.

"Can I bring somebody with me?"

"A boy?" she asked, and her voice perked up a little.

"Nah, not a boy," I said disgustedly. Who'd ever heard of taking another fellow along with you to a party? "A girl."

"Oh," she said, and her voice deflated again. Then after a moment's reflection she agreed, without any great show of enthusiasm. "I s'pose so. There was one girl short at the table, anyhow."

I couldn't wait to tell Vera about it. I came rushing up to the bench the following day, kissed her breathlessly and for once almost perfunctorily, and pulling her down onto the bench along with me, blurted out: "Know what? We've been invited to a party."

But to my surprise, instead of being pleased, she acted appalled about it at first. "Where is it?" she asked, and when I'd told her, she kept repeating almost hypnotically, "But *Riverside Drive!* I can't go *there*."

"What's so wonderful about Riverside Drive?" I said, shrugging uncomprehendingly. "I've been to their place lots of times. In the wintertime they get all the ice-cold wind blowing in from the river. And in the summer, when it *would* be cooler than other parts of town, they're not there to enjoy it anyway."

But temperature wasn't the deterrent, some kind of monetary denominator—or differential—was. Her mind evidently magnified it and couldn't rid itself of the fixed idea. I had never taken this into account myself, so I wasn't in a position to see her point of view.

"That isn't what I mean!" she said impatiently. "Only rich people live there."

"What difference does it make?" I said. "You're going with *me*. You're not worried about *me*, are you? Then why worry about them?"

"But you're different," she said, groping to find the right words. "I never think about you in that way, maybe because I'm used to you. You're *friendly*, and you never seem to dress up much. And besides, you're a fellow, and it's not the fellows that worry me as much as it is the girls."

"What about them? They're a bunch of drips. You've got more real personality than all of them put together," I said loyally.

But I couldn't seem to overcome her misgivings.

"And what about a dress? What kind are they going to wear?"

"I d'no," I said vaguely. "Dresses for dancing in, I guess. Haven't you got one of those?"

"When do I go dancing?" she said, almost resentfully.

When we separated that evening, I still hadn't been able to bring her to the point of agreeing to come. The most I could get her to say was "I'll think it over, and I'll let you know."

The next time we met it was the same thing, and the time after. As far as I could judge her attitude, it wasn't coyness or wanting to be coaxed. She seemed attracted to the idea of going, and yet at the same time something seemed to keep holding her back. One time she even made the outrageous suggestion: "I'll walk down there with you as far as the door, and then you go in by yourself. I could even meet you later, after you leave." Then before I had time for the heated protest that I felt this deserved, she quickly recanted it, saying, "No, that would be foolish, wouldn't it?"

I finally told her, another time, "Let's forget about it. If you're not going, then I'm not either. Who needs the party?"

But she wouldn't hear of this either. "No, I'm not going to dish you out of the party. You're expected there, and if you don't show up, I'll get the blame. You'll have to go. I won't meet you that night, I won't come out at all, so if you don't go, you'll be all by yourself."

"We go together, or we stay away together," I insisted stubbornly, as I had right along.

This went on for nearly the whole week or eight days preceding the controversial little event. Then on the very night before, after I'd already just about given up all further hope of persuading her and was ready to quit trying once and for all, she suddenly said—not at the very first, but after we'd been sitting there together for quite some time—"I'm going to tell you something that'll please you. Want to hear it?"

I told her sure, sure I did.

"I'm going with you tomorrow night."

I bounced to my feet, took hold of her two hands in my two, and swung them vigorously in and out, to give vent to my elation.

"I made up my mind several days ago," she admitted, smiling at my enthusiasm, "but I didn't tell you until now because I wanted to keep it as a surprise."

The dinner had been set for "somewhere between seven-thirty and eight" (Janet's words), so we arranged to meet three-quarters of an hour earlier, in order to give ourselves time enough to get there without hurrying. She told me to wait for her at the bench, she'd come there, and I gave in to that readily enough. I didn't like the idea of having to pass in review before her whole family, anyway.

By six-fifteen the following evening, all aglow, I'd completed my rather uncomplicated toilette, which included the by-now semi-weekly rite of a light overall shave, more in tribute to the future than a present necessity, and put on my one dark blue suit. I stopped in to see my mother for a minute, before leaving.

"Are you taking her anything?" she asked me. "Because I have a little unopened bottle of cologne you could have. It would save you the expense of buying something."

"I'll pick her up a box of candy on the way," I said evasively. I knew I wouldn't; I didn't think that much of Janet.

"I'd like to take her a baseball bat, and give it to her over the head!" I added darkly.

She was laughing, accommodatingly but a little unsurely, as I left her.

I was ahead of time, Vera wasn't there yet, when I got to the bench.

I sat down to wait for her, and at first I whistled and was relaxed, one knee cocked up high in front of me and my hands locked around it. But the minutes came, the minutes went, more minutes came, more went, and still she didn't arrive. Pretty soon I wasn't carefree anymore, I was on needles and pins. I turned and I twisted and I shifted; I constantly changed position, as though by doing that I would bring her there faster. I crossed my legs over one way, then over the other. I swung my hoisted foot like a pendulum. I drummed the bench-seat with my fingers like the ticking away of a fast-moving taxi meter. I raked my nails through my hair, wrecking its laboriously achieved sleekness. I clasped my hands at the back of my neck and let my elbows hang from there. I probably smoked more than in any comparable length of time up to that point in my short young life.

I even combined two positions into one, so to speak—the sitting and the standing—using the top of the bench-back for a seat and planting my feet on the seat itself.

It was while I was in this last hybrid position that I heard a skittering sound, like raindrops spattering leaves, and a small figure came rushing out of the lamp-spiked darkness toward me. A figure smaller than Vera, anyway. It was the little girl who'd been up in the flat that first day I went there, and who seemed to tag around after Vera a good deal. I'd glimpsed her more than once hanging around, helping Vera pass the time while she was waiting for me on the bench, and then when I came along she'd discreetly drift off, probably at a confidential word from Vera.

She seemed to have run all the way, judging by her breathlessness; it was no inconsiderable distance for a youngster her size. Or maybe it was only feasible for that very reason, because of her young age.

"What happened?" I asked, hopping down from the bench-back. "Why didn't she meet me here like she said she was going to?"

But she only repeated verbatim the message she had been given, evidently having been told nothing else. "She says come right away. She's waiting for you at her house."

I bolted off without even giving the poor little thing time to stand still a minute and catch her breath. She turned and faithfully started back the way she had just come, following me. But my long legs soon outdistanced her shorter ones, and after falling behind more and more, she finally bleated out: "Don't go so fast! I can't keep up with you!"

I stopped a couple of times to let her catch up, but finally I shouted back to her, rather unfeelingly: "You're holding me up! I can't stand and wait for you each time. Come back by yourself!" And I sprinted off and soon left her completely behind.

When I got to the building that housed Vera's flat, I ran up the whole six flights without a pause even at landings—but if you can't do it at that age, then you never can do it at all—and finally, half-suffocating, I rapped on the door with tactful restraint (remembering the terrible thump Frankie had given it that first day, and trying not to repeat it).

The door opened, but there was no one standing there alongside it. Then Vera's voice said, from in back of it: "Come on in, but keep walking straight ahead and don't turn your head. Hold your hands over your eyes."

I thought, for a minute, she hadn't finished dressing yet, and wondered why she'd admitted me so quickly in that case. I heard her close the door.

Then she said: "Now you can turn. But don't look yet."

Obediently I turned, eyelids puckered up, exaggeratedly tight, as though normal closing in itself wasn't a sufficient guarantee.

"Now!" she said triumphantly. "Now look."

I opened my eyes and looked, and she was all dressed up for the party.

"How do you like me?" she asked eagerly.

It was blue, I'm almost sure. I *was* sure then, but I'm not sure now anymore. But I think it must have been blue. She was a blonde, and it would have been blue more likely than anything else.

"My aunt ran it up for me on her machine," she went on breathlessly. "We bought the material at Koch's, on a-Hunner-twenty-fifth. We only needed four yards, and we even had some leftover for a lampshade when we got through."

Looking at it, I could well believe it. They were wearing them short and skimpy that year.

"But that isn't all I've got to show you. Just wait'll you see this!" She went hurrying into one of the other rooms, a bedroom, I guess, and then paper crackled in there. It didn't rustle softly, as tissue paper would have; it crackled sharply, more as stiff brown wrapping paper would.

Then she came back, something swirling blurrily about her as it settled into place.

"What've you got to say now?" she cried.

The blue party-shift had disappeared from view, and she had glossy fur wrapped all around her, covering her everywhere, except her face and legs. She was hugging it tight to her, caressing it, luxuriating in it, in a way I can't describe. I'd never seen a girl act that way over something inanimate before. She even tilted her head and stroked one cheek back and forth against it, over and over and over again. She made love to it, that's about all I can say.

I don't know what kind it was. I didn't know anything about furs then. Years later, when it had gotten so that I could identify mink, simply by dint of constant sight-references ("Mink," somebody would say, and then I would look at it), I realized in retrospect that whatever it had been, it hadn't been mink. It hadn't been that dark a shade of brown. It had been more a honey-colored kind of brown. Anyway:

"Holy mackerel!" I cried in excitement, or something equally fatuous but equally sincere, and I took a step backward in a parody of going off balance that was only partly pretense.

She kept turning from side to side, and then pivoting all the way around like a professional model, showing it to me from all angles. Her little eyebrows were arched in the cutest expression of mimic hauteur I'd ever seen then or ever have since.

"But it must have cost a pile of money," I said anxiously. "How'd you ever get them to . . . ?"

"Oh, it's not all paid for," she said facilely. "We made a down payment on it, and they let us take it home on approval. If we're not satisfied we can return it, and they'll give us our money back."

"I didn't know they did that with fur coats," I said, impressed. But then I didn't know much about the fur-coat traffic anyway. "It's the cat's meow," I said, which was the utmost you could give to anything in commendation.

We kissed, I in ecstatic admiration, she in jubilant satisfaction at being so admired. "Don't spoil my mouth, now," she cautioned, but even that didn't mar the kiss, for though she withheld her lips protectively from mine, she held my head between her two hands in affectionate pressure.

"We all set, now?" I asked.

"Just one thing more," she said. She produced a tiny glass vial, not much thicker than a toothpick, and uncapped it. She stroked herself with it at several preordained places: at the base of her throat and in back of both ears. "Woolworth's," she said. "But it's good stuff. You only get a couple of drops for twenty-five cents."

It smelled very good to me, that was all I knew. Like a hundred different flowers ground up into a paste and leavened with honey.

"Don't let me forget to turn out all the lights," she said with a final look around. "They'll raise cain if I do. It costs like the devil when you leave the electh-tricity on all night." I remember how she said it. That was how she said it. Electh-tricity. It sounded even better than the right way.

That taken care of, we closed the door after us and went rattling down the stairs, on our way at last.

"Have you got a key for when you come home, or will you have to wake them up?" I asked her on the way down.

"My aunt gave me hers for tonight," she said. "I don't think they'll be back until after we are. They went to a wake, and you know how long those things last."

I didn't, but I nodded knowingly, so she wouldn't know I didn't.

When we reached the street-entrance, she stopped short, and even seemed to shrink back within its recesses for a moment, almost as though she were afraid to come out into the open, you might say. "How're we going down there?" she asked.

"Why, in a taxi, of course," I answered loftily. "I wouldn't take you any other way, dressed the way you are."

"Well then you go out ahead and get one, and bring it back to the door with you," she said. "I'll wait inside here until you do. I don't want any of the neighbors to see me standing around on the sidewalk dressed like this. Then by tomorrow, it'll be all over the house."

"What's that their business?" I asked truculently, but I went ahead and did what she'd suggested.

I got one about a block away, got in, and rode back to the doorway in it. Then I got out and held the door open for Vera.

There was a moment's wait, like when you're gathering yourself together to make a break for it. Then Vera came rushing out headlong and scurried in. I never saw anyone get into a waiting taxi so fast. She was like a little furry animal scampering for cover.

She pushed herself all the way over into the corner of the seat, out of sight. "Put the light out," she whispered urgently.

The closing of the door, as I got in after her, cut it off automatically. I heard her give a deep, heartfelt sigh as it went out, and thought it was probably one of contentment because we were finally on the last lap of our way to the party.

I told the driver Janet's address, and we started off, she and I clasping hands together on the seat between us.

The lights came at us and went by like shining volleyballs rolling down a bowling alley, and it was great to be young, and to be sitting next to your girl in a hustling taxi, and to be going to a party with her. It's never so much fun in your whole life afterward as it is that first time of all.

I remember thinking: This is only the beginning. I'll go to other parties with Vera, like this. Every party I ever go to from now on, I'll go to only with Vera.

I can no longer recall too many of the particulars of the party, at this distance, just its overall generalities. It was about average for its time and for its age group, I guess: like any other party then, and probably still pretty much like any such party now, given a few insignificant variations in tricks of dress and turns of dance and turns of speech. The basic factor remains the same: the initial skirmishing of very young men and girls in preparation for the pairing off of later life. Learning the rules for later on. The not-quite-fully mature, trying to act the part of grown-ups. No, that's not wholly accurate, either. For we were enclosed in our own world, and therefore we *were* what we seemed to ourselves to be, in every sense of the word. We reacted to one another on that plane, and that made it a fact. Those outside that world were not the real grown-ups, they were simply aliens, and their viewpoint had no validity among us. The wall of the generations.

She had a fleeting moment or two of uncertainty, of faltering self-confidence, as we stood facing the door, waiting for it to be opened. I could tell it by the whiteness of her face, by the strained fixity of her eyes. Then as the room spread itself out before us like a slowly opening, luminous, yellow and ivory fan, alive with moving figures and flecks of disparate color—the party—her lack of assurance passed and she swept forward buoyantly, almost with a lilt to her step, not more than two or three fingers lightly touching the turn of my arm in token indication that I was her escort. And from then on, all the rest of the evening, that was the word to describe her: buoyant. Whether she was standing or sitting still, dancing or just moving about without music; whatever she was doing. She seemed to skim over the floor instead of being held to it like the rest of us.

She was well liked at once, it was easy to see that. All the very first words that followed my pronunciation of her name each time were warm and friendly and interested and showed a real eagerness on the speaker's part to become better acquainted with her, over and above the formal politeness that the occasion indicated. We weren't much on formal politeness anyway, at our ages.

I had expected the boys to like her, but the girls very patently did too. For a boy will like almost any girl except the most objectionable, that's part of his make-up, but to be liked by her own kind is the real test of popularity for a girl. Within an hour or two of the start of the affair, Vera was a beckoned-to and sought-after and arms-about-waists member of each successive little group and coterie that went inside to the bedroom to giggle and chatter and powder its collective noses away from the boys for a few moments' respite. She was as incandescent as a lighted lamp swinging from the ceiling of an old-fashioned ship's cabin and darting its rays into the farthest corners.

But Janet was the big surprise of it all. I had fully expected her to be her usual prickly self, and though for my own part this wouldn't have fazed me in the least (I even welcomed it, for it put us on a more even footing of mutual ill will, of verbal give-and-take with no holds barred), I had intended to do all I could to protect Vera from her quills. But it turned out not to be necessary at all. Janet seemed to take to her from the moment that she first stepped forward to welcome her, sizing her up in one quick, comprehensive, head-to-foot look, the kind even very young girls her age are fully capable of giving. She obviously liked her, whatever her reasons. From then on, she made her the exception to the entire group. She was quite simple, natural, unaffected, cordial, and hospitable toward her, with just a touch of self-effacement. Her smiles were elfin, but at least they were real smiles. Her remarks had no rusty razor blades embedded in them. A new Janet I had never seen before began to peer shyly forth.

I caught myself thinking as I watched her: Well, I'll be darned. Sometimes you know people for years, and then suddenly you find out you don't really know them at all. Somebody new comes along who brings out another side to them that you didn't even suspect was there, simply because it never had been shown to you before. This is how she would be if she had really liked anyone before. She feels about all of us exactly as I feel about her; she's known us all too long and well, and she sees only our unappealing qualities by now.

We had dinner first, and then afterward we danced. We played records on the phonograph and danced to them: "Kalua," which was just going out, and "April Showers," which was just coming in, and others which were in-between. The phonographs of the day were upright consoles, generically called victrolas, although other manufacturers in addition to the Victor Company marketed them. The average one still had to be cranked by hand, although a few of the costlier ones could now be operated on electrical current, but that was as far as mechanization had gone. They stopped after just one record each time, and a new one had to be put on by hand. We were uncomplaining, though. Our older brothers and sisters, or at least the younger ones among our parents, had had to rely for the most part on player pianos and hand-played pianos, and squeaky, open-topped little turntables with tremendous tulip-horn amplifiers, when they wanted to dance in their homes.

We had dinner and we danced, and that's all there really was to the party.

We were the last ones to leave, Vera and I. I think we would have stayed on even longer if it weren't for the fact that we were now reduced (from my point of view, at least) to being alone with the unpleasing Janet. Vera seemed not to mind how long we stayed. She was so keyed up and animated from the hours-long peak of stimulation whipped up by the party (just like an actress is after an opening night, I suppose) that she kept talking away without a let-up, as if there were still dozens of people there and not just three of us.

Janet, whom I had frequently known to be quite ungracious and even blunt in her dismissals (she had once said to a whole group of us, holding the door back at full width, "All right, everybody out; go home now"), seemed to enjoy having her stay. She sat beside Vera, an arm about her shoulder, nibbling at something from the refreshment table, drinking in everything she said with little nods and grins of accord. But it was close to one o'clock, which was still a fairly raffish hour for us at that stage of our lives, and I finally suggested to Vera she'd better let me take her home.

"Oh, what a lovely party that was!" she burst out as we emerged from the glowingly warm building into the cold, bracing night air, which immediately formed little wisps of steamy breath in front of our faces. "I never dreamed I'd have such a good time. My head's still swimming from it." And while I was busy scanning the street for a cab, she spread her coat and dress out wide between her out-stretched hands and executed a succession of little whirling dance steps, waltz-turns, there on the sidewalk, turning, reversing, then turning back again.

Back at her house, we hustled all the way up those six flights of stairs, and then stopped suddenly almost at the top, and threw our arms around each other, as much in high spirits as in love. We stood there, and we kissed, and we whispered so low that no one standing right beside us could have heard, even if there had been someone standing right beside us.

Something more could have happened; she would not have opposed it. She was stirred by the party, intoxicated by her success at it, and this would have been part of that, and that would have been part of this. There is an unspoken understanding, a wordless language, at certain times, and even a youngster such as I was then, can sense and translate it. The half-turn her head made against my shoulder, lying inert, passive, submissive, the way her hand dropped off my arm and hung down loose, the play of her breath as soft as the ebb and flow of breath-mist on a mirror, against my face, were words enough, no real ones were needed. This is part of the race's instinct.

But I didn't want it to happen. I did, but I didn't. And I made the didn't master the did. She had me accustomed now, conditioned now. I wanted her this way, the way she was, the way she had been on the bench that night. I had this image of her. I wanted to keep it, I didn't want to take anything away from it. (I didn't realize until years later that that's all there are, are our images of things. There are no realities. There are only the hundred different approximations of reality that are our images of it, no two the same, from man to man, from case to case, from place to place.)

There was a breathless springtime charm about her this way, a fragile sway she exerted over me, which would have been gone at a touch. Maybe a more heated, more grown love would have taken its place. But only for a while. Then that would have gone too, as it always does in such cases. And nothing would have been left. Not the first, not the second.

It wasn't a mere matter of purity or non-purity. Even that young, I wasn't narrow-minded. That was a mere cuticle-distinction.

It was partly possessive: You have something that belongs to you, that you value, like a bright new necktie or a leather wallet or a chrome lighter with your initials on it, and you don't want to get a stain on it, you don't want to deface it.

There was part self-esteem in it, I think. Your girl had to be better than any other girl around, or what was the use of her *being* your girl? You were so good yourself that you rated only the best, nothing less would do. Caesar's sweetheart.

But it was idealistic, mostly. If you're not going to be idealistic at that age, you're never going to be idealistic at all.

I don't know. I didn't know then, I still don't now. Who can explain the heart, the mind, the things they make you do?

I dropped one foot down to the step below, and took my arms off her.

"You better get inside, Vera." I said. "You better say good-night to me."

And then I said again, "You better hurry up and get inside, Vera."

"Aren't you going to kiss me good-night first?" she said softly.

"No, say it from up there. Not down here."

She went up the three or four remaining steps to the level, and took her key out and opened the door with it. Then she turned and looked at me as she went in. I saw her put the backs of a couple of her fingers across her lips, then she tipped them toward me in a secretive kissing sign. Still looking at me to the last, she slowly drew the door closed past her face, very slowly and very softly, almost without a sound.

She didn't come to the bench the next afternoon. I waited there for her for several hours, with that slowly fading afterglow you're left with on the day after a party, wanting to share it with her by talking the whole thing over, but she didn't come. Finally, when the early winter twilight had closed down and turned the whole world into a sooty, charcoal line drawing, all of black and gray, I got up and left, knowing she wasn't coming anymore this late, and knowing just as surely I'd see her the following day. I didn't even stop by her house to find out what had kept her away, because I felt sure it was nothing more than a case of her being overtired from the night before, and of having slept late as a result.

But the next day she didn't come again, either, and I wondered about it. I wondered if she'd stayed out too late with me to suit her family, and they were keeping her away from me for a few days to show their disapproval. But they hadn't been home yet themselves, to all appearances, when I'd brought her back.

Then I wondered if something had happened at the party that had offended or displeased her, something that she hadn't told me about. But I remembered how she'd danced in exuberance out on the sidewalk after we'd left, so it didn't seem likely it was that.

The third time she disappointed me, it was already the start of a new week, the party was already three or four days in back of us now, and I didn't wait any longer. The only possible explanation left was that she'd been taken ill; she might have caught cold that night, she'd been thinly dressed and it had been stingingly cold from what I remembered. And if she was ill, I wanted her at least to know I'd asked for her, and not let her think I'd been completely indifferent. So after a forlorn half-hour's token vigil on the bench, with no real anticipation even at the start, I got up again and went over to her house to see if I could find out anything.

I don't recall any longer whether I made two visits over there on two successive days, on the first of which I merely loitered about in front of the place, in hopes either of catching sight of her or else of questioning somebody who might possibly know her (such as the little girl who had carried her message the night of the party), and on the second of which I finally went all the way up the stairs as far as her door; or whether the two telescoped themselves into one and the same occasion. But I do know that, all else having failed, I finally stood at the top of the six flights of stairs and I finally knocked at her door.

After a moment's wait I heard a single heavy crunch of the flooring just on the other side of it; I imagine the one board that had been trodden on creaked, while all the rest of them did not.

A voice asked: "Who's that?" A woman's, but that was all I recognized about it.

"Me," I said. "Vera's friend, Con." (To my own ears, it sounded like a faltering quaver that came out of me.)

The door opened, and her mother stood there.

Her face wasn't friendly. I couldn't decipher exactly what was on it at first, but it was set in bleak, grim lines and no smile broke on it.

"And is it Vera you're asking after?" she said, and I can still remember the thick Irish twist of speech she gave it.

I nodded and swallowed a lump of self-consciousness in my throat.

Her voice grew louder and warmer, but not the warmth of congeniality, the warmth of glittering, spark-flying resentment. "You have the nerve to come here and ask for her? You have the nerve to come here to this door? You?"

She kept getting louder by the minute.

"I should think you'd have the decency to stay home, and not show your face around here. Isn't it enough you've done? Well, isn't it?" And she clamped her hands to the sides of her head, as when you're trying to stifle some terrible recollection.

I drew back a step, stunned, congealed with consternation. Only one explanation was able to cross my mind. I knew nothing had happened on the stairs that night. But maybe they didn't, maybe they thought something had. And if they did, what way was there I could ever—

"Now go on about your business!" she said sternly. The expression "Get lost" had not yet come into general parlance, but she used an approximation of it. "Take yourself off," I think it was.

By that time I was partly down the stairs already, and then had stopped again and half-turned around to her to hear the rest of it out.

"Stay away from here. There's no Vera here for you."

The door gave a cataclysmic bang, and that was the end of it. There was no Vera there for me.

I have often wondered since why it was such a long time after that before I ran into Frankie again. Maybe it actually wasn't, but it seemed so at the time. Weeks, if not quite months. But our paths didn't happen to cross, I guess, for we each had differing interests by now. The hero-worship stage was long a thing of the past. I had probably grown out of it by myself; I don't think my friendship with Vera had anything to do with ending it. And I hadn't sought him out, because it had never occurred to me that he might be in a better position than I to pick up the neighborhood rumors and gossip, his ear being closer attuned to it than mine, in a way.

Anyway, one day we came along on opposite sides of the same street, he going one way, I the other. He threw up his arm to me, I flung up mine to him, and he crossed over to me. Or we met in the middle, whichever it was.

We made a couple of general remarks, mostly about his current boxing activities (he was still in the amateur category, he told me, but about ready to become pro; all he needed was to find the right manager). Then he suddenly said: "That was tough about your friend, wasn't it?"

I must have sensed something serious was about to come up; I quickly became alerted, even before the conversation had gotten any further. "Vera? What was tough? What was?" I asked tautly.

"About her getting caught up with like that."

"Caught up with how?" I insisted.

"What are you, serious?" he said impatiently. "I thought you knew about it. The whole block knows. How come you don't know about it, when you been going around with her so much lately? Practically steady."

"All of a sudden I didn't see her anymore," I tried to explain. "She dropped out of sight, and I couldn't find out why. Nobody told me."

"I could'a' told you," he said. "Why di'ntya come to me?"

"Well, what is it?" I urged. "What?"

"She was picked up," he said flatly.

I didn't understand at first; I thought he meant a flirtatious pickup, by some stranger on the street.

"Picked up by some fellow? She wasn't that kind. I know her too well."

"I don't mean picked up by some fellow. Picked up by the cops. She was taken in."

I felt as though one of his best punches had hit me squarely between the eyes. All I could see for a minute were swirls in front of them. Like a pair of those disks with alternate black and white circular lines that keep spinning into a common center, but they never come to an end, they always keep right on coming.

"For what?" I managed to get out when they'd finally thinned somewhat and started to fade away. "What for?"

I guess he could see by my face the kind of effect he had had on me; it seemed to make him feel regretful that he'd told me. "Don't take it like that," he said contritely. "I wounna told you, if I knew it was going to get you like that."

"But why?" was all I kept saying, tearful without any tears, querulous, resentful, all those things at once. "What'd she *do*? They can't just come along like that and haul anybody in they want to."

He didn't stop to argue that with me; evidently he felt the facts did it for him. "You know the old lady she worked for part-time, the rich old lady on West End Avenue—? She ever tell you about her?"

"Yeah, I knew she worked for her," I said marginally.

"The old lady put in a complaint about her to the cops. She called them up and told them there was an expensive fur coat missing out of her closet, and she accused Vera of swiping it. So they went over there to Vera's place, looking for it, at eight o'clock in the morning. She was still in bed, but they found it folded up underneath her mattress."

"She had one she was paying for on time—" I tried to say in her defense.

"Na," he said juridically. "The old lady identified it, it had the same labels on it."

"Then what'd they do?" I faltered, sickish in the throat with backed-up salty fluid.

"They made her get dressed, and they took her with them. She claimed she just borrowed it to wear for one night, and was going to bring it right back the next day. The trouble was she couldn't prove that, because they caught up with her too quick and she still had it in the room with her when they got there."

An excruciating little mental image crossed my mind, of her coming out the street-doorway of her house, that same doorway where she hadn't wanted the neighbors to see her "all dressed up," but now with two men alongside her, people looking on from windows and from the steps, holding her head down, and with tears probably, tears almost certainly, gliding down her shame-flushed face.

"But if the old lady got her coat back, why didn't she just let her go?" I wailed querulously.

"She wanted to teach her a lesson, I guess. She said she'd been very good to Vera, and Vera had repaid her by stealing from her behind her back." And he interpolated sagely: "You know, them old ladies can be very mean sometimes, especially when it comes to losing something like a fur coat."

"I know," I assented mournfully. To both of us, I suppose, a woman of forty would have been what we considered an old lady.

"She was sore, and she wouldn't drop the charges. They brung Vera up before a magistrate—I doanno if it was in juvenile court or where, but I guess it was there, because she's still a minor—and he committed her to a reformatory for six months. She's up there now, at some farm they got upstate."

And he added, quite unnecessarily, "That's why you haven't seen her around anymore."

After a wordless pause of several moments, I started to move away from him.

"Hey, come back here," he said. "Come back here." He was trying to be sympathetic, consolatory, in a gruff sort of way, which was the only way he knew how.

I kept on going, drifting away from him.

Then he tried to come after me and rejoin me. I didn't see him because I didn't turn to look, but I knew he was, because I could tell by the sound of his feet, coming along behind me. I motioned to him with a backward pass of my hand to leave me alone, to go on off.

I didn't want him to see my face.

I felt like a dog that's just had its paw stepped on real hard, and it goes limping off on three feet and is leery of everyone, doesn't want anyone to come near it for a while. The only thing I didn't do was whimper like one.

All the winter long I'd pass there now and then, and every time I passed I'd seem to see her standing there in the doorway. Just the way I'd seen her standing sometimes when we'd met by her door instead of at the park bench.

Complete, intact in every detail: looping her tamoshanter around by its headband on the point of one finger. Much more than an illusion: a life-size cut-out, like those figures they sometimes stood up outside of theaters. So real that the checks of her coat hid the grubby brownstone doorway-facing behind where they were. So real that even the remembered position of her feet repeated itself on the brownstone doorstep, and they seemed to be standing there once again just as they once had: one planted flat out a little way before her so that the shank of her leg curved gracefully outward a little to reach it, the other bent backward behind her, and planted vertically against the sideward part of the doorway. And as I'd once noticed, when she thrust a door closed behind her with a little kick-back of her heel, here again she gave grace, not grotesqueness, to this odd little posture.

But then as I'd look and look, and look some more, longingly (not so much with love—for what did I know of love at nineteen? Or for that matter, what did I know of it at thirty-nine or forty-nine or fifty-nine?—as with some sense of isolation, of pinpointed and transfixed helplessness under the stars, of being left alone, unheard and unaided to face some final fated darkness and engulfment slowly advancing across the years toward me, that has hung over me all my life), the brownstone-facing would slowly peer back through the checks of her coat, the doorstep would be empty of her disparately placed feet, and I'd have to go on my way alone again. As all of us have to go alone, anywhere that we go, at any time and at any place.

The young, I think, feel loneliness far more acutely than the older do, for they have expected too much, they have expected everything. Those older never expect quite everything, or more than just a little at best, and when loneliness strikes, their lack of complete expectation in the first place dulls the sharp edge of it somewhat.

The spring came again, and then that warmed itself into early summer, and by now it was a year since I had first met her. I still thought of her very often, but I no longer thought of her all the time. Her immediacy had faded.

One night in June I was passing along Eighth Avenue again, and as the corner of One-hundred-fourteenth Street came abreast of me and opened up the side-street into view, it suddenly seemed to blaze up from one end to the other like a rippling straw-fire, an illusion produced by scores of light bulbs strung criss-cross from one side of the street to the other, and fidgeting in the slight breeze. Vehicular entry had been blocked off by a wooden traffic horse placed at the street entrance. People were banked on both sidewalks looking on, and between them, out in the middle, tightly packed couples were dancing. They were holding a block party on the street.

Block parties were nothing new. In fact, by this time they were already well on their way out. They had first originated about four years before, at the time of the mass demobilization, when each individual block celebrated the return to its midst of those young men who had seen service overseas by holding a community homecoming party in their honor out in the street (because that was the only place that could conveniently accommodate all the participants).

But this was the early summer of 1923, not 1919 any longer; the last soldiers had finished coming back long ago; the only ones left were regulars, on garrison duty along the Rhine, at the Koblenz bridgehead. Another thing: The climate of public opinion had noticeably changed in the meantime. The naive fervor of the first postwar year or two had now given place to that cynicism toward all things military and patriotic that characterized the remainder of the decade. So the occasion for this particular party must have been something else: a church benefit or charity affair of some kind.

I moved in among the onlookers and stood there with my shoes tipping over the edge of the curb, watching. The music wasn't very good, but it was enthusiastic and noisy, and that was the mood the crowd was in, so that was all that mattered. They were probably amateurs who lived on the block themselves, and each one had brought his particular instrument down into the street with him, and joined forces with the others. But they were so uneven they were almost good, because the music of the moment was supposed to be played in just that sort of jagged, uneven time, anyway. I can still remember them blaring and blatting away at two of the current favorites: "Dearest, You're the Nearest to my Heart" and "Down, Down Among the Sleepy Hills of Ten, Ten, Tennessee."

Then as I stood there on the lip of the curbing, taking it all in, she was suddenly there in front of me. I never knew afterward which direction she'd come from, because I didn't have time to see. She was just suddenly there, that was all, and I was looking at Vera again.

She hadn't changed much. The even-all-around cut might have been missing from her hair, but I can't be sure, for I didn't look up at it, just looked at her. She had on a fresh, summery little dress, orchid in color, that much I seem to remember. It was both gauzy and crisp at the same time, most likely what they call organdy.

But there was one thing I did notice clearly, as we looked straight into one another's eyes, one thing that hadn't been there before. There was a little diagonal crevice, like a nick or slit, traced downward from the inside corner of each eye, slanted like an accent mark and just as brief as one. It couldn't have been called a crease, for she was too young to have creases yet. It wasn't a furrow either, it wasn't deep enough for that.

Studying her, I wondered what had caused it. Tear-tracks, maybe, from excessive crying? No, not tears alone. Tears maybe, but something else as well. Long, sleepless nights of brooding, of frustration and rebellion.

If they grew longer, deeper, I sensed somehow they would

change the expression of her face, give her eyes a hardened, crafty aspect. But it was too soon to do that yet. All they were so far was a mark of hurt; they gave her eyes an apprehensive, reproachful look.

I don't know what we said first. Probably I said her name, and she said mine.

Then she moved her mouth upward toward me a little, and we kissed.

"It's been an awful long time I last saw you," I said, skipping the "since" in the hurry of my speech. Tactless, without meaning to be. But what else could I have said? I hadn't seen her just yesterday.

"I've been away," she said reticently.

I wondered if she knew I knew. I hoped she didn't. I would have liked to tell her that I didn't know, but I couldn't figure out a way that wouldn't tell her that I did know.

"Working," she added even more reticently.

"You still live here on the block?" I asked her.

She answered that with less constraint. "Not anymore," she said. "I just came around tonight to see what the old neighborhood looked like."

Then, as if to break the chain-continuity of questions, she suddenly suggested: "Dance with me. It's too hard to try to talk with all that noise they're making."

I stepped down to the asphalt roadbed she was standing on, which had been powdered over with something to make it less abrasive to the dancers' feet.

We moved a few steps, a few steps only, and then even that was taken away from me.

A girl came jostling and thrusting her way through the mangle of dancers, someone I had never seen before. She touched Vera on the back or something, I couldn't see what it was, to attract her attention.

"What're you doing?" she demanded in a tone of urgency. "Don't you know they're waiting for us?"

"I just met an old friend," Vera told her happily, and she indicated me with her head, about to introduce us.

The other girl brushed that aside, as if to say: This is no time for that now. She didn't even look toward me.

"This is the second time they've sent me out to look for you," she went on rebukingly. "How much longer you going to be? You must have seen everything you wanted to by now. What's there to see around here, anyway? They won't like it if you keep them waiting much longer."

"All right, I'm coming," Vera said with a sort of passivity, as though she were used to being told what to do.

"I guess I have to go now," she said, turning to me, with a regretful little smile that, whether she meant it or not, was a pleasant balm to my feelings.

She turned aside from my still-upheld arms and followed the other girl back through the crowd. And after a moment, I went after the two of them, more slowly.

Once up on the sidewalk and in the clear, they broke into a choppy little quick-step that girls sometimes use, not quite a run but more than a walk, Vera still a trifle in back of the other one.

"But when am I going to see you again?" I called out after her, bewildered by the rapidity with which I'd found her, only to lose her again.

She turned her head around, but without breaking stride in the little jogging trot she was engaged in, and called back reassuringly: "Real soon, Con. And that's a promise."

Then they both made the turn of the corner and whisked from sight. I went down there after them, not to try to stop them, for I knew that wouldn't have worked, but simply to see if I could get a look at who it was they were hurrying so to join.

As I put my head around the corner, a pale-stockinged after-leg was drawing from sight into a car that was standing there, and then the car door cracked shut with that flat sound they always have.

It was standing, oh I don't know, about ten yards along from the corner, and there were a number of men in it, exactly how many I couldn't tell, maybe three, possibly four, but certainly more than just two to pair off with the girls. They were older men, not youths my own and Vera's age. This was more a matter of outline than anything else, since I couldn't see their faces to the slightest degree, but the impression of maturity was unmistakable. The massiveness of their shoulders gave it to me, and the breadth of the backs of their necks, and they were all alike wearing rather too dressy snap-brim felt hats (and this was already June). One of them was smoking a cigar, I saw it glow for a moment in the darkness under the roof of the car, and the livid concentric swirl it made was much larger than a mere cigarette ember would have been, particularly if seen from a distance like that.

And finally, the car itself was not of a type that young men would have owned or cared to own or habitually been found driving around in. It was no runabout or roadster or rattling, motto-inscribed "flivver." It was a closed car, a black sedan, a very heavy-set, high-powered affair. It almost looked custom-made. It had more than the usual amount of burnished hardware on the outside (door handles, headlights, and a smaller, cone-shaped swivel light up alongside the windshield). If it weren't for the wheels, it could have resembled a coffin.

I don't know who or what they were, and I never will. Maybe they were just hard-bitten older men, older than the two girls with them, toughened up by years of wresting every hard-fought buck from a reluctant world. Without grace, without compunction, without laughter. Harmless otherwise in general (except of course to young girls such as those). Non-lethal, or I should say, non-illicit.

And then again maybe not. About two or three years after that, around '25 or '26, when an awareness of the new type of public violence, which the First War and Prohibition had bred between them, finally percolated through to the public consciousness from the specialized areas to which it had been confined until now—the police-files, crime- and police-reporters, certain politicians, speakeasy operators, and the like—and new words like *gangster* and *racketeer* and *public enemy* began to sprinkle the pages of the newspapers more and more often, along with accounts of nocturnal ambuscades and machine-gun fusillades and murders in garages and warehouses and concrete-weighted drownings along the water's edge . . . Every time I'd come across one of them, something brought back the picture of that car to my mind's eye.

And I'd wonder then, as I still wonder now, was it men of that kind she and her friend had gone off with that night? Some of their earlier prototypes, their very first vanguard? Or was there just a superficial resemblance there that fooled my untrained, unknowledgeable eye?

And I'd hope, every time I thought about it, that that was what it was, and nothing more.

But I never could be sure.

It didn't even have a tail-light on, to follow its recession by. But like a great big inky patch against the paler night it grew smaller and smaller as it dwindled down the street, stealthily, without sound, until it had contracted into extinction and was there no more.

We never saw each other again, in this world, in this lifetime. Or if we did, we didn't know each other.

Late in 1932 or early the following year, Woolrich moved out of 239 West 113th Street and into a cheap hotel, determined to survive as a professional writer in the pit of the Depression without his mother or the Tarler estate to fall back upon. The third chapter of *Blues of a Lifetime* describes—with how much an admixture of fiction we'll never know—what life was like for him in the year his literary career seemed dead in the water, and how he struggled to complete a new novel while scraping by on small change and trying desperately to stall on paying his long overdue back rent. Nothing in *Blues of a Lifetime* gives us a hint of what happened after the events of the following chapter, but clearly the only option left for Woolrich was to tuck his tail between his legs and go back to his mother. Soon afterward the children of George Abelle Tarler sold the house on 113th Street and Woolrich with his mother moved into the Hotel Marseilles on Broadway and 103rd Street. Their suite in that building was to be his home, or more precisely his prison cell, during the years when, like lava from an erupting volcano, there poured out of him at white heat the powerful suspense novels and stories that entitle him to be called the Hitchcock of the written word.

EVEN GOD FELT
THE DEPRESSION

I'd hardly made a cent that whole year. Or for that matter the one before, or the one before that. The Depression had become stabilized by this time. It was now accepted as a permanent condition. The sharp downgrade had come to an end, and it had leveled off, but with that had also ended all the earlier hopes of an upturn, of a magic-wand dismissal, of a just-around-the-corner mirage of a picture-postcard goddess called Prosperity spilling roses and gold pieces indiscriminately out of a brimming cornucopia. People had given up hoping. It was now a part of everyday existence, and everyday existence is the most difficult thing of all to change; all the emperors, kings and conquerors have found that out. It was the Present, it was the Thirties, you couldn't have one without the other. Even the songs were tinged with it. "Brother, Can You Spare a Dime?"; "I'll never be the same, Stars have lost their meaning for me—"; "No more money in the bank—"; "Potatoes are cheaper, tomatoes are cheaper—." For the first time, love, in this context, ran a poor second.

As the new decade plodded dejectedly on, holding an apple for sale in one hand, an upturned hat in the other, it became hard even to remember the time when there hadn't been a depression. That time was legend, not reality anymore. There'd been a time when there'd been Indians and colonists. There'd been a time when the states warred against each other.

So too had there been a time when you went to parties and speakeasies. And the only thing that mattered, if you were a girl then, was to wear the shortest possible haircut and the shortest possible skirts. And if you were a young man, to know the greatest number of speakeasies so long and so well that you were called by your first name there and admitted on sight when the small grille first opened and an eye looked out at you, without having to present one of those meaningless, ubiquitous little cards that seemed to be floating around by the thousands and said, "Charlie sent me," or "John," or "Joe"; only the uninitiated had to do that any longer, by the time the period reached its crest. That was for visitors, out-of-towners, strangers, and even they were seldom refused. Even a policeman would now and then drop in, not for purposes of inspection—for he was on their payroll, so to speak—but to have a friendly drink; and on one occasion at least, at which I was present, to sing "Silver Threads Among the Gold" in a beautiful baritone for the entertainment of the other customers, who then passed around the hat.

During the twenties, there was always money around somewhere near at hand, somehow. If not right in your pocket, then over in your room, or your apartment. If not in your apartment, then around at the bank. If not around at the bank, then in some friend's pocket, until there was once more some around at the bank. Never a matter of more than a few days or a week at the most.

Of course it didn't just grow on trees, no. You worked for it. But the work was so easy and the pay was so large. And the working part of the day seemed so short and inconsequential compared to the long, delectable speakeasy nights and dawnings. And if you were dissatisfied with the work (and it was the worker who was dissatisfied more often than those he worked for) you simply went on to another place where the pay was even larger. Only absolute ineptitude or a personal feud with a superior seemed able to cost anyone his job against his own volition. And if you were a writer, or at least an entertainment-writer, such as I had started out to be, you shared in this general run of things. The work was easy and the pay was large.

Those were marvelous times. Not even the time before the French Revolution equaled them in splurge and squander: For then the poor had been discontented. Now there were no poor at all. (Until the bottom fell out of the whole world, and everyone was poor together.)

But all that was long ago, dimmed by the mists of time. Those days had been whisked backward out of the memory as though they had been forty years before and not just four.

And now, it was no time in which to be a writer. Food and shelter were the essentials. They could no longer be just taken for granted, they had to be struggled for now. And thousands had even lost them altogether. Whole families had broken up. The wives and children, because women are less fit for a nomadic life, went back under their parents' roofs, if they were lucky enough to have parents who still had roofs. To live it out somehow, to bide their time, until the dreadful thing should pass, if it ever did pass. The men built colonies of shacks, of cartons and of packing cases and gasoline drums and whatever they could get their hands on, and drew their drinking water from the nearest comfort station (because they could be sure at least it was sterile there) and got their food standing in endless, dejected lines outside of public soup kitchens and other charitable hand-out places.

These shacks along the river banks, and whatever other public unrestricted ground they were allowed to trespass upon, were commonly called Hoovervilles, in unjust deprecation of the man who had not at all caused the situation but simply inherited it.

No, it was no time in which to be a writer. Magazines were expiring all over, dropping off like autumn leaves falling from trees. Who had time for books, for magazines? Who had the money to waste on fairy tales of a world that had vanished? The two great mutually antipathetic forces in this life have never been love and death, but love and hunger. Whichever gains the ascendancy, the other suffers by it.

No one cared who got the girl in the story anymore. They knew he couldn't keep her very long, nowadays.

On the other hand, the new times were too new to be written about yet. Those who would write about them a little later on were still busy living them now.

I had given my situation as a writer in these indigent times much thought. I had had to. There was no money coming in anymore, absolutely not a single penny. My last sale had been late in 1932, already nearly half a year back by this time (counting from the check and not the acceptance date, which were not the same thing by any means), to a magazine called *Illustrated Love Stories*, which had had the great advantage, if nothing else, of being displayed and sold throughout the widespread and popular Woolworth five-and-ten-cent store chain. But even that money by now had fallen by the wayside and was no more.

At the time of the memorable bank closure of February 1933 I had had exactly sixty-one dollars to my name in one of the locked-up banks. This amount I can stake my word on, because I distinctly recall a friend of mine saying he envied me having even that much, as he himself had had only sixteen left in, and then we both noticed that the figures were reversible, that is, interchangeable if turned around. When the banks reopened I quickly took the sixty-one out, mainly because I'd already pledged a good part of it toward my daily needs, and the remainder because I was apprehensive, as many others were, that the banks might reclose again any day as unexpectedly as they had the first time, and I wanted the few dollars out in the open where I could put my hands on them.

By now, about two months later, this sixty-one dollars was all gone, but I'd found various ways of tiding myself over in the interim. There was a beautiful gold watch my father's younger brother had left me. This was constructed in such a way that I managed to live off it for some time, in the way that you eat an artichoke, leaf by leaf. It had two thick outer casings, one on each side, and then two somewhat thinner ones inside, making four altogether. All of the finest purest gold. Its works were heavily jeweled, and then a massive gold fob went with it, such as they had worn in those days.

At intervals which I spaced as widely as I could, I used to take it downtown, near the foot of Wall Street, over toward the river, to an assay office that bought precious metals, and have them carefully pry off one lid, so that the rest wouldn't be damaged, and have that weighed and sell it to them. I got surprisingly liberal amounts each time, too; when the nineties made something of gold, they weren't stingy with the gold. Still, I felt bad each time I had to part with some more of it—nostalgic, wistful, penitent— and surprisingly, considering that it was the gift of a man whom I hadn't seen since my early boyhood.

When the last of it was all gone finally, and only a scrap of black grosgrain ribbon was left to show what it had been, I started in on my books and sold them piecemeal as well. I had a considerable number of limited editions given to me as gifts at Christmastime by the publishers themselves, during the course of the years, all numbered, inscribed, rag-papered, gilt-edged, and beautifully bound.

I used to get a miserable couple of dollars for one of them each time: for a thing which could not have been obtained on the open market at any price. I had a little red-and-black tiered bookcase in my room, and the increasing gaps in its various compartments used to stare out at me accusingly, like wide-open eyes, and I'd want to turn my head away.

Then one night, right after I'd parted with a costly deluxe edition of *The Life of Isadora Duncan*, I happened to go by a bar. It was one of those bland, springlike evenings that always seemed to stir a longing for recreation even more than at other times. The lights looked inviting, and there was the pulse-beat of music coming from inside. So I went in, and bought a beer, and stood there with it for a while.

Then just as I was about to order a second one, the thought suddenly came to me: This is someone's life you're drinking down. Her glories and her triumphs, her aspirations and her strivings, her heartaches and her happiness. Should this be the end result of all that? Is this all she lived for? Is this all the transmutation her life deserves? Cheap rank-smelling beer going down some brash young guy's gullet? And afterward maybe, in some foul washroom, to turn into something even worse.

How would you like it if, someday after you're gone, and have left behind you (if you do) just one worthwhile book, one thing you put everything into, one thing to live on after you, one thing to show you'd ever been around in the first place; then how would you like it if some young fellow who never had heard of you, and wouldn't have cared if he had, stood up one night and did that to your life's work?

I winced, and put down my glass, and got out of there fast, and I never repeated that again. Not on the proceeds of anyone else's book, anyone else's lifeblood, at least.

But I was starved for recreation, and had to get it the best way I could, even if I had no money to pay for it.

There was a rooftop motion picture theater nearby at that time called Japanese Gardens (most likely because its overhead aisle-lights were encased in a few pseudo-Japanese lanterns; there was never anything else Japanese that I could notice about it). It was not an open-air theater, but simply a roofed over one on the top floor of the building. The great advantage of the place was this: If you bought an admission and entered legitimately, so to speak, which I could not do because I couldn't afford the twenty-five cents, you were carried from the street-level lobby by elevator up to the theater itself. But in compliance with fire department regulations there was an enclosed safety-staircase that ran down from above and gave onto the street by means of a heavy metal door, which could not be opened from the outside, but could easily be pushed aside from the inside. The elevator was slow in coming up, and very often people who had finished seeing the show and wanted to leave were too impatient to wait for it and would come down the stairs instead. I used to hang around the outside of this staircase door and watch it like a hawk, and when I saw it start to swing open, I'd hook my hand to it and keep it akimbo until I could get in myself. Those leaving never offered any objection; they seemed tolerant that way. I didn't mind climbing up the five or six flights. It meant nothing to me; I considered it well worth-while. They changed the bill twice a week, and for several weeks I took in each new show and managed to see a fair sampling of the best feature pictures of the early thirties.

But one night, careless from long immunity, I timed myself wrong, and the usher on duty must have spotted me without my knowing it, as I crossed the vulnerable open space between the stairhead and the last row of seats. He waited until I'd picked out a nice comfortable aisle seat, then I felt a rock-hard tap on my shoulder, and when I looked up, he grimly and wordlessly swung his thumb back and forth a few times toward the staircase.

He didn't actually take hold of my arm, but he insisted on escorting me all the way down the stairs again to where I had orig-inally entered. The sound of his slapping footsteps counterpointing mine down five or six whole flights irritated me for some reason.

"All right," I protested, offended. "I'm going. You don't have to come all the way down to the bottom with me."

He came back at me with a catch-phrase popular at the time: "You're telling *me* you're going? No, I'm telling *you!*"

When we were both on the outside, he securely reclosed the front door from that side and then he himself reentered by the front way, in order to be able to ride the elevator up, leaving me standing by myself on the dismal sidewalk, heaving and as cracklingly indig-nant as though I had been unjustly put upon.

And this was the way things had been going with me right then. It was, as I said at the beginning, no time in which to be a writer.

But I knew I had to be. It was something I couldn't help being. It was something that had been in me all my life, from the time that I was a kid and first kept a schoolboyish diary. It was something that I couldn't push aside until later, when I would know the real meaning of unhappiness, not these little trials and tribulations I knew now. I used to round my fist, and swing it with all my might into my other palm, whenever I received a disappointment or a rejection, and mutter doggedly: "I'll beat this game yet! I'll beat it yet!"

I thought about it, and thought about it, and finally I came to a decision. There was one solution and only one. There was one way to make enough money all at one time to tide me over, take the curse off this hand-to-mouth existence I was leading, give me a start back onto my feet at least. Books wouldn't do it, they weren't selling. Magazines wouldn't do it, they weren't buying.

But there was one medium of profit left. The motion-picture industry. Although its earnings, too, had gone down greatly, it was so worldwide, so universal, had become such a standby of modern-day living, that it alone managed to keep its head well above the general inundation. Many a man without work or hope of work (or after a while even the desire for it) managed somehow to find a stray quarter and go into some small moviehouse at noon when it opened, and spend the rest of the day in there trying to forget that he had no work or hope of work. Smoking, eating a stale roll, watching the anesthetic up on the screen.

The motion-picture industry still bought from writers. It needed them, it fed upon them, they were its fodder. And when it bought, it still paid, not by the hundreds of dollars but by the thousands.

The problem, though, was to offer them something that stood a good chance of acceptance, that was likely to be bought. To come up with anything else would be just a waste of time. All the things I had on hand, already done, were as stale as the speakeasies and the knee-length skirts; I knew no one would touch them.

Then when I least expected it I came across, quite by accident, something that seemed to have just the right possibilities. Opening my valise one day to scramble through it for something (it always made me wistful to bring it out into the open and see the travel- and hotel-stickers still all over it—"Red Star Line," "Holland- America Line," "Hotel Colón, Barcelona," "Pension Isabella, Muenchen"—from the carefree days now gone), I upturned the first few pages of a novel I had started in Paris two years before and never gone ahead with.

It was called *I Love You, Paris,* a title which would have been invalidated a couple of decades later by the hit song from *Can Can.* There was very little of it done, just an opening chapter, but I found when I reread it that what I had intended to do with it was still fresh enough in my mind, and in any case there was a key- sheet along with it, with a skeleton plot-framework outlined on it.

My volatile optimism (at least where my own material was con- cerned) immediately blazed up on reading it over, and it seemed to me to be the very thing I was looking for, the best possible bet for what I had in mind. For one thing, the period I had picked for it—pre-war Paris, 1912—was still completely untouched as far as the pictures were concerned, and I felt that should make a very good selling point. The screen was known to be always on the lookout for new, unhackneyed settings for its stories.

My protagonists were a pair of professional ballroom dancers, the man much older than the girl, his pupil and protégée, one of a long succession he has had throughout his career, whom he has taught to dance, made famous, and who then have repaid him by leaving him for some other, younger man. He is in love with his current partner, but she looks upon him only as a father and mentor.

Along comes a younger man the girl's own age, and he and she fall in love. Then the young people have a misunderstanding and fall out again. She disappears, and he goes looking for her every- where and cannot find her. Then, on her opening night, the night of her professional debut, he happens to pass the place where she is to appear and recognizes her from a photograph in the foyer. He goes in to watch her, thinking this will be the last time he will ever see her.

She has an enormous and dazzling success, and instantly

becomes the sensation of Paris. But she has recognized him sitting out front, and immediately after the performance she runs out to him, throws her success over her shoulder, and they go off together.

Her partner, who has really got a bad deal out of the whole thing, accepts it with graceful resignation (he is used to it by now) and goes back to his former partner, who has been intermittently sending off sparks of jealousy in the background throughout the story. The implication is that they will continue to bicker like cat and dog, as they did the first time, but at least will understand each other.

There were also a couple of subplots to help fill the thing out, in a more or less comic vein. A rich fat maharajah becomes enamored of the girl, though he already has a retinue of vivacious young Parisiennes who follow him around all over, and a middle-aged American lady tourist from the Middle West, also well-to-do and speaking hilarious (I hoped) broken French, mistakes the young man for a gigolo and pursues him almost to distraction.

If all this sounds pretty bad, all I can say is it was. But we are always so much wiser in retrospect, all of us. I would have died to defend its merits then. At least it was no worse than anything else that was to be seen on the screen those days.

The format in which to present it had to be considered. I decided that a shortcut, simply to save myself work, wouldn't be advisable, would lessen its chances. That a synopsis or outline, what they called a short "treatment," wouldn't do any good. I felt it might be pigeonholed and forgotten, as they received literally thousands of such things. Moreover, to avoid later accusations of plagiarism, many of the studios, it was my understanding, refused to accept them, returning them unopened. Therefore, the only sensible thing to do would be to complete it first as a book, to write it out at full, toilsome length no matter how much labor was involved, to try to get it published by a book firm to start with, to give it that much more prestige, attract that much more attention to it, and then to immediately try to sell it from there, perhaps from the galley-proofs alone, without even waiting for formal publication.

This meant, and I knew it well, anywhere from six weeks to two months of the most driving, uninterrupted drudgery, amounting almost to self-immolation. To give up everything else, all thought of recreation. And to continue living in the meantime as I had been doing all the while: scraping along tooth and nail almost without any money to speak of, only nickels and dimes in my pocket. When you look back toward a certain age, two months isn't long. But when you *are* that certain age, two months is eternity.

It was a gamble, and a very great one. All or nothing. But I decided to take it. If I didn't try it, I still had nothing. But if I did try it, and I succeeded, then I had just about everything. The money problem would be over, for years to come. What other choice was there for me anyhow? I asked myself. I wasn't equipped for anything else. To wait on customers, sell things over a counter, either in a haberdashery or a grocery? There were thousands who could do it much better than I, and they couldn't get those jobs themselves, jobs like that weren't to be had. This was the only thing I knew how to do. So I tightened my belt, took a last regretful look at the coruscating, titillating world around me, and sat down and grimly bent to work.

As far as the book-publishing stage of it was concerned, that didn't worry me too much. I had a promising opening, or at least potential opening, waiting for me there. A man in the editorial field whom I'd dealt with in the past had, just shortly before this, been taken on at one of the smaller publishing houses—probably displacing somebody else, which was the only way it was done at this time. I'd known him in the halcyon days of four or five years before, and then lost track of him until now. I'll call him Irwin, since I've never been sure exactly what part he played in what happened later on, and have no wish even at this late date to do him an injustice. His own first name began with the same capital letter, at any rate.

I'd noticed a little squib about his new alignment in the book notes which the *Times* habitually ran on its daily book page, and I promptly got in touch with him and told him I'd started working on something. He sounded very encouraging and hospitable, and urged me to let him see it as soon as I'd finished doing it. This of course might have been no more than the ordinary professional courtesy he would have extended to any published author, but I took a sanguine view of it.

There was of course no question of an advance before its completion, and I knew enough not to ask him for one, although it would have solved all my problems beautifully. If the thing was no good, I would have had no way of repaying it, and we both realized it. Publishers weren't using their money to speculate on anything sight unseen in those parlous days, except in the case of a big name, perhaps, and I was a writer of too dubious a stature to warrant it. I was fairly well known, but on the strength of fairly little accomplished. I wasn't by any means what could have been called a good risk at the time.

I had everything lined up now, and the rest was up to me. I worked, and I worked, and I worked. I worked in the morning, I worked in the afternoon, I worked at night. I don't think typewriter keys ever took such a hammering before. Perhaps stenographically, but never creatively.

The spring was advancing, and tantalizingly beautiful days came; there seemed to be an endless succession of them, as if purposely sent to plague me. New York may not be notable for its weather, but when it does turn out a fine day, no place else can top it. And just enough of that first delicate, immaculate green showed through its concrete crevices here and there to put nature's official seal on the season, adding a decorative touch, like the parsley on the omelette or the mint sprig in the lemonade. Each day had the effect on me of a champagne cocktail: golden and tingling and heady. And I couldn't even touch it, had to pass it by.

The nights were even more excruciating. To me those long lines of lights that flamed along the avenues as far as the eye could see were never garish (as they probably were) but glamorous, seeming to hold out a promise of wonderment and magic, and I wanted to be out where they were. Everyone else was, in droves; I could see them passing the corner, from my window, in two continuous opposite-moving streams, and there I sat, in a solitary room, locked in the lonely pool of light cast by a desk lamp.

But I wouldn't leave the desk. I almost had to grab it with both hands and hang onto it for dear life, almost had to hook my ankles around its legs to stay on the chair, but I wouldn't leave it, no I wouldn't leave it. Consummation had to come first.

During this whole time I was having a great deal of difficulty with the hotel manager, Mr. Drew. Difficulty avoiding him, I mean. I was chronically anywhere from a month to a month and a half behind in my room rent, and though I paid installments on it as often as I could, the gap was so great that I never could seem to bridge it and bring myself up to date. It was like a sort of hopeless treadmill. By the time I finished up one month, a new one would be over already.

Mr. Drew was a corpulent, apoplectic man and, in my case at least, a great believer in the personal appeal as far as rent-lag was concerned, always accompanied by numerous histrionic gestures such as clapping his forehead and flapping his hands about in a woebegone way. I suppose he had learned by now that all the standard methods, such as reminders from clerks, notations at the foot of bills, and even telephone calls, were of no avail in my case; they weren't, because there was nothing I could do to remedy the situation myself. He had come up through the ranks in the hotel business, starting first as a waiter, then maître d', and so on, and I think basically we liked each other, but if we did, no two people who liked each other ever had such a scrappy, turbulent relationship as we.

The hotel had an elevator that used to continue on down below the lobby floor, where the desk was, and bring you out at the back of a drugstore that the building housed. From there you could gain the street, without having to pass the front desk and Mr. Drew's watchful eye.

I used this means of escape with great frequency until, as Drew became familiar with the tactic, its usefulness began to wane. For the elevator, unfortunately, had an old-fashioned lattice-work draw-gate securing it, which could be looked through, and when he would spot me in the interior of the car, trying to make myself as inconspicuous as possible as I continued on down below, he would dash out from around in back of the desk, chase down the entrance-steps, out the main entrance, and around the corner to the drugstore doorway, and I would walk right into his arms, so to speak, when I came quick-stepping out a minute later.

After several of these half-supplicating, half-stormy sidewalk fracases, I gave up coming out the side entrance, as an expedient that had outlived its usefulness. I couldn't give him his money, because I didn't have it to give in the first place, but I stopped trying to evade him, and he had to fall back on his original (and wholly unproductive) technique of bombarding me with countless bills, all with lurid crimson-ink "Past Due" stamps on them, and calling me in my room on the phone at varied hours of the day and night, ranging from eight in the morning until midnight. He only stopped then because he went to bed around that hour himself, I suppose. I did more angrily severe banging up of the telephone receiver in those days than I have ever done in my life, before or since.

Thus we stalemated one another, and finally relapsed into a state of sullen, armed truce.

One night there was a knock at my door around nine or so, and when I took my hands off the keys and went over and opened it, Drew was standing there.

I raised my arms and slapped my hands against my sides fumingly. "For the love of Pete," I burst out. "You're not going to start in at this hour of the night, are you? I've told you over and over, as soon as I get something I'll give it to you. Can't you let up for one day at least?"

"Now wait a minute, wait a minute, don't get your back up," he tried to calm me. "D'you want to go to the movies?"

"What d'you mean, do I want to go to the movies?" I asked suspiciously.

He took a slip of paper out of his pocket. "I have a pass here for the R.K.O. Eighty-first Street. They send me one each week for letting them display their advertising down at the desk."

"It's for two," I said, glancing at it. "Are you coming with me?"

"I can't leave the hotel," he said. "My boss might take it into his head to call up or even drop around, and it would look bad if I weren't on the job. Take someone else with you. Take some girl."

"I can't take a girl," I said inflexibly. "It means an orangeade or a soda afterwards, that's the least you can do, and I can't even afford that much right now. It's too late to call anyone up at the last minute like this, anyway."

"Go by yourself then," he urged. "It'll do you good, relax you, take your mind off. You're leading an old man's life, C'nell, shut up in here day and night, night and day. You're only young once, mark my word, you'll regret it someday."

"No I won't," I contradicted him. "I've figured it all out. It's got to be now or later. I'd rather have it now and over with, and do my playing later."

But I took the pass from him and closed the door.

I buttoned up my shirt collar, put on a tie, slung my jacket across my arm, and went out—for the first time (except for just a hurried meal) in I don't know how many weeks.

I got as far as the corner, and then my feet seemed to lock themselves rigid on the pavement, wouldn't go on any further. I couldn't do it. I longed to see the show, as much as any school kid ever did who's only allowed to go once a week to a Saturday matinee—longed for a little fun and recreation, was almost famished for it—but I couldn't do it. My conscientiousness about first finishing the work I was doing was as rigid as an iron poker; I couldn't seem to bend it in the slightest.

I turned around and went back inside the hotel again and up to my room.

The door of the lady who lived on the other side of the hall from me was slightly ajar, and I could hear Drew's voice in there talking to her, as I came off the elevator.

He was taking his leave, and as he slowly came out backward, he didn't see me.

"—never lets up," she was complaining in a low, mournful voice. "Starts in at nine in the morning, and goes on all day long, sometimes until after twelve o'clock at night. I get the most splitting headaches from it. I've called down until I'm blue in the face, and it doesn't seem to do any good."

"Well, you won't have to listen to it tonight, at least," he promised her in a soothing voice. "I got rid of him for one night, anyway, by giving him a pass to a movie. Wish I'd have thought of it sooner."

"That's what you think!" I called out stridently.

He jumped almost a half-foot off the floor, and whirled around, and his normally ruddy face got almost the color of a raspberry.

I shied the pass across the hall in his direction, keyed open my door, slammed it shut behind me, and went back to the typewriter keys again, with the renewed vigor of rancor now added to everything else.

Then suddenly one day there was a mystifying change in Mr. Drew's attitude. He beamed, his expression was cherubic, as we came unexpectedly face to face. He clapped my shoulder, he asked how I was, he winked at me to show a special geniality.

When I saw his extended hand, waiting for mine, I said with overemphasized weariness, "Now, please. *Don't* start that again. I've told you over and over: when I can, as soon as I can."

He looked hurt that I should misconstrue his friendliness. He creased his forehead ruefully. "C'nell, I haven't said a word. C'nell, have I said a word? Why do you jump on me like this?"

"No, but you're going to," I said skeptically.

"All I wanted to say was, now that you're caught up, try to stay that way. Don't let it run so far behind the next time."

"Next time?" I said dumbfounded. "What happened to this time?"

"Don't worry about it—" he started to say blandly.

"Don't worry about it?" I flared. "Now I *am* going to worry about it more than ever, because it's not like you to be so easygoing. There's something up. You're just trying to put me off my guard. I'll probably find my door plugged up when I come back."

"C'nell," he protested, horrified, raising a sanctimonious pudgy pink palm. Then he asked me, "Have you gotten a bill, all this week? Tell the truth now, have you?"

I suddenly realized I hadn't; they'd stopped. I was so used to ignoring them anyway, I hadn't noticed the difference.

"There you are," he went on. "You're in the clear. All paid up. Forget about it."

"Paid up?" I called after him loudly. "How can I be? Since when? Aren't you always dinning it into my ears that you don't know what you'll tell the owner when he comes around to collect his rents, that you don't know how you'll face him?"

But he was now, I could see, in as much of a hurry to get away from me as he had been before to approach me. I followed him a few steps, but I couldn't get another word out of him.

I couldn't make head nor tail out of this wholly improbable turn of events. I knew he was too good a hotel man to have mixed my account up with somebody else's, although for a moment that gratifying thought did cross my mind. I decided there was only one way to find out for sure, and that was to get a look at the hotel's bookkeeping ledger with my own eyes.

I knew that neither of the two daytime clerks would be likely to allow me to do that. They were too much under Drew's thumb. But the midnight-to-morning desk-man, Mr. Mack, was a far more unfettered spirit where Drew was concerned, since their hours did not coincide and they rarely saw one another. I might just possibly get him to do it if I went about it in the right way.

So late that night, shortly after he'd come on duty, I approached the desk, leaned negligently on my elbow and chatted with him for a while. Then after I'd offered him a cigarette, I asked casually, "By the way, how does my bill stand? Do I still owe anything on it?"

He got out the bulky ledger, thumbed its pages over, scanned one, and then looked up at me. "You're paid up until the thirtieth of this month," he said.

"Let me see that," I exclaimed.

Caught off guard, just as I'd hoped, he let me turn it around my way without protest and trace my finger along the page. The entry was there as clear as day; the entire amount outstanding against me had been paid up, a matter of some five or six days earlier.

I didn't say anything more to him. I turned around and went back up to my room, almost in a daze.

I sat down and tried to think the thing out logically in my mind. The more I thought about it, the more convinced I became there was only one possible explanation, until finally I was sure I must be right.

Late the next afternoon, after I'd finished my daytime stint and before beginning my evening one, I went over to my mother's house to see her. I shouldn't actually call it her house; it had belonged to my grandfather, who had died six or seven years before, and his daughters had stayed on in it after that, both having lost their husbands. My mother was the older, and (I suppose) the titular head of the small establishment.

The chow dog they kept in the house, Blong (or "Blong Mei," pidgin for "Belongs to Me," the name on his pedigree papers), always rushed clamoring against the door at anyone's ring, and then, when he'd hear my voice, would subside. But I always got the impression it was in a miffed sort of way, as though he felt cheated of having a chance to show his valor off before the two ladies who were in his charge.

"Are you going to have something with us?" was the first thing my mother asked after we'd kissed.

"No, I have to get right back," I told her. "You know I'm working on that thing."

"You're working too hard. You'll kill yourself. You've got to eat better."

And my aunt, tilting her head sideward to study me, concurred (as usual) with a plaintive "You don't look good. You looked better the last time you were here."

"Oh," I said impatiently, "I'll have all the rest of my life to eat in.

The work comes first right now." Then I said to my mother, "I came over because I wanted to talk to you about something."

As soon as we were alone together in the other room, I told her: "I found out what you did."

A momentary flicker of guilt showed on her face, reminding me of the expression on a little girl's face when she has been found out doing something she knows she shouldn't. Then a look of quiet hurt took its place.

"That just shows you how reliable Mr. Drew is. He promised he wouldn't say anything."

"Drew didn't tell me," I said, and found myself for once in the odd position of defending my arch-enemy. "I got the night man to show me the ledger."

She didn't say anything to that.

"You don't carry that much around with you in your handbag at one time," I added. "You must have taken it out of your savings account."

"I went down to the bank the next day, after he'd spoken to me the last time I was over to see you, and I stopped off with it on my way home."

But I could only see it from my own point of view, no other. "I don't want to be helped," I insisted. "Don't you understand? I want to do this all on my own, prove to myself that I can do it, without any help from anyone. If you help me now, and I succeed afterward, then you've taken that much away from my success, made it that much less. I want it to be all mine. That's the only way I can really enjoy it if it comes." And I added with all that sublime, ridiculous cocksureness of one's young years, "I'm not going to sponge off anyone—not even my own mother."

I saw tears form in her eyes, but she kept them back.

"I don't understand you, the way you talk sometimes," she said quietly. "I only did it because I thought I would be helping you keep up your morale that way."

"But it's just the opposite; it's bad for my morale, instead of being good for it. Don't you have confidence in me?"

She came to me, put her arms around me, and pressed me fervently to her. "Every confidence!" she breathed. "You've got too much in you not to be recognized someday. I only hope I live to see it, that's my one prayer."

"I know I'll make it," I chanted raptly. "I'm going to, and I will. I know this thing will work out right. It's got to." Then I said in a softer voice, "Promise me you won't do anything like that again."

"I won't, if you don't want me to," she said submissively. "But will you be all right?" she added with a touch of anxiety.

"Sure I will. I'm not afraid of Drew," I scoffed. "He's a great big coward, fat as he is."

"But he did turn the lights in your room off once, you told me."

"He won't try that again in a hurry," I assured her. "You should have seen me chase him all around the desk, in front of everybody standing there, until he sent the mechanic up and had him put the fuse back in again. It was like slapstick comedy; I'd go running in at one end and he'd come running out at the other, then he'd go running in again at the opposite end as I came out once more at the first one."

In retrospect, I can tell she didn't see the humor in it that I did. "I don't like you to be bad friends with him" was all she said, demurely.

Now that I'd gained my way in the major matter, I gave in on the minor one, not an uncommon trait in human nature. I stayed and had my meal with them, and they waited on me and handed me things at the table and made a lot of fuss over me, as they always did, and made me feel altogether like a king. Or at least like the lord of a manor visiting among his loyal and devoted tenantry.

But late that night when I was back in my own room, and through with my work, and going to bed, I thought again of what she, my mother, had done, and saw it in a different, truer perspective than I had at first, and the tears came to my own eyes for a moment, just as they had to hers.

I understood always, my whole life through, how much she

loved me. And I think she understood, surely must have, how very much the same I felt about her.

On the night I finally came to the end of it, it was well on into the early morning hours. It seemed so quiet all at once, so smotheringly, stiflingly still, after all those days and nights and weeks of cricketlike chattering of the keys. Almost as though a thick eiderdown quilt had fallen down all over me, muffling everything. My ears couldn't seem to get used to it. They felt stunned, they almost seemed to be ringing with the emptiness. I'd stopped many times before this of course, stopped each night, and several times each day. But that was different, because then I knew I'd have to go on again each time. Now there was nothing more to come, the last keys had been struck, "The End" was lettered at the bottom of the final page, it was over. That's why, I suppose, I noticed the silence so much more than I had those other times. It was a psychological silence as much as an auditory one.

The hotel was asleep all around me. It was a quiet, drowsy sort of place anyway, most of the time. And even the street outside, which in that part of New York was, as a rule, never still, day or night, this night seemed to be so too, as if to blend itself in with my mood, just an occasional taxi-horn barking somewhere a block or so off. And the muffled surge of a lonely, passing subway train would now and then come up through the ventilating grids on the sidewalk and be plainly heard in the stillness of the streets above.

I turned the light out first, to cool my poor overworked eyes. It had been on so long, so steadily, that the heat of the glowing bulb extended all the way down the chain-pull to its very tip. When I touched that, it was hot enough to make me quickly take my fingers away. I sat there slumped before the desk in the dark for a while, too tired even to get up and leave the chair. Then after a while I made room by pushing things aside, and I laid my head down on the desktop, forehead first. I must have jarred the typewriter carriage slightly, and the little bell that always signaled the end of a line tinkled faintly, I remember. I thought it was a fitting coda to the whole thing. *Ping*, like that: and then unbroken silence.

I wanted desperately to go to sleep, and yet I was too keyed up, my nerves were too taut from the last long stint I'd put in, for me to be able to. Then suddenly hunger came. It struck me like a blow, almost. One moment there was no thought of food in my head, the next I was ravening.

I'd never felt hunger so strong, I'd never known it could be. It couldn't wait another moment, sleep was an impossibility until it was fed. It was agonizing. It was the actual pang I'd so often read of, but that I had never fully realized the meaning of before. It was like the teeth of an animal caught into you and refusing to let go their hold.

I dug into the linings of my pockets, quite unnecessarily. I'd already known I had no money. I had none. But this is not poetic license or retouching of a fact simply to point up, play up, a plight. This was literal: I had not one single, solitary penny of money on me, or in the room about me, or anywhere in the world, at that moment. The next day there would be some way of getting a little, there always was. But hunger couldn't wait until the next day. This wasn't one night's hunger, this was two months'. Even more, for that matter. I hadn't been eating well, even long before I'd first begun the book.

Now I thought of the poor strays who had come up to me on the street occasionally and asked me for enough money to get something to eat, and I was glad of the few times I'd been able to give it and sorry for the many times I'd had to refuse. But like most New Yorkers I'd been cynical, and thought they just wanted it for a drink. Tonight I knew better; there must have been some of them at least who felt like I did now.

I got up, left the room, and closed the door behind me, about to do very much the same thing they had myself. Not on the streets, perhaps, but right here in the hotel itself—that was about the only difference. I went up to Drew's floor, two floors above my own, stood there for a moment mustering my courage, and then knocked on his door. I don't know yet—even as I stood there at the time I didn't—where I got the amazing gall, the effrontery, to single him out, of all people. Beneath all our squabbling and differences, there must have been some sense of empathy there.

It required quite some knocking, and of a steadily increasing caliber, before anything happened. Finally I heard his voice ask blurredly on the inside: "Who is it?"

For some indefinable reason, possibly a feeling of embarrassment, I couldn't bring myself to give my name, I just repeated my knock.

He opened the door and looked out at me, face puffed up, rounded more than ever with the swellings of sleep, eyes closed into slits, and in a dingy bathrobe.

"Help me out, will you?" I burst out impetuously. "I've got to have something to eat, I can't stand it—and I haven't got a cent. Lend me something, and I'll give it back to you. Even fifty cents. Anything."

He looked at me as though he thought he hadn't heard me right. "C'nell, are you crazy?" he gasped.

"Not crazy," I said, glowering at him. "Hungry. I'm crazed with hunger, yes."

He looked searchingly into my face, and I think he must have detected that I was practically drooling with the need for food. If my chin wasn't actually wet, the inside of my mouth kept filling with a saliva that I couldn't seem to dispose of.

Suddenly his wife called out from within their bedroom, "Charlie, who is that?"

"C'nell," he said, turning his head aside. The two of us looked at each other with a sort of telepathic understanding. Husbandlike, he must have given her a faithful transcription of all our difficulties and all my derogations of him, and she could hardly have been a great admirer of mine.

Not realizing that I could hear her where I was, or perhaps not caring, she called out, annoyed: "Tell him to go to grass!"

He made an inscrutable sign to me, and muffled his voice in precaution. "Too bad you woke her up. Wait here a minute. I'll see if I can get you something without letting her see me."

I stood there by the half-open door, and he went back toward the bedroom.

I heard her ask suddenly, as distinctly as ever, "Charlie, what are you doing over there?"

I quailed for a moment, as I know he too must have.

"I'm looking for my cigarettes, Cass," I heard him say to her.

Then he came back to the door again and, with his head turned watchfully in her direction, put a dollar bill into my hand.

I didn't know what to say to him. "I'm sorry" was all I could think of. "I'm sorry about all the times I've rowed with you and insulted you. It won't happen anymore, after this."

"Forget about it, boy," he said, and he gave me one of the usual claps on the shoulder, but at the same time I saw him shaking his head to himself. "I didn't realize. You really are hard up, aren't you?"

Her final voicing aloud put an end to our bathos-redolent reconciliation scene. "Charlie, come back to bed!" she called out in no uncertain terms.

He quickly closed the door, and I as quickly went away from it.

I went up the street one block and across, where there was a cafeteria that stayed open all night. I ordered scrambled eggs and coffee and sat down to them, moaning under my breath with a peculiar mixture of pain and pleasure. The tabletops were white glazed, and stained with unwiped food marks. The sugar was caked in the sugar sifters. The coffee had been reboiled a hundred times. Still, I'd eaten a thousand times before then, and I've eaten a thousand times since then, but no food I've ever had tasted as good as the coffee in that inch-thick mug and the eggs on that greasy cracked plate that I ate in that cheap cafeteria at three or four o'clock that morning. It tasted the way food should taste. I almost wanted to cry with gratitude, it tasted so good.

Then I went back to my room and fell into the bottomless, prostrated sleep of release from months of accumulated fatigue and overwork.

I took the book downtown the next day and turned it over to Irwin, and the rest was only to wait.

I found the waiting harder than the working almost. For my life hadn't changed; the same scrimping, scraping, cutting down on meals to save a penny went on as before. Never any money, at least not enough all at a time to do anything with. And now that the solar plexus of the book had been taken out of my life, there was a great big hole left in the middle of it. I didn't know what to do with myself. I couldn't start working on something else because there wasn't the remotest possibility of selling anything else right then, and even if there had been, I still couldn't have; I was too drained by the effort I had just put in, I needed a breathing spell first.

Every night I would go out walking, killing time, merged in the drifting crowd I used to glimpse so longingly from my window. Yes, people still strolled the avenues in the Depression evenings, even if they couldn't do anything else. The lights were as gay as ever, the voices as animated, the smiles as ready, even if the hearts weren't quite as light anymore. The lights would be rippling on the picture-theater marquees like sprays of colored water, glinting in furriers' show-windows, which were coated with amber-tinted cellophane (a new decorative device then). The lights would be sizzling on casefuls of zircons and rhinestones like glassed-in fireworks displays. The lights would be shining from below upward, like submerged crocuses, at the feet of posturing mannequins garbed in the by-now universal silhouette of the new day: skirts to the shin and shoulders squared off and padded like those of a football player's uniform. And hair brushed flat from side to side across the top like that of a little girl of seven.

Even when they couldn't buy half the things they looked at, it was nice just to look, and the same went for me.

Then when they were tired of walking, they could always go back home and listen to the Kate Smith program, or the Eddie Cantor show, or Burns and Allen, and that was free of charge, too. I could do that too; the only difference was I couldn't sit down or take my coat off. I'd sold my little Emerson portable radio long before, but I used to get all the programs by standing in the entrances of hospitable music stores that had their loudspeakers turned on over the doorway. The jokes were just as funny there.

Life was as good as ever, as good as it's always been, to me and to those strolling with me. The only difference was you needed money more than you once had, for there was now far less of it around. But there wasn't one of us in that promenading-to-nowhere-and-back crowd who would have changed it, changed life, for anything else.

Each night when I went to bed, I said to myself, "Maybe tomorrow he'll call." Then the day came, and he didn't, and the night came, and again: "Maybe tomorrow. Maybe tomorrow."

A dozen times, a half a hundred times, I started to call him instead, and I kept from doing so. A dozen times I already had my nickel in the pay slot, and I pressed down the arm and brought it back to me again. Once I even got through to his office, and then I wouldn't name myself to the switchboard operator, hung up before she could put me through.

For I knew it wouldn't help any, wouldn't hasten it any, might even detract from it if I become too importunate or impatient. One call would bring on a second, then a third, and each time less and less gained. He would call me when he was ready, when the decision had been reached, and he wouldn't call me before. My calling him wouldn't make the decision; only his calling me would.

So until then it had to be "Maybe tomorrow he'll call me. Maybe tomorrow he'll call."

And then suddenly one morning he did. Very early, very unexpectedly, about 9:30 in the morning. It must have been almost as soon as he reached his desk. I'd jumped straight to the phone from my bed, and it was only as the film strips of sleep peeled slowly off my mind one by one that I realized whose the voice was. I stood there, holding up my pajama pants with one hand, the phone in the other.

"You sound half-awake," I heard him say. "Can you come down here later in the day?" he said. "I'd like to talk to you. I'd ask you to lunch, only I'm doing without lunches these days."

I was fully awake by now and almost bursting with excitement. "Forget lunch!" I told him. "What about the book? Is it in? Is it in?"

"Wait'll you get your eyes open, then come down," he hedged. "I don't like talking on the phone anyway. It's much more satisfactory when you get together personally." And he hung up.

I tried to click him back on again, but he was off for good and I couldn't get him back.

I let go my pajama waistband and it fell down to the floor and I had to bend over and hoist it up again.

It can't be a rejection, I kept thinking as I dressed, and then later as I rode the excruciatingly slow subway, or he would have told me then and there. I knew editors well enough by now; in that case he would rather *not* have had me come down and see him.

When I stepped into his office, the first thing I noticed was that it wasn't in evidence, he didn't have it there on his desk ready to give back to me, and my hopes rose even higher still.

He started in by mentioning its good points, bouncing a pencil on its end as he remarked each one.

"It's gay, it's jaunty.

"There's only one trouble. It's no longer valid.

"That Paris is gone."

"That Paris'll never be gone," I retorted resentfully, much as you refute a slander against the personality of your first sweetheart—such as that she's aging, no longer what she used to be.

"Yes it is," he insisted. "It's as dead as the New York that used to send half its own population over there to visit every summer. That's beside the point anyway. We're not selling the book in Paris, we're selling it right here in New York. People aren't going to read it there, they're going to read it here. And the New York that used to want to read about that Paris doesn't exist anymore."

He was right; I could see with my own eyes that it didn't.

"It's out," I murmured, releasing a long, mournful sigh.

He didn't answer.

"Well, where is it, then?" I finally wanted to know. "I may as well take it home with me."

He opened his desk drawer and fumbled around a little, but more as though making time than actually looking for something which he really didn't know where to locate. Then instead of the thick 300-odd-page typescript, he brought out a single sheet of paper with a few lines typed on it.

"I know you want to make money on it," he remarked.

I didn't answer that; it was too obvious.

He handed me the slip of paper to read.

It very briefly stated, in no more than two or three typed lines: In the event of a sale of my book, *I Love You, Paris* to X-Studios on the recommendation of Mr. Y, associate producer at that studio, I agreed to divide the profits of the sale fifty-fifty with Mr. Irwin—.

"You keep all the other rights just as much as ever," he hastened to assure me. "In fact, they might even reconsider here and do it as a book, if a successful motion picture comes out of it. That's been done before. A successful motion picture helps to sell a book, you know."

Then he went on to tell me that he knew this Mr. Y, and was sure that if he liked it a sale could be made on the strength of his recommendation to the studio heads. It was not like sending it to an agent. This was a direct contact with the studio itself.

I didn't need much more urging than that. I signed it and he put it back where he'd taken it from.

Then and only then he told me, "It's already out there. We ought to hear any day now. I know you need the money, don't want to be held up too long waiting."

We shook hands, and my hopes went way up again, even higher than they'd been before.

On that note I left him and went home.

I knew I hadn't been too astute, but I felt I hadn't had much choice in the matter, and anyone else in my position would have done pretty much as I had. Certainly, I was giving away half my potential profits. But I was giving away half of nothing, for without him and his associate producer friend Mr. Y, there would be no chance of a sale at all, I knew. Half a cake, to be La Rochefoucauldian about it, was better than none.

At that, he could have been much more demanding, or let's say much more flagrant, about it. By that I mean he could have insisted on a half-share of any picture sale at all that was made, and not just a sale to the one studio that was specified. Or worse still, he could have bought the book outright from me, all rights to it, for a thousand dollars or even five hundred dollars of his own (which I'm not sure I would have been able to refuse) and thus stand to collect the entire amount when the sale came. But I suppose, to be completely objective about it, he didn't have the thousand or five hundred in his own pocket, and couldn't very well ask the publishers for it since they'd already turned the book down.

I think all it amounted to was that he saw a chance to make some money on his own account out of something that had fortuitously come his way, and took it. And who is to blame him? I could see his logic, and I didn't resent it in the least.

I'm only trying to be fair. It doesn't matter now anymore, but it mattered terribly then.

I went home again to wait. This second wait was even worse than the first, for it was added to the first, was a continuation of it, and therefore seemed to have gone on twice as long as it actually had. But I outlasted it, I outlived it. Everything comes to an end, and at last it did, too.

When he called me this time, he did it indirectly. He had his assistant—he seemed to have attained the status of having his own secretary by now, or perhaps it was just the general operator for the office—put the call through for him, and he didn't get on himself. She asked if I could come down that afternoon, said he'd like to see me. I said I would, of course, but when I asked if I could talk to him himself, she told me that he was either tied up in a meeting or had stepped out of the office for a short while, I forget now which it was. Which could have been perfectly true, after all.

I let it go at that; what difference did an extra hour or two make, after all those leaden-footed days and weeks I'd put in waiting?

On my way to his office from the subway stop, I took a shortcut through a side-street. As I was moving briskly along through it, the figure of a middle-aged woman descending a short flight of stone steps just ahead of me caught my eye. She was shrouded completely in black, apparently in widow's weeds, but the brief glimpse I had of her face as she turned away and went up the street before me had showed a serenity, a passivity, that struck me. It was a sad cast of expression with its downlidded eyes, but it was completely at peace, that much couldn't be doubted.

I glanced at the steps, and then up above them. The cool, dingy and yet dignified façade of a church met my eyes. I had never yet been inside one. Neither for any joyous occasion nor any sad one. Neither for a wedding nor a funeral, a baptism nor a confirmation nor a mass.

I stopped, and turned halfway, and stood there looking at it. Then I moved slowly back again the few steps past it that I'd gone, and stood and looked some more.

People went into them for help; why shouldn't I? That woman I'd seen just now had, and you could tell by her face that she'd found it, been given what she asked.

But, something inside me argued, that woman's concerns are with death, her black garb shows that. Yours are with life and life only; it isn't the same thing.

I loitered around out there thinking the thing out, a sort of sidewalk loafer in front of a church, my hands deep in my pockets in uncertainty, the inevitable cigarette clenched in my mouth.

My sense of fair play, my sense of good manners, told me: You shouldn't go in just when you have something to ask for. You should have been going in steadily all along before now. Then you would be entitled to go in now and ask for your favor. This way you're not. You're only trying to use God. It's your problem, you should keep it to yourself.

Everyone uses God. Why shouldn't I? Every prayer that was ever sent up is asking God a favor. Why shouldn't my prayer go up too, along with all the other millions? I'm entitled to my happiness as much as anyone else.

Then another thought came to further cloud the issue: You wouldn't let your mother help you. You claimed it would take something away from you. Then why are you willing to let God help you? Won't that also take something away from you?

It's not the same thing, I answered in thought. My mother is weaker than I am, God is stronger. My mother looks up to me, admires me. God certainly doesn't. When you let the weaker help you, you detract from yourself. When you let the stronger help you, you don't. If you see a small child fall flat and lie there on the ground bawling, and you go over and help it back to its feet, do you detract from that child?

I threw my cigarette over my shoulder, jerked my hands out of my pockets, and ran tautly up the steps, neck slightly bent, as though they were a springboard into a pool of icy-cold water.

I had a fleeting impression of a marble-floored vestibule with a stone basin of water (was that what they called holy water? I wondered) set between two massive inner doors, and then I was standing stock still in the dim interior, as suddenly as I'd surged forward from outside just now.

The hush was the first thing I noticed about it. There was some sort of an inner quiet here that other buildings didn't have, for surely its walls were no thicker than many of theirs and yet they lacked it. The absence of windows? I asked myself. Far ahead, it seemed, there were little taper-lights. They seemed to be up on the wall, although I knew they actually weren't. They reminded me of shimmering teardrops and little ruddy drops of blood that had trickled down a certain distance, and then stopped and stayed there, pulsing, each one where it was.

Finally I moved again. I didn't go too far forward, I was too timid to. I think subconsciously I was fearful somebody would come out from the side, down there by the altar, and ask me what I was doing in there, what right I had to be in there.

I chose about the fourth or fifth row from the back, entered it, and sat down three or four seats from the outside. I clasped my hands and rested them on the back of the seat in front of me, and just sat for a while, my head respectfully lowered a trifle, but taking everything in from under my eyelids. It had a tragic grandeur to it, and yet an infinite loneliness too. I wondered if the next world was going to be this lonely. People took your loneliness away; God made you feel vastly lonely. I wondered why that was; it should be the other way around, I thought, shouldn't it?

My unaccustomed mundane eye, no conscious irreverence intended, kept traveling in the direction of the altar and expecting to come up against a big, blank picture-screen that was not to be found there. The cavernous grandiloquence was like that of a large motion-picture palace before the audience has filed in and the cameras have started turning in the projection room. I kept trying to put the thought out of my head, but it kept coming back again each time. It was the only comparison my past experience could conjure up.

I brought one knee down to the floor, but since that was an awkward position—there wasn't space enough there to comfortably allow the length of a bent leg—I finally brought the other one down beside it, and crouched there like that, my forehead pillowed against my clasped hands.

I had common sense enough to realize that formula didn't matter, it wasn't what counted. I knew no stylized prayers or forms of addressing God, because I'd never used any. And even words, that is, unspoken words within my mind, were difficult to marshal. So I contented myself with offering my prayer in thought form only, letting the smooth-flowing current of my thoughts carry it along far more evenly and naturally than any word-forms could have.

It was about like this:

"Dear God: Nature or You—if you are separate, and I don't think you are, or both—have put an unusually strong love of life in me. Everybody has it, I know, but I have it to an inordinate degree. And by love of life, I don't mean just the act of breathing and the wish not to stop breathing. I mean having fun, having a good time.

"My youthfulness is about to end, and I myself robbed it of many of the years it was entitled to.

"That's why I ask you: Let me have this money now, while I can still enjoy it as it should be enjoyed, to the hilt. Five years from now will be too late. Or even four. Even three.

"I don't want it for security. I don't want it to hoard, or put away in a musty bank, or count over, or scheme with. I want it to live with.

"Let me have it now.

"Now.

"Now, or not at all."

I noticed a strange thing immediately afterward. I felt strangely emptied out, weak, as when you've just expended all the energy you're capable of. I knew by that, whatever my prayer's merits, whatever its importunity, whatever its impertinence, it had been at least sincere, not feigned, not superficial, not play-acting.

I stayed there as I was for some time afterward, too limp to move, and I noticed that there were beads of perspiration on my forehead, and I felt moist under the arms.

After a while I passed my sleeve across my forehead and dried it off, and got stiffly and clumsily back to a sitting position. I say again, I meant that prayer with all my heart and all my soul.

Finally, as the pressures of the outside world began to circle closer around me again, and particularly as the imminence and importance of my appointment with Irwin came back to mind, I got to my feet and moved haltingly backward out of the space between the seats. Why backward, I haven't any idea. Possibly I thought it was the proper etiquette.

I went up the aisle and outside into the streets, and the sudden onset of their life-noises was almost like being buffeted by a howling storm, the first few minutes, after the unearthly silence inside there.

The effect (not of the noise but of the emotion spent) hadn't altogether worn off yet even by the time I reached Irwin's office. I could tell that by the meek, almost limp way I went in, when the girl ushered me, and shook hands and submissively sat down opposite him, instead of rushing in with all sorts of questions popping from my lips as I ordinarily would have.

He came directly to the point, now that he had me in front of him. (And I have never been able to understand that telephonic indirectness, evasiveness, of his, then or since.)

"Cornell," he said, "I wish I had something good to tell you. It's back. It came in this morning."

"Oh," I said almost inaudibly. "It's turned down."

"Turned down," he repeated. And then he went on to discuss their viewpoint briefly. The post-mortem was of no value even then, and still less now, so there is no point in repeating it.

Finally he said, "I want to show you that I'm trying to be fair about this," and he took out the single sheet of paper granting him half-share of the rights which I had signed the previous time, had me glance at it, then tore it into four pieces and dropped them into his wastebasket.

I think this only made me feel worse, instead of reassuring me as he had probably intended it to, for it only pointed up to my mind how hopeless from a sales angle he must consider the thing to be, to do that.

True, the grant had been valid only in this one instance, but I was in no mood to derive any comfort from that. If he had thought there was any further chance, he wouldn't have relinquished it so easily.

"It was a one-shot," he pointed out. "And when a one-shot goes wrong, it goes wrong, and that's all there is."

"Yeah," I assented bitterly.

The thing was beginning to sink slowly in, and I could feel myself hardening up. I realized the best thing I could do was get out of there, before I started taking it out on him. He actually hadn't done anything wrong, I kept reminding myself, only what I had intended doing myself from the beginning; if anything, he'd expedited it.

The last thing I recall saying to him was: "I even went into a church and prayed I'd have luck with it."

I've never forgotten what he answered to that. "You must have picked the wrong church," he smiled cynically.

So I left there, as the defeated always leave the place of their defeat: heavy-hearted, leaden-footed, the world all black and stormy around me, not a ray of light in it anywhere.

All that hard work for nothing. All those wearisome drudging weeks. A whole big chunk taken out of my life and thrown away, wasted. But far worse than the disappointment itself was the timing of it. My instinct told me very surely that this marked the ending of something or other in me. Call it being young, call it being completely carefree. Call it being wholeheartedly foolish, even; that has its place in life, too. And I knew that that was the real reason why I'd prayed. Not just for the money itself, for its own sake. (That would have been too presuming even for my non-theological turn of mind.) But to be given the money now, when every penny would have brought a dollar's worth of zest and enjoyment, and not later, when every dollar would bring only a penny's worth, maybe not even that much.

I noticed an ashcan standing by the curb as I came out of the building and made my downcast way along the street. I opened the clasp-envelope he had so bountifully given me and took my manuscript out of it.

I took the title page, which had my name on it, off it first, and crumpled that into a ball and jammed it down into my pocket. Then I dropped the rest of it, just as it was, bodily into the ashcan.

Then I scooped some of the powdery white ash over it and covered it up. Buried it, as it were.

Then I went on without it, but I felt heavier, not lighter, than when I'd been carrying it.

I came across a bar, and I went in. What more natural place to go, at such a time and in such a frame of mind? But I couldn't even drown my sorrows adequately. I had just enough for one beer on me, plus the nickel required for the long subway trip up to the hotel.

There was no one else in the place at that hour of the afternoon, and the bartender must have unnoticeably taken in my dismal expression as I lingered there, head bowed numbly over the lone beer until it was gone. I suppose he guessed my dejection had to do with money in one way or another. Everyone's did in those days.

When he saw me start to sidle off the stool about to go, he called over from where he was standing: "Have another."

"I can't," I said. "That's all I have enough for."

"Have one on me, then," he invited, and I glimpsed a rueful cast of compassion on his face for just a moment as he brought it over and set it down before me. That told me it wasn't just business goodwill that prompted him, it was human sympathy. Sympathy for a kid, of an older man who's gone through the same thing himself and knows what it's like. Nothing further was said by either one of us. When I finished it, I nodded to him and went out. But the trifling little act of human fellowship had made me feel better.

Not much, just an infinitesimal bit better. Like when your leg is broken, and you're lying there, and somebody pats his handkerchief to your moist forehead. It doesn't make the pain any less, but at least you're not alone in the pain.

A moment after, I turned around and went back to the place again.

I flung the door forcefully inward without, however, releasing my hold on it, not wanting it to strike back and break his glass.

"Y'know something, mister?" I called in to him.

He turned, startled slack-jawed.

"No, wh-what?" he quavered, half-frightened, I could tell, by my unexpected vehemence.

"You're better, even, than God. Because God didn't give me a ten-cent glass of beer free. But you did!"

And I reclosed the door and went on my bitter, beaten, homeward way, freed forever of any further religious beliefs.

There is a brief postscript to this story. Somewhat under a year later, which would bring it up to about 1934, a new picture opened in one of the first-run picture houses downtown. It had the word "Paris" somewhere in its title, that much I can recall. But that was nothing; the important thing about it was the reviews, which I read the next day just as I always did after any new opening. They were not overly enthusiastic about it, but they all alike mentioned that at least one thing in its favor, if not the only one, was that it brought a fresh and hitherto untouched period to the screen: the 1912 epoch.

I immediately went down there to see it. There were variations in it here and there, of course; there always are in any film derivation, even when its source has been bought and paid for. But its two leading characters were still a pair of ballroom dancers, and they still danced their highlight number to the rhythm of Ravel's "Bolero" just as I had specified in my script. As for the dialogue, much of that had been transposed almost verbatim. Not just a few random remarks, but whole stretches, especially in the key scenes. I couldn't fail to recognize it. I had worked too hard to try to make it witty, scintillating, brittle. It came out now sounding flat and dull to my discouraged ears, but it was still my dialogue, superimposed upon a very close approximation of my plot, set in the Paris of, not the year 1911, not the year 1913, but 1912. In fact, throughout it bore such an unabashed verisimilitude to my piece that it almost looked as though somebody had been paid for it. But it certainly hadn't been I.

I came out of there with a sullen scowl on my face, but actually it no longer hurt. That had been last year's grief and heartache. I was already starting on the way up again myself by now. I had no time for last year's grief, I was too taken up in this year's hopes and plans. And there was this note of consolation to be derived from it too: Whoever had stolen it, had stolen it as much from Irwin as from me. It had, in actuality, been stolen twice over. The biter had been bitten in turn.

It no longer hurt.